THE HOUND OF THE
BASKERVILLES

THE HOUND OF THE BASKERVILLES

Retold by Russell Punter

Based on the story by Sir Arthur Conan Doyle

Illustrated by Andrea da Rold

Series editor: Jane Chisholm

Consultant: Mike Collins

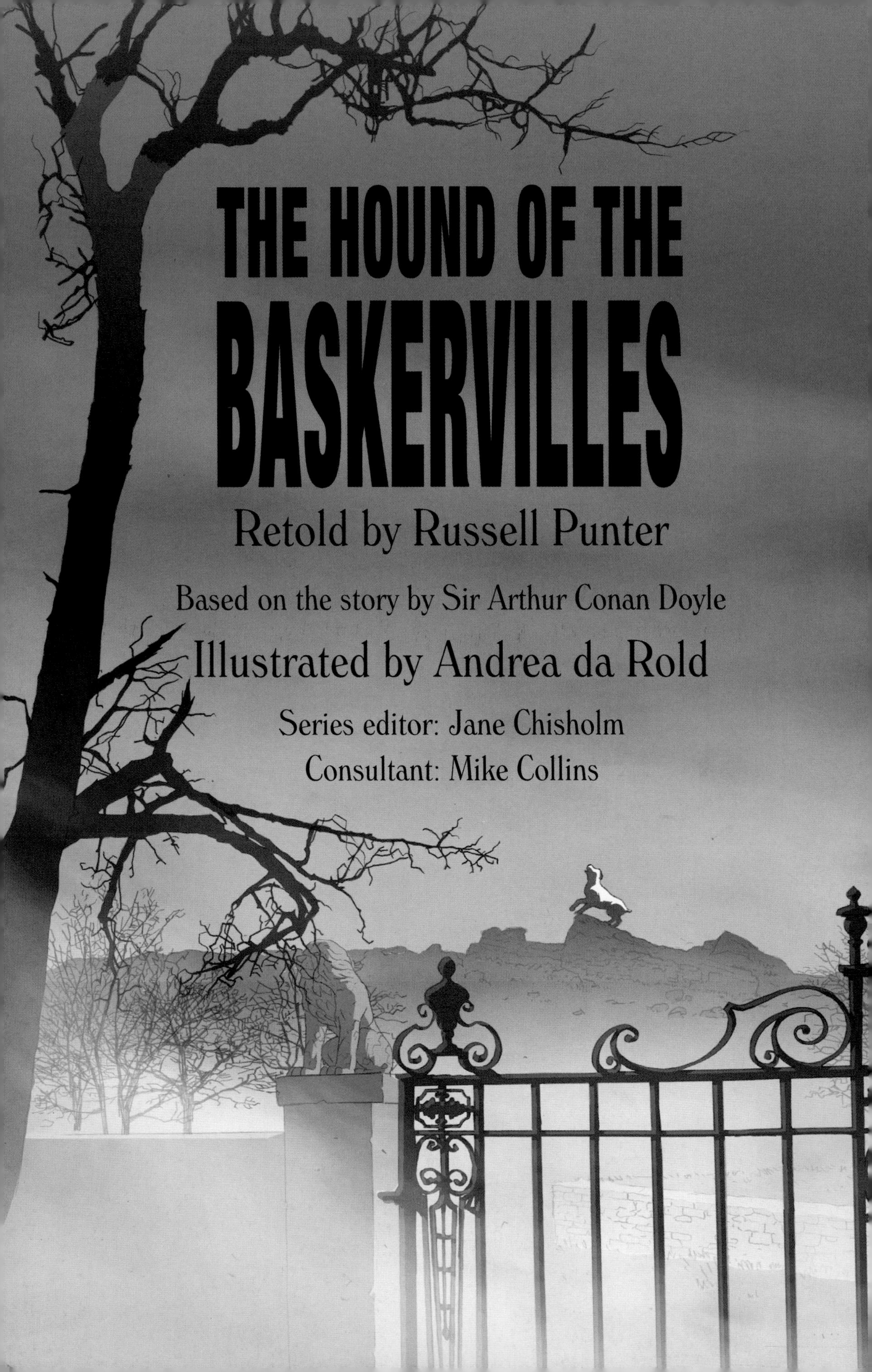

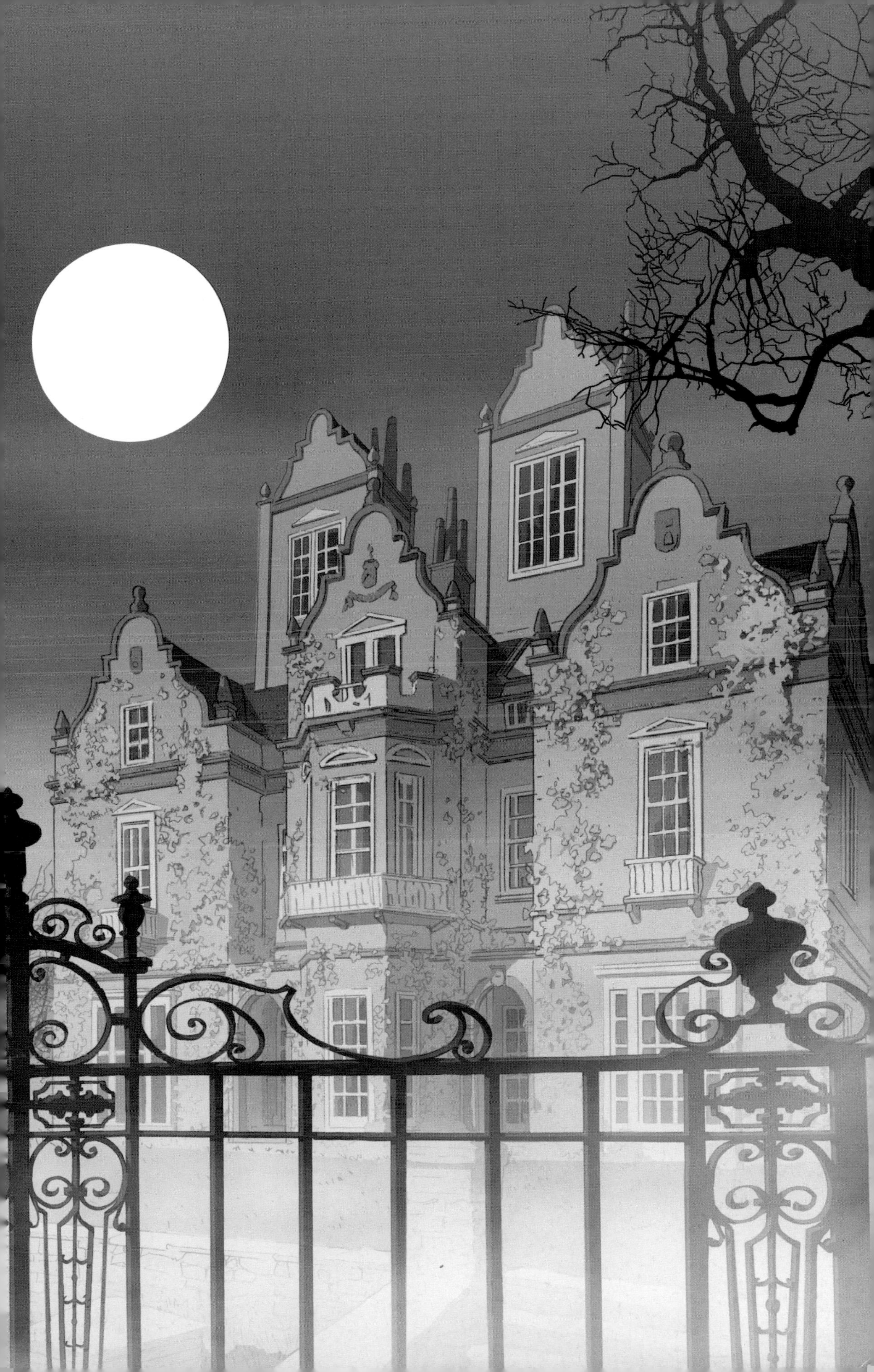

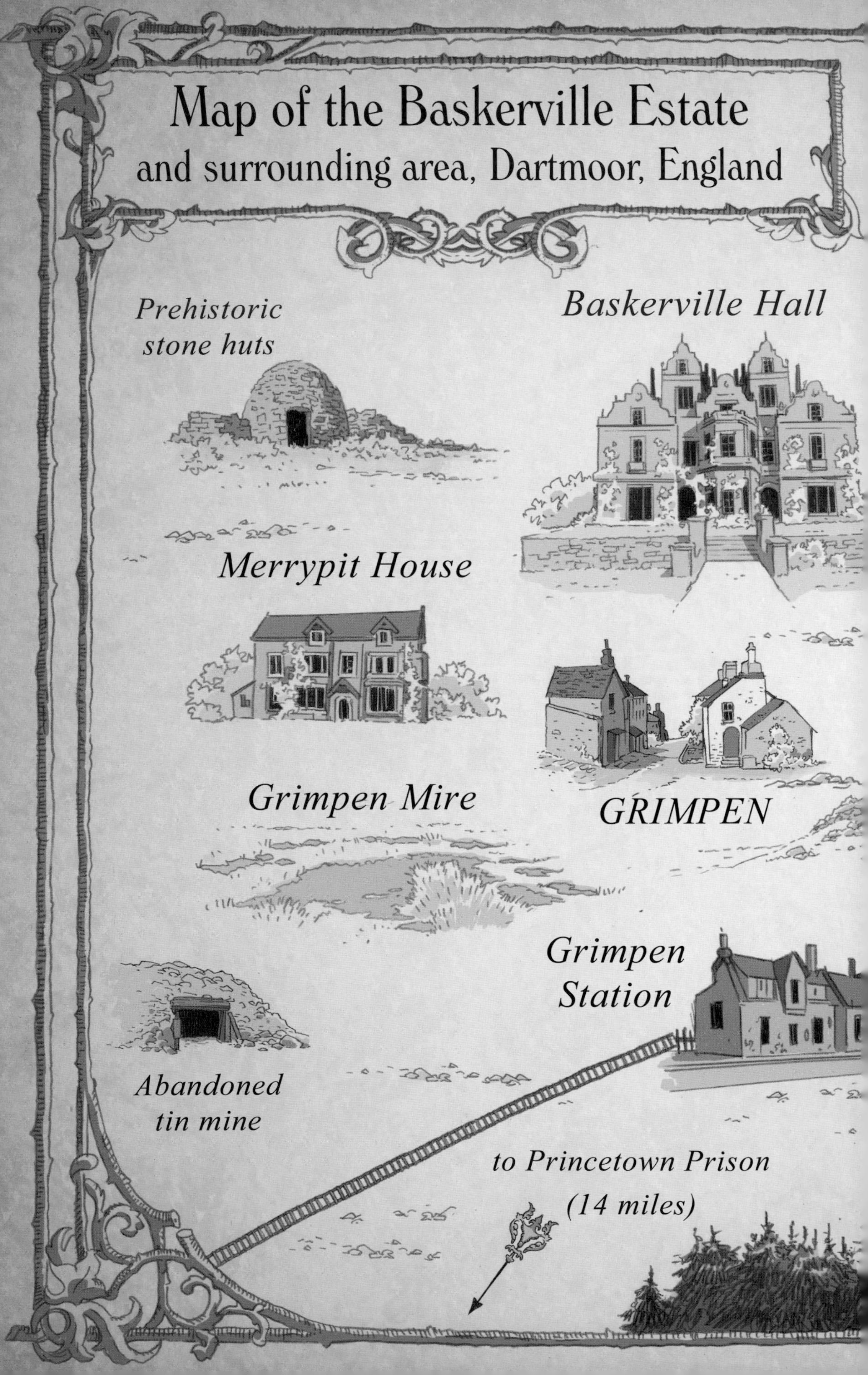
Map of the Baskerville Estate
and surrounding area, Dartmoor, England
Prehistoric stone huts
Baskerville Hall
Merrypit House
Grimpen Mire
GRIMPEN
Grimpen Station
Abandoned tin mine
to Princetown Prison (14 miles)

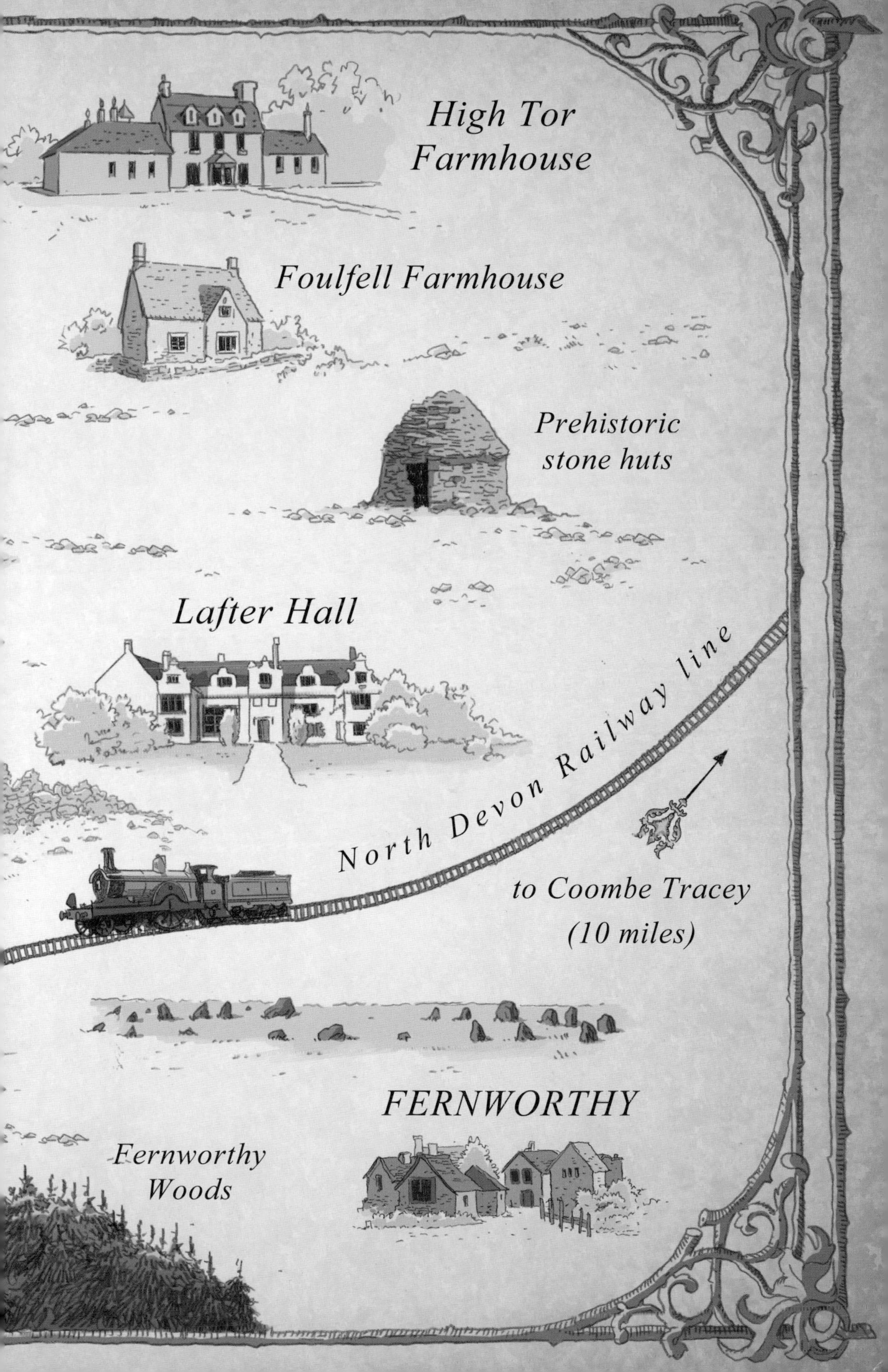
High Tor Farmhouse
Foulfell Farmhouse
Prehistoric stone huts
Lafter Hall
North Devon Railway line
to Coombe Tracey (10 miles)
FERNWORTHY
Fernworthy Woods

My name is Dr. John Watson. For many years, it has been my privilege to share in the adventures of the world-famous detective, Mr. Sherlock Holmes.

Perhaps the most well-known case that Holmes was ever called upon to investigate began one bright morning in September 1889.

As I made my way through the bustling byways of London towards Holmes' rooms at 221B Baker Street, little could I have imagined the bizarre and terrifying events that lay ahead of us...

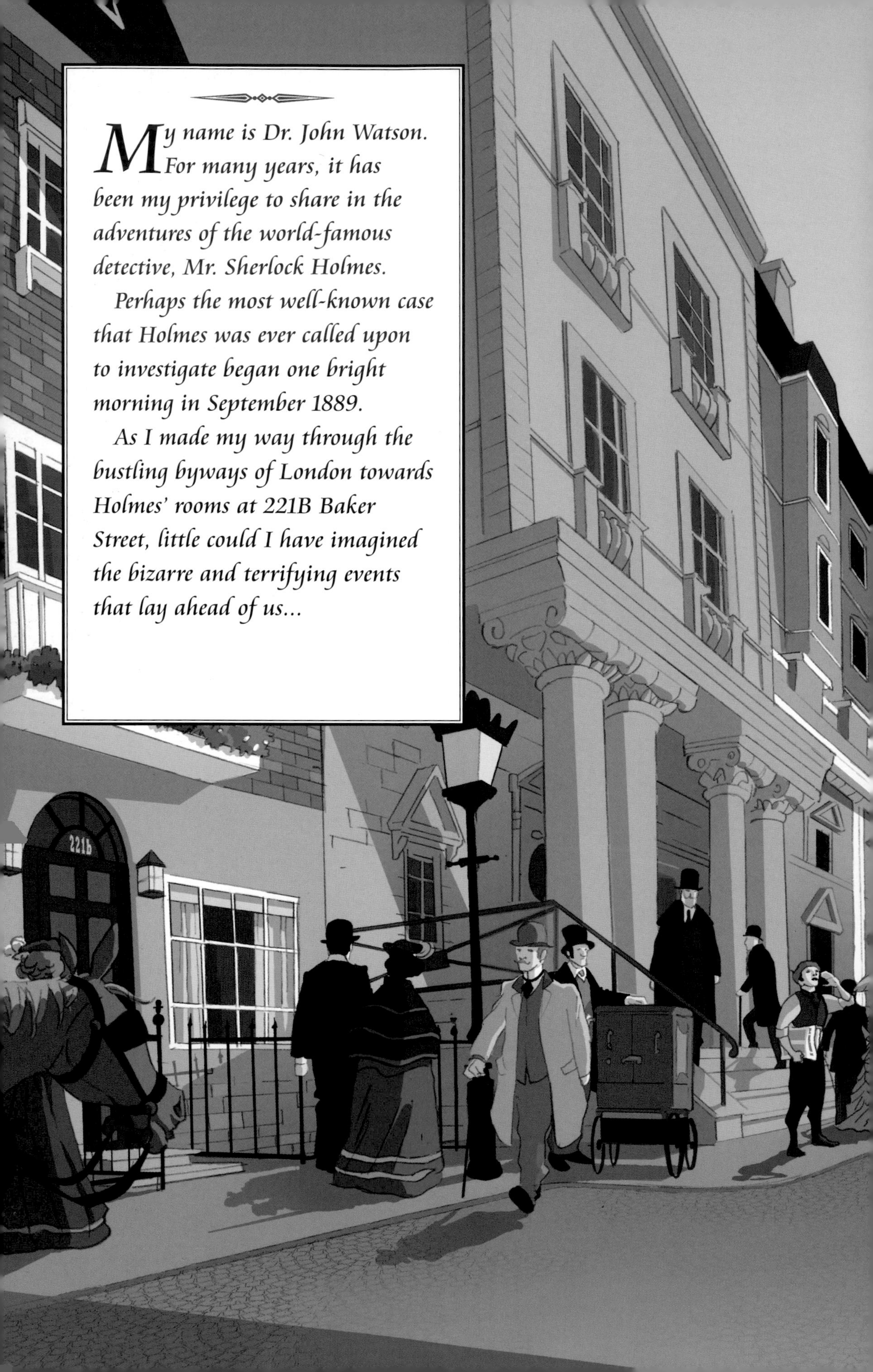
221b

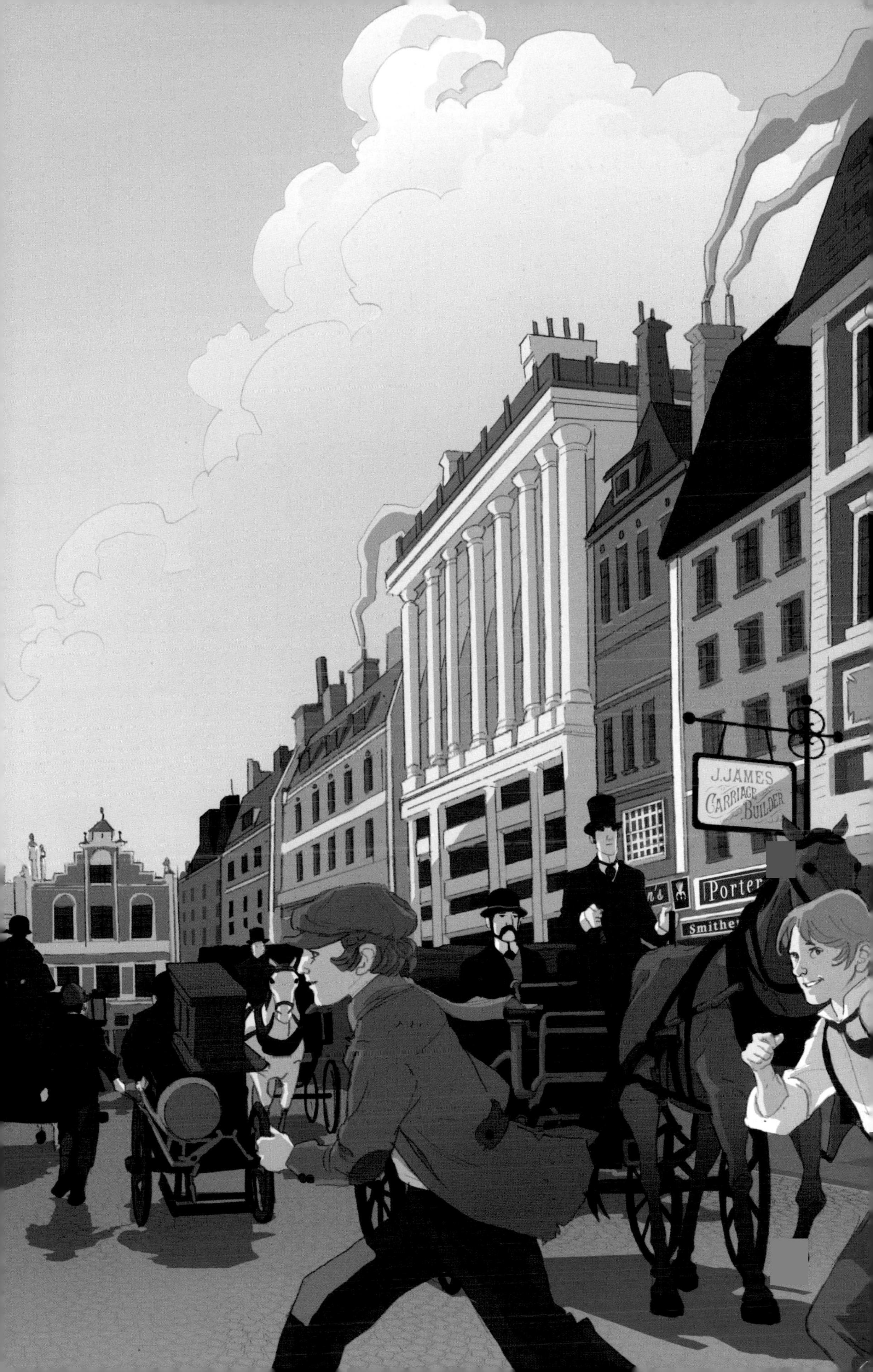

J. JAMES
CARRIAGE BUILDER
Porter
Smither

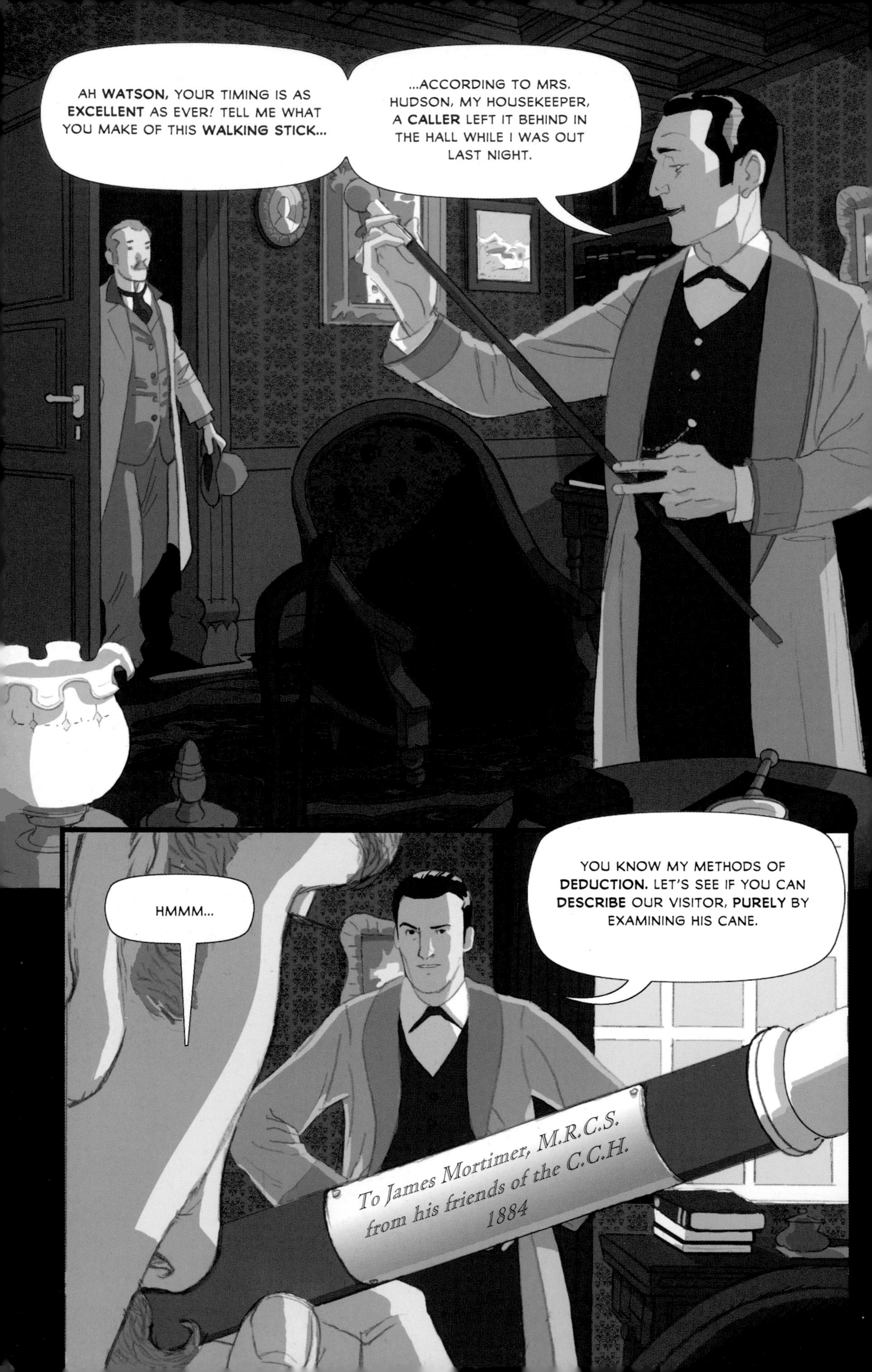
AH WATSON, YOUR TIMING IS AS EXCELLENT AS EVER! TELL ME WHAT YOU MAKE OF THIS WALKING STICK...
...ACCORDING TO MRS. HUDSON, MY HOUSEKEEPER, A CALLER LEFT IT BEHIND IN THE HALL WHILE I WAS OUT LAST NIGHT.
YOU KNOW MY METHODS OF DEDUCTION. LET'S SEE IF YOU CAN DESCRIBE OUR VISITOR, PURELY BY EXAMINING HIS CANE.
HMMM...
To James Mortimer, M.R.C.S. from his friends of the C.C.H. 1884

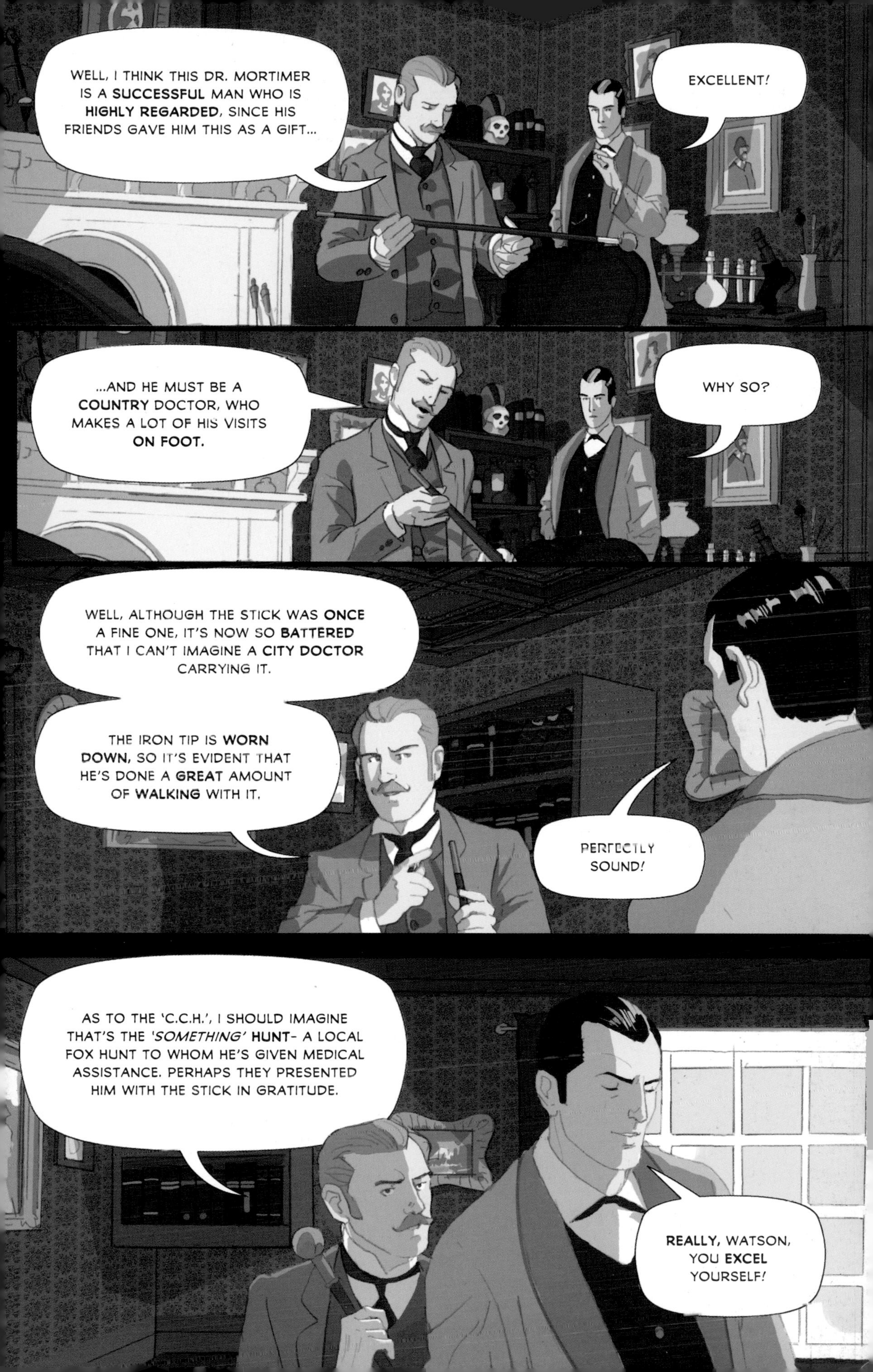
WELL, I THINK THIS DR. MORTIMER IS A SUCCESSFUL MAN WHO IS HIGHLY REGARDED, SINCE HIS FRIENDS GAVE HIM THIS AS A GIFT...
EXCELLENT!
...AND HE MUST BE A COUNTRY DOCTOR, WHO MAKES A LOT OF HIS VISITS ON FOOT.
WHY SO?
WELL, ALTHOUGH THE STICK WAS ONCE A FINE ONE, IT'S NOW SO BATTERED THAT I CAN'T IMAGINE A CITY DOCTOR CARRYING IT.
THE IRON TIP IS WORN DOWN, SO IT'S EVIDENT THAT HE'S DONE A GREAT AMOUNT OF WALKING WITH IT.
PERFECTLY SOUND!
AS TO THE 'C.C.H.', I SHOULD IMAGINE THAT'S THE 'SOMETHING' HUNT- A LOCAL FOX HUNT TO WHOM HE'S GIVEN MEDICAL ASSISTANCE. PERHAPS THEY PRESENTED HIM WITH THE STICK IN GRATITUDE.
REALLY, WATSON, YOU EXCEL YOURSELF!

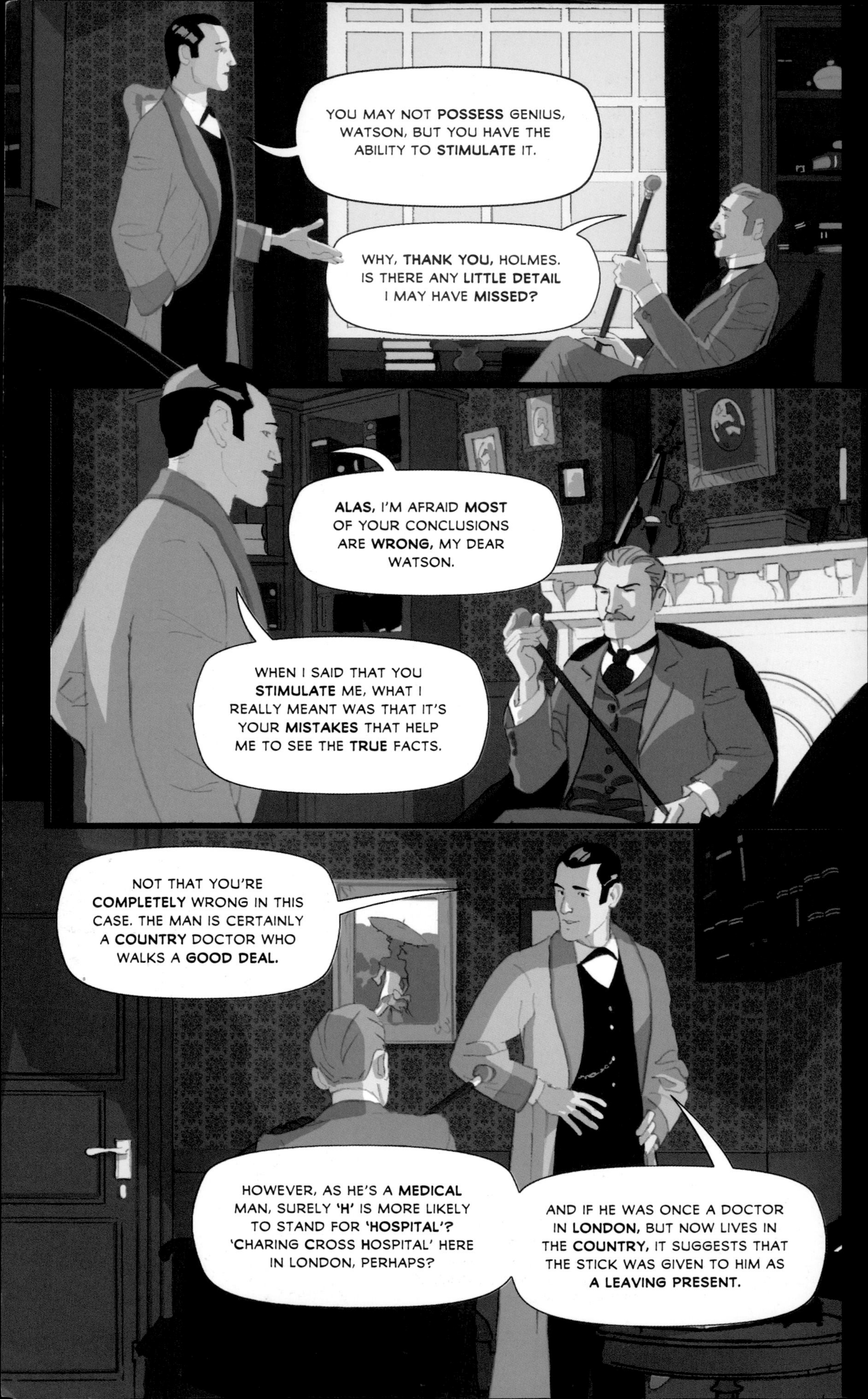
YOU MAY NOT POSSESS GENIUS, WATSON, BUT YOU HAVE THE ABILITY TO STIMULATE IT.
WHY, THANK YOU, HOLMES. IS THERE ANY LITTLE DETAIL I MAY HAVE MISSED?
ALAS, I'M AFRAID MOST OF YOUR CONCLUSIONS ARE WRONG, MY DEAR WATSON.
WHEN I SAID THAT YOU STIMULATE ME, WHAT I REALLY MEANT WAS THAT IT'S YOUR MISTAKES THAT HELP ME TO SEE THE TRUE FACTS.
NOT THAT YOU'RE COMPLETELY WRONG IN THIS CASE. THE MAN IS CERTAINLY A COUNTRY DOCTOR WHO WALKS A GOOD DEAL.
HOWEVER, AS HE'S A MEDICAL MAN, SURELY 'H' IS MORE LIKELY TO STAND FOR 'HOSPITAL'? 'CHARING CROSS HOSPITAL' HERE IN LONDON, PERHAPS?
AND IF HE WAS ONCE A DOCTOR IN LONDON, BUT NOW LIVES IN THE COUNTRY, IT SUGGESTS THAT THE STICK WAS GIVEN TO HIM AS A LEAVING PRESENT.

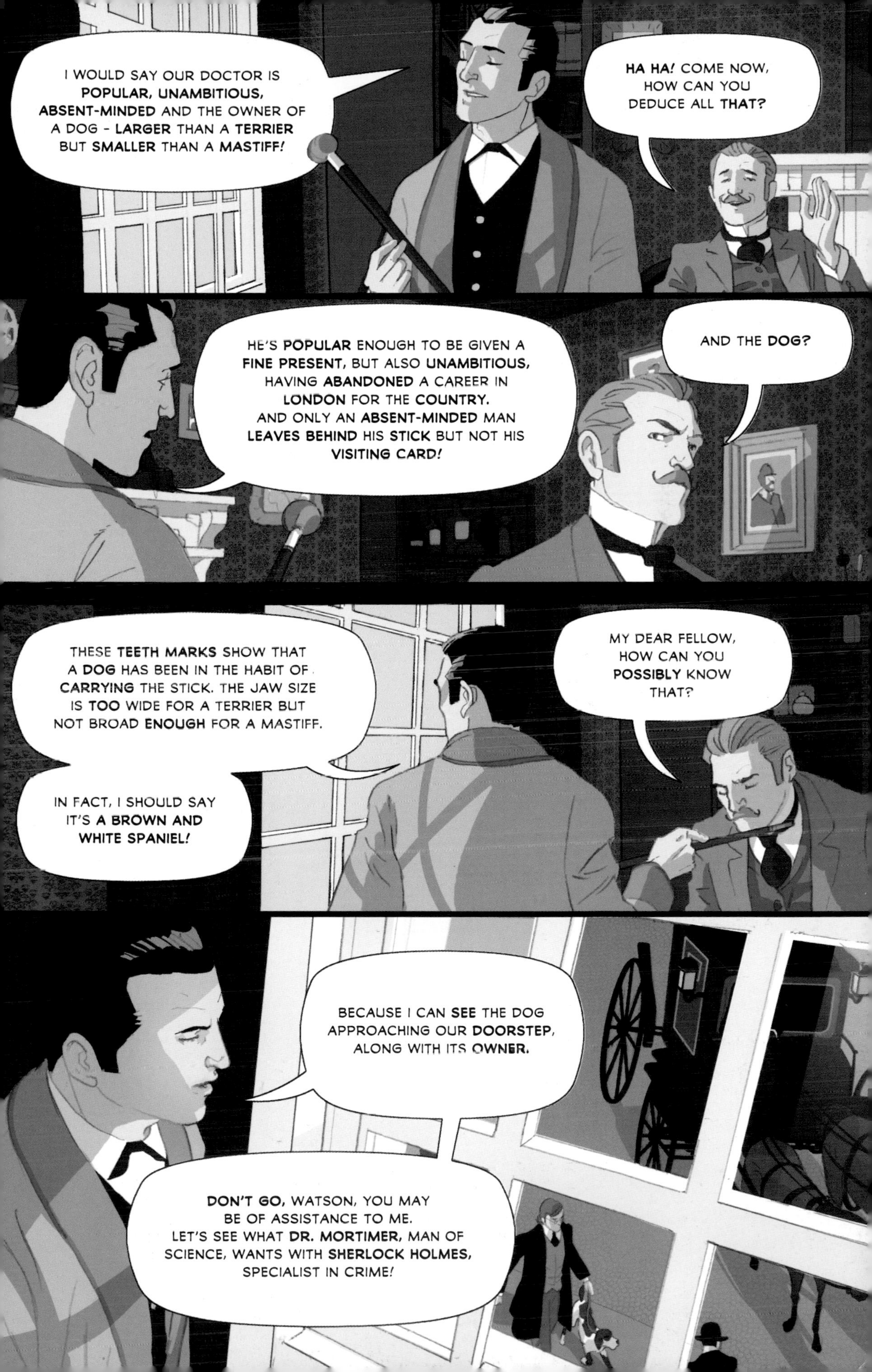
I WOULD SAY OUR DOCTOR IS POPULAR, UNAMBITIOUS, ABSENT-MINDED AND THE OWNER OF A DOG - LARGER THAN A TERRIER BUT SMALLER THAN A MASTIFF!
HA HA! COME NOW, HOW CAN YOU DEDUCE ALL THAT?
HE'S POPULAR ENOUGH TO BE GIVEN A FINE PRESENT, BUT ALSO UNAMBITIOUS, HAVING ABANDONED A CAREER IN LONDON FOR THE COUNTRY. AND ONLY AN ABSENT-MINDED MAN LEAVES BEHIND HIS STICK BUT NOT HIS VISITING CARD!
AND THE DOG?
THESE TEETH MARKS SHOW THAT A DOG HAS BEEN IN THE HABIT OF CARRYING THE STICK. THE JAW SIZE IS TOO WIDE FOR A TERRIER BUT NOT BROAD ENOUGH FOR A MASTIFF.
IN FACT, I SHOULD SAY IT'S A BROWN AND WHITE SPANIEL!
MY DEAR FELLOW, HOW CAN YOU POSSIBLY KNOW THAT?
BECAUSE I CAN SEE THE DOG APPROACHING OUR DOORSTEP, ALONG WITH ITS OWNER.
DON'T GO, WATSON, YOU MAY BE OF ASSISTANCE TO ME. LET'S SEE WHAT DR. MORTIMER, MAN OF SCIENCE, WANTS WITH SHERLOCK HOLMES, SPECIALIST IN CRIME!

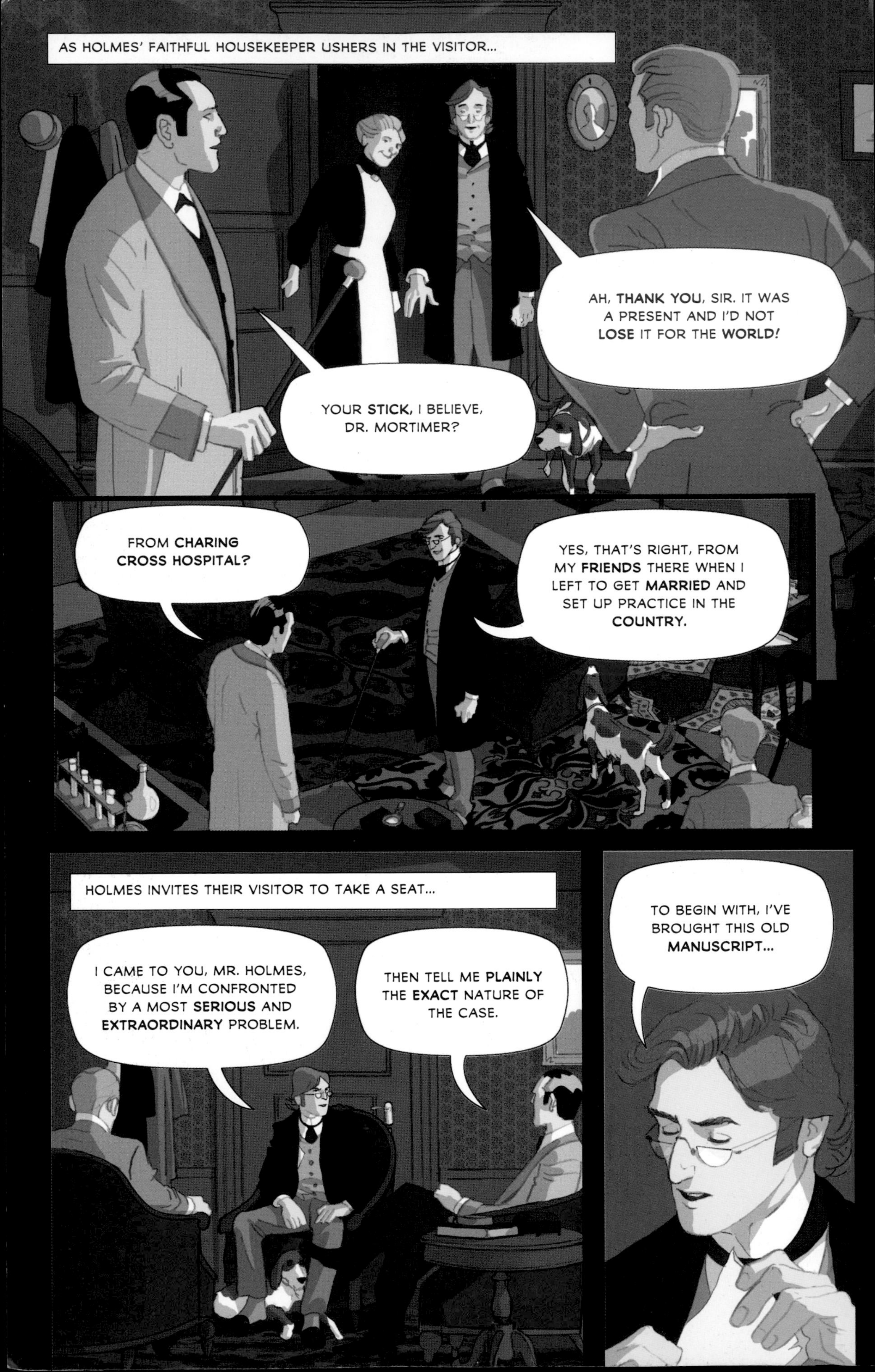
AS HOLMES' FAITHFUL HOUSEKEEPER USHERS IN THE VISITOR...
YOUR STICK, I BELIEVE, DR. MORTIMER?
AH, THANK YOU, SIR. IT WAS A PRESENT AND I'D NOT LOSE IT FOR THE WORLD!
FROM CHARING CROSS HOSPITAL?
YES, THAT'S RIGHT, FROM MY FRIENDS THERE WHEN I LEFT TO GET MARRIED AND SET UP PRACTICE IN THE COUNTRY.
HOLMES INVITES THEIR VISITOR TO TAKE A SEAT...
I CAME TO YOU, MR. HOLMES, BECAUSE I'M CONFRONTED BY A MOST SERIOUS AND EXTRAORDINARY PROBLEM.
THEN TELL ME PLAINLY THE EXACT NATURE OF THE CASE.
TO BEGIN WITH, I'VE BROUGHT THIS OLD MANUSCRIPT...

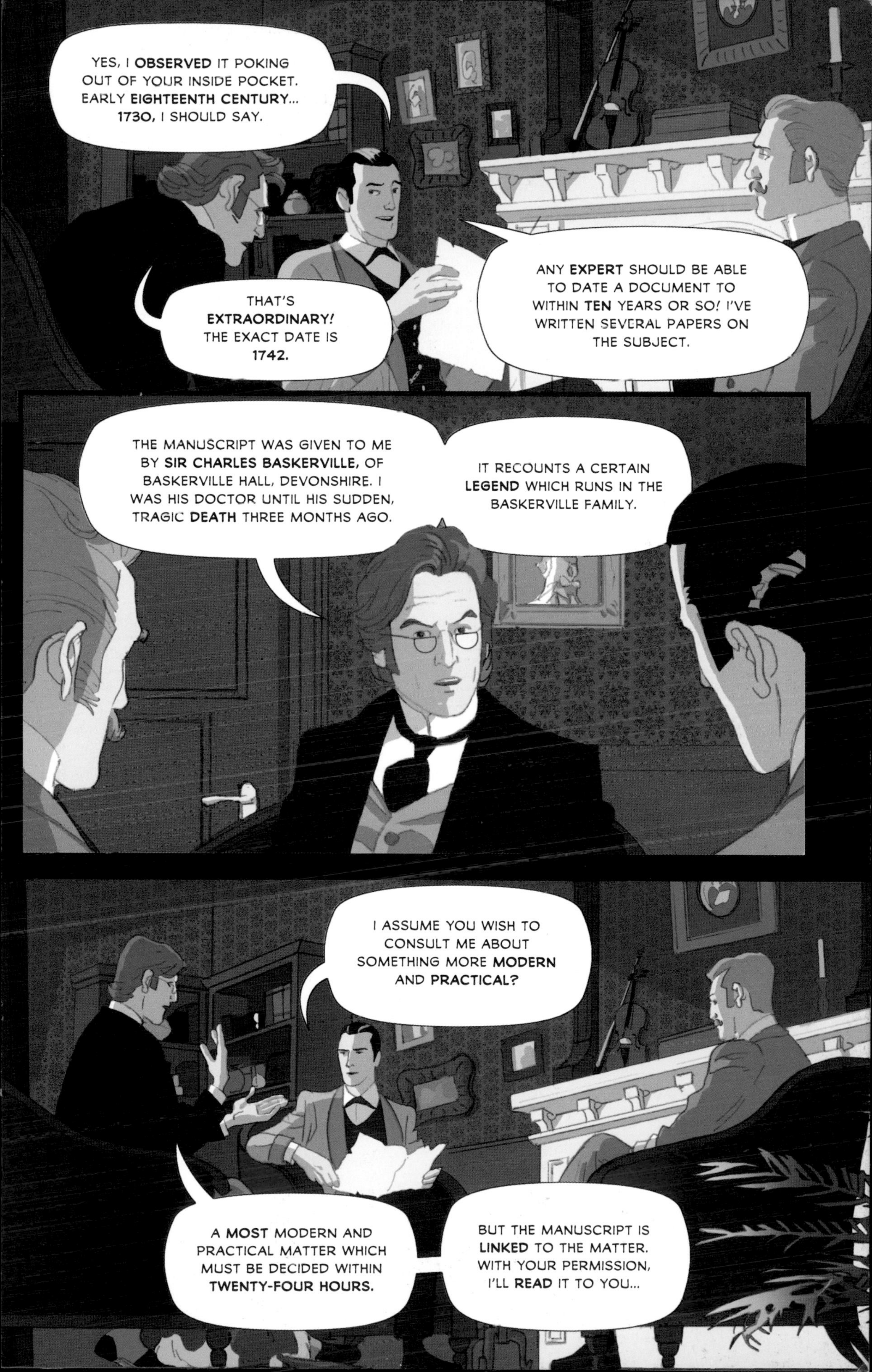
YES, I **OBSERVED** IT POKING OUT OF YOUR INSIDE POCKET. EARLY **EIGHTEENTH CENTURY**... **1730,** I SHOULD SAY.
THAT'S **EXTRAORDINARY!** THE EXACT DATE IS **1742.**
ANY **EXPERT** SHOULD BE ABLE TO DATE A DOCUMENT TO WITHIN **TEN** YEARS OR SO! I'VE WRITTEN SEVERAL PAPERS ON THE SUBJECT.
THE MANUSCRIPT WAS GIVEN TO ME BY **SIR CHARLES BASKERVILLE,** OF BASKERVILLE HALL, DEVONSHIRE. I WAS HIS DOCTOR UNTIL HIS SUDDEN, TRAGIC **DEATH** THREE MONTHS AGO.
IT RECOUNTS A CERTAIN **LEGEND** WHICH RUNS IN THE BASKERVILLE FAMILY.
I ASSUME YOU WISH TO CONSULT ME ABOUT SOMETHING MORE **MODERN** AND **PRACTICAL?**
A **MOST** MODERN AND PRACTICAL MATTER WHICH MUST BE DECIDED WITHIN **TWENTY-FOUR HOURS.**
BUT THE MANUSCRIPT IS **LINKED** TO THE MATTER. WITH YOUR PERMISSION, I'LL **READ** IT TO YOU...

From Hugo Baskerville to his sons Rodger and John, with instructions that they say nothing thereof to their sister Elizabeth.

There have been many statements regarding the origin of the Hound of the Baskervilles. However the following version has been handed down from previous generations of our family. As such, I believe it to be true. It tells the story of our ancestor with whom I share my name, Hugo Baskerville. I lay it down so that future generations may learn from the mistakes of that evil man...

One hundred years ago, this Manor of Baskerville was owned by one Hugo of that name. He was a wild and cruel man who became obsessed with the daughter of a local farmer, though she felt nothing for this most wicked of men.

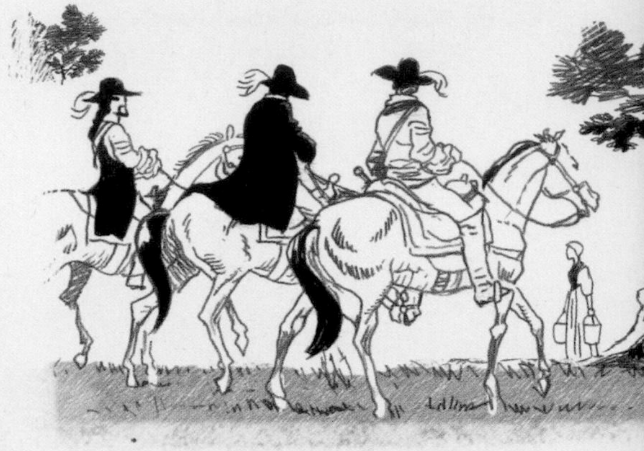

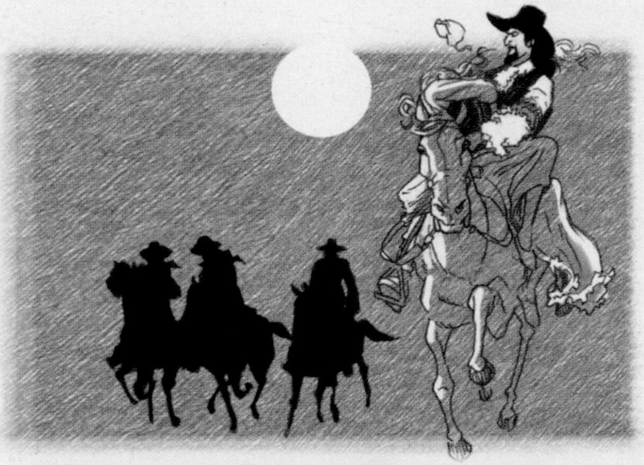

One night, Hugo and his companions stole the maiden away from her home and carried her back to Baskerville Hall, where Hugo locked her in an upper chamber.

Fearing for her life, she climbed down the ivy which covered the wall below the room. Then she ran across the moor towards her father's farm. When Hugo found her gone, he let loose his hounds and rode off in pursuit of the girl across the moonlit moor.

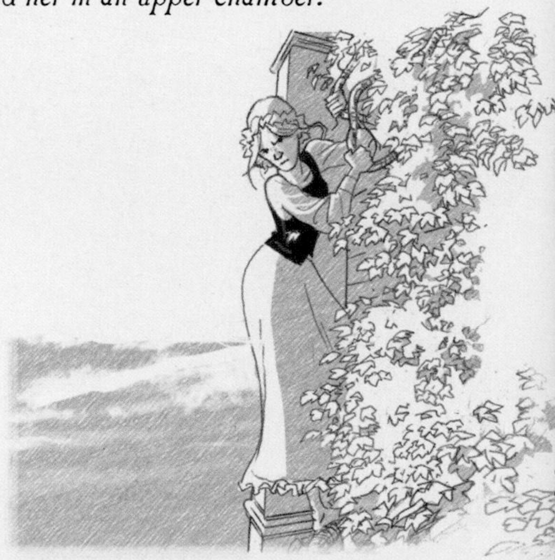

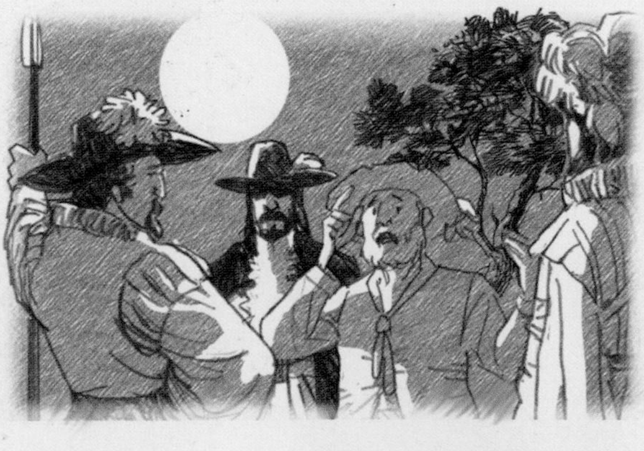

The companions he left behind came to their senses and followed Hugo with the aim of saving the poor girl. On their way, they met a terrified shepherd who told them that Hugo Baskerville had indeed passed by, pursued by an unearthly hound.

The men's skins turned cold, as Hugo's horse came galloping across the moor, its saddle empty. They rode on until they found Hugo's hounds whimpering and gazing down the narrow valley before them.

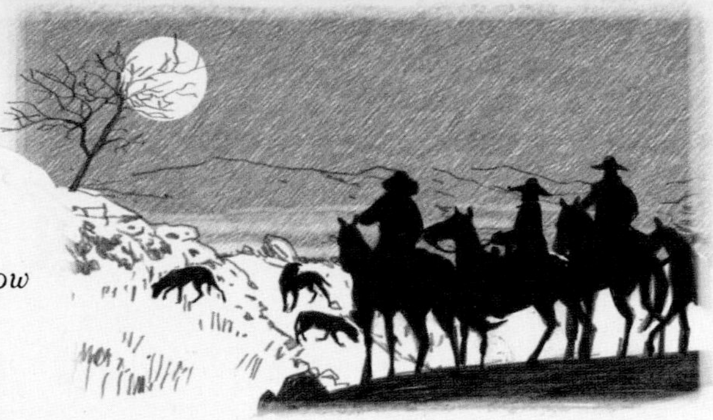

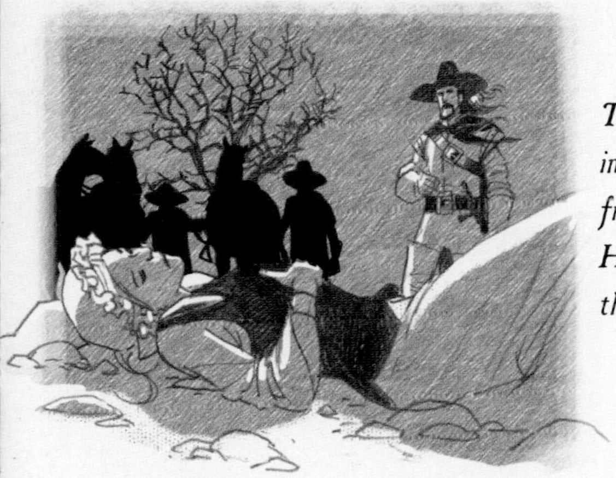

Three of the men rode on into the valley. There in the moonlight lay the body of the maid, dead from fear and fatigue. Nearby lay the body of Hugo Baskerville. But it was not these sights that raised the hair upon their heads...

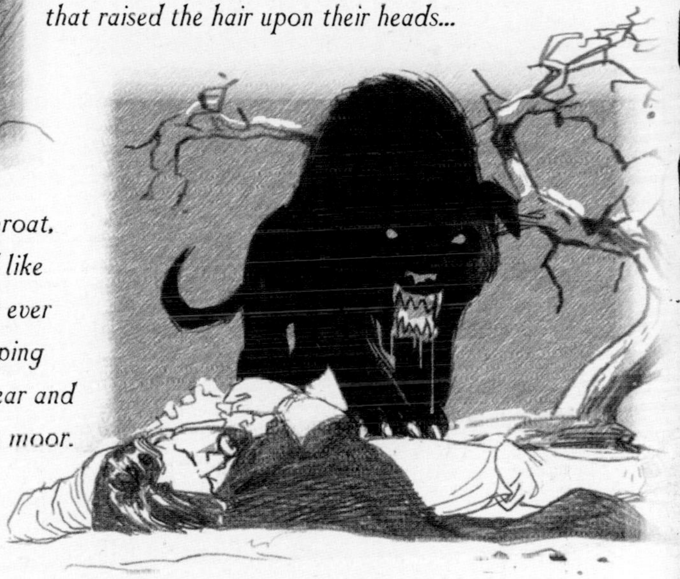

...standing over Hugo, plucking at his throat, there stood a great, black beast, shaped like a hound, yet larger than any hound that ever lived. It turned its blazing eyes and dripping jaws upon the men, who shrieked with fear and rode for dear life, screaming, across the moor.

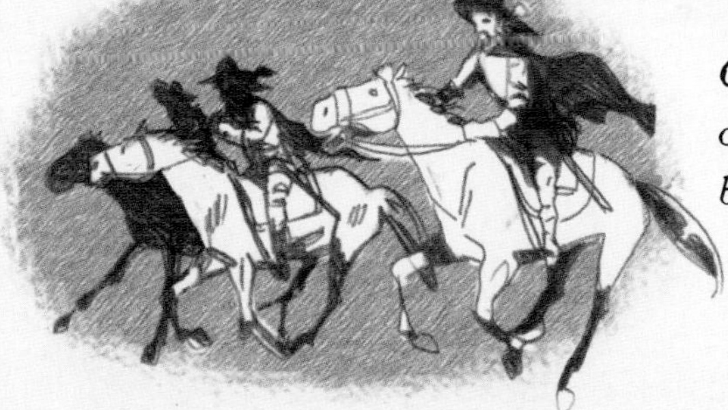

One of them, it is said, died that very night of what he had seen. The other two were broken men for the rest of their days.

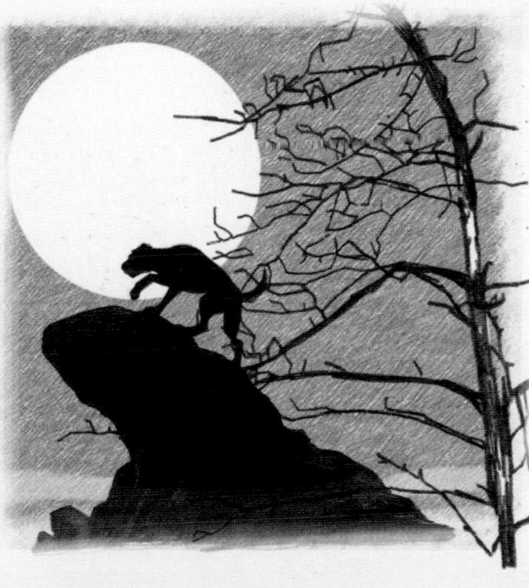

Such is the tale, my sons, of the coming of the hound which is said to have plagued our family ever since. Many of the family have suffered sudden, bloody and mysterious deaths. I hereby caution you not to cross the moor in those dark hours when the powers of evil are at their height.

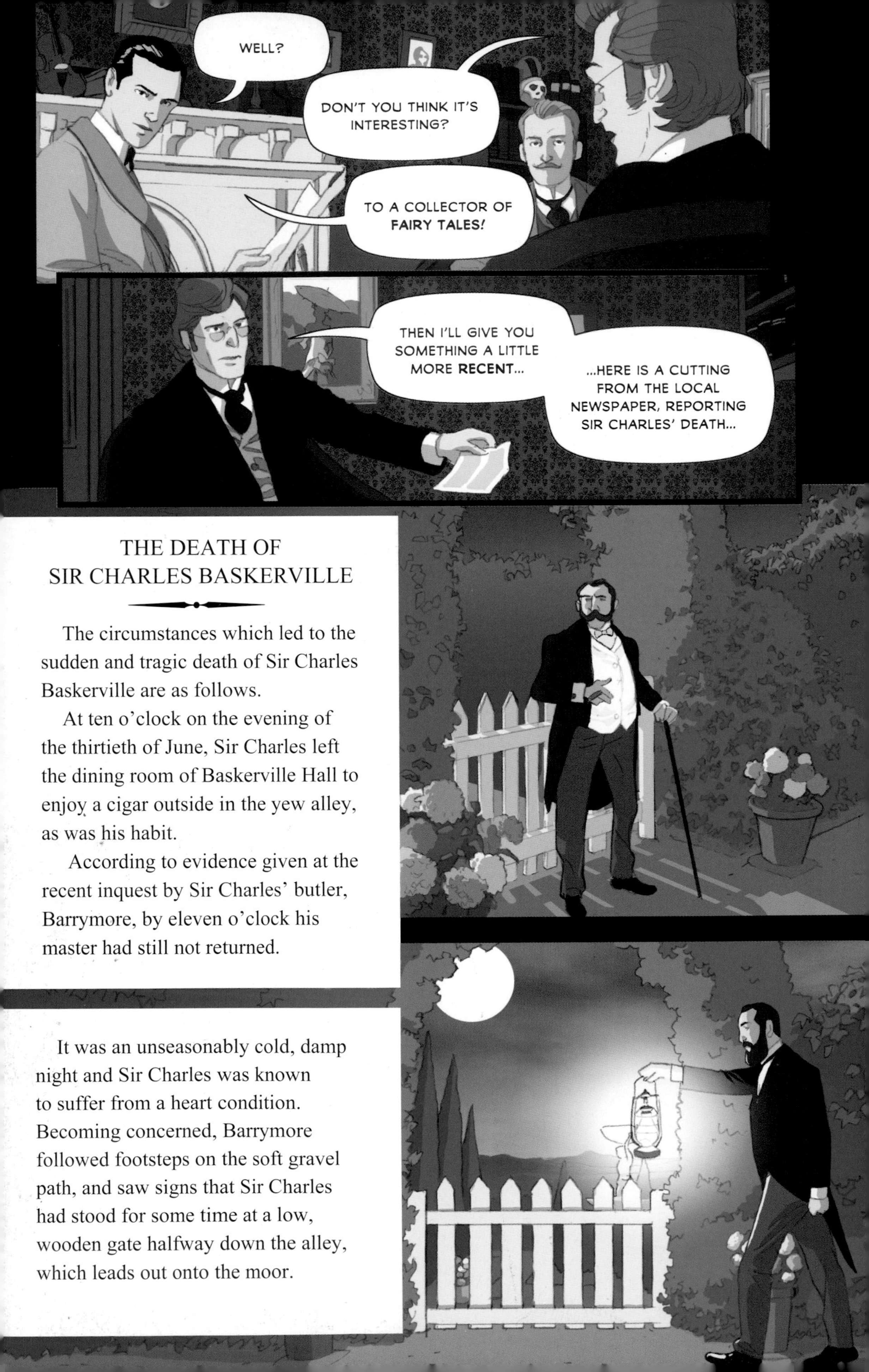
WELL?
DON'T YOU THINK IT'S INTERESTING?
TO A COLLECTOR OF FAIRY TALES!
THEN I'LL GIVE YOU SOMETHING A LITTLE MORE RECENT...
...HERE IS A CUTTING FROM THE LOCAL NEWSPAPER, REPORTING SIR CHARLES' DEATH...
THE DEATH OF SIR CHARLES BASKERVILLE
The circumstances which led to the sudden and tragic death of Sir Charles Baskerville are as follows.
At ten o'clock on the evening of the thirtieth of June, Sir Charles left the dining room of Baskerville Hall to enjoy a cigar outside in the yew alley, as was his habit.
According to evidence given at the recent inquest by Sir Charles' butler, Barrymore, by eleven o'clock his master had still not returned.
It was an unseasonably cold, damp night and Sir Charles was known to suffer from a heart condition. Becoming concerned, Barrymore followed footsteps on the soft gravel path, and saw signs that Sir Charles had stood for some time at a low, wooden gate halfway down the alley, which leads out onto the moor.

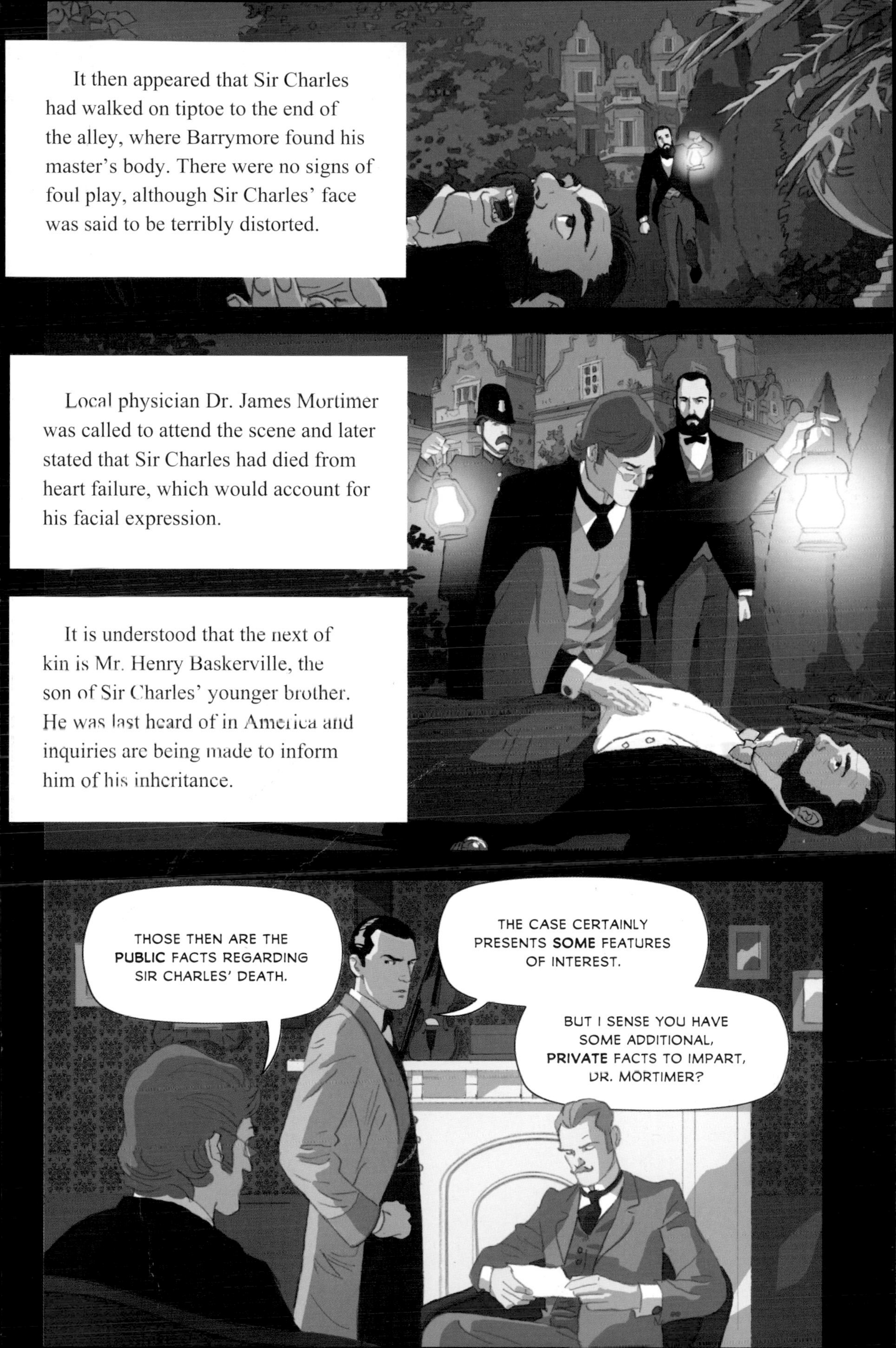
It then appeared that Sir Charles had walked on tiptoe to the end of the alley, where Barrymore found his master's body. There were no signs of foul play, although Sir Charles' face was said to be terribly distorted.
Local physician Dr. James Mortimer was called to attend the scene and later stated that Sir Charles had died from heart failure, which would account for his facial expression.
It is understood that the next of kin is Mr. Henry Baskerville, the son of Sir Charles' younger brother. He was last heard of in America and inquiries are being made to inform him of his inheritance.
THOSE THEN ARE THE **PUBLIC** FACTS REGARDING SIR CHARLES' DEATH.
THE CASE CERTAINLY PRESENTS **SOME** FEATURES OF INTEREST.
BUT I SENSE YOU HAVE SOME ADDITIONAL, **PRIVATE** FACTS TO IMPART, DR. MORTIMER?

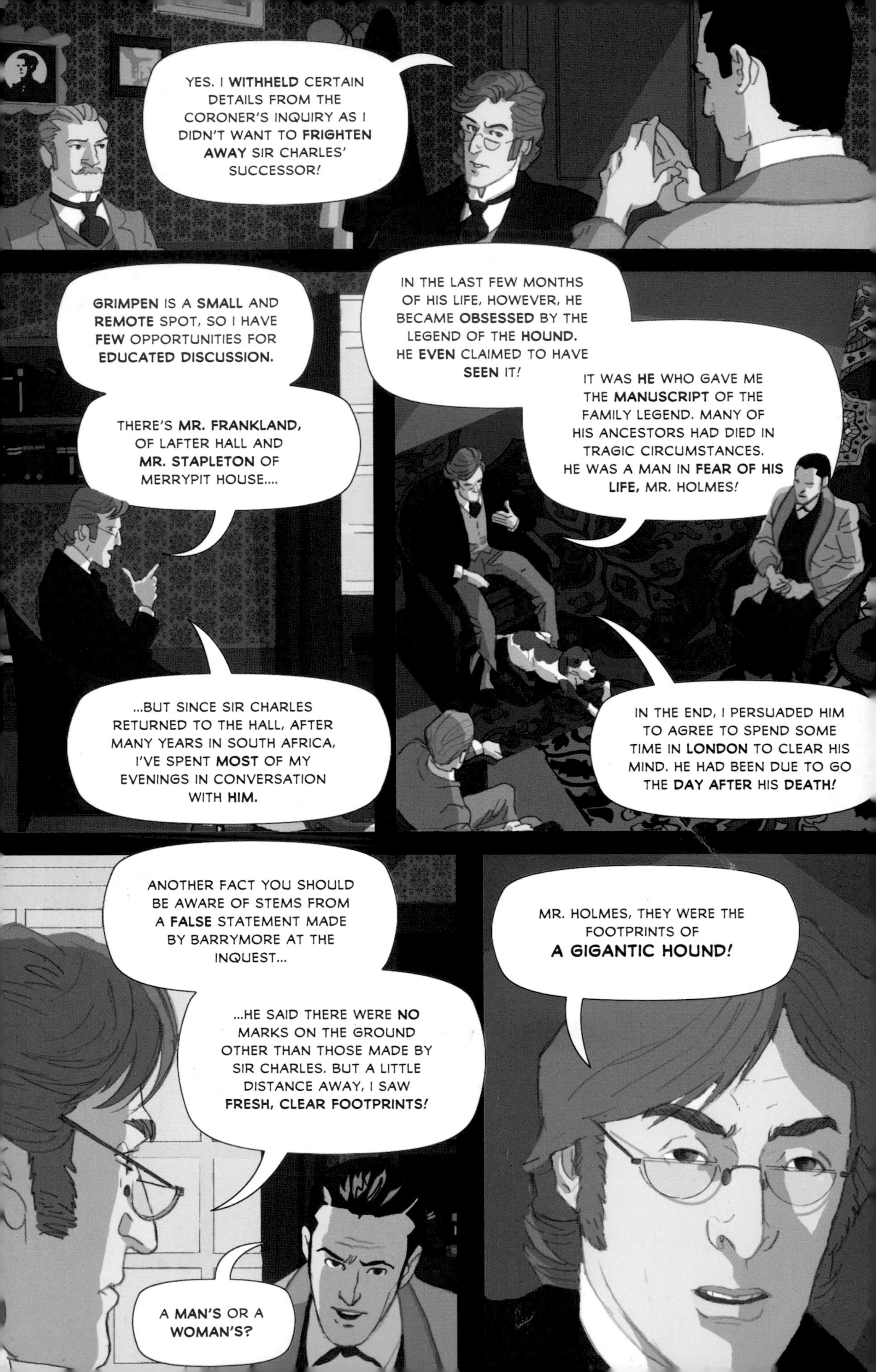
YES. I WITHHELD CERTAIN DETAILS FROM THE CORONER'S INQUIRY AS I DIDN'T WANT TO FRIGHTEN AWAY SIR CHARLES' SUCCESSOR!
GRIMPEN IS A SMALL AND REMOTE SPOT, SO I HAVE FEW OPPORTUNITIES FOR EDUCATED DISCUSSION.
THERE'S MR. FRANKLAND, OF LAFTER HALL AND MR. STAPLETON OF MERRYPIT HOUSE....
...BUT SINCE SIR CHARLES RETURNED TO THE HALL, AFTER MANY YEARS IN SOUTH AFRICA, I'VE SPENT MOST OF MY EVENINGS IN CONVERSATION WITH HIM.
IN THE LAST FEW MONTHS OF HIS LIFE, HOWEVER, HE BECAME OBSESSED BY THE LEGEND OF THE HOUND. HE EVEN CLAIMED TO HAVE SEEN IT!
IT WAS HE WHO GAVE ME THE MANUSCRIPT OF THE FAMILY LEGEND. MANY OF HIS ANCESTORS HAD DIED IN TRAGIC CIRCUMSTANCES. HE WAS A MAN IN FEAR OF HIS LIFE, MR. HOLMES!
IN THE END, I PERSUADED HIM TO AGREE TO SPEND SOME TIME IN LONDON TO CLEAR HIS MIND. HE HAD BEEN DUE TO GO THE DAY AFTER HIS DEATH!
ANOTHER FACT YOU SHOULD BE AWARE OF STEMS FROM A FALSE STATEMENT MADE BY BARRYMORE AT THE INQUEST...
...HE SAID THERE WERE NO MARKS ON THE GROUND OTHER THAN THOSE MADE BY SIR CHARLES. BUT A LITTLE DISTANCE AWAY, I SAW FRESH, CLEAR FOOTPRINTS!
A MAN'S OR A WOMAN'S?
MR. HOLMES, THEY WERE THE FOOTPRINTS OF A GIGANTIC HOUND!

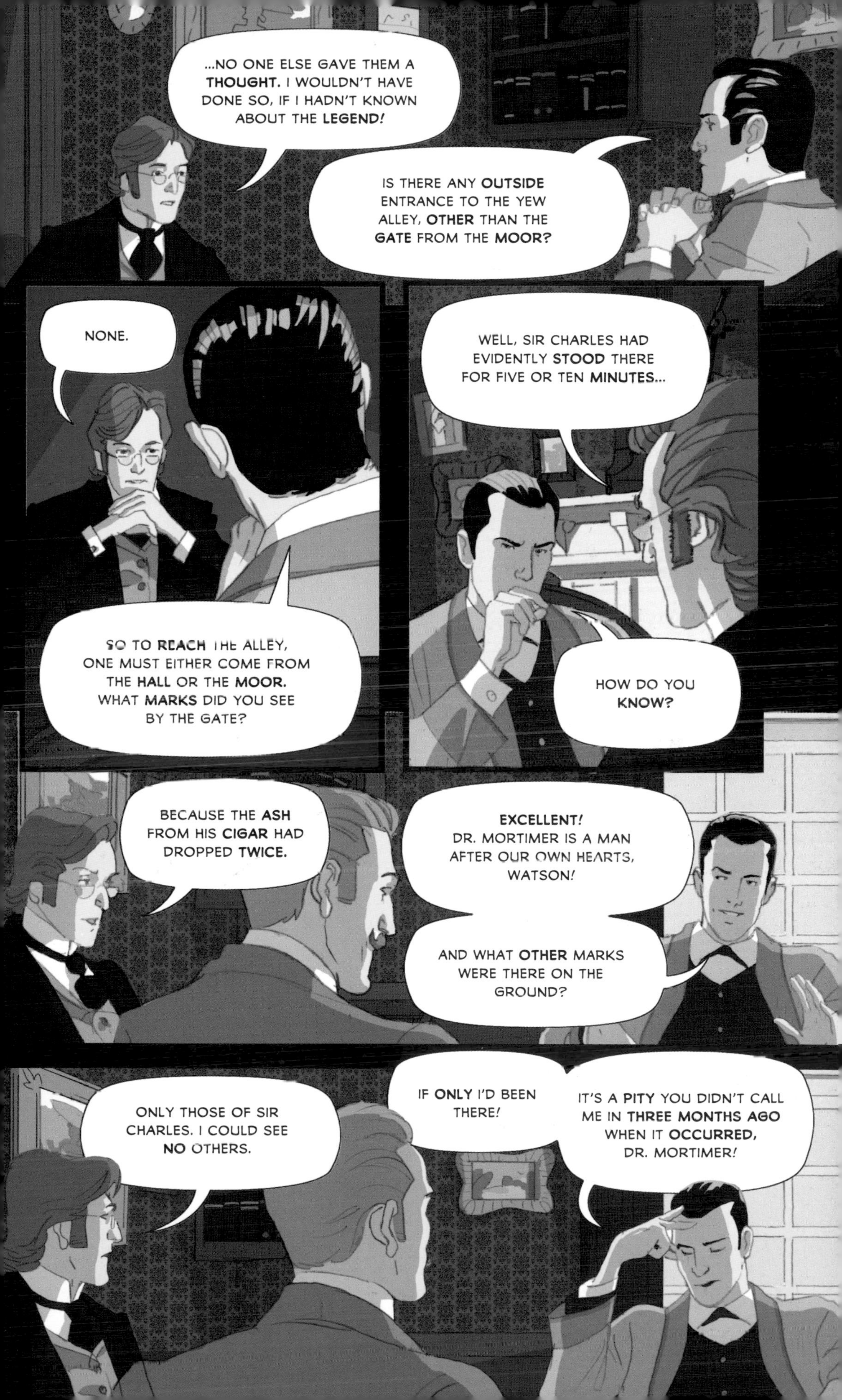
...NO ONE ELSE GAVE THEM A THOUGHT. I WOULDN'T HAVE DONE SO, IF I HADN'T KNOWN ABOUT THE LEGEND!
IS THERE ANY OUTSIDE ENTRANCE TO THE YEW ALLEY, OTHER THAN THE GATE FROM THE MOOR?
NONE.
SO TO REACH THE ALLEY, ONE MUST EITHER COME FROM THE HALL OR THE MOOR. WHAT MARKS DID YOU SEE BY THE GATE?
WELL, SIR CHARLES HAD EVIDENTLY STOOD THERE FOR FIVE OR TEN MINUTES...
HOW DO YOU KNOW?
BECAUSE THE ASH FROM HIS CIGAR HAD DROPPED TWICE.
EXCELLENT! DR. MORTIMER IS A MAN AFTER OUR OWN HEARTS, WATSON!
AND WHAT OTHER MARKS WERE THERE ON THE GROUND?
ONLY THOSE OF SIR CHARLES. I COULD SEE NO OTHERS.
IF ONLY I'D BEEN THERE!
IT'S A PITY YOU DIDN'T CALL ME IN THREE MONTHS AGO WHEN IT OCCURRED, DR. MORTIMER!

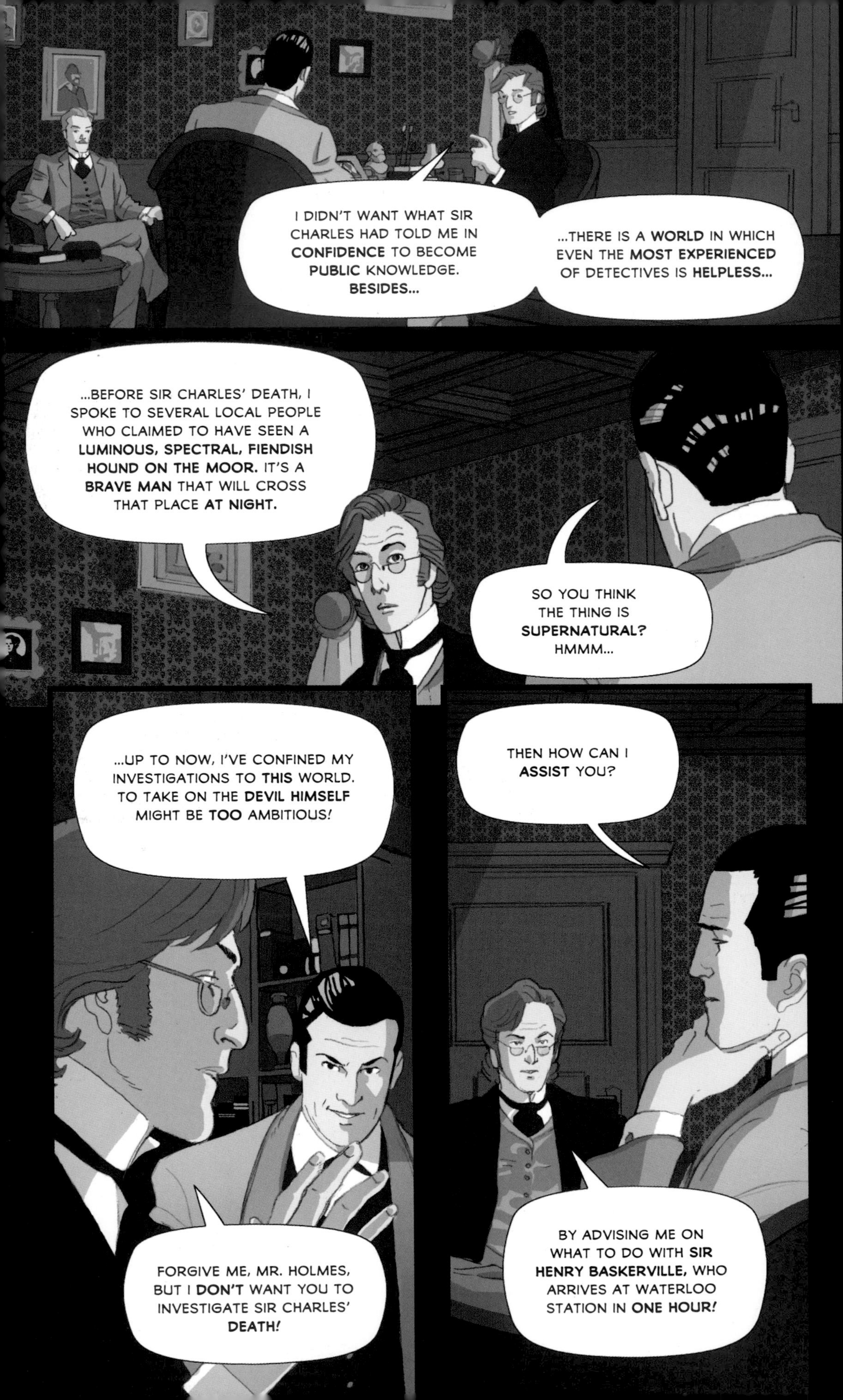
I DIDN'T WANT WHAT SIR CHARLES HAD TOLD ME IN CONFIDENCE TO BECOME PUBLIC KNOWLEDGE. BESIDES...
...THERE IS A WORLD IN WHICH EVEN THE MOST EXPERIENCED OF DETECTIVES IS HELPLESS...
...BEFORE SIR CHARLES' DEATH, I SPOKE TO SEVERAL LOCAL PEOPLE WHO CLAIMED TO HAVE SEEN A LUMINOUS, SPECTRAL, FIENDISH HOUND ON THE MOOR. IT'S A BRAVE MAN THAT WILL CROSS THAT PLACE AT NIGHT.
SO YOU THINK THE THING IS SUPERNATURAL? HMMM...
...UP TO NOW, I'VE CONFINED MY INVESTIGATIONS TO THIS WORLD. TO TAKE ON THE DEVIL HIMSELF MIGHT BE TOO AMBITIOUS!
FORGIVE ME, MR. HOLMES, BUT I DON'T WANT YOU TO INVESTIGATE SIR CHARLES' DEATH!
THEN HOW CAN I ASSIST YOU?
BY ADVISING ME ON WHAT TO DO WITH SIR HENRY BASKERVILLE, WHO ARRIVES AT WATERLOO STATION IN ONE HOUR!

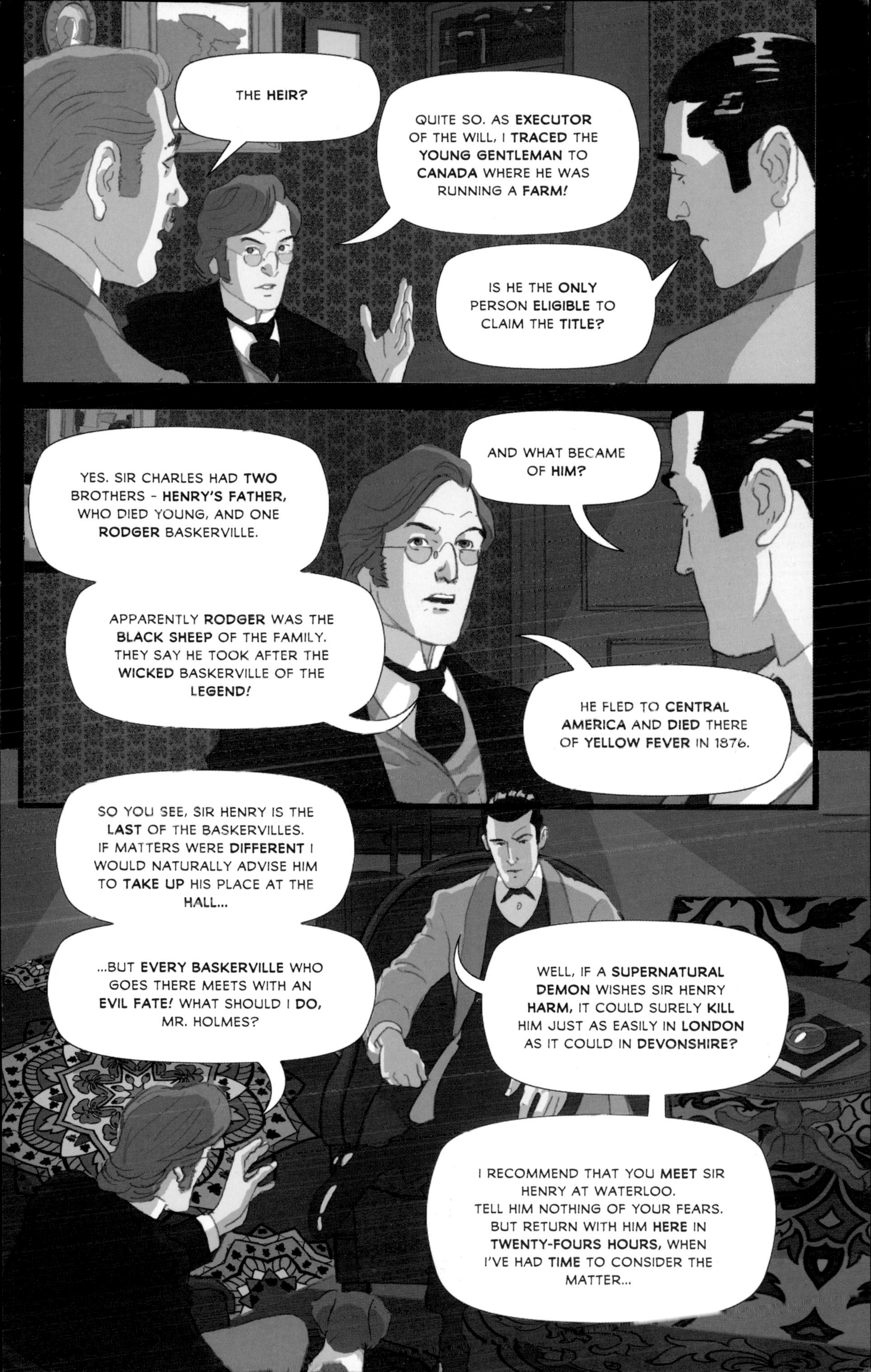
THE HEIR?
QUITE SO. AS EXECUTOR OF THE WILL, I TRACED THE YOUNG GENTLEMAN TO CANADA WHERE HE WAS RUNNING A FARM!
IS HE THE ONLY PERSON ELIGIBLE TO CLAIM THE TITLE?
YES. SIR CHARLES HAD TWO BROTHERS - HENRY'S FATHER, WHO DIED YOUNG, AND ONE RODGER BASKERVILLE.
AND WHAT BECAME OF HIM?
APPARENTLY RODGER WAS THE BLACK SHEEP OF THE FAMILY. THEY SAY HE TOOK AFTER THE WICKED BASKERVILLE OF THE LEGEND!
HE FLED TO CENTRAL AMERICA AND DIED THERE OF YELLOW FEVER IN 1876.
SO YOU SEE, SIR HENRY IS THE LAST OF THE BASKERVILLES. IF MATTERS WERE DIFFERENT I WOULD NATURALLY ADVISE HIM TO TAKE UP HIS PLACE AT THE HALL...
...BUT EVERY BASKERVILLE WHO GOES THERE MEETS WITH AN EVIL FATE! WHAT SHOULD I DO, MR. HOLMES?
WELL, IF A SUPERNATURAL DEMON WISHES SIR HENRY HARM, IT COULD SURELY KILL HIM JUST AS EASILY IN LONDON AS IT COULD IN DEVONSHIRE?
I RECOMMEND THAT YOU MEET SIR HENRY AT WATERLOO. TELL HIM NOTHING OF YOUR FEARS. BUT RETURN WITH HIM HERE IN TWENTY-FOURS HOURS, WHEN I'VE HAD TIME TO CONSIDER THE MATTER...

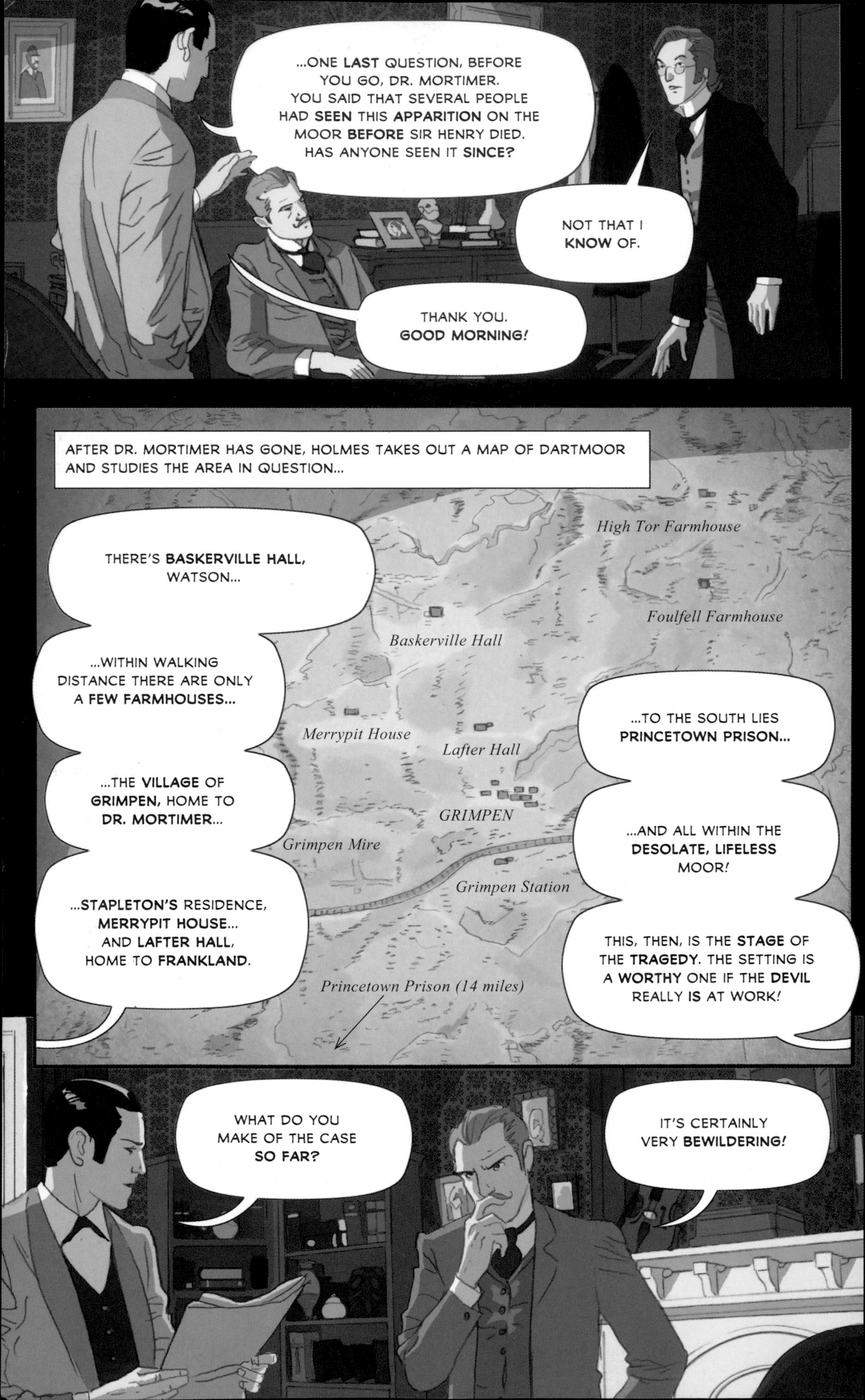
...ONE LAST QUESTION, BEFORE YOU GO, DR. MORTIMER. YOU SAID THAT SEVERAL PEOPLE HAD SEEN THIS APPARITION ON THE MOOR BEFORE SIR HENRY DIED. HAS ANYONE SEEN IT SINCE?
NOT THAT I KNOW OF.
THANK YOU. GOOD MORNING!
AFTER DR. MORTIMER HAS GONE, HOLMES TAKES OUT A MAP OF DARTMOOR AND STUDIES THE AREA IN QUESTION...
THERE'S BASKERVILLE HALL, WATSON...
...WITHIN WALKING DISTANCE THERE ARE ONLY A FEW FARMHOUSES...
...THE VILLAGE OF GRIMPEN, HOME TO DR. MORTIMER...
...STAPLETON'S RESIDENCE, MERRYPIT HOUSE... AND LAFTER HALL, HOME TO FRANKLAND.
...TO THE SOUTH LIES PRINCETOWN PRISON...
...AND ALL WITHIN THE DESOLATE, LIFELESS MOOR!
THIS, THEN, IS THE STAGE OF THE TRAGEDY. THE SETTING IS A WORTHY ONE IF THE DEVIL REALLY IS AT WORK!
High Tor Farmhouse
Foulfell Farmhouse
Baskerville Hall
Merrypit House
Lafter Hall
GRIMPEN
Grimpen Mire
Grimpen Station
Princetown Prison (14 miles)
WHAT DO YOU MAKE OF THE CASE SO FAR?
IT'S CERTAINLY VERY BEWILDERING!

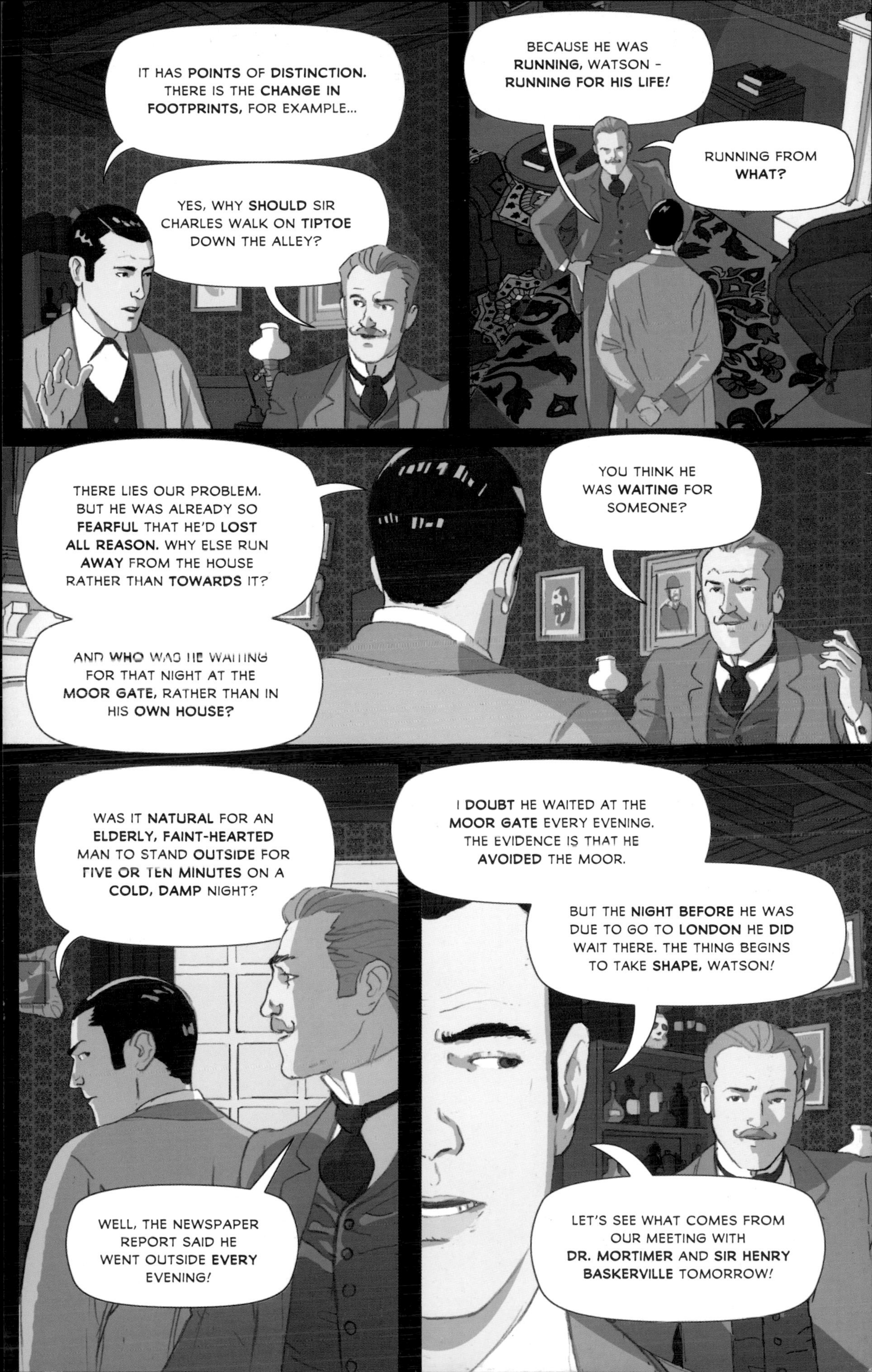
IT HAS POINTS OF DISTINCTION. THERE IS THE CHANGE IN FOOTPRINTS, FOR EXAMPLE...
YES, WHY SHOULD SIR CHARLES WALK ON TIPTOE DOWN THE ALLEY?
BECAUSE HE WAS RUNNING, WATSON - RUNNING FOR HIS LIFE!
RUNNING FROM WHAT?
THERE LIES OUR PROBLEM. BUT HE WAS ALREADY SO FEARFUL THAT HE'D LOST ALL REASON. WHY ELSE RUN AWAY FROM THE HOUSE RATHER THAN TOWARDS IT?
AND WHO WAS HE WAITING FOR THAT NIGHT AT THE MOOR GATE, RATHER THAN IN HIS OWN HOUSE?
YOU THINK HE WAS WAITING FOR SOMEONE?
WAS IT NATURAL FOR AN ELDERLY, FAINT-HEARTED MAN TO STAND OUTSIDE FOR FIVE OR TEN MINUTES ON A COLD, DAMP NIGHT?
WELL, THE NEWSPAPER REPORT SAID HE WENT OUTSIDE EVERY EVENING!
I DOUBT HE WAITED AT THE MOOR GATE EVERY EVENING. THE EVIDENCE IS THAT HE AVOIDED THE MOOR.
BUT THE NIGHT BEFORE HE WAS DUE TO GO TO LONDON HE DID WAIT THERE. THE THING BEGINS TO TAKE SHAPE, WATSON!
LET'S SEE WHAT COMES FROM OUR MEETING WITH DR. MORTIMER AND SIR HENRY BASKERVILLE TOMORROW!

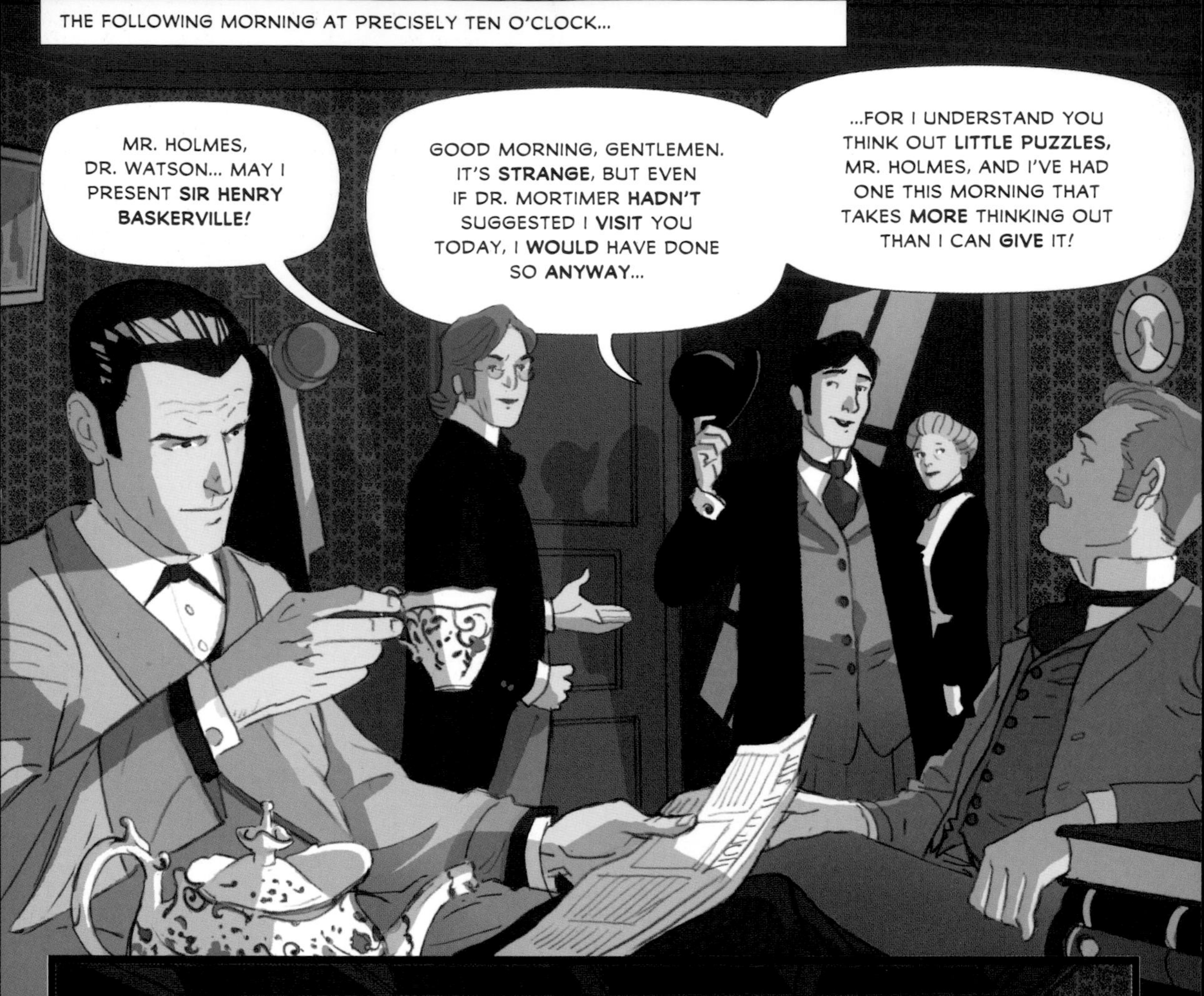
THE FOLLOWING MORNING AT PRECISELY TEN O'CLOCK...
MR. HOLMES, DR. WATSON... MAY I PRESENT **SIR HENRY BASKERVILLE!**
GOOD MORNING, GENTLEMEN. IT'S **STRANGE**, BUT EVEN IF DR. MORTIMER **HADN'T** SUGGESTED I **VISIT** YOU TODAY, I **WOULD** HAVE DONE SO **ANYWAY**...
...FOR I UNDERSTAND YOU THINK OUT **LITTLE PUZZLES,** MR. HOLMES, AND I'VE HAD ONE THIS MORNING THAT TAKES **MORE** THINKING OUT THAN I CAN **GIVE** IT!

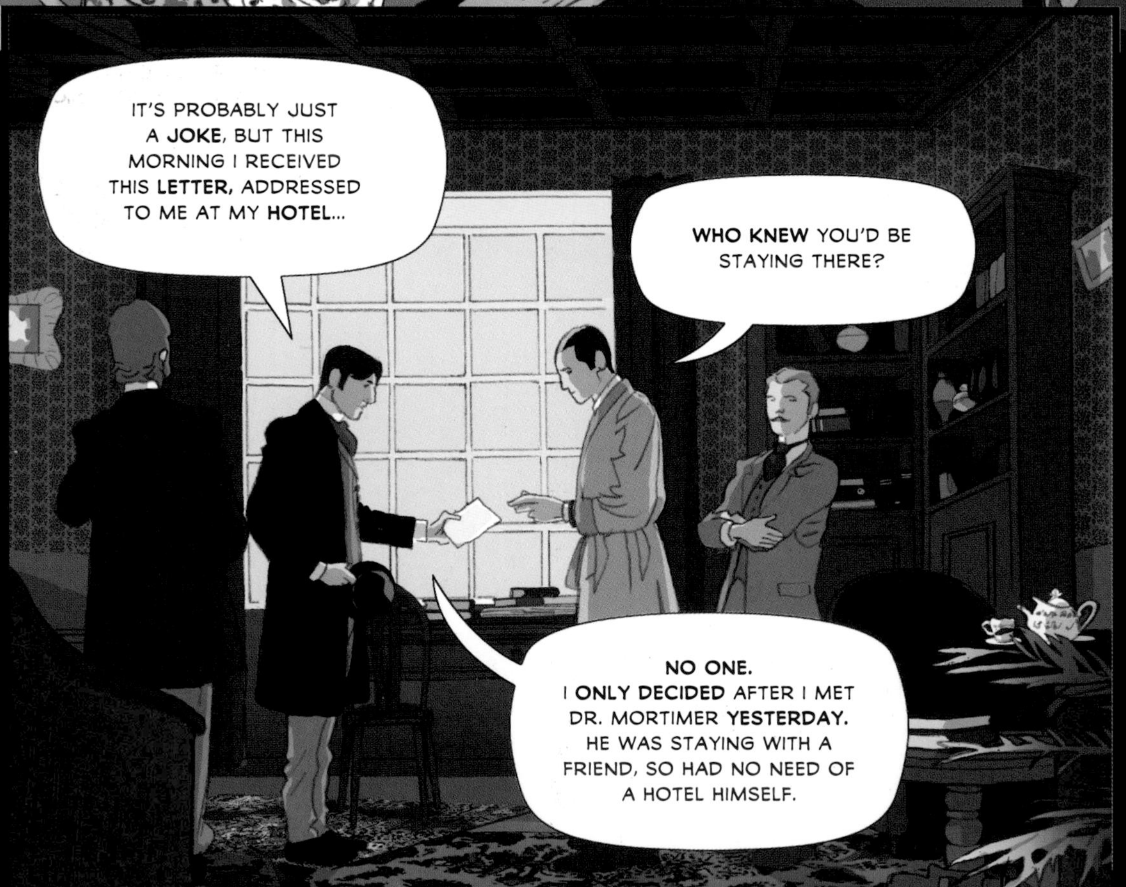
IT'S PROBABLY JUST A **JOKE**, BUT THIS MORNING I RECEIVED THIS **LETTER,** ADDRESSED TO ME AT MY **HOTEL**...
WHO KNEW YOU'D BE STAYING THERE?
NO ONE. I **ONLY DECIDED** AFTER I MET DR. MORTIMER **YESTERDAY.** HE WAS STAYING WITH A FRIEND, SO HAD NO NEED OF A HOTEL HIMSELF.

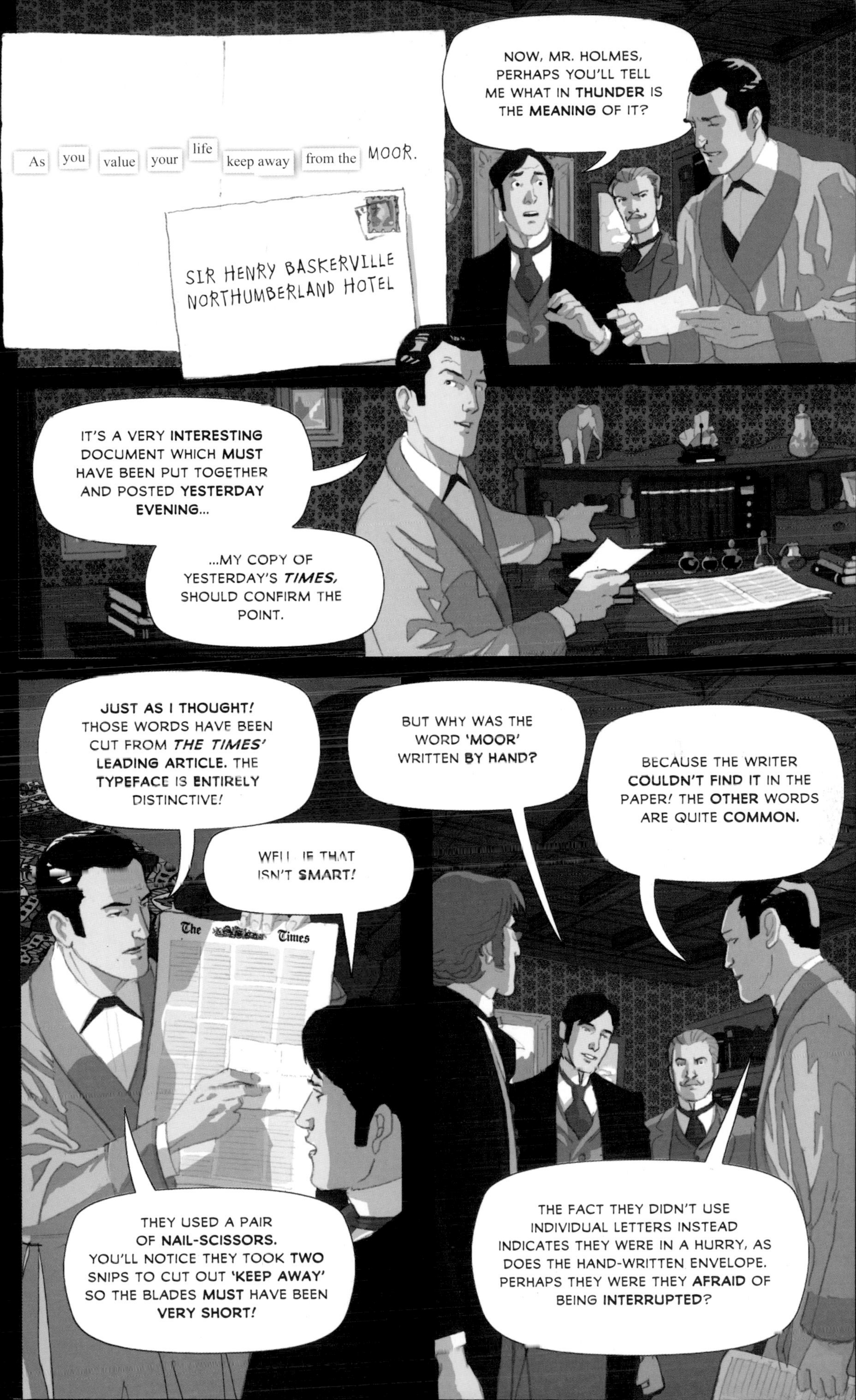
As you value your life keep away from the MOOR.
SIR HENRY BASKERVILLE NORTHUMBERLAND HOTEL
NOW, MR. HOLMES, PERHAPS YOU'LL TELL ME WHAT IN **THUNDER** IS THE **MEANING** OF IT?
IT'S A VERY **INTERESTING** DOCUMENT WHICH **MUST** HAVE BEEN PUT TOGETHER AND POSTED **YESTERDAY EVENING...**
...MY COPY OF YESTERDAY'S ***TIMES,*** SHOULD CONFIRM THE POINT.
JUST AS I THOUGHT! THOSE WORDS HAVE BEEN CUT FROM ***THE TIMES'* LEADING ARTICLE.** THE **TYPEFACE** IS **ENTIRELY** DISTINCTIVE!
WELL, IF THAT ISN'T **SMART!**
BUT WHY WAS THE WORD **'MOOR'** WRITTEN **BY HAND?**
BECAUSE THE WRITER **COULDN'T FIND IT** IN THE PAPER! THE **OTHER** WORDS ARE QUITE **COMMON.**
THEY USED A PAIR OF **NAIL-SCISSORS.** YOU'LL NOTICE THEY TOOK **TWO** SNIPS TO CUT OUT **'KEEP AWAY'** SO THE BLADES **MUST** HAVE BEEN **VERY SHORT!**
THE FACT THEY DIDN'T USE INDIVIDUAL LETTERS INSTEAD INDICATES THEY WERE IN A HURRY, AS DOES THE HAND-WRITTEN ENVELOPE. PERHAPS THEY WERE THEY **AFRAID** OF BEING **INTERRUPTED**?

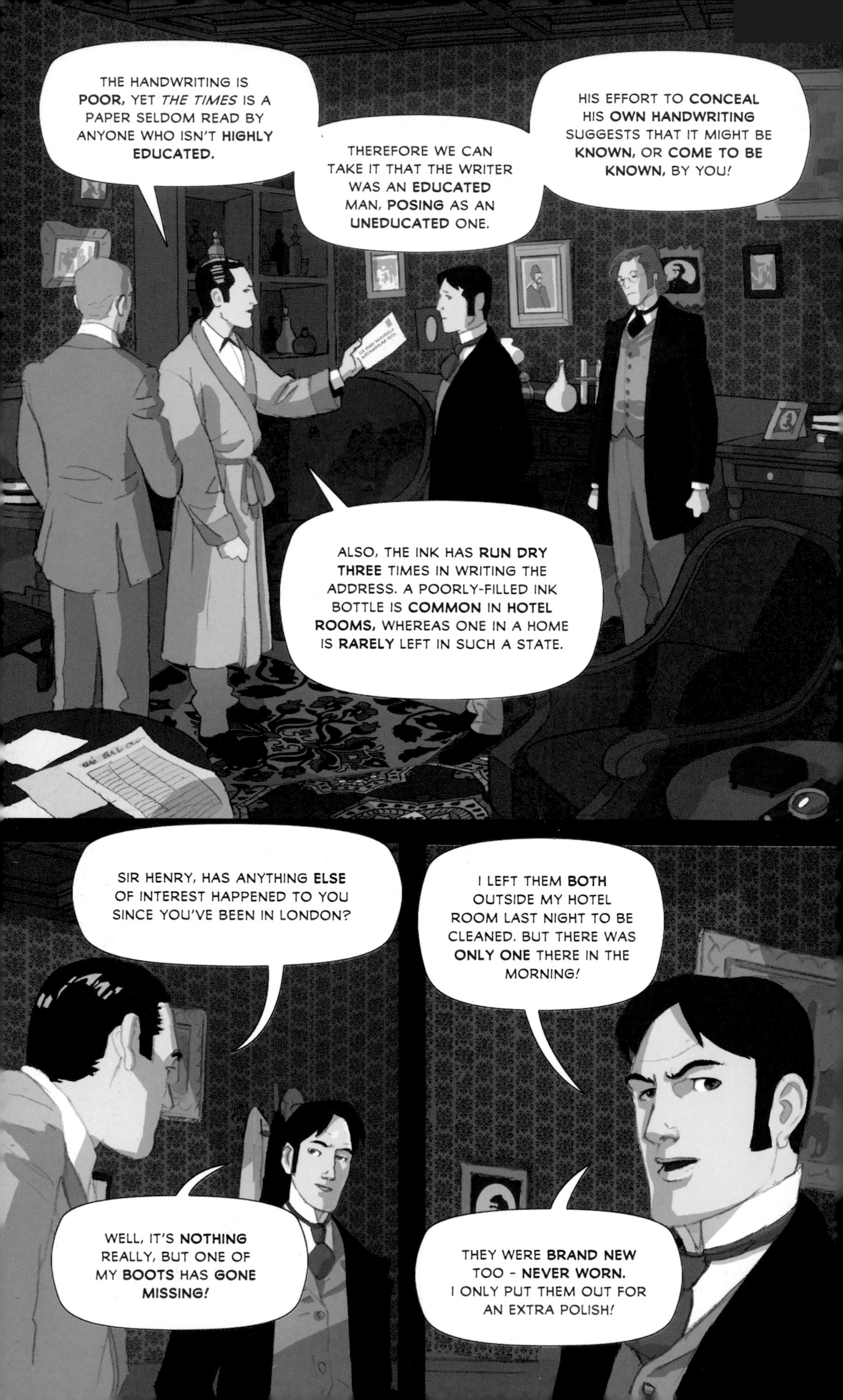
THE HANDWRITING IS **POOR,** YET *THE TIMES* IS A PAPER SELDOM READ BY ANYONE WHO ISN'T **HIGHLY EDUCATED.**
THEREFORE WE CAN TAKE IT THAT THE WRITER WAS AN **EDUCATED** MAN, **POSING** AS AN **UNEDUCATED** ONE.
HIS EFFORT TO **CONCEAL** HIS **OWN HANDWRITING** SUGGESTS THAT IT MIGHT BE **KNOWN,** OR **COME TO BE KNOWN,** BY YOU!
ALSO, THE INK HAS **RUN DRY THREE** TIMES IN WRITING THE ADDRESS. A POORLY-FILLED INK BOTTLE IS **COMMON** IN **HOTEL ROOMS,** WHEREAS ONE IN A HOME IS **RARELY** LEFT IN SUCH A STATE.
SIR HENRY, HAS ANYTHING **ELSE** OF INTEREST HAPPENED TO YOU SINCE YOU'VE BEEN IN LONDON?
WELL, IT'S **NOTHING** REALLY, BUT ONE OF MY **BOOTS** HAS **GONE MISSING!**
I LEFT THEM **BOTH** OUTSIDE MY HOTEL ROOM LAST NIGHT TO BE CLEANED. BUT THERE WAS **ONLY ONE** THERE IN THE MORNING!
THEY WERE **BRAND NEW** TOO - **NEVER WORN.** I ONLY PUT THEM OUT FOR AN EXTRA POLISH!

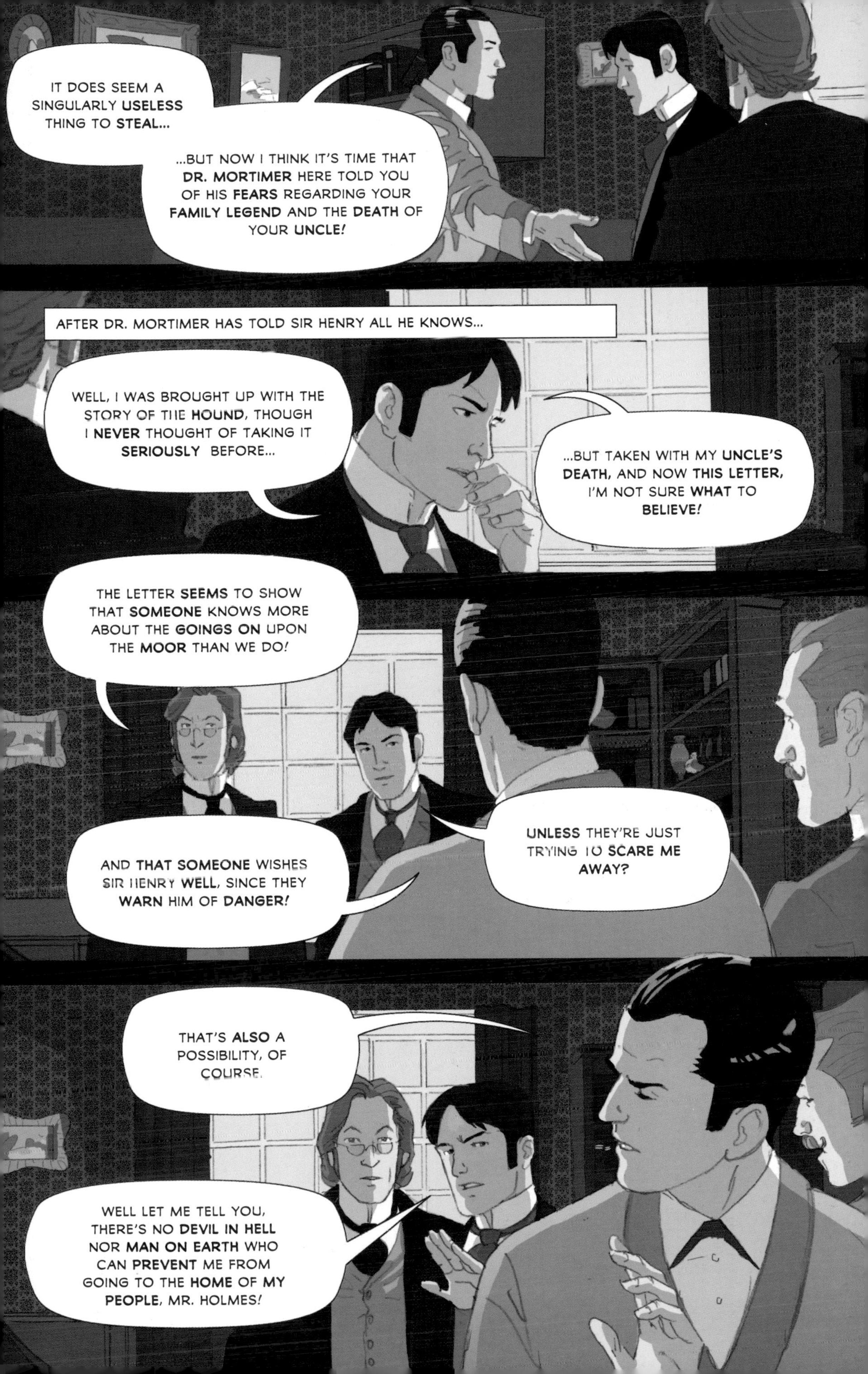
IT DOES SEEM A SINGULARLY USELESS THING TO STEAL...
...BUT NOW I THINK IT'S TIME THAT DR. MORTIMER HERE TOLD YOU OF HIS FEARS REGARDING YOUR FAMILY LEGEND AND THE DEATH OF YOUR UNCLE!
AFTER DR. MORTIMER HAS TOLD SIR HENRY ALL HE KNOWS...
WELL, I WAS BROUGHT UP WITH THE STORY OF THE HOUND, THOUGH I NEVER THOUGHT OF TAKING IT SERIOUSLY BEFORE...
...BUT TAKEN WITH MY UNCLE'S DEATH, AND NOW THIS LETTER, I'M NOT SURE WHAT TO BELIEVE!
THE LETTER SEEMS TO SHOW THAT SOMEONE KNOWS MORE ABOUT THE GOINGS ON UPON THE MOOR THAN WE DO!
AND THAT SOMEONE WISHES SIR HENRY WELL, SINCE THEY WARN HIM OF DANGER!
UNLESS THEY'RE JUST TRYING TO SCARE ME AWAY?
THAT'S ALSO A POSSIBILITY, OF COURSE.
WELL LET ME TELL YOU, THERE'S NO DEVIL IN HELL NOR MAN ON EARTH WHO CAN PREVENT ME FROM GOING TO THE HOME OF MY PEOPLE, MR. HOLMES!

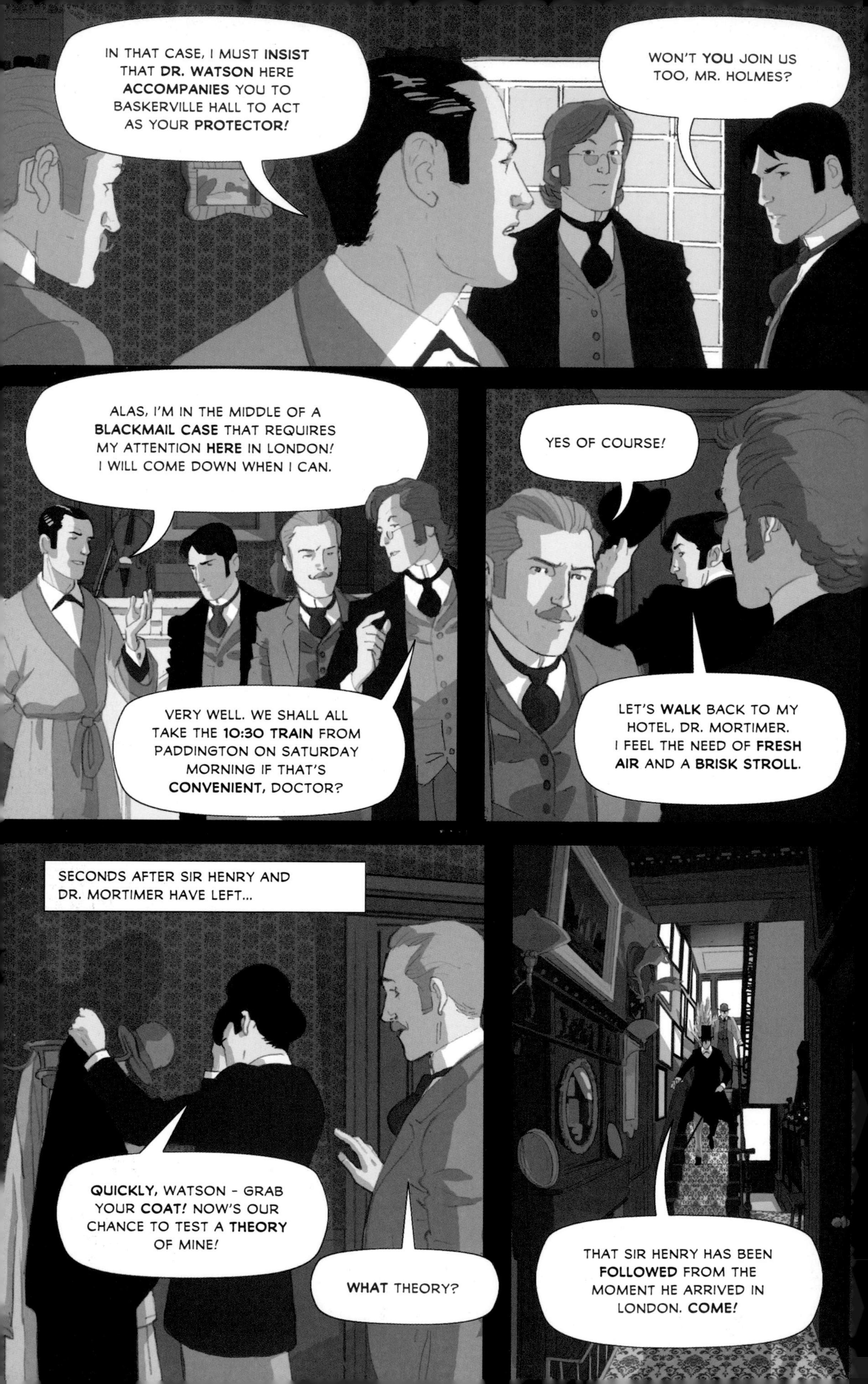
IN THAT CASE, I MUST INSIST THAT DR. WATSON HERE ACCOMPANIES YOU TO BASKERVILLE HALL TO ACT AS YOUR PROTECTOR!
WON'T YOU JOIN US TOO, MR. HOLMES?
ALAS, I'M IN THE MIDDLE OF A BLACKMAIL CASE THAT REQUIRES MY ATTENTION HERE IN LONDON! I WILL COME DOWN WHEN I CAN.
VERY WELL. WE SHALL ALL TAKE THE 10:30 TRAIN FROM PADDINGTON ON SATURDAY MORNING IF THAT'S CONVENIENT, DOCTOR?
YES OF COURSE!
LET'S WALK BACK TO MY HOTEL, DR. MORTIMER. I FEEL THE NEED OF FRESH AIR AND A BRISK STROLL.
SECONDS AFTER SIR HENRY AND DR. MORTIMER HAVE LEFT...
QUICKLY, WATSON - GRAB YOUR COAT! NOW'S OUR CHANCE TO TEST A THEORY OF MINE!
WHAT THEORY?
THAT SIR HENRY HAS BEEN FOLLOWED FROM THE MOMENT HE ARRIVED IN LONDON. COME!

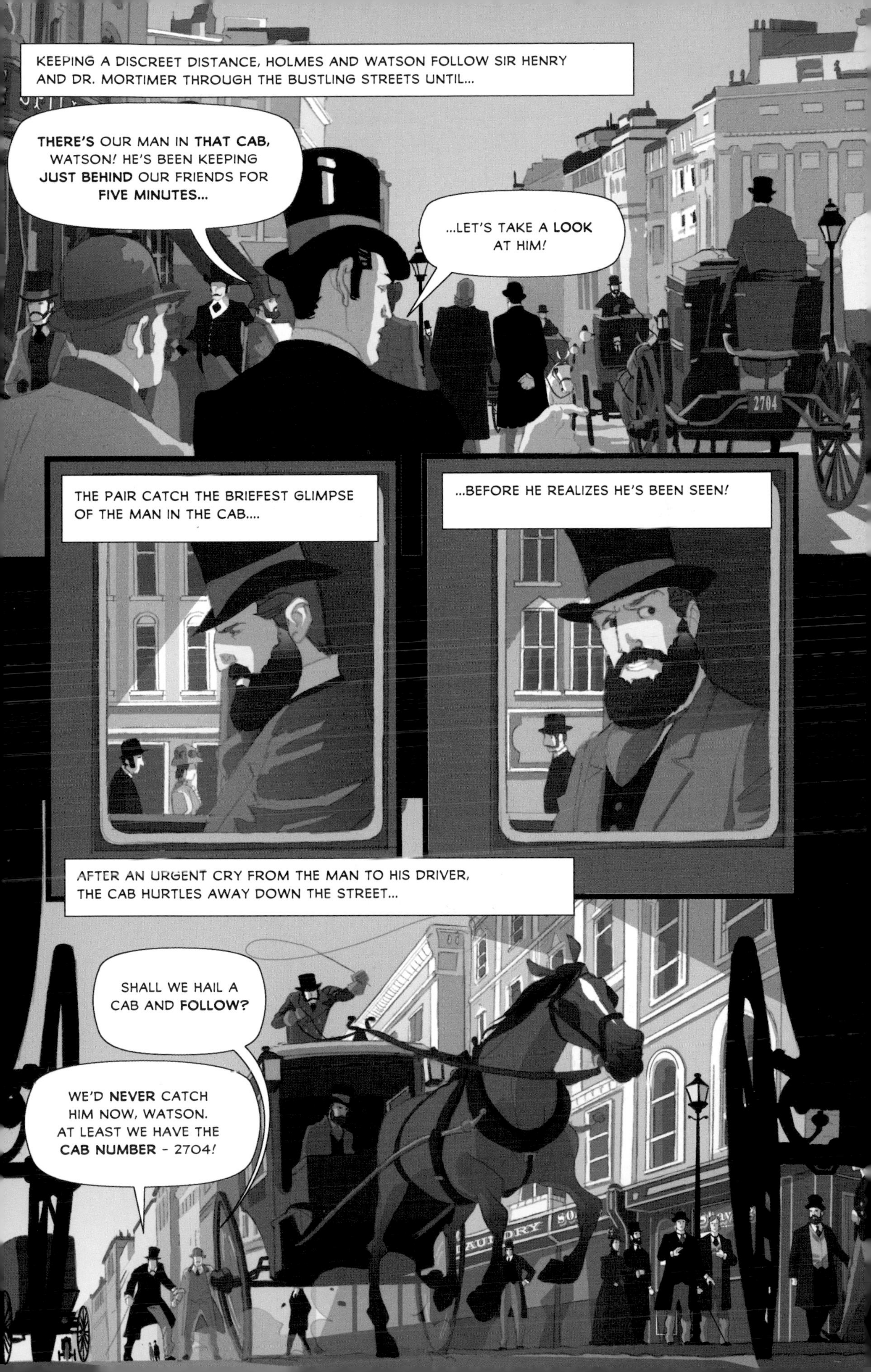

KEEPING A DISCREET DISTANCE, HOLMES AND WATSON FOLLOW SIR HENRY AND DR. MORTIMER THROUGH THE BUSTLING STREETS UNTIL...
THERE'S OUR MAN IN THAT CAB, WATSON! HE'S BEEN KEEPING JUST BEHIND OUR FRIENDS FOR FIVE MINUTES...
...LET'S TAKE A LOOK AT HIM!
2704
THE PAIR CATCH THE BRIEFEST GLIMPSE OF THE MAN IN THE CAB....
...BEFORE HE REALIZES HE'S BEEN SEEN!
AFTER AN URGENT CRY FROM THE MAN TO HIS DRIVER, THE CAB HURTLES AWAY DOWN THE STREET...
SHALL WE HAIL A CAB AND FOLLOW?
WE'D NEVER CATCH HIM NOW, WATSON. AT LEAST WE HAVE THE CAB NUMBER - 2704!
LAUNDRY

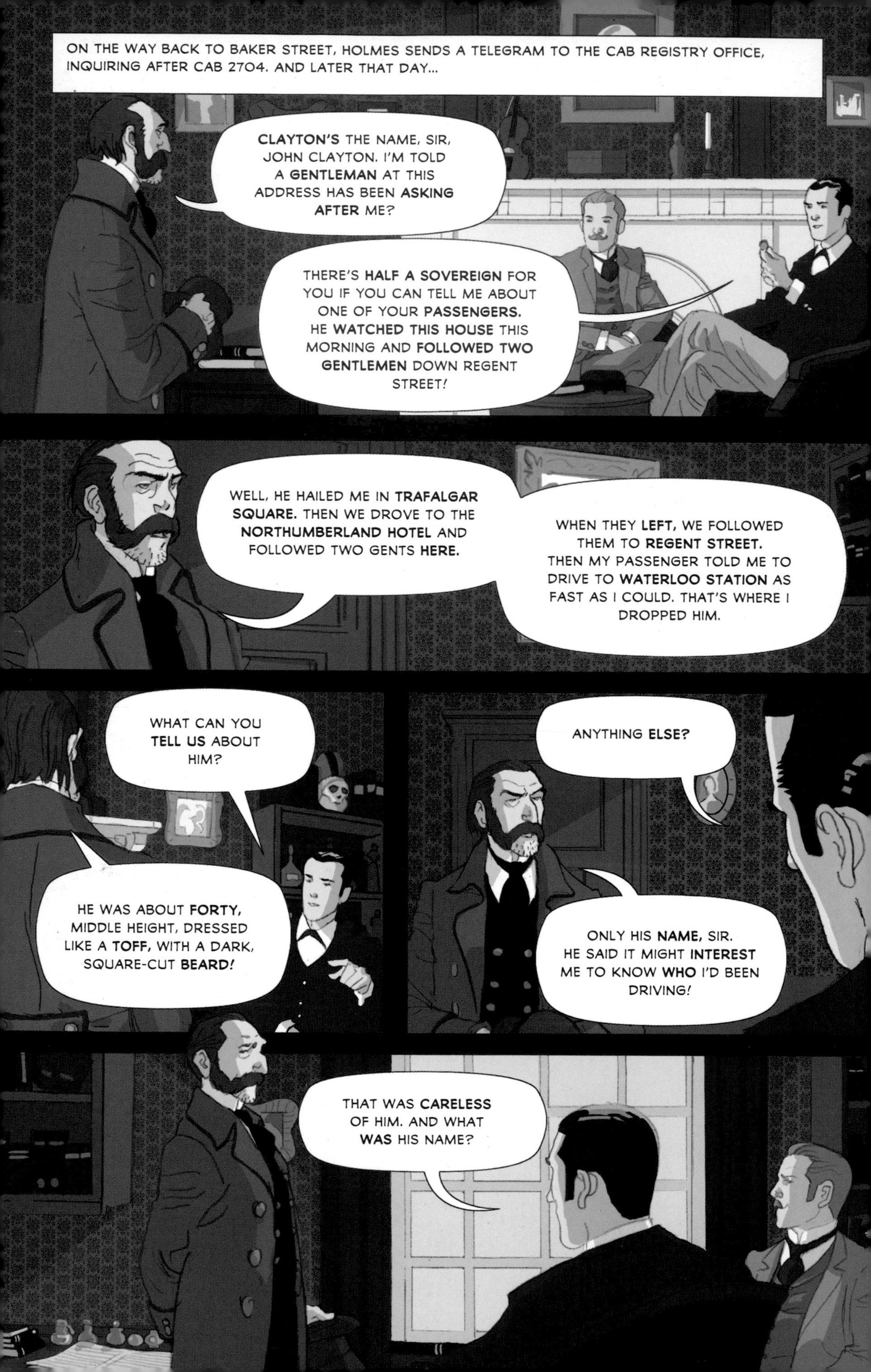

ON THE WAY BACK TO BAKER STREET, HOLMES SENDS A TELEGRAM TO THE CAB REGISTRY OFFICE, INQUIRING AFTER CAB 2704. AND LATER THAT DAY...
CLAYTON'S THE NAME, SIR, JOHN CLAYTON. I'M TOLD A GENTLEMAN AT THIS ADDRESS HAS BEEN ASKING AFTER ME?
THERE'S HALF A SOVEREIGN FOR YOU IF YOU CAN TELL ME ABOUT ONE OF YOUR PASSENGERS. HE WATCHED THIS HOUSE THIS MORNING AND FOLLOWED TWO GENTLEMEN DOWN REGENT STREET!
WELL, HE HAILED ME IN TRAFALGAR SQUARE. THEN WE DROVE TO THE NORTHUMBERLAND HOTEL AND FOLLOWED TWO GENTS HERE.
WHEN THEY LEFT, WE FOLLOWED THEM TO REGENT STREET. THEN MY PASSENGER TOLD ME TO DRIVE TO WATERLOO STATION AS FAST AS I COULD. THAT'S WHERE I DROPPED HIM.
WHAT CAN YOU TELL US ABOUT HIM?
HE WAS ABOUT FORTY, MIDDLE HEIGHT, DRESSED LIKE A TOFF, WITH A DARK, SQUARE-CUT BEARD!
ANYTHING ELSE?
ONLY HIS NAME, SIR. HE SAID IT MIGHT INTEREST ME TO KNOW WHO I'D BEEN DRIVING!
THAT WAS CARELESS OF HIM. AND WHAT WAS HIS NAME?

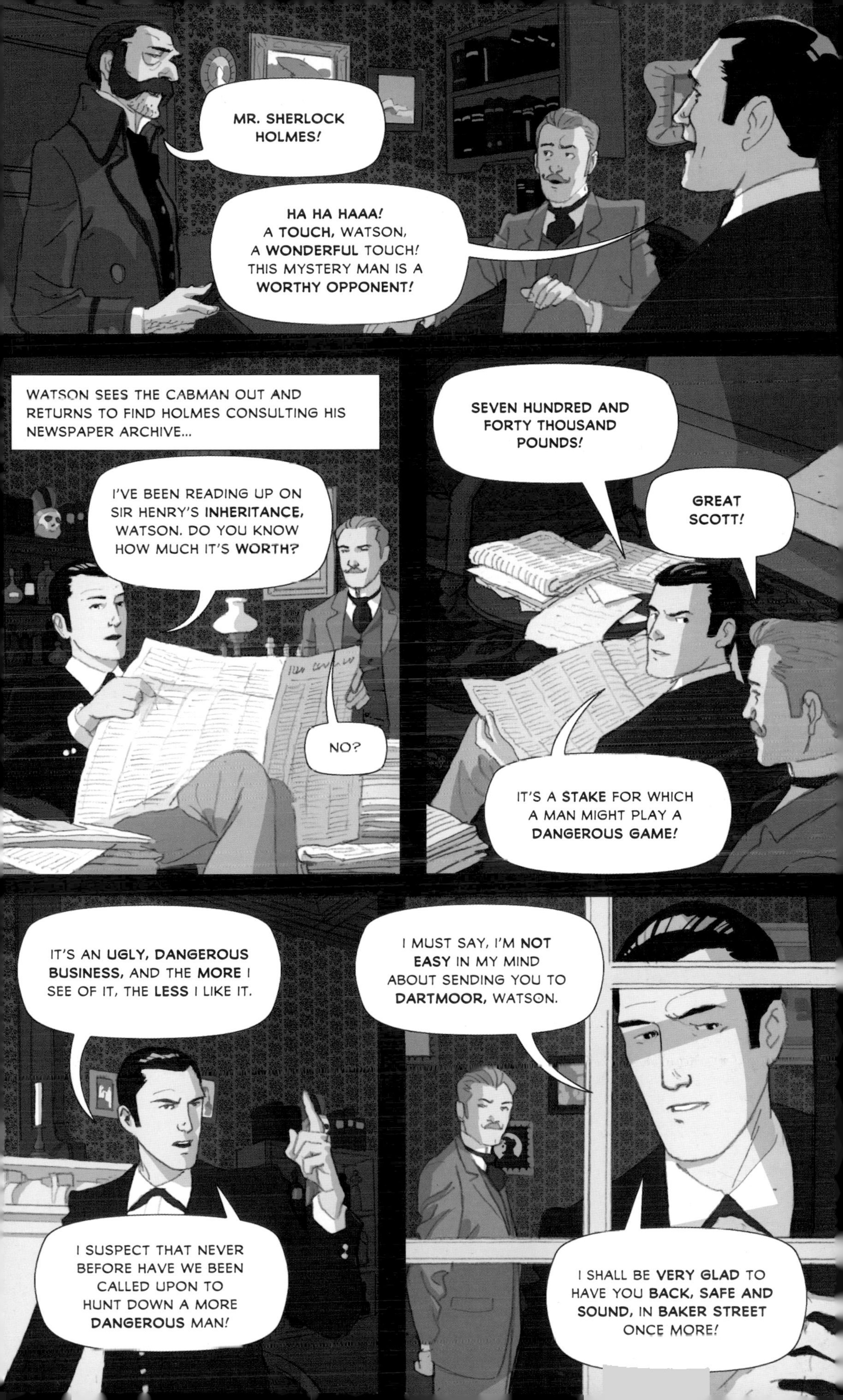
MR. SHERLOCK HOLMES!
HA HA HAAA! A TOUCH, WATSON, A WONDERFUL TOUCH! THIS MYSTERY MAN IS A WORTHY OPPONENT!
WATSON SEES THE CABMAN OUT AND RETURNS TO FIND HOLMES CONSULTING HIS NEWSPAPER ARCHIVE...
I'VE BEEN READING UP ON SIR HENRY'S INHERITANCE, WATSON. DO YOU KNOW HOW MUCH IT'S WORTH?
NO?
SEVEN HUNDRED AND FORTY THOUSAND POUNDS!
GREAT SCOTT!
IT'S A STAKE FOR WHICH A MAN MIGHT PLAY A DANGEROUS GAME!
IT'S AN UGLY, DANGEROUS BUSINESS, AND THE MORE I SEE OF IT, THE LESS I LIKE IT.
I SUSPECT THAT NEVER BEFORE HAVE WE BEEN CALLED UPON TO HUNT DOWN A MORE DANGEROUS MAN!
I MUST SAY, I'M NOT EASY IN MY MIND ABOUT SENDING YOU TO DARTMOOR, WATSON.
I SHALL BE VERY GLAD TO HAVE YOU BACK, SAFE AND SOUND, IN BAKER STREET ONCE MORE!

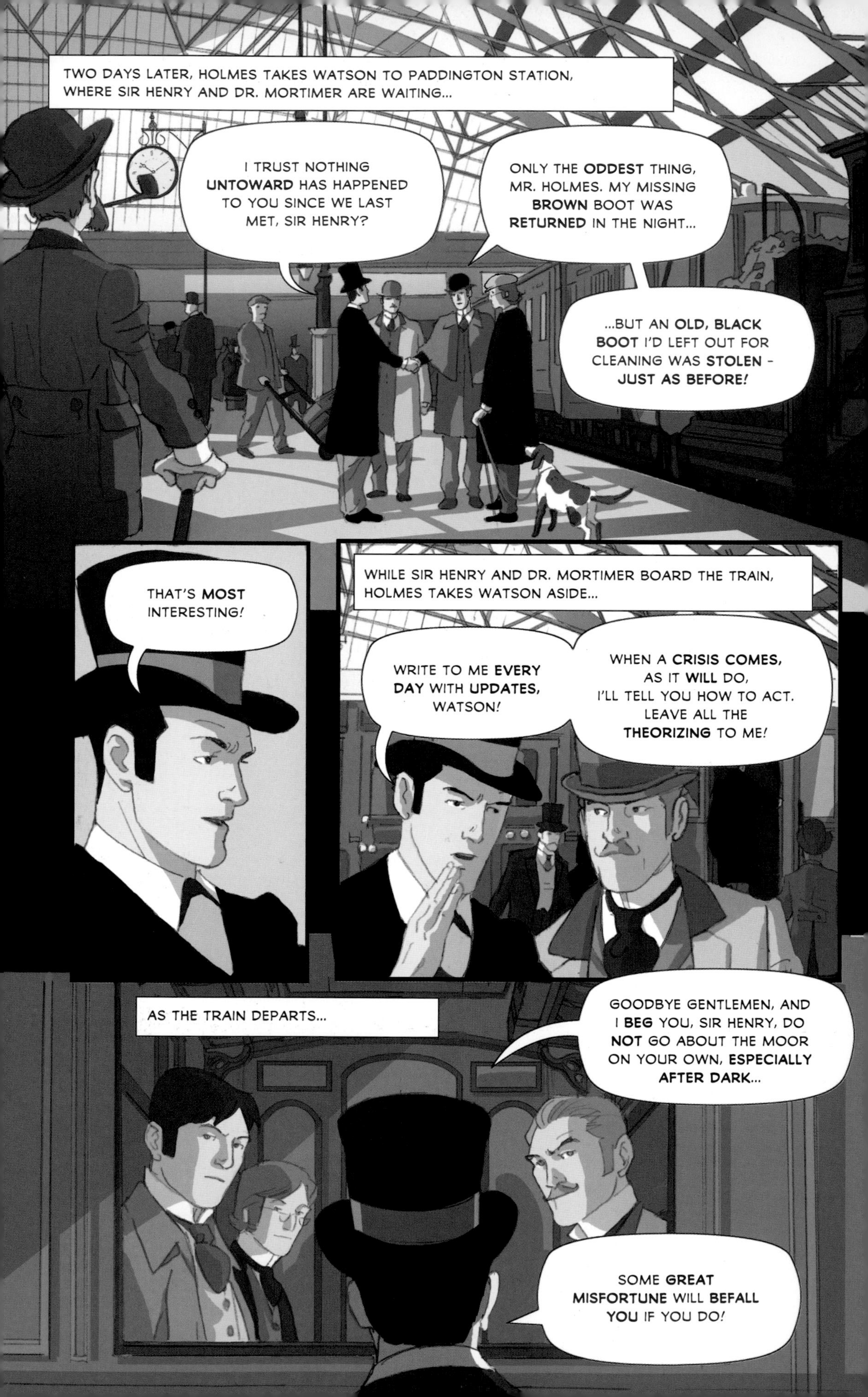
TWO DAYS LATER, HOLMES TAKES WATSON TO PADDINGTON STATION, WHERE SIR HENRY AND DR. MORTIMER ARE WAITING...
I TRUST NOTHING UNTOWARD HAS HAPPENED TO YOU SINCE WE LAST MET, SIR HENRY?
ONLY THE ODDEST THING, MR. HOLMES. MY MISSING BROWN BOOT WAS RETURNED IN THE NIGHT...
...BUT AN OLD, BLACK BOOT I'D LEFT OUT FOR CLEANING WAS STOLEN - JUST AS BEFORE!
THAT'S MOST INTERESTING!
WHILE SIR HENRY AND DR. MORTIMER BOARD THE TRAIN, HOLMES TAKES WATSON ASIDE...
WRITE TO ME EVERY DAY WITH UPDATES, WATSON!
WHEN A CRISIS COMES, AS IT WILL DO, I'LL TELL YOU HOW TO ACT. LEAVE ALL THE THEORIZING TO ME!
AS THE TRAIN DEPARTS...
GOODBYE GENTLEMEN, AND I BEG YOU, SIR HENRY, DO NOT GO ABOUT THE MOOR ON YOUR OWN, ESPECIALLY AFTER DARK...
SOME GREAT MISFORTUNE WILL BEFALL YOU IF YOU DO!

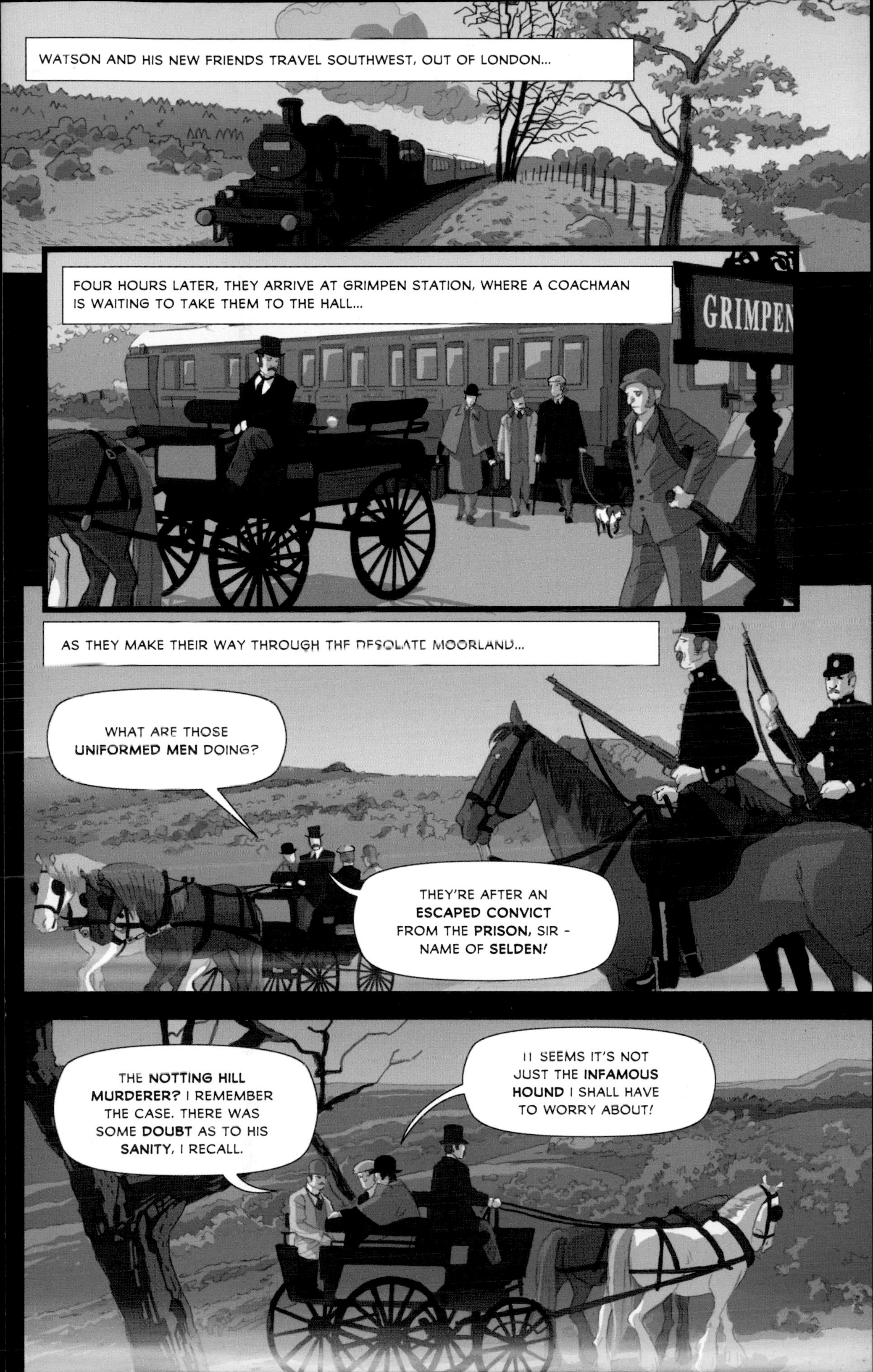
WATSON AND HIS NEW FRIENDS TRAVEL SOUTHWEST, OUT OF LONDON...
FOUR HOURS LATER, THEY ARRIVE AT GRIMPEN STATION, WHERE A COACHMAN IS WAITING TO TAKE THEM TO THE HALL...
GRIMPEN
AS THEY MAKE THEIR WAY THROUGH THE DESOLATE MOORLAND...
WHAT ARE THOSE UNIFORMED MEN DOING?
THEY'RE AFTER AN ESCAPED CONVICT FROM THE PRISON, SIR - NAME OF SELDEN!
THE NOTTING HILL MURDERER? I REMEMBER THE CASE. THERE WAS SOME DOUBT AS TO HIS SANITY, I RECALL.
IT SEEMS IT'S NOT JUST THE INFAMOUS HOUND I SHALL HAVE TO WORRY ABOUT!

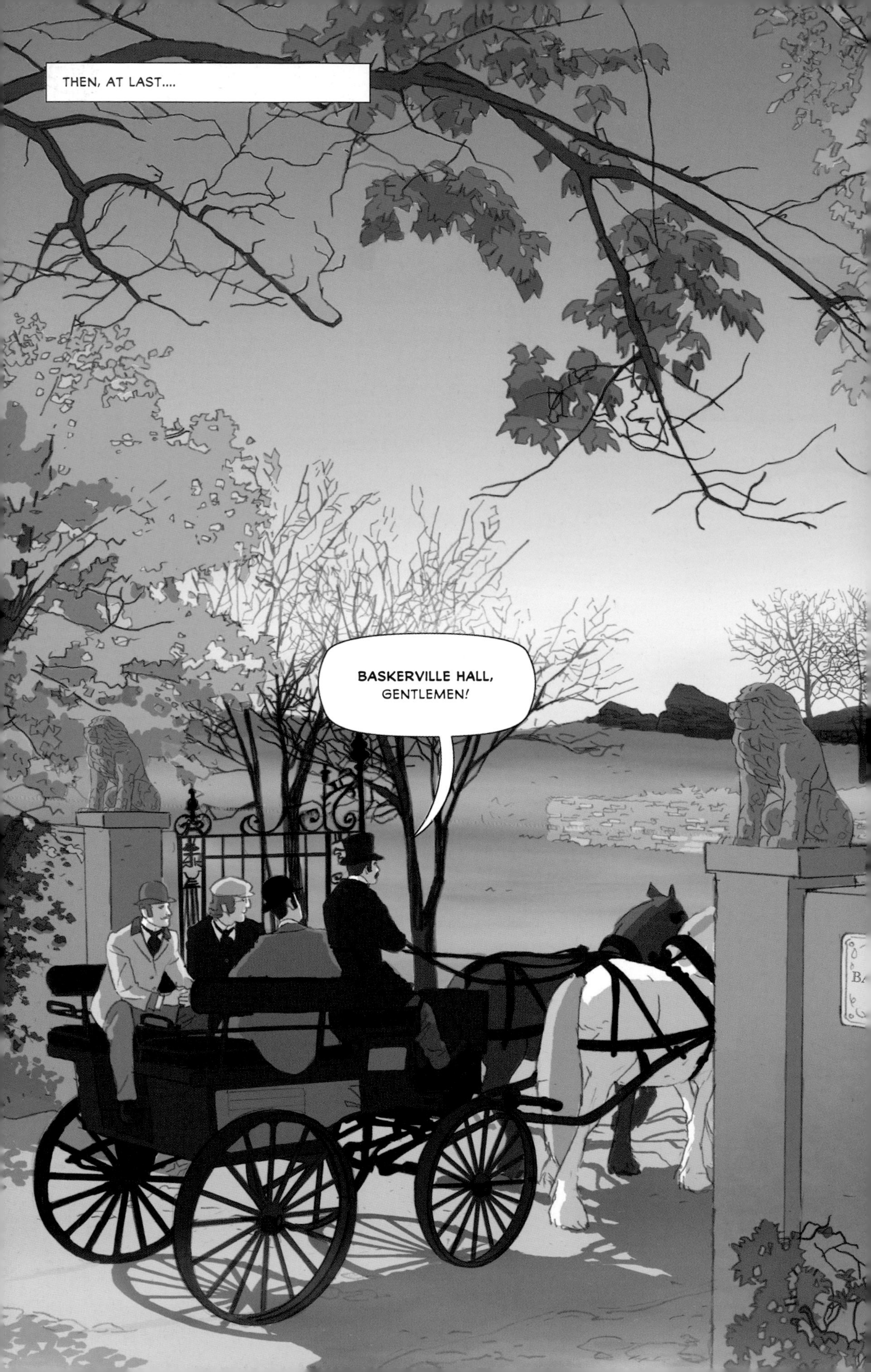
THEN, AT LAST....
BASKERVILLE HALL, GENTLEMEN!

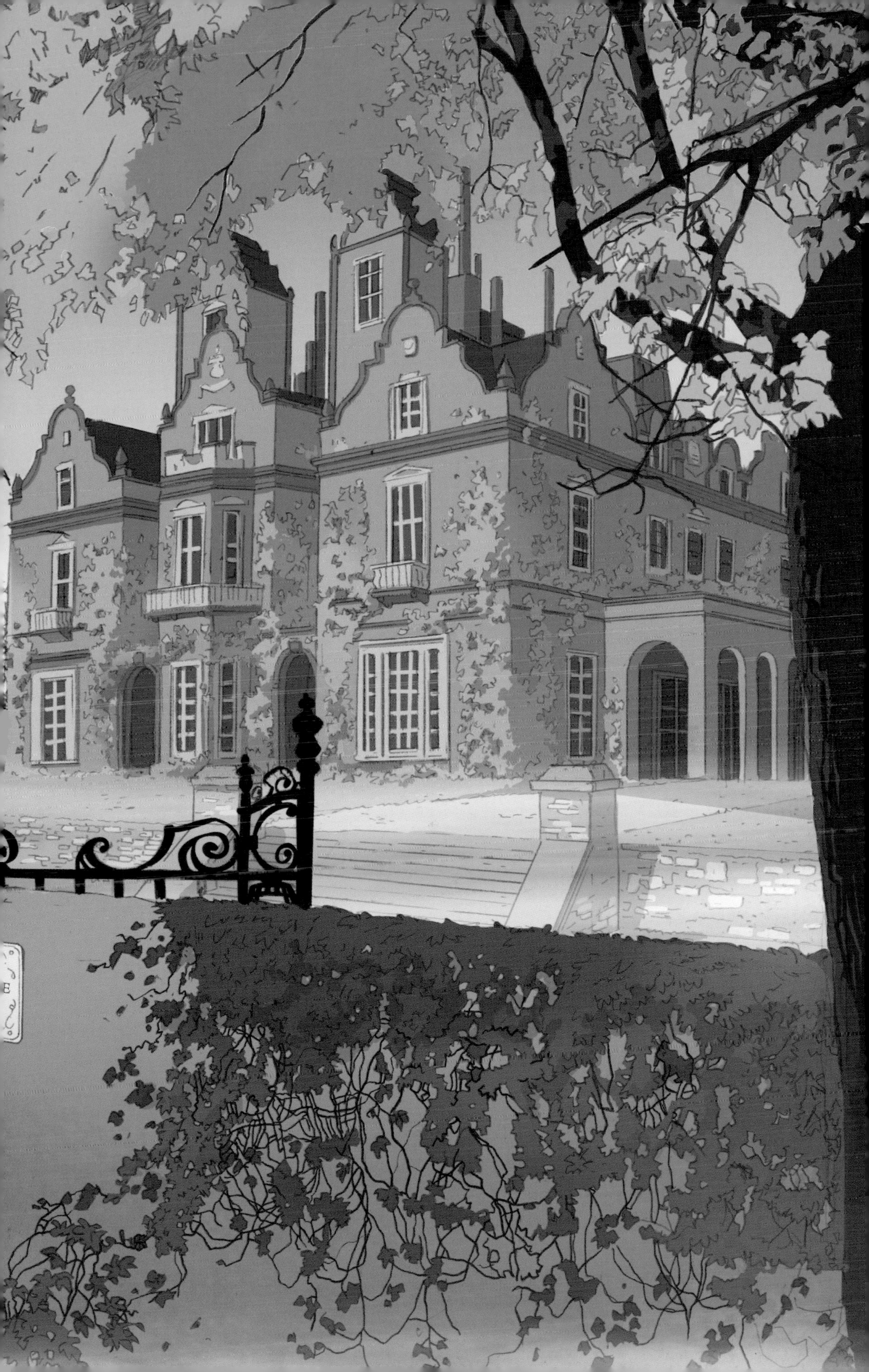

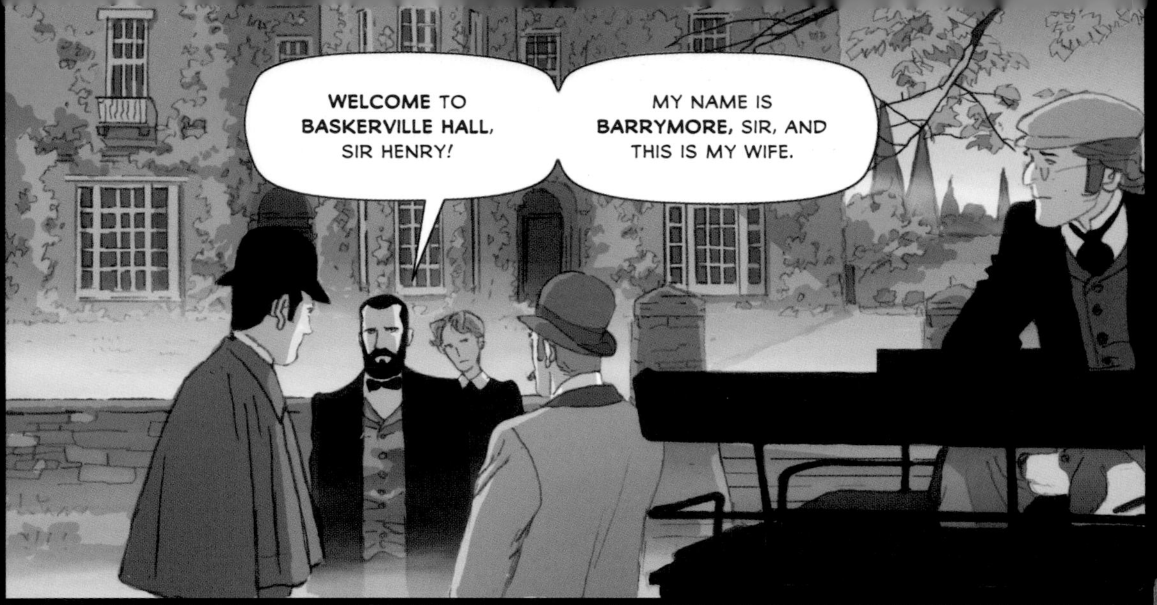
WELCOME TO BASKERVILLE HALL, SIR HENRY!
MY NAME IS BARRYMORE, SIR, AND THIS IS MY WIFE.

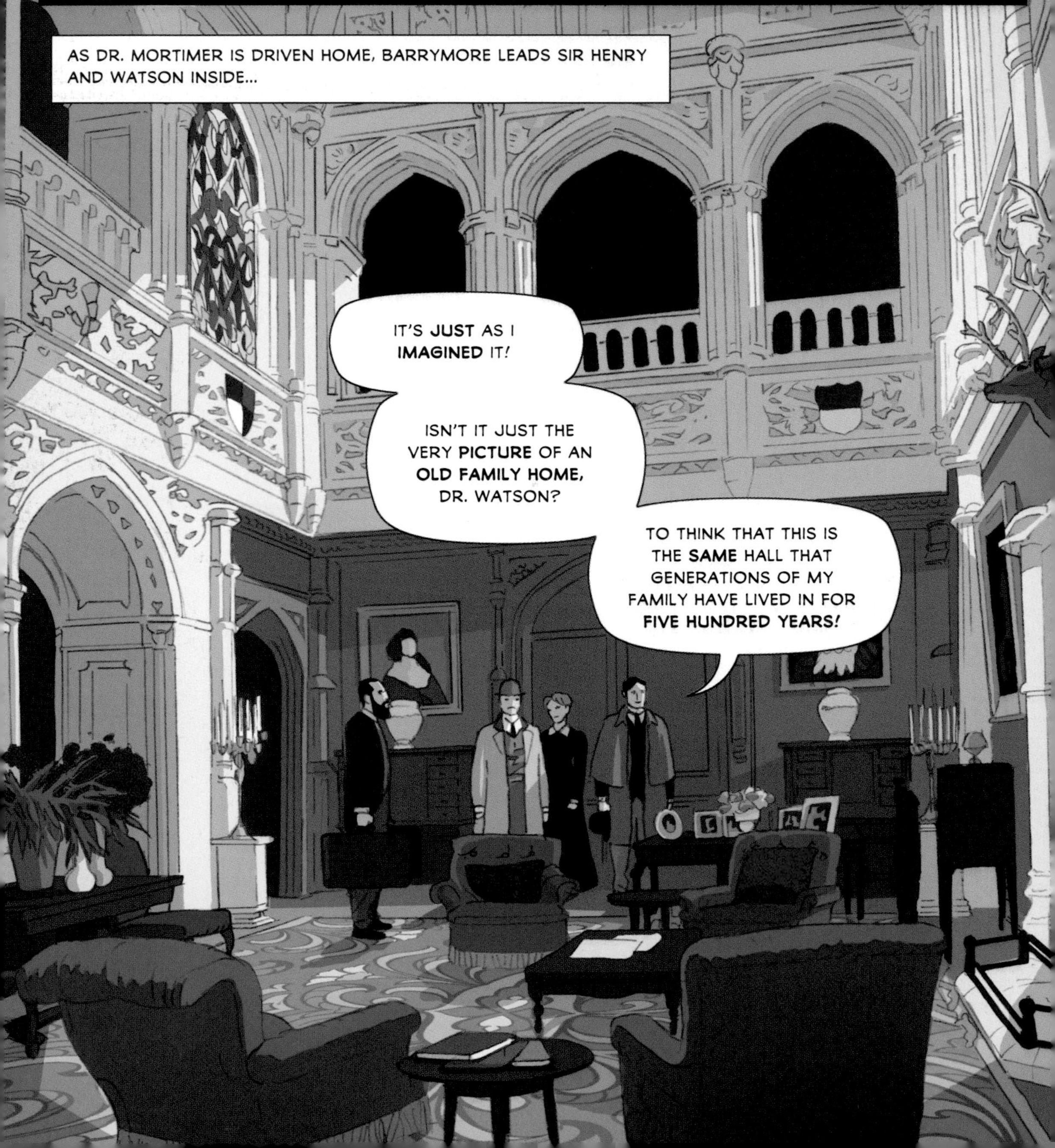
AS DR. MORTIMER IS DRIVEN HOME, BARRYMORE LEADS SIR HENRY AND WATSON INSIDE...
IT'S JUST AS I IMAGINED IT!
ISN'T IT JUST THE VERY PICTURE OF AN OLD FAMILY HOME, DR. WATSON?
TO THINK THAT THIS IS THE SAME HALL THAT GENERATIONS OF MY FAMILY HAVE LIVED IN FOR FIVE HUNDRED YEARS!

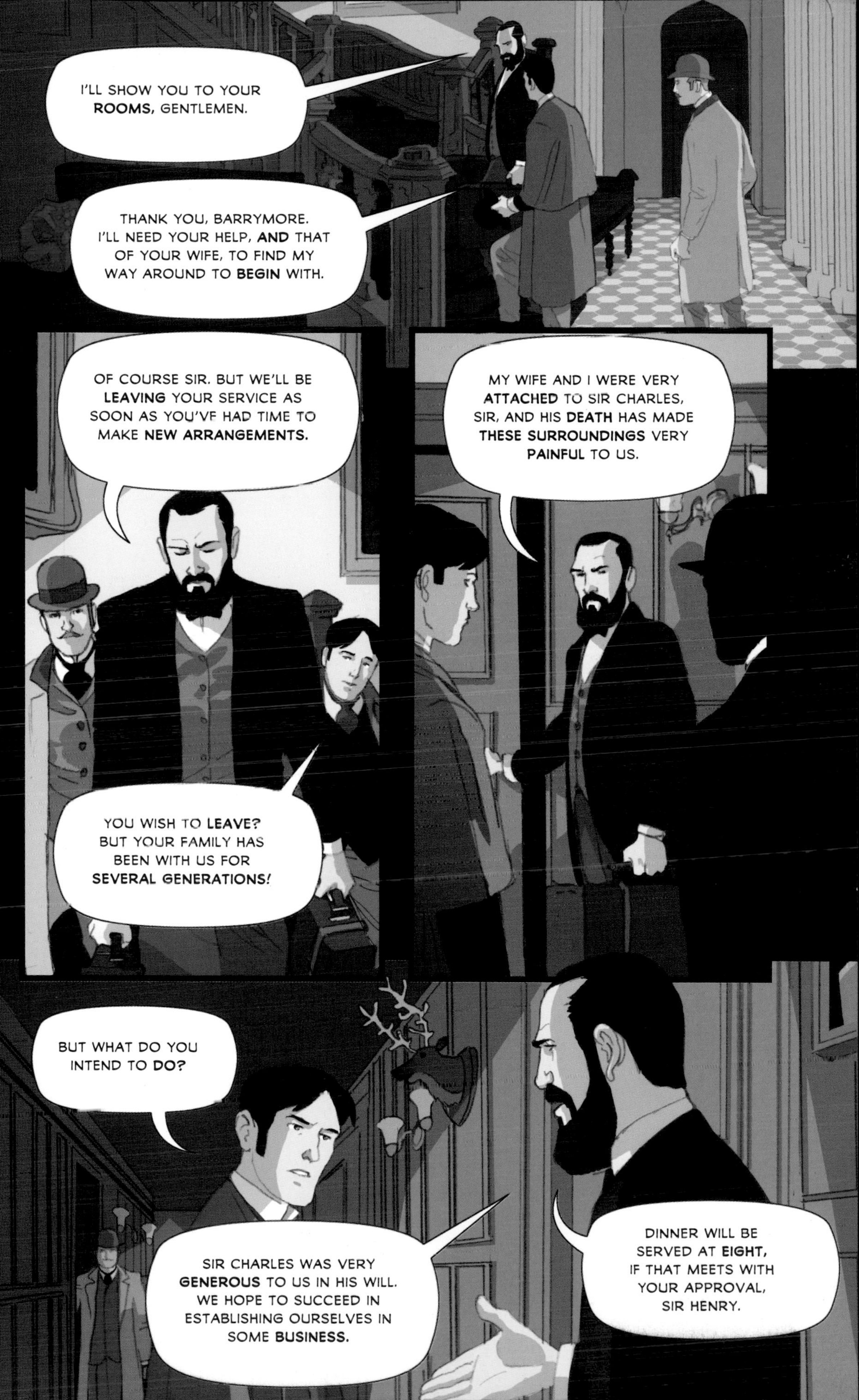
I'LL SHOW YOU TO YOUR ROOMS, GENTLEMEN.
THANK YOU, BARRYMORE. I'LL NEED YOUR HELP, AND THAT OF YOUR WIFE, TO FIND MY WAY AROUND TO BEGIN WITH.
OF COURSE SIR. BUT WE'LL BE LEAVING YOUR SERVICE AS SOON AS YOU'VE HAD TIME TO MAKE NEW ARRANGEMENTS.
YOU WISH TO LEAVE? BUT YOUR FAMILY HAS BEEN WITH US FOR SEVERAL GENERATIONS!
MY WIFE AND I WERE VERY ATTACHED TO SIR CHARLES, SIR, AND HIS DEATH HAS MADE THESE SURROUNDINGS VERY PAINFUL TO US.
BUT WHAT DO YOU INTEND TO DO?
SIR CHARLES WAS VERY GENEROUS TO US IN HIS WILL. WE HOPE TO SUCCEED IN ESTABLISHING OURSELVES IN SOME BUSINESS.
DINNER WILL BE SERVED AT EIGHT, IF THAT MEETS WITH YOUR APPROVAL, SIR HENRY.

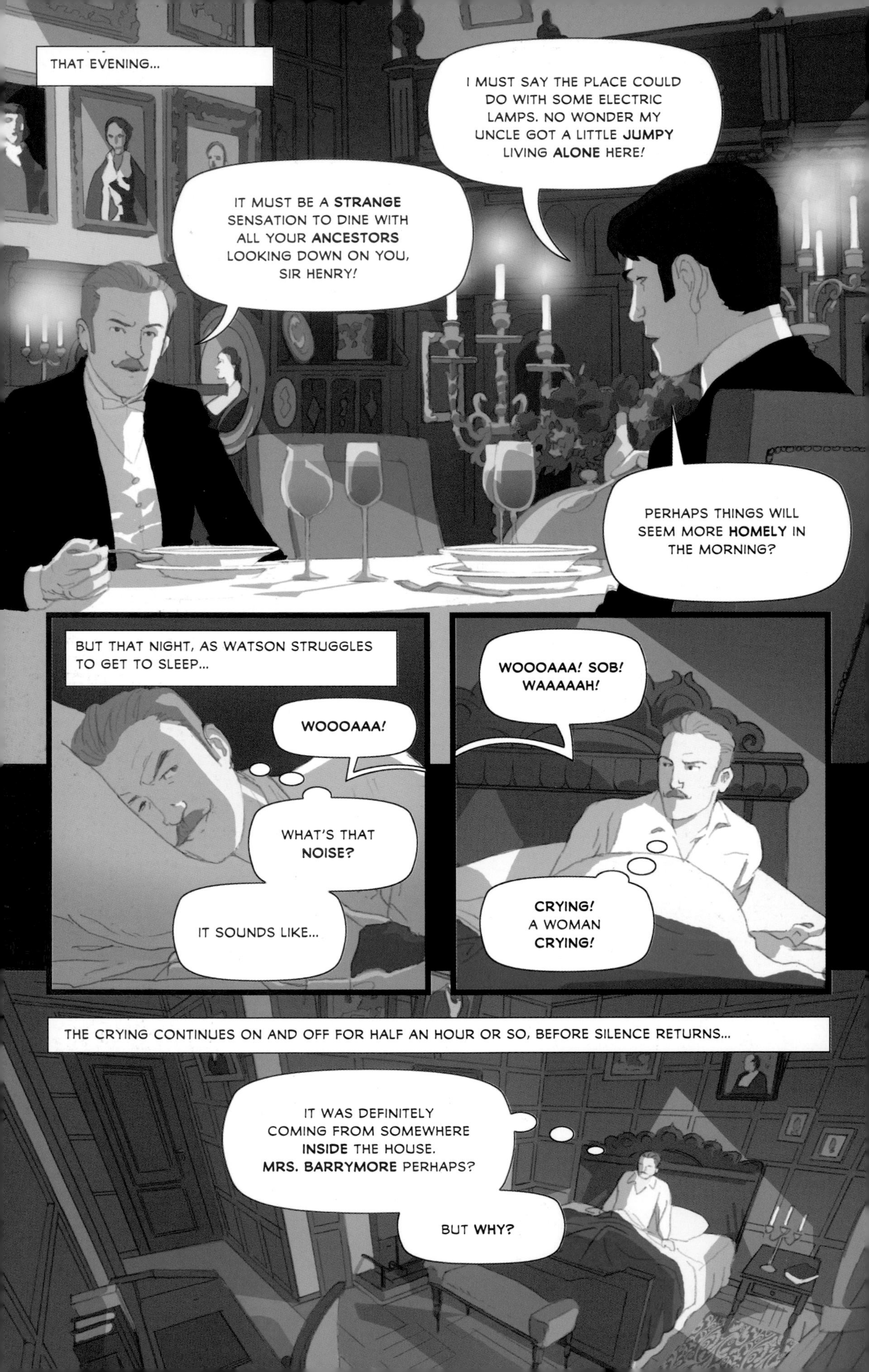
THAT EVENING...
IT MUST BE A STRANGE SENSATION TO DINE WITH ALL YOUR ANCESTORS LOOKING DOWN ON YOU, SIR HENRY!
I MUST SAY THE PLACE COULD DO WITH SOME ELECTRIC LAMPS. NO WONDER MY UNCLE GOT A LITTLE JUMPY LIVING ALONE HERE!
PERHAPS THINGS WILL SEEM MORE HOMELY IN THE MORNING?
BUT THAT NIGHT, AS WATSON STRUGGLES TO GET TO SLEEP...
WOOOAAA!
WHAT'S THAT NOISE?
IT SOUNDS LIKE...
WOOOAAA! SOB! WAAAAAH!
CRYING! A WOMAN CRYING!
THE CRYING CONTINUES ON AND OFF FOR HALF AN HOUR OR SO, BEFORE SILENCE RETURNS...
IT WAS DEFINITELY COMING FROM SOMEWHERE INSIDE THE HOUSE. MRS. BARRYMORE PERHAPS?
BUT WHY?

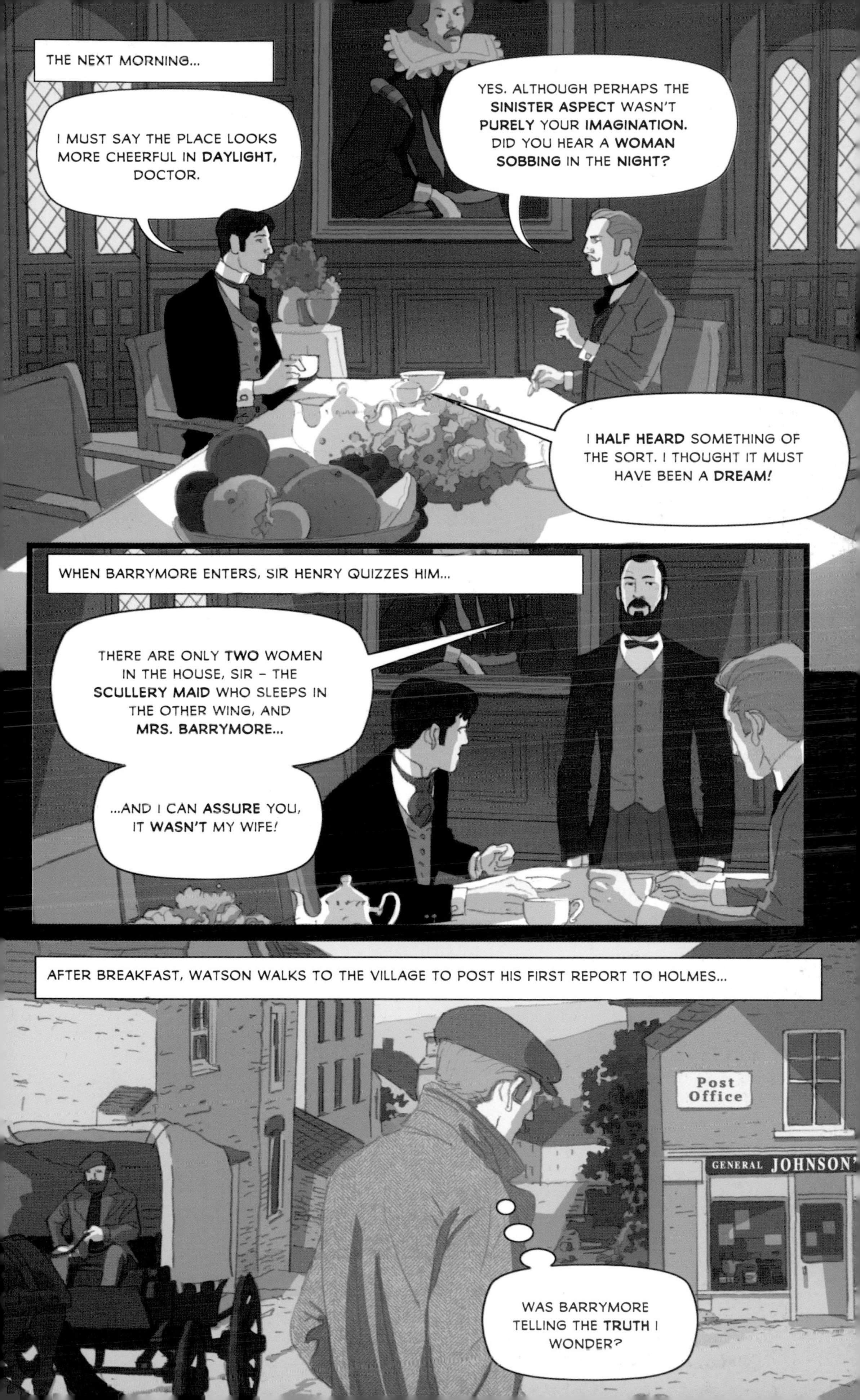
THE NEXT MORNING...
I MUST SAY THE PLACE LOOKS MORE CHEERFUL IN DAYLIGHT, DOCTOR.
YES. ALTHOUGH PERHAPS THE SINISTER ASPECT WASN'T PURELY YOUR IMAGINATION. DID YOU HEAR A WOMAN SOBBING IN THE NIGHT?
I HALF HEARD SOMETHING OF THE SORT. I THOUGHT IT MUST HAVE BEEN A DREAM!
WHEN BARRYMORE ENTERS, SIR HENRY QUIZZES HIM...
THERE ARE ONLY TWO WOMEN IN THE HOUSE, SIR – THE SCULLERY MAID WHO SLEEPS IN THE OTHER WING, AND MRS. BARRYMORE...
...AND I CAN ASSURE YOU, IT WASN'T MY WIFE!
AFTER BREAKFAST, WATSON WALKS TO THE VILLAGE TO POST HIS FIRST REPORT TO HOLMES...
Post Office
GENERAL JOHNSON'
WAS BARRYMORE TELLING THE TRUTH I WONDER?

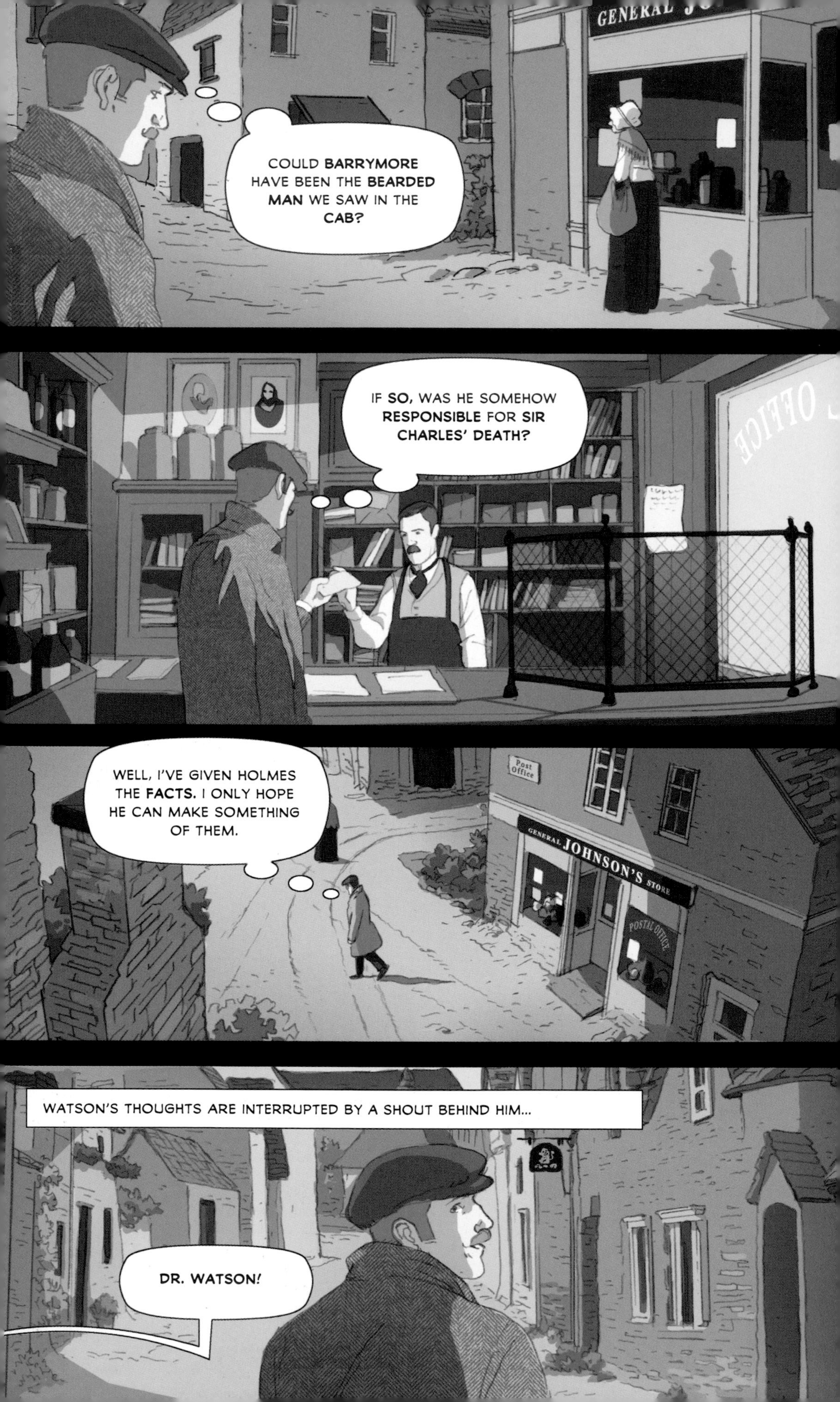
COULD BARRYMORE HAVE BEEN THE BEARDED MAN WE SAW IN THE CAB?
IF SO, WAS HE SOMEHOW RESPONSIBLE FOR SIR CHARLES' DEATH?
WELL, I'VE GIVEN HOLMES THE FACTS. I ONLY HOPE HE CAN MAKE SOMETHING OF THEM.
Post Office
GENERAL JOHNSON'S STORE
POSTAL OFFICE
WATSON'S THOUGHTS ARE INTERRUPTED BY A SHOUT BEHIND HIM...
DR. WATSON!

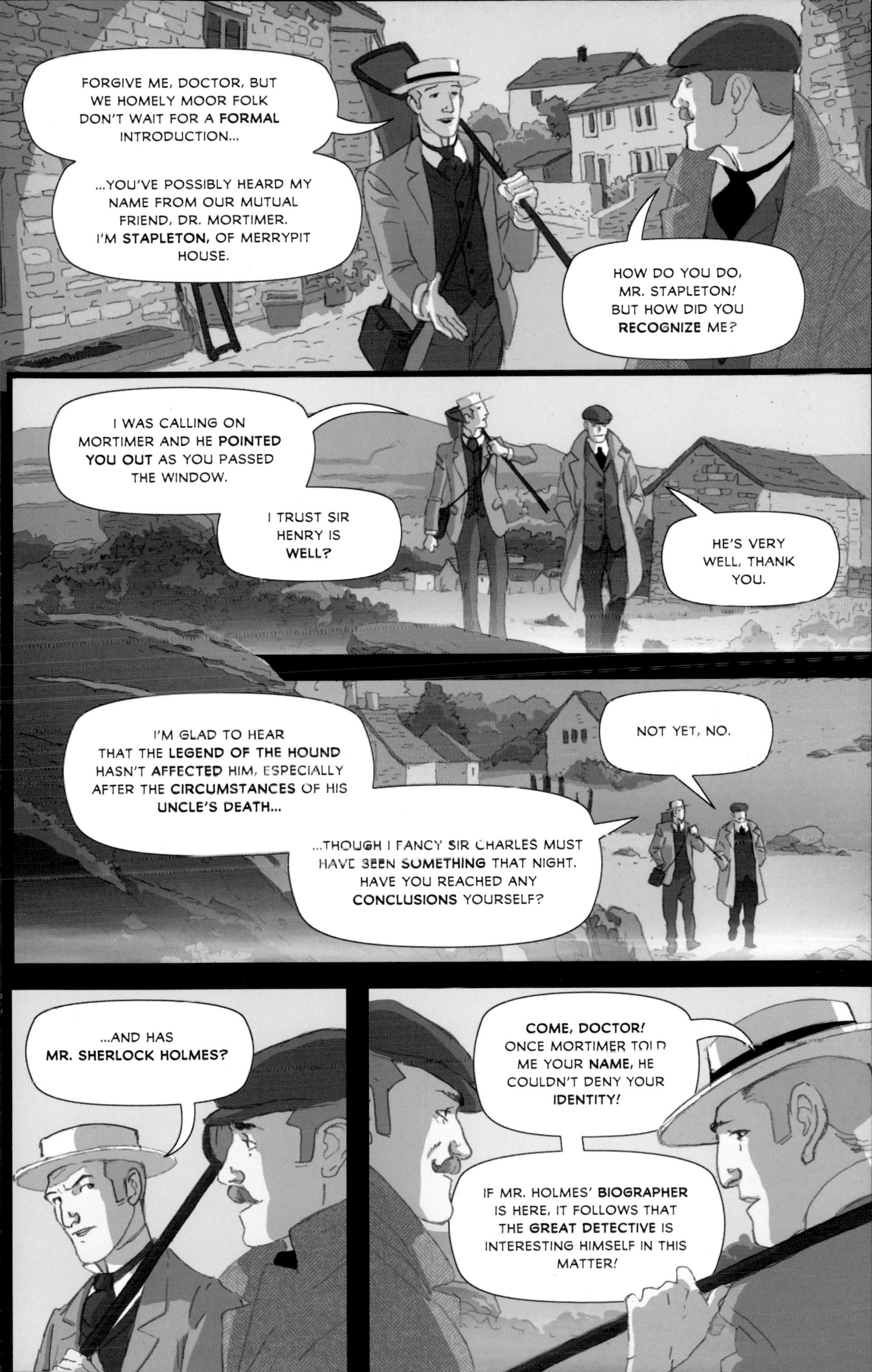
FORGIVE ME, DOCTOR, BUT WE HOMELY MOOR FOLK DON'T WAIT FOR A **FORMAL** INTRODUCTION...
...YOU'VE POSSIBLY HEARD MY NAME FROM OUR MUTUAL FRIEND, DR. MORTIMER. I'M **STAPLETON,** OF MERRYPIT HOUSE.
HOW DO YOU DO, MR. STAPLETON! BUT HOW DID YOU **RECOGNIZE** ME?
I WAS CALLING ON MORTIMER AND HE **POINTED YOU OUT** AS YOU PASSED THE WINDOW.
I TRUST SIR HENRY IS **WELL?**
HE'S VERY WELL, THANK YOU.
I'M GLAD TO HEAR THAT THE **LEGEND OF THE HOUND** HASN'T **AFFECTED** HIM, ESPECIALLY AFTER THE **CIRCUMSTANCES** OF HIS **UNCLE'S DEATH...**
...THOUGH I FANCY SIR CHARLES MUST HAVE SEEN **SOMETHING** THAT NIGHT. HAVE YOU REACHED ANY **CONCLUSIONS** YOURSELF?
NOT YET, NO.
...AND HAS **MR. SHERLOCK HOLMES?**
COME, DOCTOR! ONCE MORTIMER TOLD ME YOUR **NAME,** HE COULDN'T DENY YOUR **IDENTITY!**
IF MR. HOLMES' **BIOGRAPHER** IS HERE, IT FOLLOWS THAT THE **GREAT DETECTIVE** IS INTERESTING HIMSELF IN THIS MATTER!

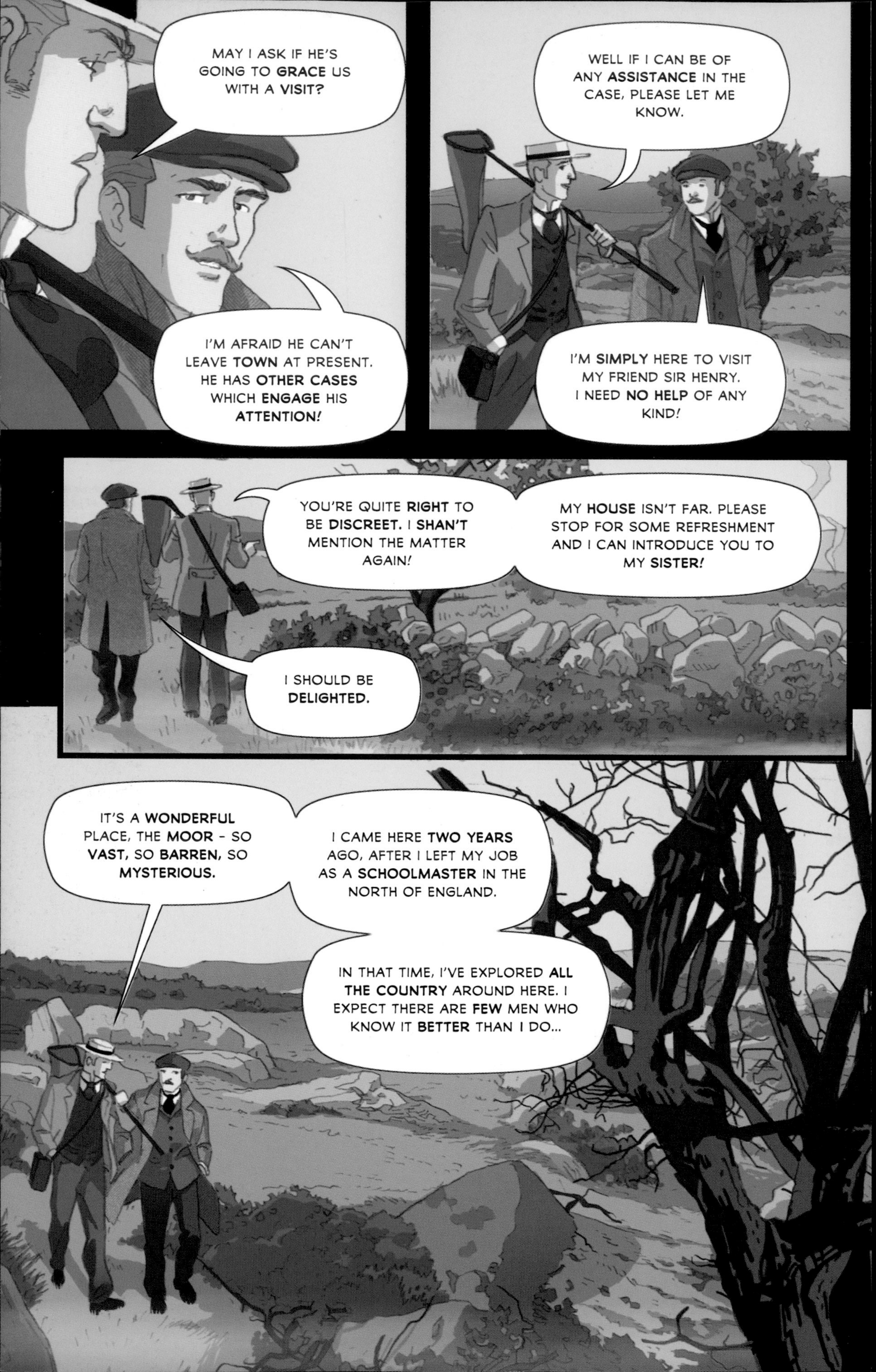
MAY I ASK IF HE'S GOING TO GRACE US WITH A VISIT?
I'M AFRAID HE CAN'T LEAVE TOWN AT PRESENT. HE HAS OTHER CASES WHICH ENGAGE HIS ATTENTION!
WELL IF I CAN BE OF ANY ASSISTANCE IN THE CASE, PLEASE LET ME KNOW.
I'M SIMPLY HERE TO VISIT MY FRIEND SIR HENRY. I NEED NO HELP OF ANY KIND!
YOU'RE QUITE RIGHT TO BE DISCREET. I SHAN'T MENTION THE MATTER AGAIN!
MY HOUSE ISN'T FAR. PLEASE STOP FOR SOME REFRESHMENT AND I CAN INTRODUCE YOU TO MY SISTER!
I SHOULD BE DELIGHTED.
IT'S A WONDERFUL PLACE, THE MOOR - SO VAST, SO BARREN, SO MYSTERIOUS.
I CAME HERE TWO YEARS AGO, AFTER I LEFT MY JOB AS A SCHOOLMASTER IN THE NORTH OF ENGLAND.
IN THAT TIME, I'VE EXPLORED ALL THE COUNTRY AROUND HERE. I EXPECT THERE ARE FEW MEN WHO KNOW IT BETTER THAN I DO...

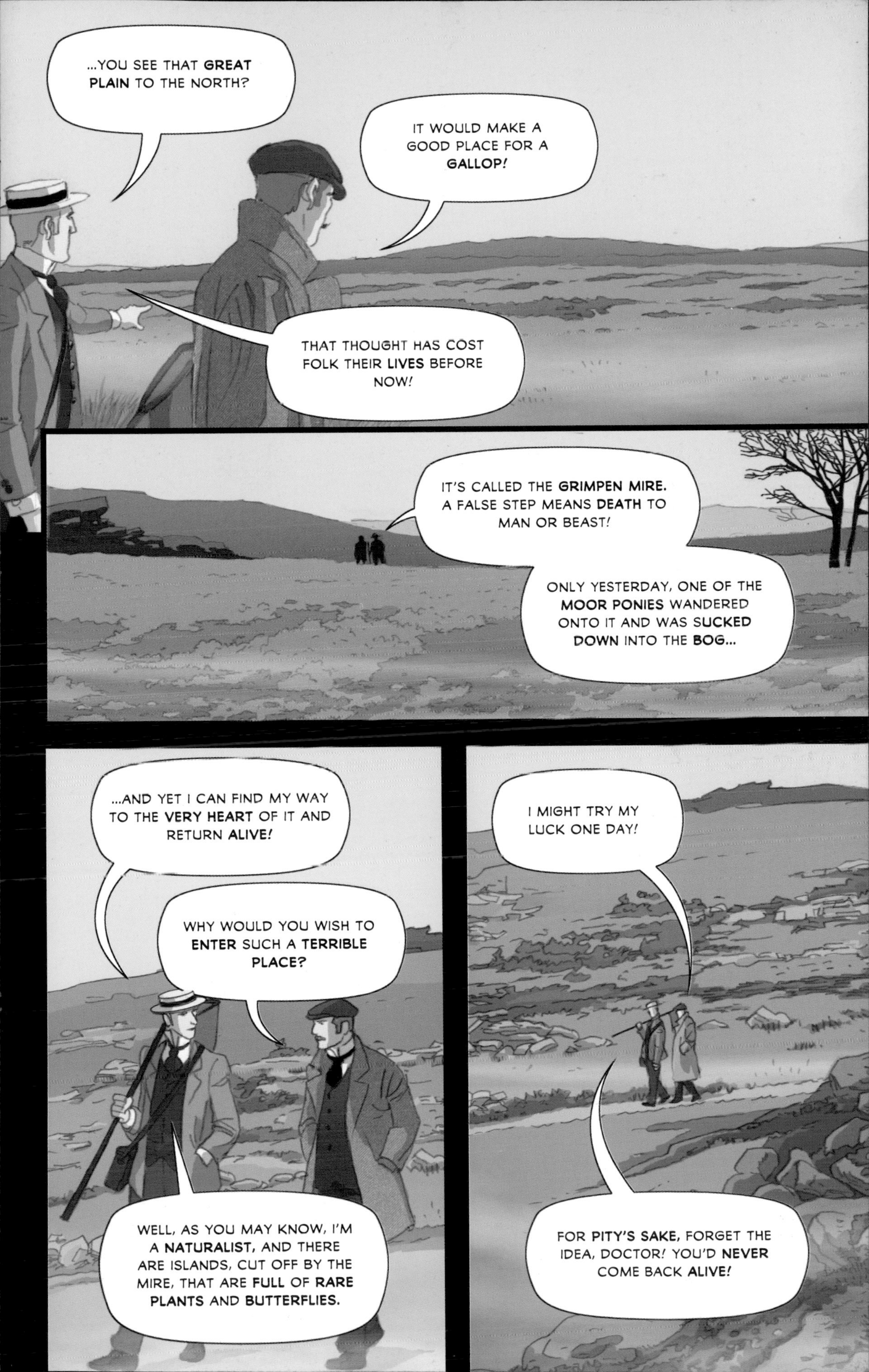
...YOU SEE THAT GREAT PLAIN TO THE NORTH?
IT WOULD MAKE A GOOD PLACE FOR A GALLOP!
THAT THOUGHT HAS COST FOLK THEIR LIVES BEFORE NOW!
IT'S CALLED THE GRIMPEN MIRE. A FALSE STEP MEANS DEATH TO MAN OR BEAST!
ONLY YESTERDAY, ONE OF THE MOOR PONIES WANDERED ONTO IT AND WAS SUCKED DOWN INTO THE BOG...
...AND YET I CAN FIND MY WAY TO THE VERY HEART OF IT AND RETURN ALIVE!
WHY WOULD YOU WISH TO ENTER SUCH A TERRIBLE PLACE?
WELL, AS YOU MAY KNOW, I'M A NATURALIST, AND THERE ARE ISLANDS, CUT OFF BY THE MIRE, THAT ARE FULL OF RARE PLANTS AND BUTTERFLIES.
I MIGHT TRY MY LUCK ONE DAY!
FOR PITY'S SAKE, FORGET THE IDEA, DOCTOR! YOU'D NEVER COME BACK ALIVE!

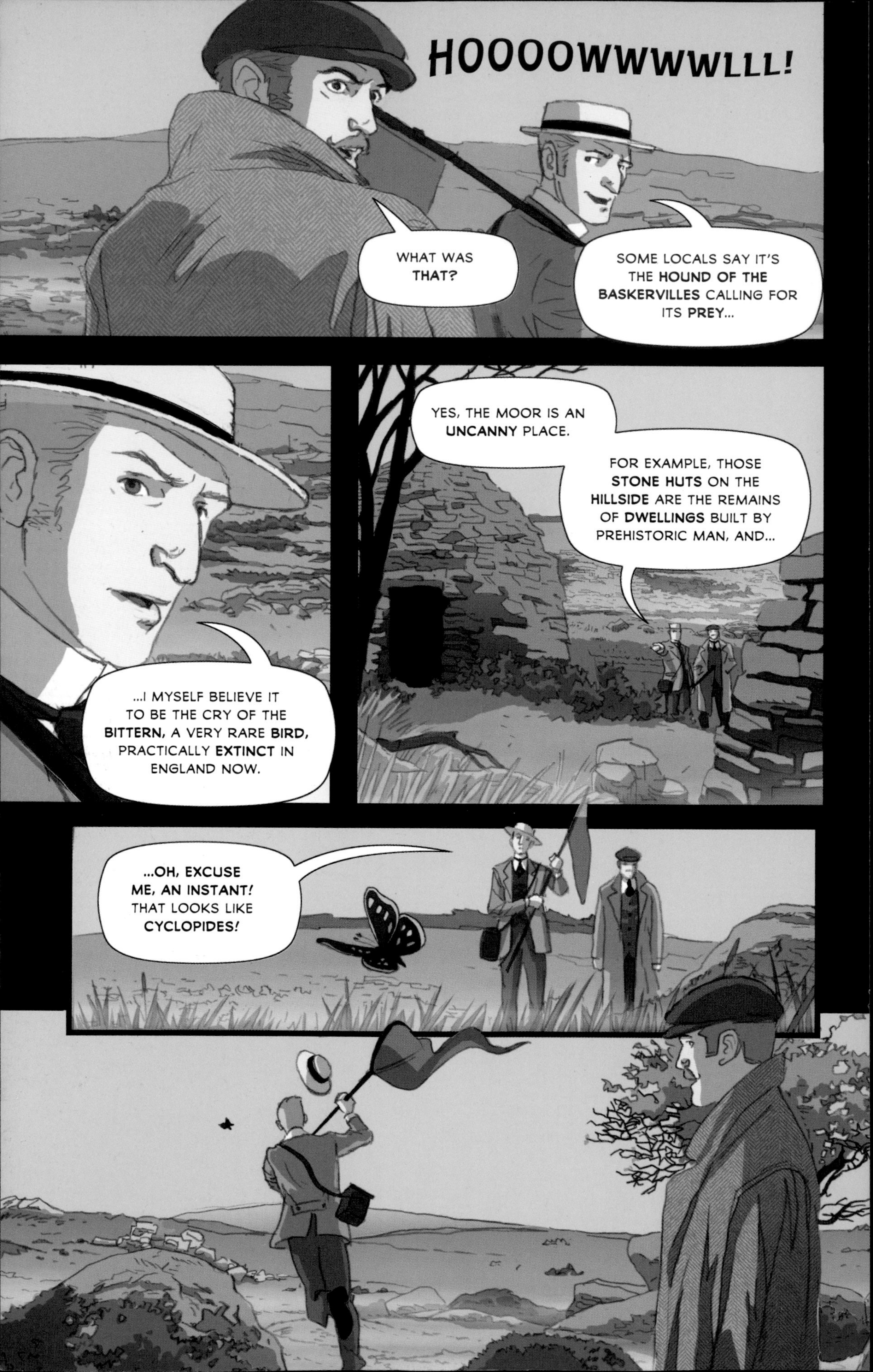
HOOOOWWWWLLL!
WHAT WAS THAT?
SOME LOCALS SAY IT'S THE HOUND OF THE BASKERVILLES CALLING FOR ITS PREY...
...I MYSELF BELIEVE IT TO BE THE CRY OF THE BITTERN, A VERY RARE BIRD, PRACTICALLY EXTINCT IN ENGLAND NOW.
YES, THE MOOR IS AN UNCANNY PLACE.
FOR EXAMPLE, THOSE STONE HUTS ON THE HILLSIDE ARE THE REMAINS OF DWELLINGS BUILT BY PREHISTORIC MAN, AND...
...OH, EXCUSE ME, AN INSTANT! THAT LOOKS LIKE CYCLOPIDES!

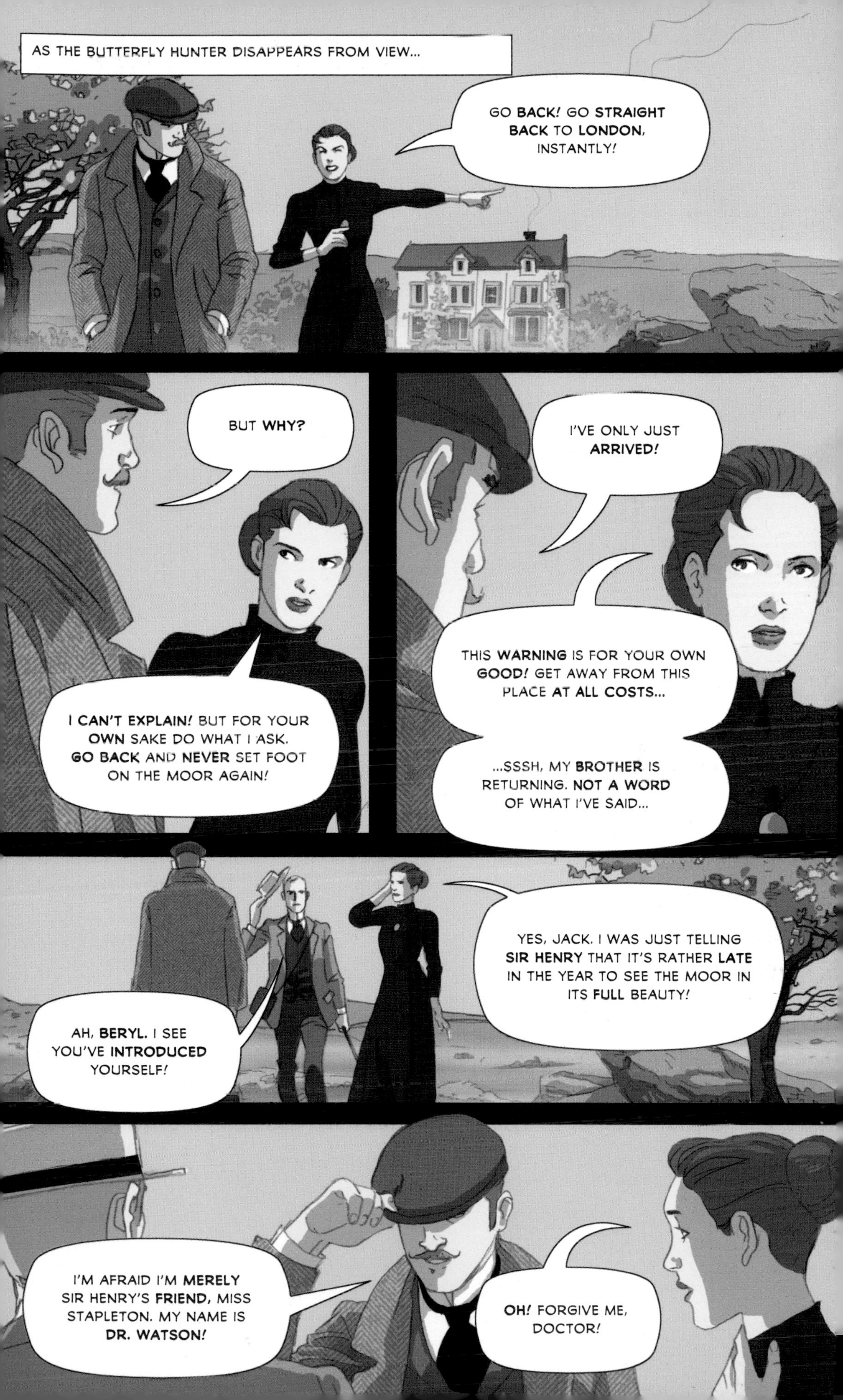

AS THE BUTTERFLY HUNTER DISAPPEARS FROM VIEW...
GO BACK! GO STRAIGHT BACK TO LONDON, INSTANTLY!
BUT WHY?
I CAN'T EXPLAIN! BUT FOR YOUR OWN SAKE DO WHAT I ASK. GO BACK AND NEVER SET FOOT ON THE MOOR AGAIN!
I'VE ONLY JUST ARRIVED!
THIS WARNING IS FOR YOUR OWN GOOD! GET AWAY FROM THIS PLACE AT ALL COSTS...
...SSSH, MY BROTHER IS RETURNING. NOT A WORD OF WHAT I'VE SAID...
AH, BERYL. I SEE YOU'VE INTRODUCED YOURSELF!
YES, JACK. I WAS JUST TELLING SIR HENRY THAT IT'S RATHER LATE IN THE YEAR TO SEE THE MOOR IN ITS FULL BEAUTY!
I'M AFRAID I'M MERELY SIR HENRY'S FRIEND, MISS STAPLETON. MY NAME IS DR. WATSON!
OH! FORGIVE ME, DOCTOR!

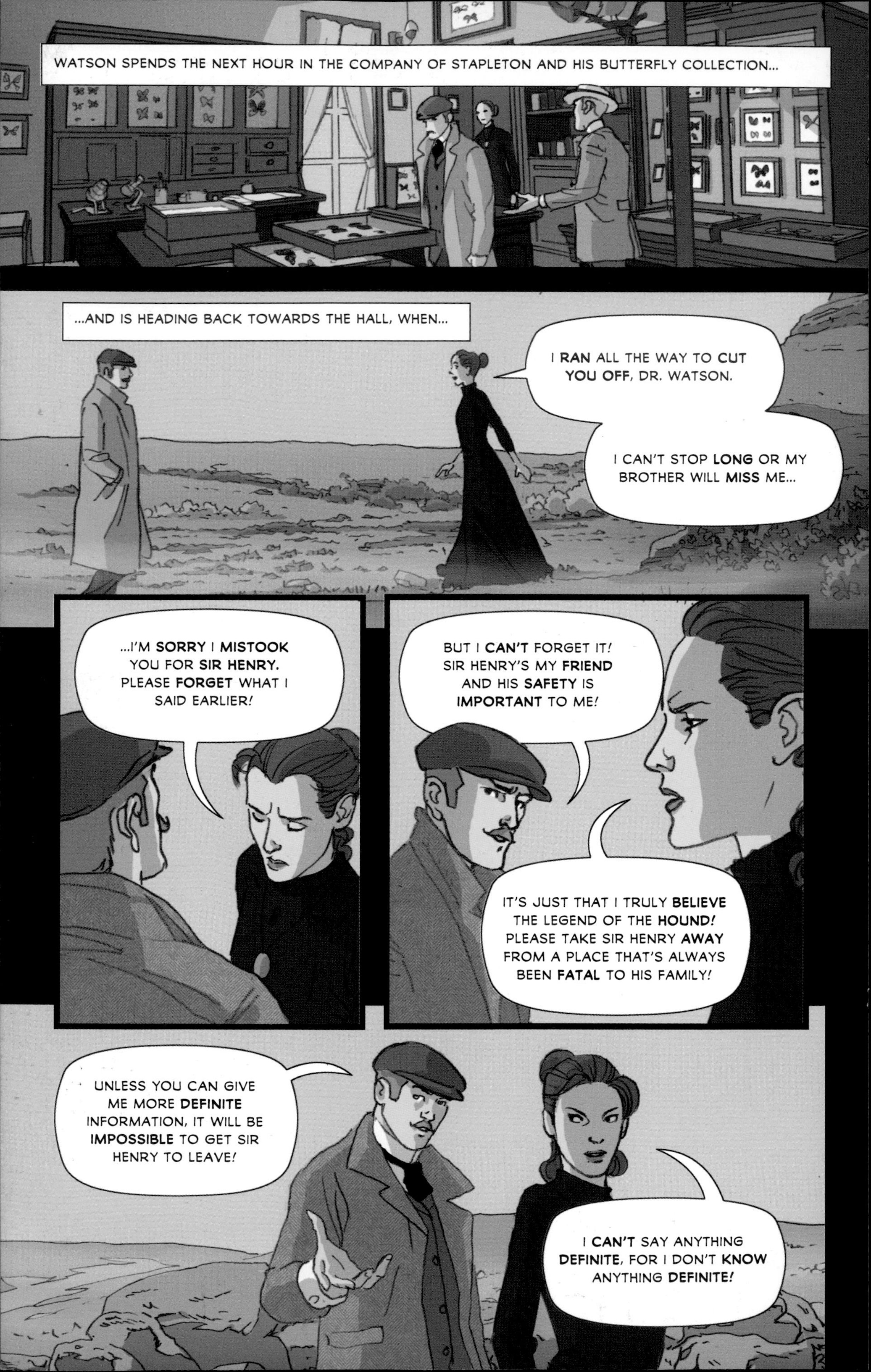

WATSON SPENDS THE NEXT HOUR IN THE COMPANY OF STAPLETON AND HIS BUTTERFLY COLLECTION...
...AND IS HEADING BACK TOWARDS THE HALL, WHEN...
I RAN ALL THE WAY TO CUT YOU OFF, DR. WATSON.
I CAN'T STOP LONG OR MY BROTHER WILL MISS ME...
...I'M SORRY I MISTOOK YOU FOR SIR HENRY. PLEASE FORGET WHAT I SAID EARLIER!
BUT I CAN'T FORGET IT! SIR HENRY'S MY FRIEND AND HIS SAFETY IS IMPORTANT TO ME!
IT'S JUST THAT I TRULY BELIEVE THE LEGEND OF THE HOUND! PLEASE TAKE SIR HENRY AWAY FROM A PLACE THAT'S ALWAYS BEEN FATAL TO HIS FAMILY!
UNLESS YOU CAN GIVE ME MORE DEFINITE INFORMATION, IT WILL BE IMPOSSIBLE TO GET SIR HENRY TO LEAVE!
I CAN'T SAY ANYTHING DEFINITE, FOR I DON'T KNOW ANYTHING DEFINITE!

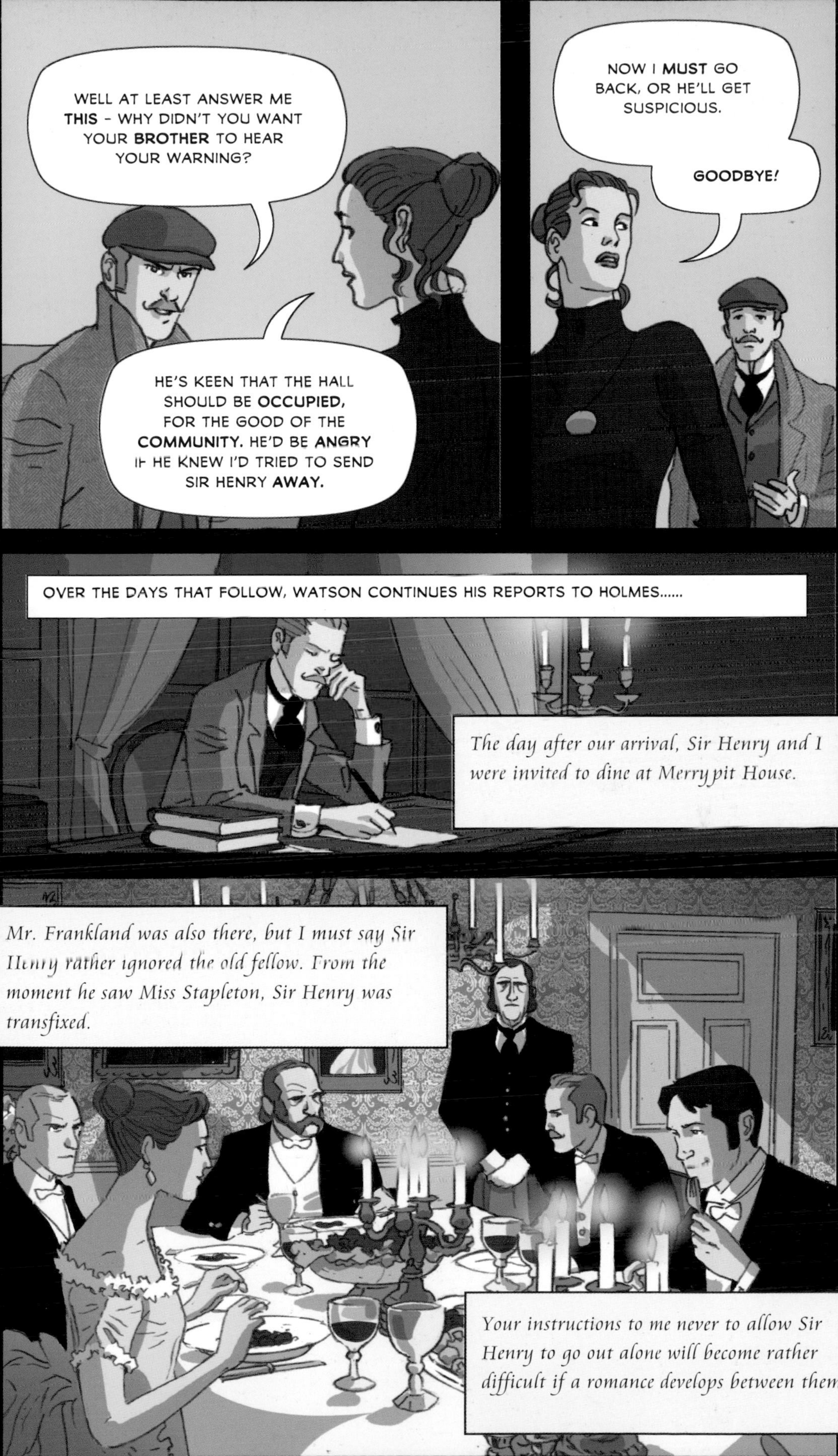
WELL AT LEAST ANSWER ME THIS - WHY DIDN'T YOU WANT YOUR BROTHER TO HEAR YOUR WARNING?
HE'S KEEN THAT THE HALL SHOULD BE OCCUPIED, FOR THE GOOD OF THE COMMUNITY. HE'D BE ANGRY IF HE KNEW I'D TRIED TO SEND SIR HENRY AWAY.
NOW I MUST GO BACK, OR HE'LL GET SUSPICIOUS.
GOODBYE!
OVER THE DAYS THAT FOLLOW, WATSON CONTINUES HIS REPORTS TO HOLMES......
The day after our arrival, Sir Henry and I were invited to dine at Merrypit House.
Mr. Frankland was also there, but I must say Sir Henry rather ignored the old fellow. From the moment he saw Miss Stapleton, Sir Henry was transfixed.
Your instructions to me never to allow Sir Henry to go out alone will become rather difficult if a romance develops between them.

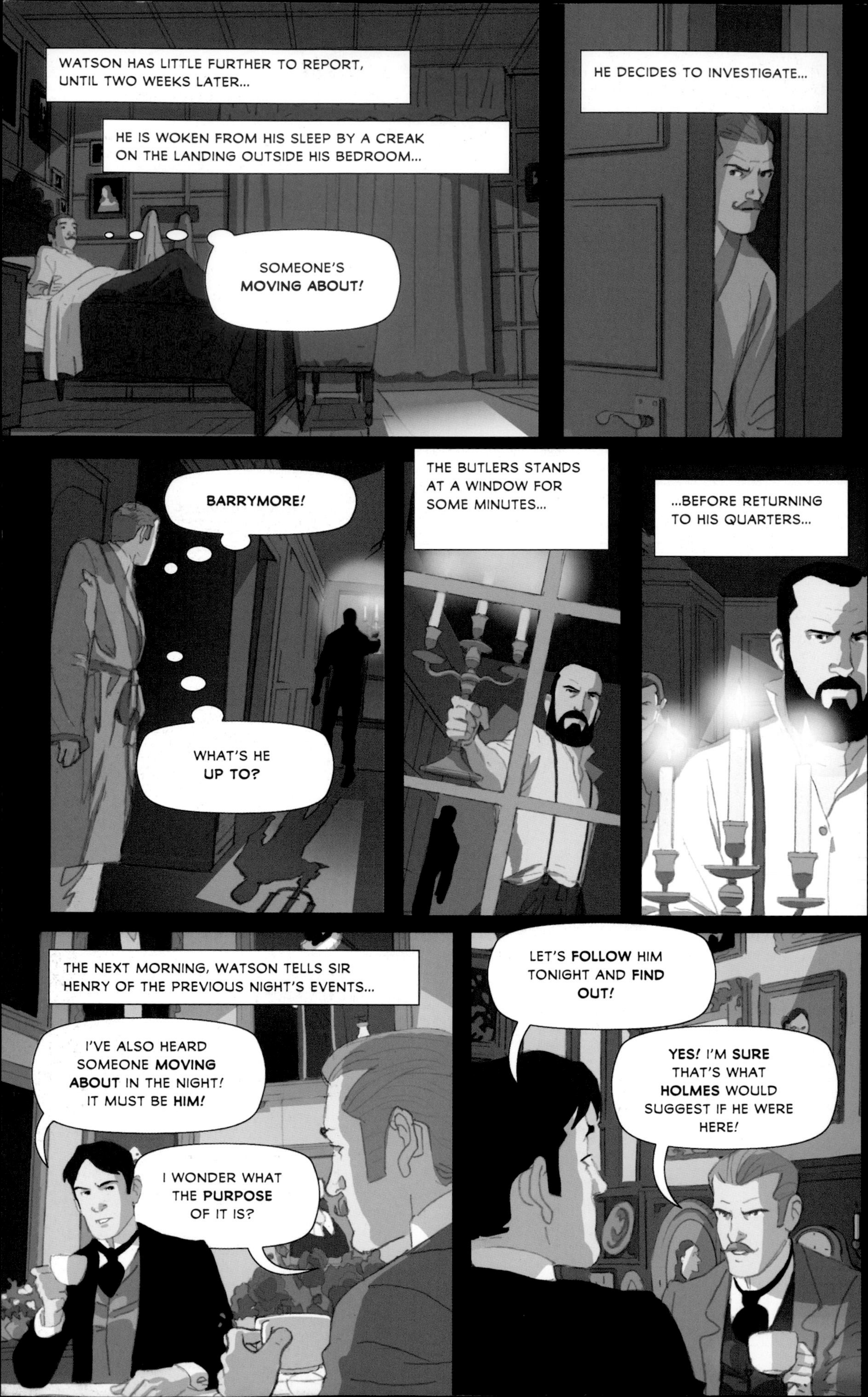
WATSON HAS LITTLE FURTHER TO REPORT, UNTIL TWO WEEKS LATER...
HE IS WOKEN FROM HIS SLEEP BY A CREAK ON THE LANDING OUTSIDE HIS BEDROOM...
SOMEONE'S **MOVING ABOUT!**
HE DECIDES TO INVESTIGATE...
BARRYMORE!
WHAT'S HE **UP TO?**
THE BUTLERS STANDS AT A WINDOW FOR SOME MINUTES...
...BEFORE RETURNING TO HIS QUARTERS...
THE NEXT MORNING, WATSON TELLS SIR HENRY OF THE PREVIOUS NIGHT'S EVENTS...
I'VE ALSO HEARD SOMEONE **MOVING ABOUT** IN THE NIGHT! IT MUST BE **HIM!**
I WONDER WHAT THE **PURPOSE** OF IT IS?
LET'S **FOLLOW** HIM TONIGHT AND **FIND OUT!**
YES! I'M **SURE** THAT'S WHAT **HOLMES** WOULD SUGGEST IF HE WERE HERE!

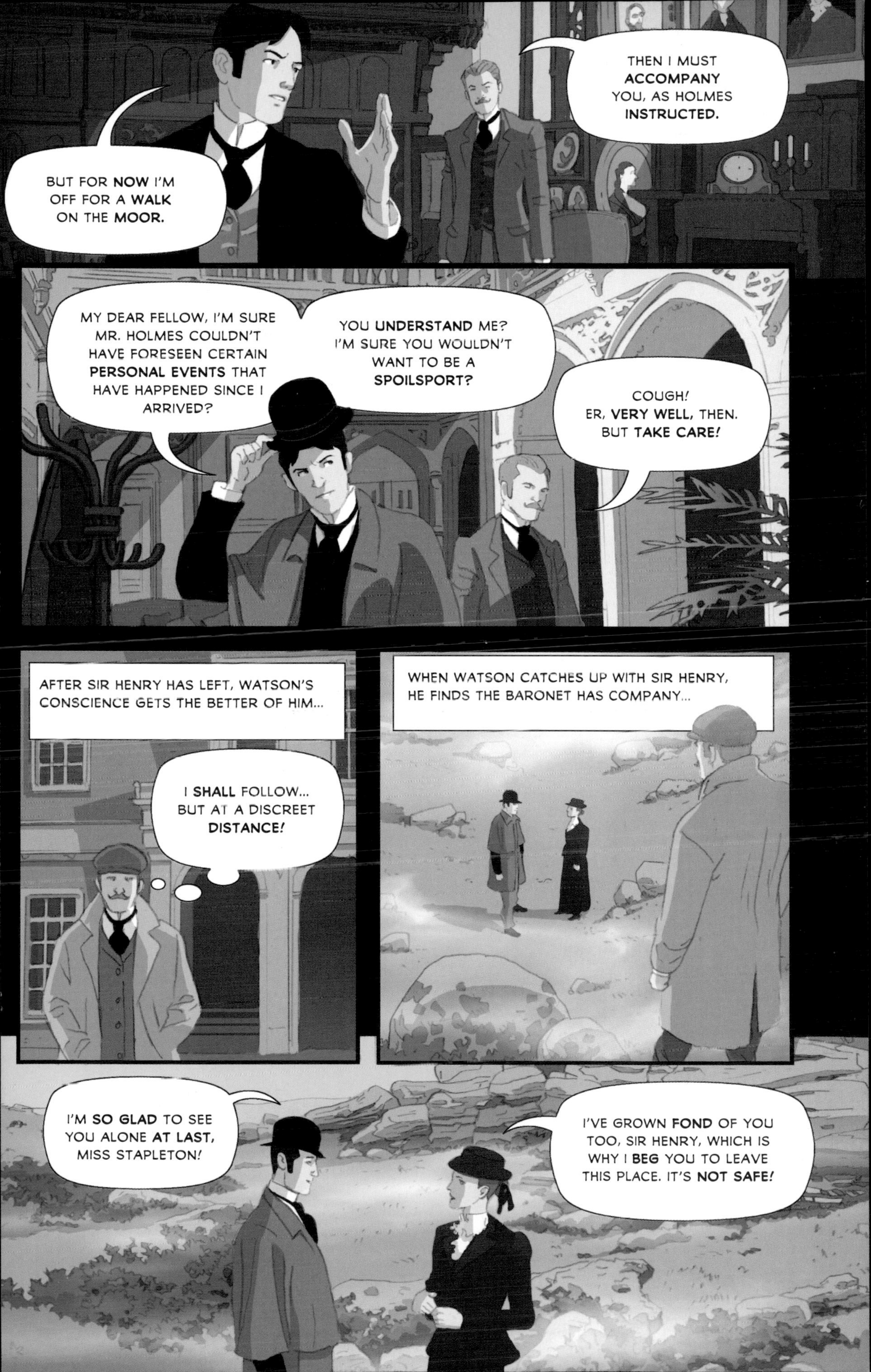
BUT FOR NOW I'M OFF FOR A WALK ON THE MOOR.
THEN I MUST ACCOMPANY YOU, AS HOLMES INSTRUCTED.
MY DEAR FELLOW, I'M SURE MR. HOLMES COULDN'T HAVE FORESEEN CERTAIN PERSONAL EVENTS THAT HAVE HAPPENED SINCE I ARRIVED?
YOU UNDERSTAND ME? I'M SURE YOU WOULDN'T WANT TO BE A SPOILSPORT?
COUGH! ER, VERY WELL, THEN. BUT TAKE CARE!
AFTER SIR HENRY HAS LEFT, WATSON'S CONSCIENCE GETS THE BETTER OF HIM...
I SHALL FOLLOW... BUT AT A DISCREET DISTANCE!
WHEN WATSON CATCHES UP WITH SIR HENRY, HE FINDS THE BARONET HAS COMPANY...
I'M SO GLAD TO SEE YOU ALONE AT LAST, MISS STAPLETON!
I'VE GROWN FOND OF YOU TOO, SIR HENRY, WHICH IS WHY I BEG YOU TO LEAVE THIS PLACE. IT'S NOT SAFE!

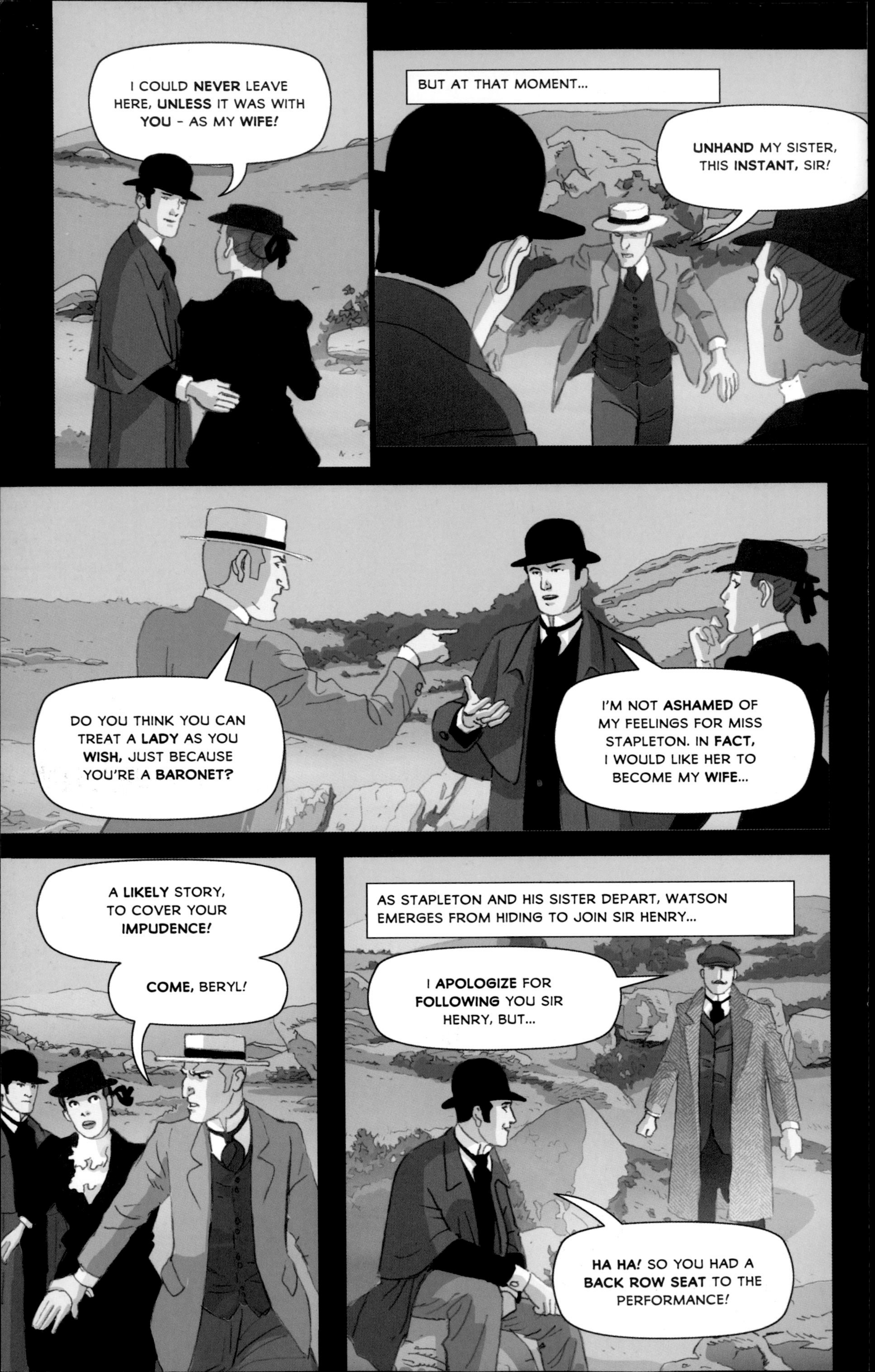

I COULD NEVER LEAVE HERE, UNLESS IT WAS WITH YOU - AS MY WIFE!
BUT AT THAT MOMENT...
UNHAND MY SISTER, THIS INSTANT, SIR!
DO YOU THINK YOU CAN TREAT A LADY AS YOU WISH, JUST BECAUSE YOU'RE A BARONET?
I'M NOT ASHAMED OF MY FEELINGS FOR MISS STAPLETON. IN FACT, I WOULD LIKE HER TO BECOME MY WIFE...
A LIKELY STORY, TO COVER YOUR IMPUDENCE!
COME, BERYL!
AS STAPLETON AND HIS SISTER DEPART, WATSON EMERGES FROM HIDING TO JOIN SIR HENRY...
I APOLOGIZE FOR FOLLOWING YOU SIR HENRY, BUT...
HA HA! SO YOU HAD A BACK ROW SEAT TO THE PERFORMANCE!

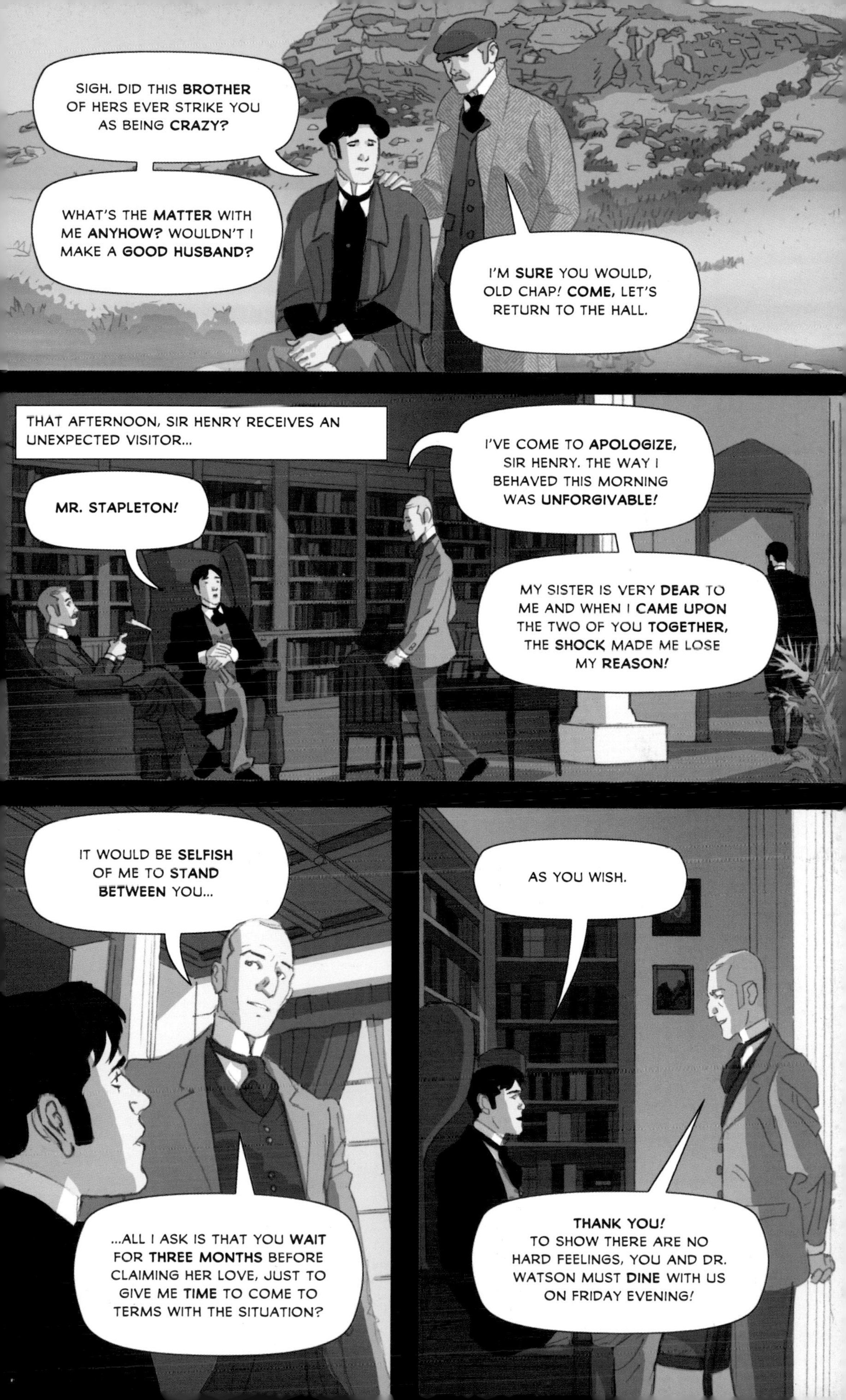
SIGH. DID THIS BROTHER OF HERS EVER STRIKE YOU AS BEING CRAZY?
WHAT'S THE MATTER WITH ME ANYHOW? WOULDN'T I MAKE A GOOD HUSBAND?
I'M SURE YOU WOULD, OLD CHAP! COME, LET'S RETURN TO THE HALL.
THAT AFTERNOON, SIR HENRY RECEIVES AN UNEXPECTED VISITOR...
MR. STAPLETON!
I'VE COME TO APOLOGIZE, SIR HENRY. THE WAY I BEHAVED THIS MORNING WAS UNFORGIVABLE!
MY SISTER IS VERY DEAR TO ME AND WHEN I CAME UPON THE TWO OF YOU TOGETHER, THE SHOCK MADE ME LOSE MY REASON!
IT WOULD BE SELFISH OF ME TO STAND BETWEEN YOU...
...ALL I ASK IS THAT YOU WAIT FOR THREE MONTHS BEFORE CLAIMING HER LOVE, JUST TO GIVE ME TIME TO COME TO TERMS WITH THE SITUATION?
AS YOU WISH.
THANK YOU! TO SHOW THERE ARE NO HARD FEELINGS, YOU AND DR. WATSON MUST DINE WITH US ON FRIDAY EVENING!

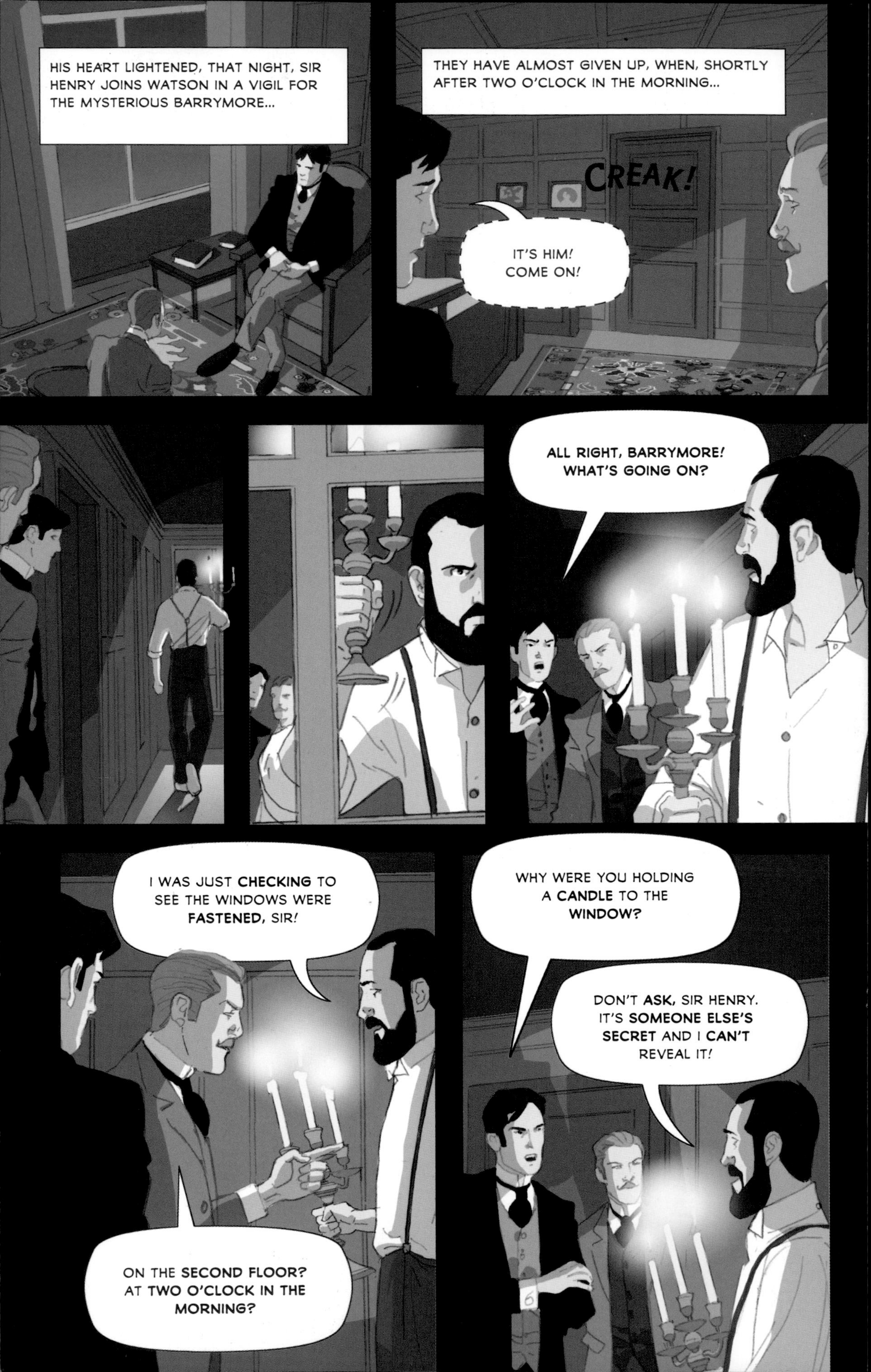
HIS HEART LIGHTENED, THAT NIGHT, SIR HENRY JOINS WATSON IN A VIGIL FOR THE MYSTERIOUS BARRYMORE...
THEY HAVE ALMOST GIVEN UP, WHEN, SHORTLY AFTER TWO O'CLOCK IN THE MORNING...
CREAK!
IT'S HIM! COME ON!
ALL RIGHT, BARRYMORE! WHAT'S GOING ON?
I WAS JUST CHECKING TO SEE THE WINDOWS WERE FASTENED, SIR!
ON THE SECOND FLOOR? AT TWO O'CLOCK IN THE MORNING?
WHY WERE YOU HOLDING A CANDLE TO THE WINDOW?
DON'T ASK, SIR HENRY. IT'S SOMEONE ELSE'S SECRET AND I CAN'T REVEAL IT!

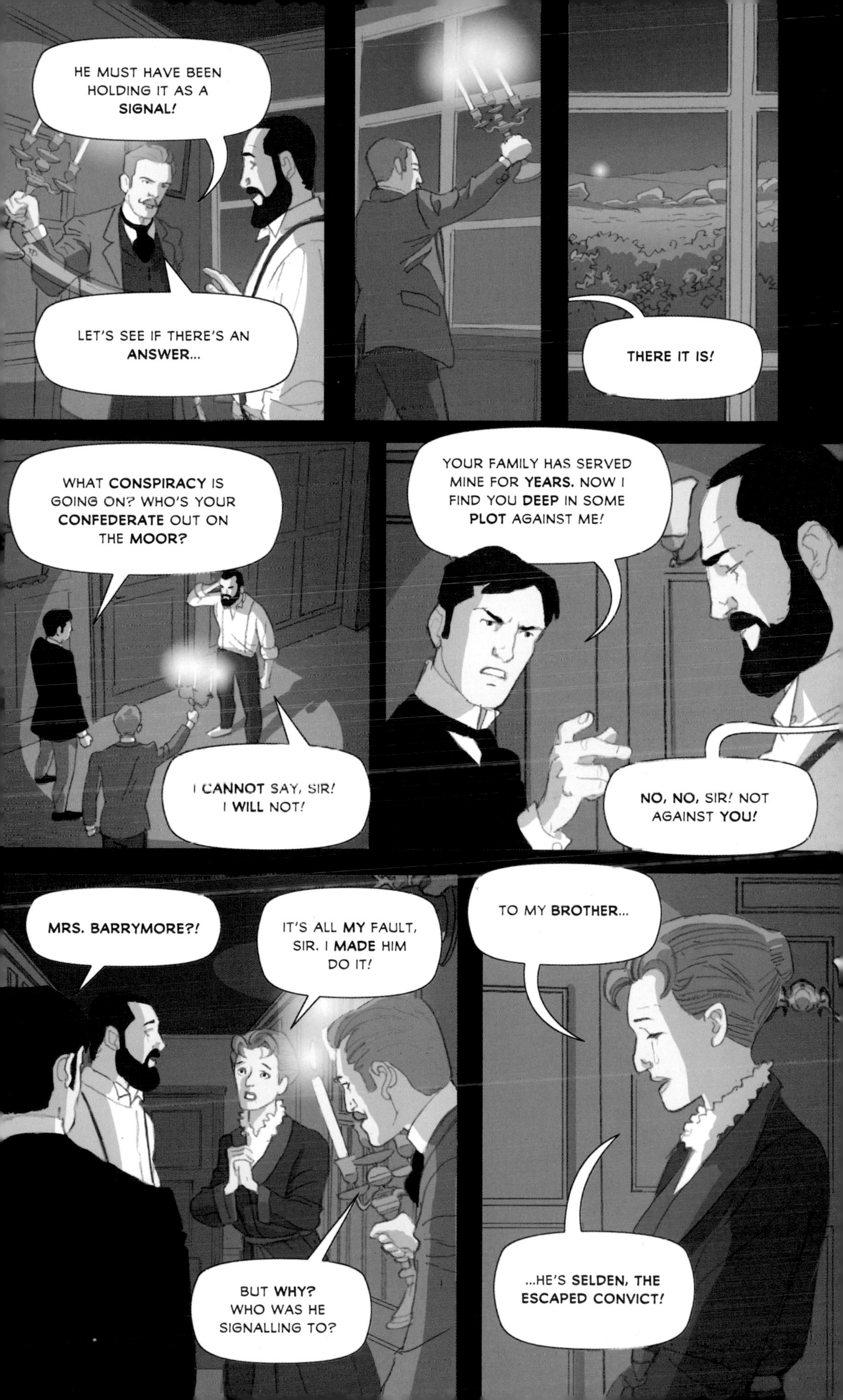
HE MUST HAVE BEEN HOLDING IT AS A SIGNAL!
LET'S SEE IF THERE'S AN ANSWER...
THERE IT IS!
WHAT CONSPIRACY IS GOING ON? WHO'S YOUR CONFEDERATE OUT ON THE MOOR?
I CANNOT SAY, SIR! I WILL NOT!
YOUR FAMILY HAS SERVED MINE FOR YEARS. NOW I FIND YOU DEEP IN SOME PLOT AGAINST ME!
NO, NO, SIR! NOT AGAINST YOU!
MRS. BARRYMORE?!
IT'S ALL MY FAULT, SIR. I MADE HIM DO IT!
BUT WHY? WHO WAS HE SIGNALLING TO?
TO MY BROTHER...
...HE'S SELDEN, THE ESCAPED CONVICT!

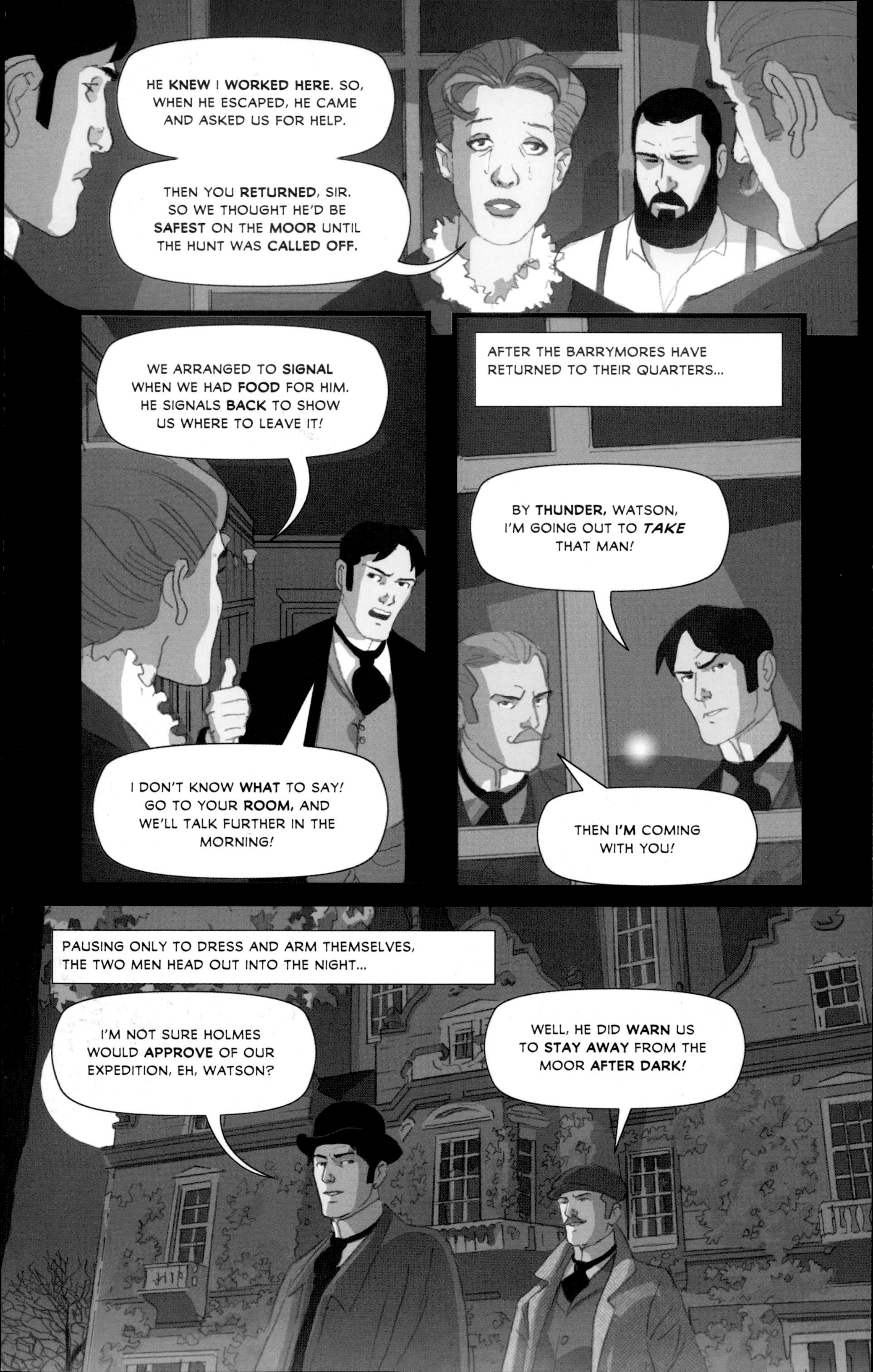
HE KNEW I WORKED HERE. SO, WHEN HE ESCAPED, HE CAME AND ASKED US FOR HELP.
THEN YOU RETURNED, SIR. SO WE THOUGHT HE'D BE SAFEST ON THE MOOR UNTIL THE HUNT WAS CALLED OFF.
WE ARRANGED TO SIGNAL WHEN WE HAD FOOD FOR HIM. HE SIGNALS BACK TO SHOW US WHERE TO LEAVE IT!
I DON'T KNOW WHAT TO SAY! GO TO YOUR ROOM, AND WE'LL TALK FURTHER IN THE MORNING!
AFTER THE BARRYMORES HAVE RETURNED TO THEIR QUARTERS...
BY THUNDER, WATSON, I'M GOING OUT TO TAKE THAT MAN!
THEN I'M COMING WITH YOU!
PAUSING ONLY TO DRESS AND ARM THEMSELVES, THE TWO MEN HEAD OUT INTO THE NIGHT...
I'M NOT SURE HOLMES WOULD APPROVE OF OUR EXPEDITION, EH, WATSON?
WELL, HE DID WARN US TO STAY AWAY FROM THE MOOR AFTER DARK!

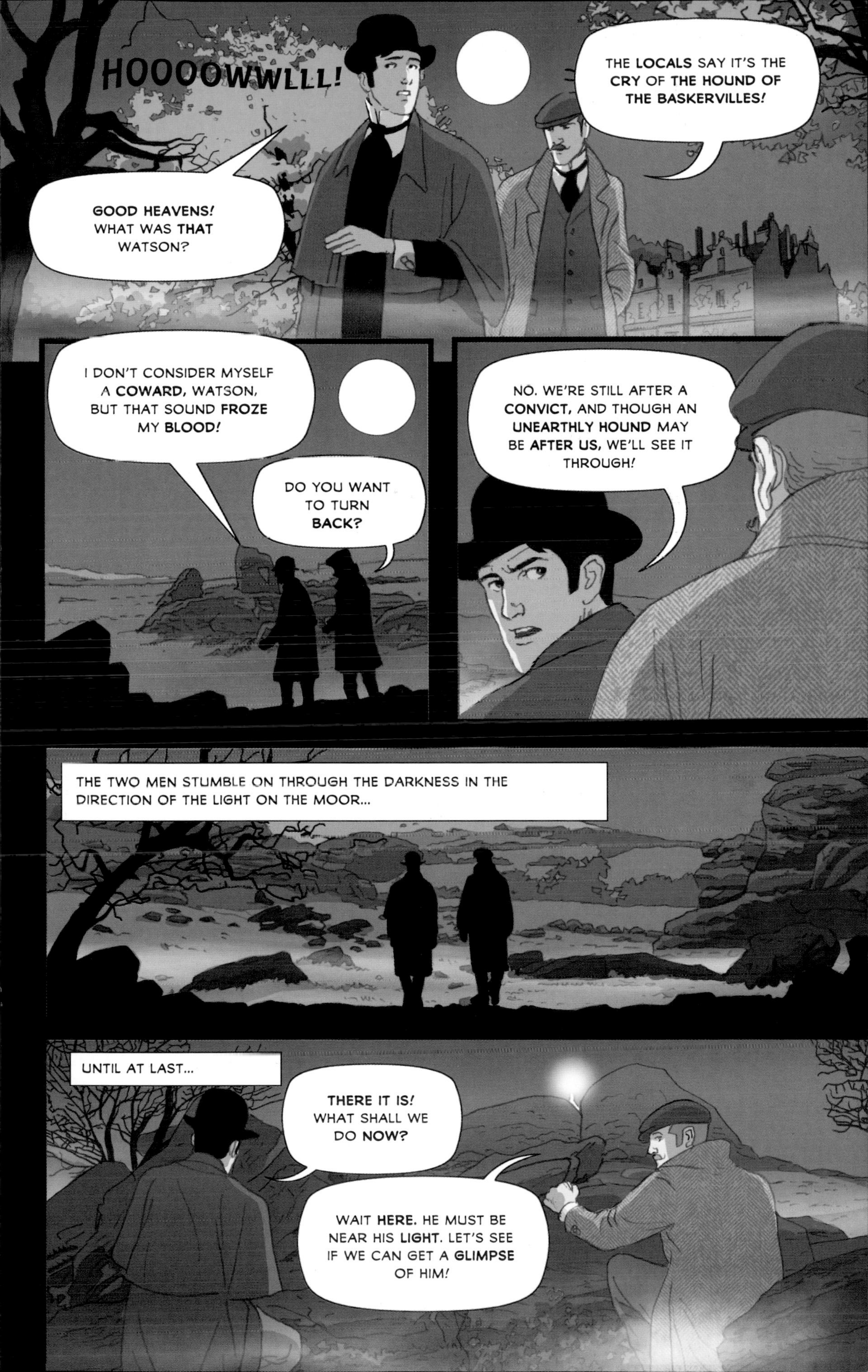
HOOOOWWLLL!
THE LOCALS SAY IT'S THE CRY OF THE HOUND OF THE BASKERVILLES!
GOOD HEAVENS! WHAT WAS THAT WATSON?
I DON'T CONSIDER MYSELF A COWARD, WATSON, BUT THAT SOUND FROZE MY BLOOD!
DO YOU WANT TO TURN BACK?
NO. WE'RE STILL AFTER A CONVICT, AND THOUGH AN UNEARTHLY HOUND MAY BE AFTER US, WE'LL SEE IT THROUGH!
THE TWO MEN STUMBLE ON THROUGH THE DARKNESS IN THE DIRECTION OF THE LIGHT ON THE MOOR...
UNTIL AT LAST...
THERE IT IS! WHAT SHALL WE DO NOW?
WAIT HERE. HE MUST BE NEAR HIS LIGHT. LET'S SEE IF WE CAN GET A GLIMPSE OF HIM!

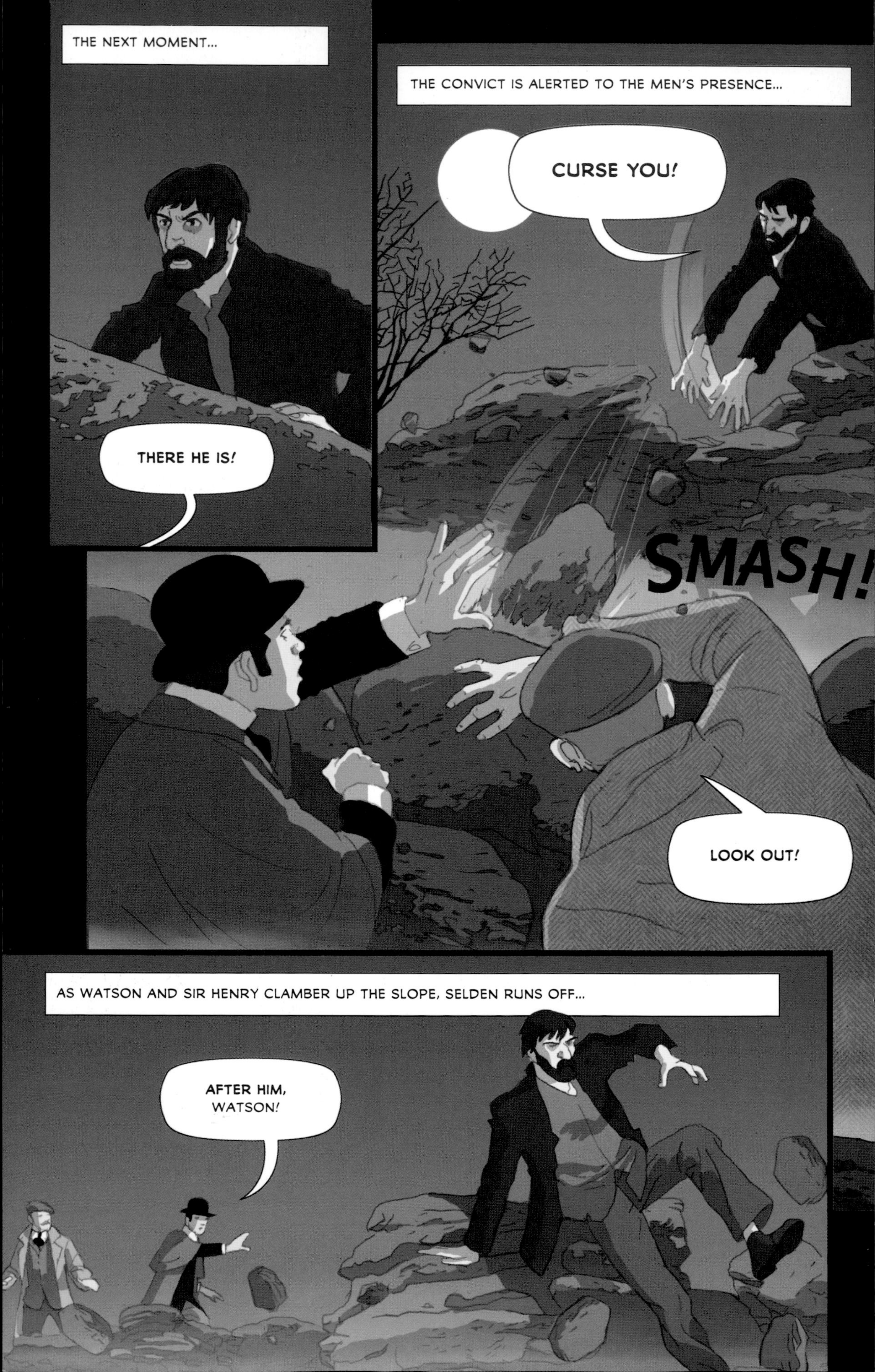
THE NEXT MOMENT...
THERE HE IS!
THE CONVICT IS ALERTED TO THE MEN'S PRESENCE...
CURSE YOU!
SMASH!
LOOK OUT!
AS WATSON AND SIR HENRY CLAMBER UP THE SLOPE, SELDEN RUNS OFF...
AFTER HIM, WATSON!

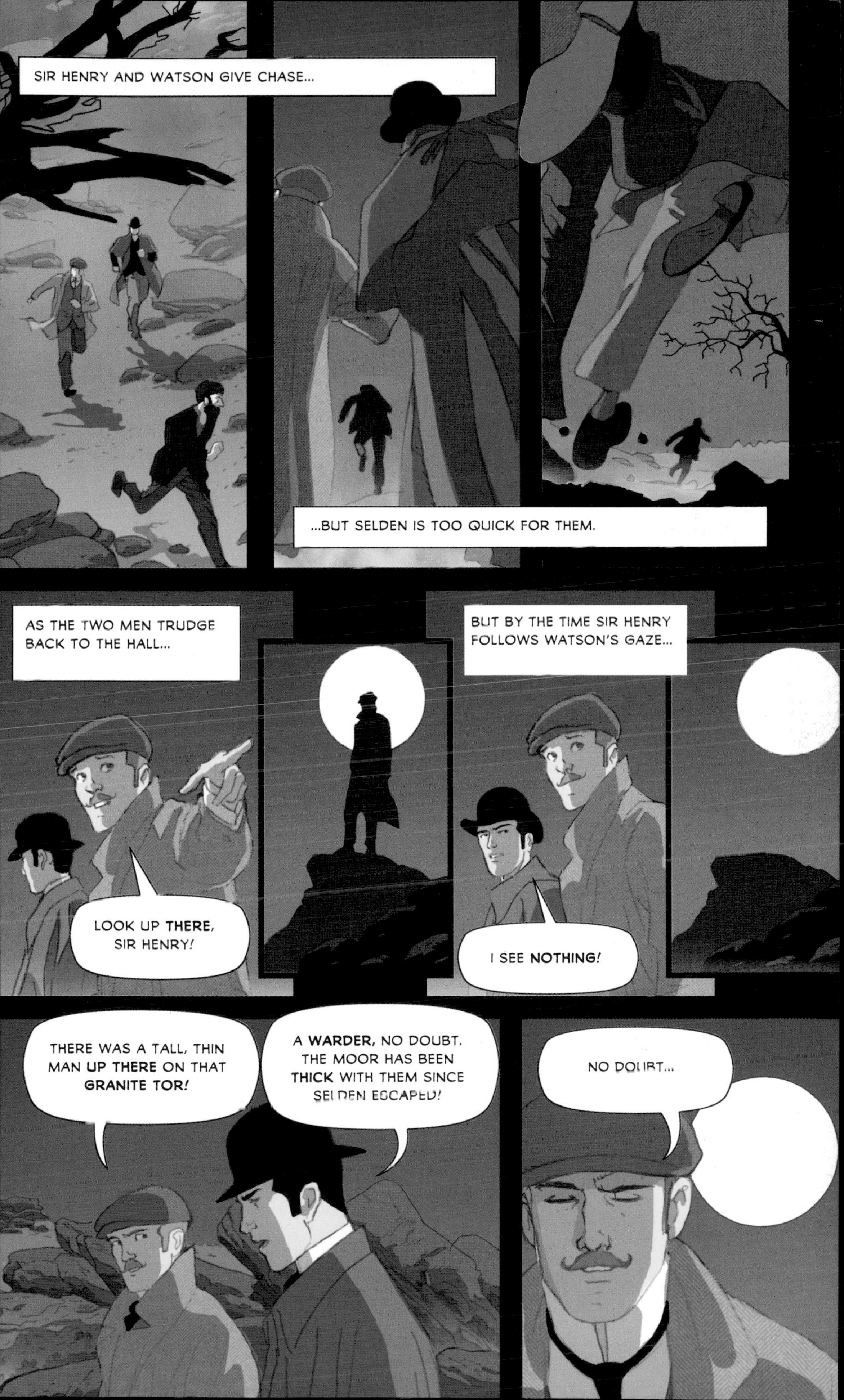
SIR HENRY AND WATSON GIVE CHASE...
...BUT SELDEN IS TOO QUICK FOR THEM.
AS THE TWO MEN TRUDGE BACK TO THE HALL...
LOOK UP THERE, SIR HENRY!
BUT BY THE TIME SIR HENRY FOLLOWS WATSON'S GAZE...
I SEE NOTHING!
THERE WAS A TALL, THIN MAN UP THERE ON THAT GRANITE TOR!
A WARDER, NO DOUBT. THE MOOR HAS BEEN THICK WITH THEM SINCE SELDEN ESCAPED!
NO DOUBT...

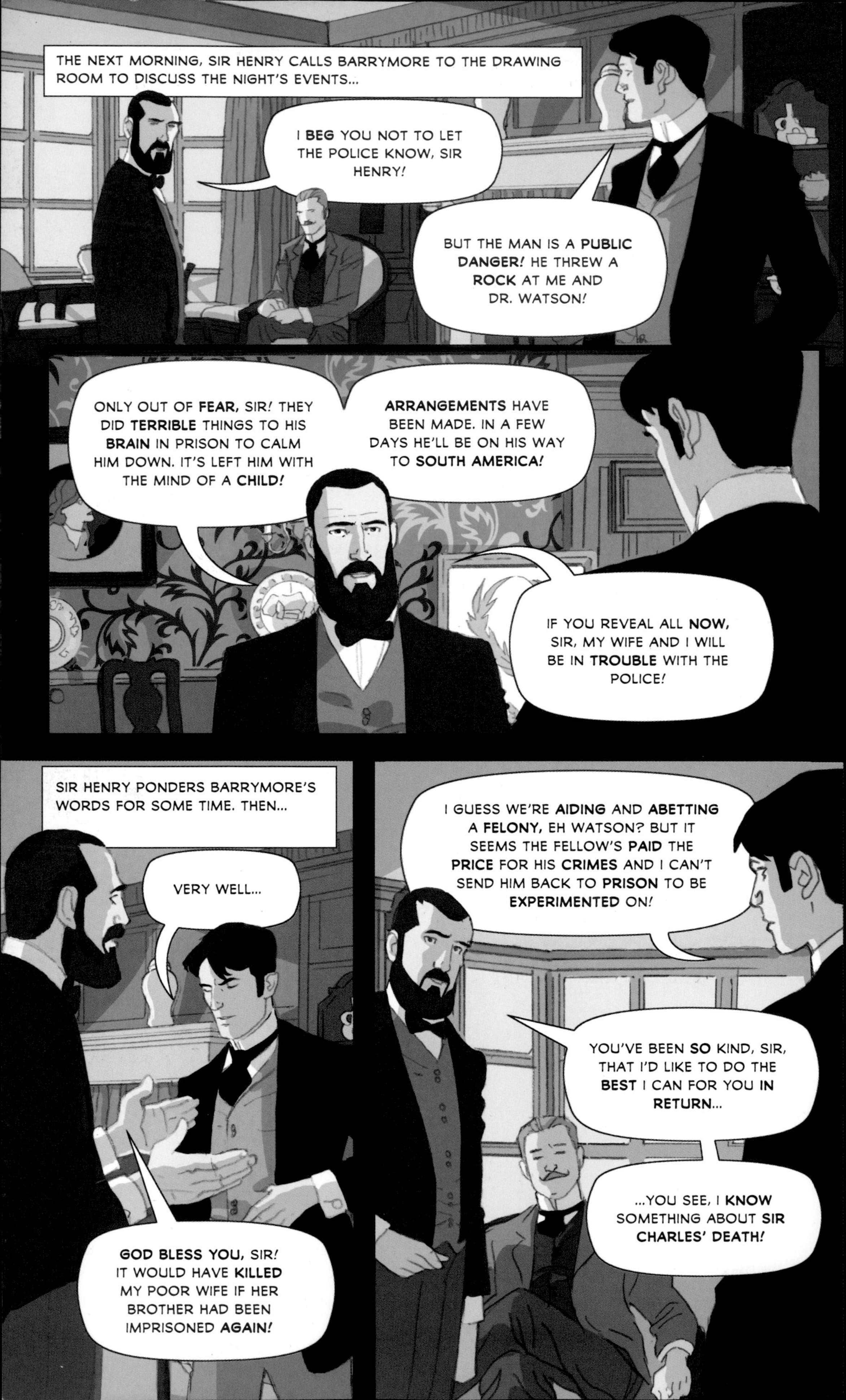
THE NEXT MORNING, SIR HENRY CALLS BARRYMORE TO THE DRAWING ROOM TO DISCUSS THE NIGHT'S EVENTS...
I BEG YOU NOT TO LET THE POLICE KNOW, SIR HENRY!
BUT THE MAN IS A PUBLIC DANGER! HE THREW A ROCK AT ME AND DR. WATSON!
ONLY OUT OF FEAR, SIR! THEY DID TERRIBLE THINGS TO HIS BRAIN IN PRISON TO CALM HIM DOWN. IT'S LEFT HIM WITH THE MIND OF A CHILD!
ARRANGEMENTS HAVE BEEN MADE. IN A FEW DAYS HE'LL BE ON HIS WAY TO SOUTH AMERICA!
IF YOU REVEAL ALL NOW, SIR, MY WIFE AND I WILL BE IN TROUBLE WITH THE POLICE!
SIR HENRY PONDERS BARRYMORE'S WORDS FOR SOME TIME. THEN...
VERY WELL...
GOD BLESS YOU, SIR! IT WOULD HAVE KILLED MY POOR WIFE IF HER BROTHER HAD BEEN IMPRISONED AGAIN!
I GUESS WE'RE AIDING AND ABETTING A FELONY, EH WATSON? BUT IT SEEMS THE FELLOW'S PAID THE PRICE FOR HIS CRIMES AND I CAN'T SEND HIM BACK TO PRISON TO BE EXPERIMENTED ON!
YOU'VE BEEN SO KIND, SIR, THAT I'D LIKE TO DO THE BEST I CAN FOR YOU IN RETURN...
...YOU SEE, I KNOW SOMETHING ABOUT SIR CHARLES' DEATH!

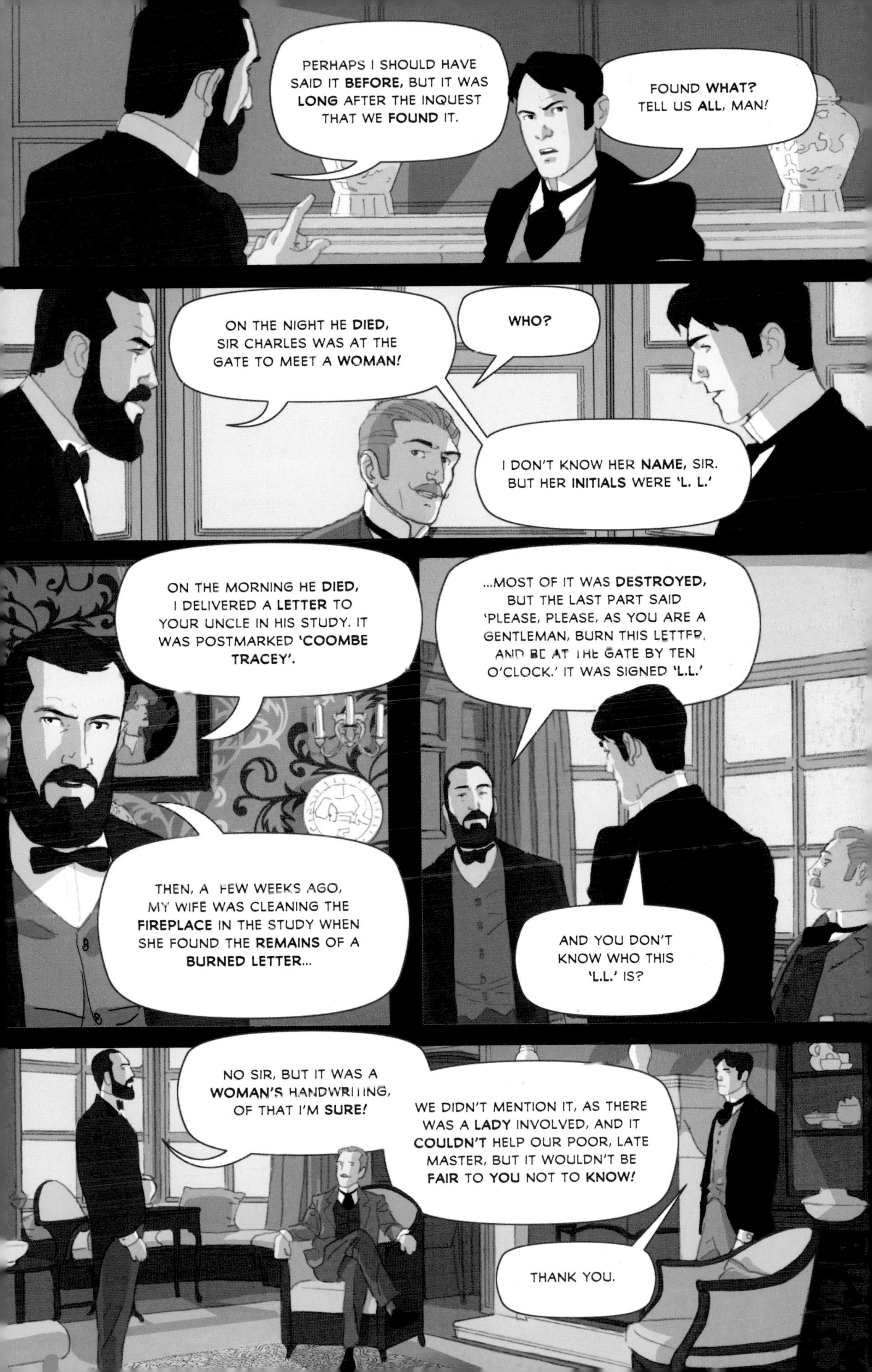
PERHAPS I SHOULD HAVE SAID IT BEFORE, BUT IT WAS LONG AFTER THE INQUEST THAT WE FOUND IT.
FOUND WHAT? TELL US ALL, MAN!
ON THE NIGHT HE DIED, SIR CHARLES WAS AT THE GATE TO MEET A WOMAN!
WHO?
I DON'T KNOW HER NAME, SIR. BUT HER INITIALS WERE 'L. L.'
ON THE MORNING HE DIED, I DELIVERED A LETTER TO YOUR UNCLE IN HIS STUDY. IT WAS POSTMARKED 'COOMBE TRACEY'.
THEN, A FEW WEEKS AGO, MY WIFE WAS CLEANING THE FIREPLACE IN THE STUDY WHEN SHE FOUND THE REMAINS OF A BURNED LETTER...
...MOST OF IT WAS DESTROYED, BUT THE LAST PART SAID 'PLEASE, PLEASE, AS YOU ARE A GENTLEMAN, BURN THIS LETTER, AND BE AT THE GATE BY TEN O'CLOCK.' IT WAS SIGNED 'L.L.'
AND YOU DON'T KNOW WHO THIS 'L.L.' IS?
NO SIR, BUT IT WAS A WOMAN'S HANDWRITING, OF THAT I'M SURE!
WE DIDN'T MENTION IT, AS THERE WAS A LADY INVOLVED, AND IT COULDN'T HELP OUR POOR, LATE MASTER, BUT IT WOULDN'T BE FAIR TO YOU NOT TO KNOW!
THANK YOU.

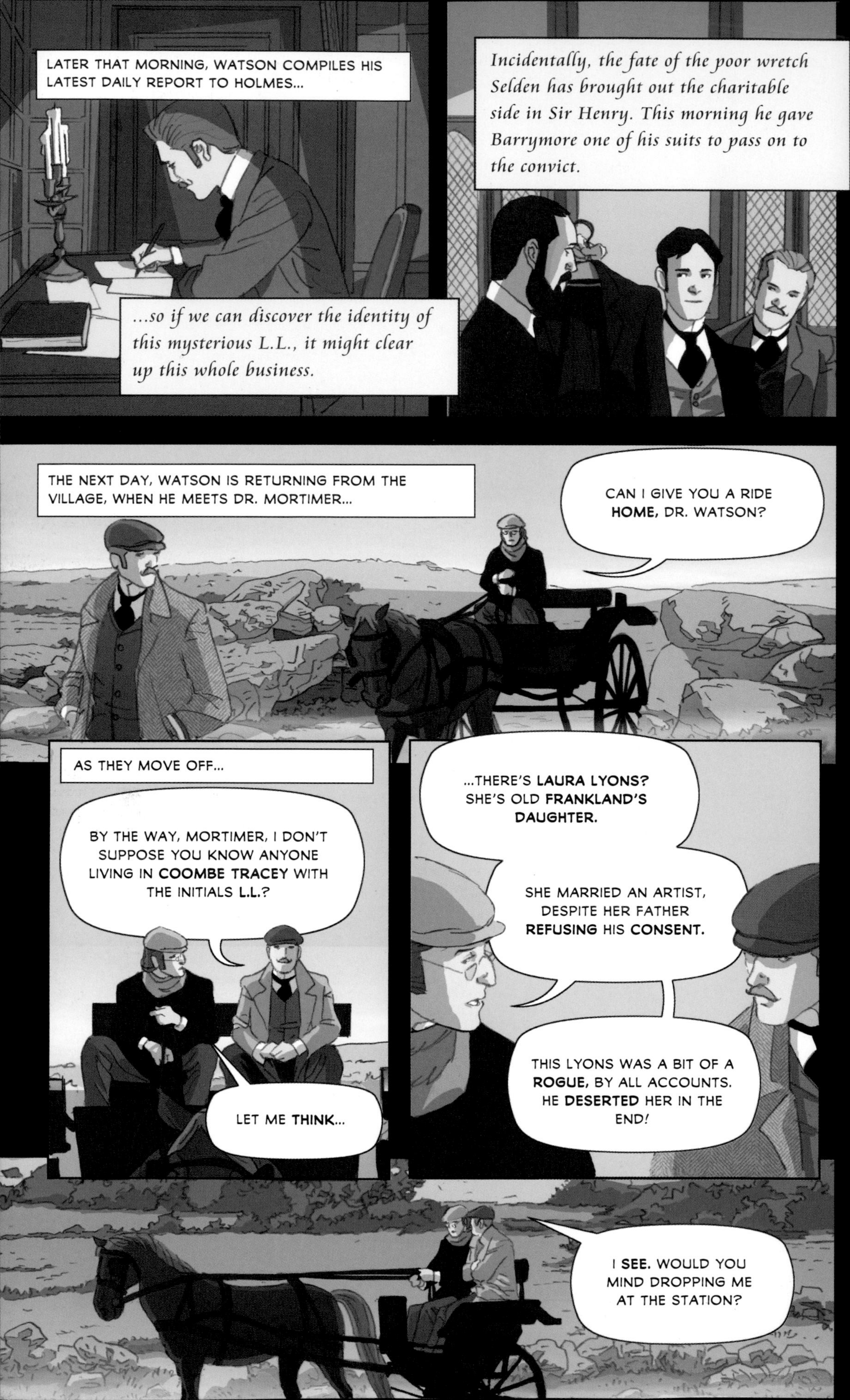
LATER THAT MORNING, WATSON COMPILES HIS LATEST DAILY REPORT TO HOLMES...
...so if we can discover the identity of this mysterious L.L., it might clear up this whole business.
Incidentally, the fate of the poor wretch Selden has brought out the charitable side in Sir Henry. This morning he gave Barrymore one of his suits to pass on to the convict.
THE NEXT DAY, WATSON IS RETURNING FROM THE VILLAGE, WHEN HE MEETS DR. MORTIMER...
CAN I GIVE YOU A RIDE **HOME,** DR. WATSON?
AS THEY MOVE OFF...
BY THE WAY, MORTIMER, I DON'T SUPPOSE YOU KNOW ANYONE LIVING IN **COOMBE TRACEY** WITH THE INITIALS **L.L.**?
LET ME **THINK**...
...THERE'S **LAURA LYONS?** SHE'S OLD **FRANKLAND'S DAUGHTER.**
SHE MARRIED AN ARTIST, DESPITE HER FATHER **REFUSING** HIS **CONSENT.**
THIS LYONS WAS A BIT OF A **ROGUE,** BY ALL ACCOUNTS. HE **DESERTED** HER IN THE END!
I **SEE.** WOULD YOU MIND DROPPING ME AT THE STATION?

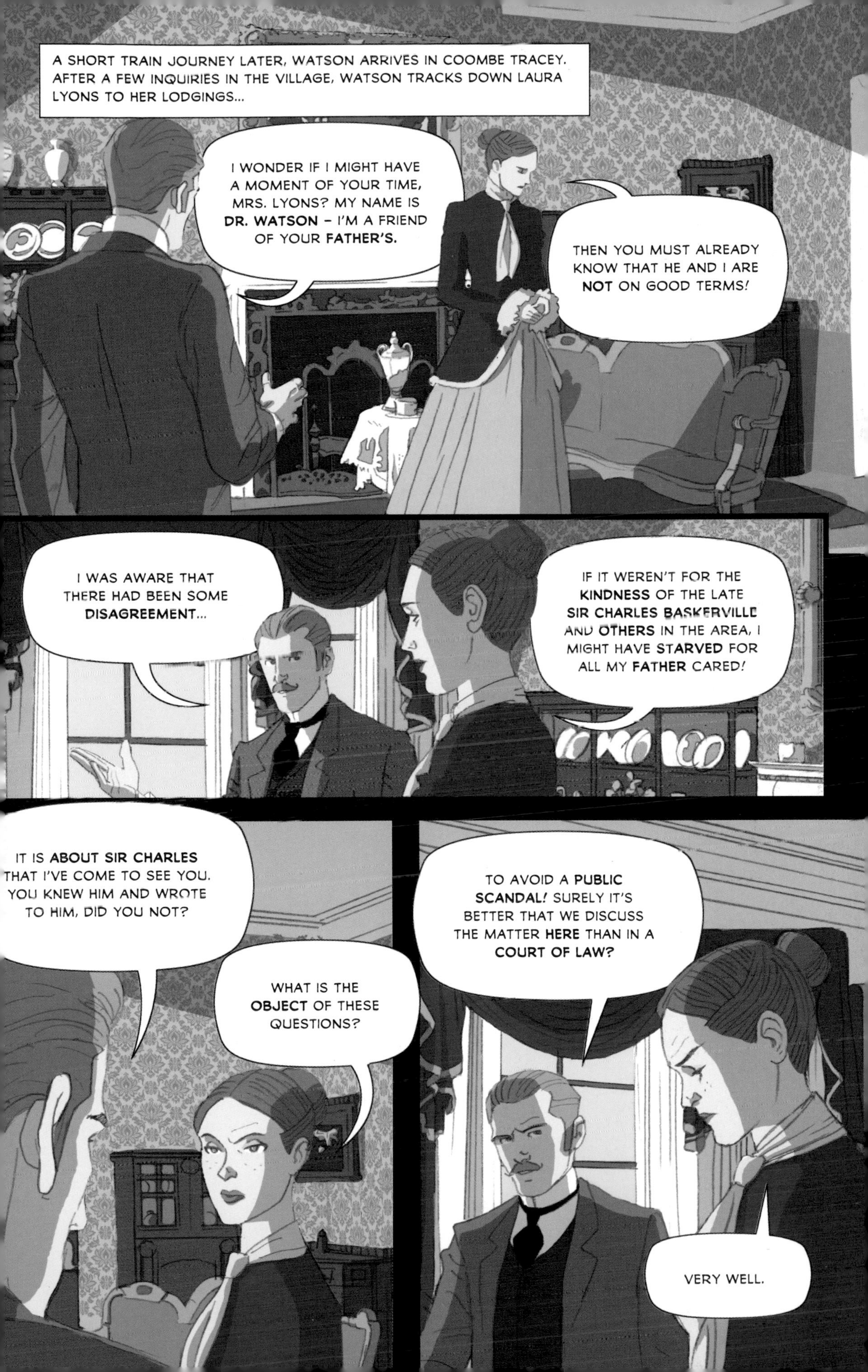
A SHORT TRAIN JOURNEY LATER, WATSON ARRIVES IN COOMBE TRACEY. AFTER A FEW INQUIRIES IN THE VILLAGE, WATSON TRACKS DOWN LAURA LYONS TO HER LODGINGS...
I WONDER IF I MIGHT HAVE A MOMENT OF YOUR TIME, MRS. LYONS? MY NAME IS DR. WATSON – I'M A FRIEND OF YOUR FATHER'S.
THEN YOU MUST ALREADY KNOW THAT HE AND I ARE NOT ON GOOD TERMS!
I WAS AWARE THAT THERE HAD BEEN SOME DISAGREEMENT...
IF IT WEREN'T FOR THE KINDNESS OF THE LATE SIR CHARLES BASKERVILLE AND OTHERS IN THE AREA, I MIGHT HAVE STARVED FOR ALL MY FATHER CARED!
IT IS ABOUT SIR CHARLES THAT I'VE COME TO SEE YOU. YOU KNEW HIM AND WROTE TO HIM, DID YOU NOT?
WHAT IS THE OBJECT OF THESE QUESTIONS?
TO AVOID A PUBLIC SCANDAL! SURELY IT'S BETTER THAT WE DISCUSS THE MATTER HERE THAN IN A COURT OF LAW?
VERY WELL.

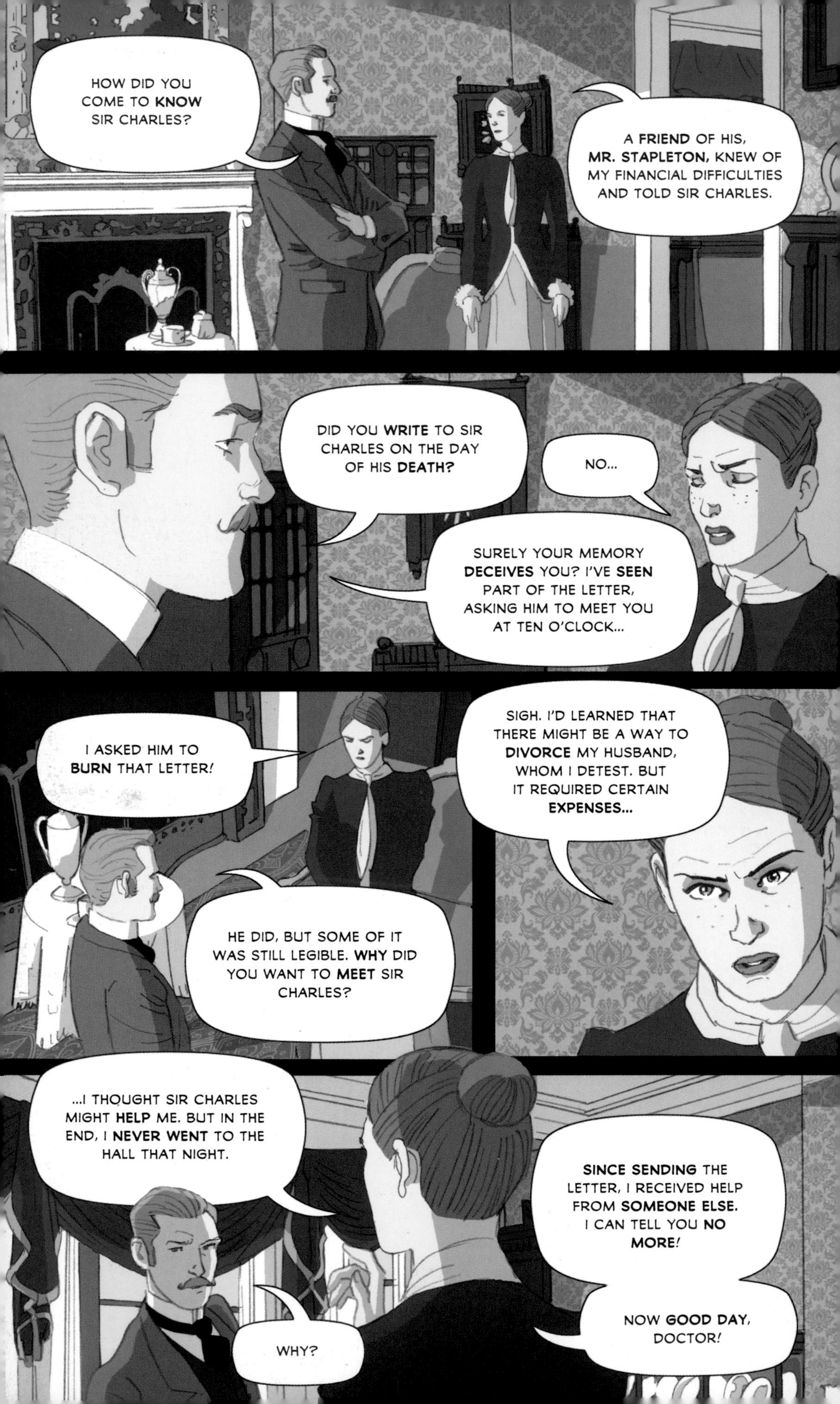
HOW DID YOU COME TO **KNOW** SIR CHARLES?
A **FRIEND** OF HIS, **MR. STAPLETON,** KNEW OF MY FINANCIAL DIFFICULTIES AND TOLD SIR CHARLES.
DID YOU **WRITE** TO SIR CHARLES ON THE DAY OF HIS **DEATH?**
NO...
SURELY YOUR MEMORY **DECEIVES** YOU? I'VE **SEEN** PART OF THE LETTER, ASKING HIM TO MEET YOU AT TEN O'CLOCK...
I ASKED HIM TO **BURN** THAT LETTER!
HE DID, BUT SOME OF IT WAS STILL LEGIBLE. **WHY** DID YOU WANT TO **MEET** SIR CHARLES?
SIGH. I'D LEARNED THAT THERE MIGHT BE A WAY TO **DIVORCE** MY HUSBAND, WHOM I DETEST. BUT IT REQUIRED CERTAIN **EXPENSES...**
...I THOUGHT SIR CHARLES MIGHT **HELP** ME. BUT IN THE END, I **NEVER WENT** TO THE HALL THAT NIGHT.
WHY?
SINCE SENDING THE LETTER, I RECEIVED HELP FROM **SOMEONE ELSE.** I CAN TELL YOU **NO MORE!**
NOW **GOOD DAY,** DOCTOR!

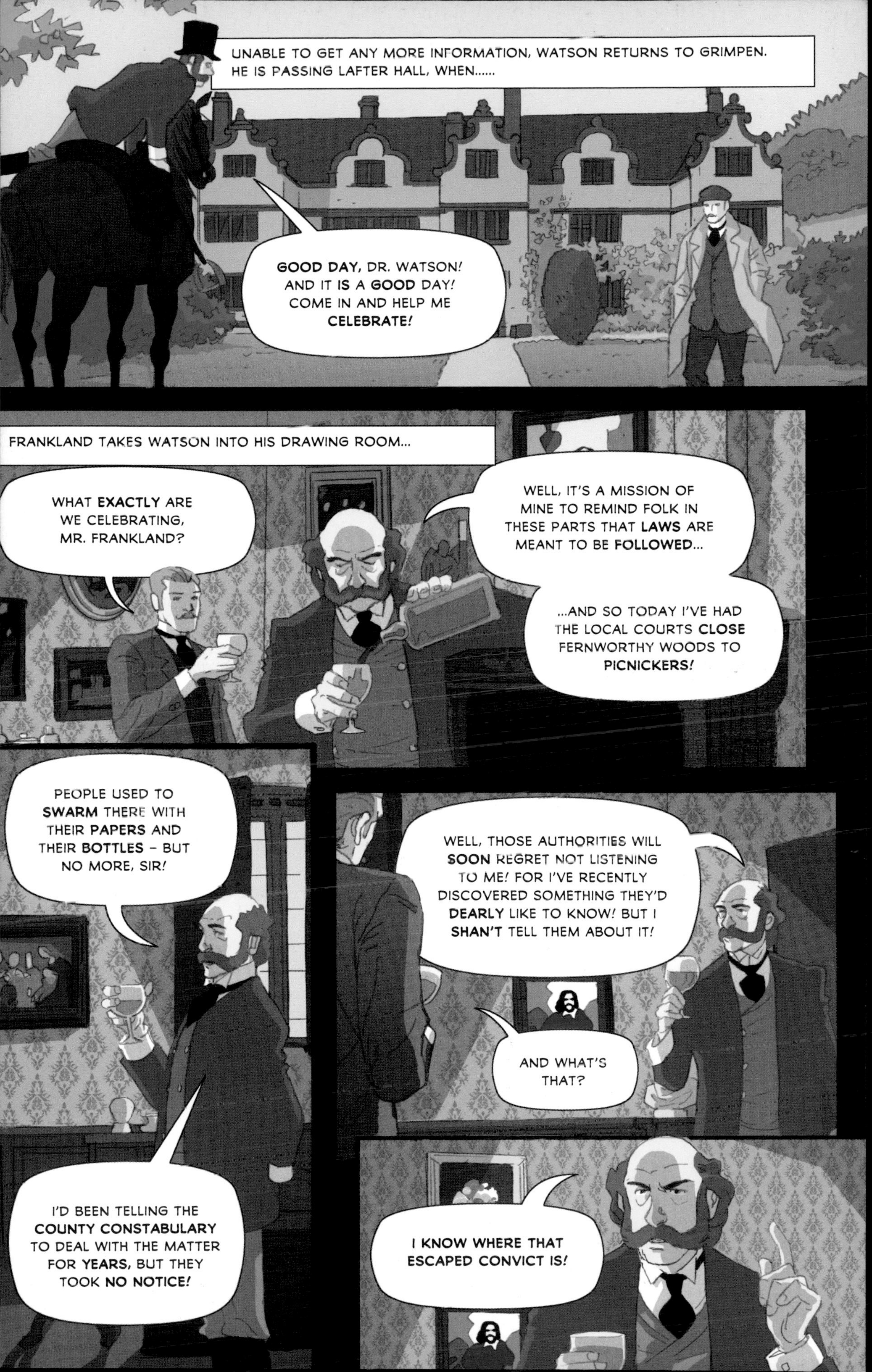

UNABLE TO GET ANY MORE INFORMATION, WATSON RETURNS TO GRIMPEN. HE IS PASSING LAFTER HALL, WHEN......
GOOD DAY, DR. WATSON! AND IT IS A GOOD DAY! COME IN AND HELP ME CELEBRATE!
FRANKLAND TAKES WATSON INTO HIS DRAWING ROOM...
WHAT EXACTLY ARE WE CELEBRATING, MR. FRANKLAND?
WELL, IT'S A MISSION OF MINE TO REMIND FOLK IN THESE PARTS THAT LAWS ARE MEANT TO BE FOLLOWED...
...AND SO TODAY I'VE HAD THE LOCAL COURTS CLOSE FERNWORTHY WOODS TO PICNICKERS!
PEOPLE USED TO SWARM THERE WITH THEIR PAPERS AND THEIR BOTTLES – BUT NO MORE, SIR!
I'D BEEN TELLING THE COUNTY CONSTABULARY TO DEAL WITH THE MATTER FOR YEARS, BUT THEY TOOK NO NOTICE!
WELL, THOSE AUTHORITIES WILL SOON REGRET NOT LISTENING TO ME! FOR I'VE RECENTLY DISCOVERED SOMETHING THEY'D DEARLY LIKE TO KNOW! BUT I SHAN'T TELL THEM ABOUT IT!
AND WHAT'S THAT?
I KNOW WHERE THAT ESCAPED CONVICT IS!

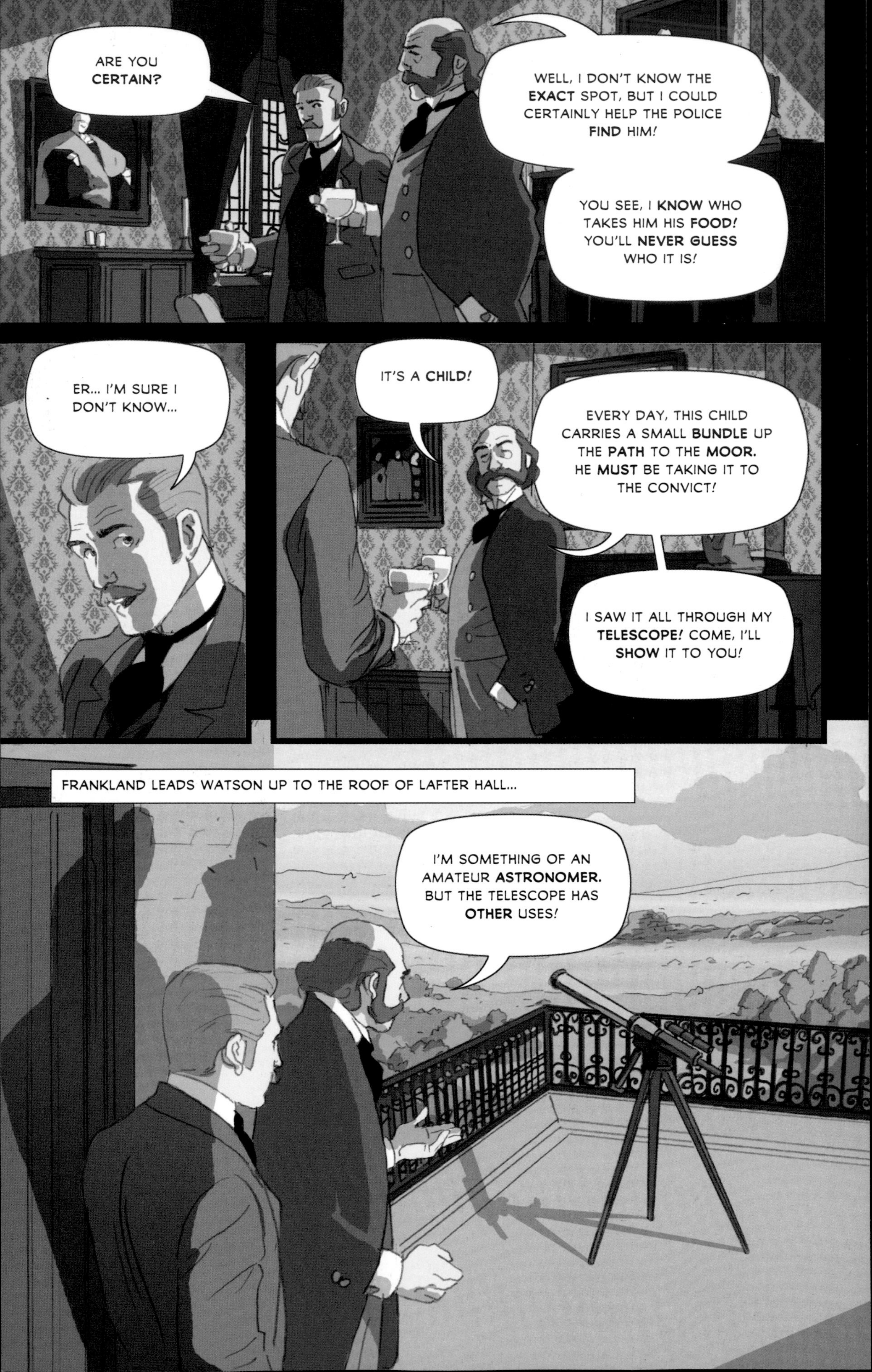
ARE YOU CERTAIN?
WELL, I DON'T KNOW THE EXACT SPOT, BUT I COULD CERTAINLY HELP THE POLICE FIND HIM!
YOU SEE, I KNOW WHO TAKES HIM HIS FOOD! YOU'LL NEVER GUESS WHO IT IS!
ER... I'M SURE I DON'T KNOW...
IT'S A CHILD!
EVERY DAY, THIS CHILD CARRIES A SMALL BUNDLE UP THE PATH TO THE MOOR. HE MUST BE TAKING IT TO THE CONVICT!
I SAW IT ALL THROUGH MY TELESCOPE! COME, I'LL SHOW IT TO YOU!
FRANKLAND LEADS WATSON UP TO THE ROOF OF LAFTER HALL...
I'M SOMETHING OF AN AMATEUR ASTRONOMER. BUT THE TELESCOPE HAS OTHER USES!

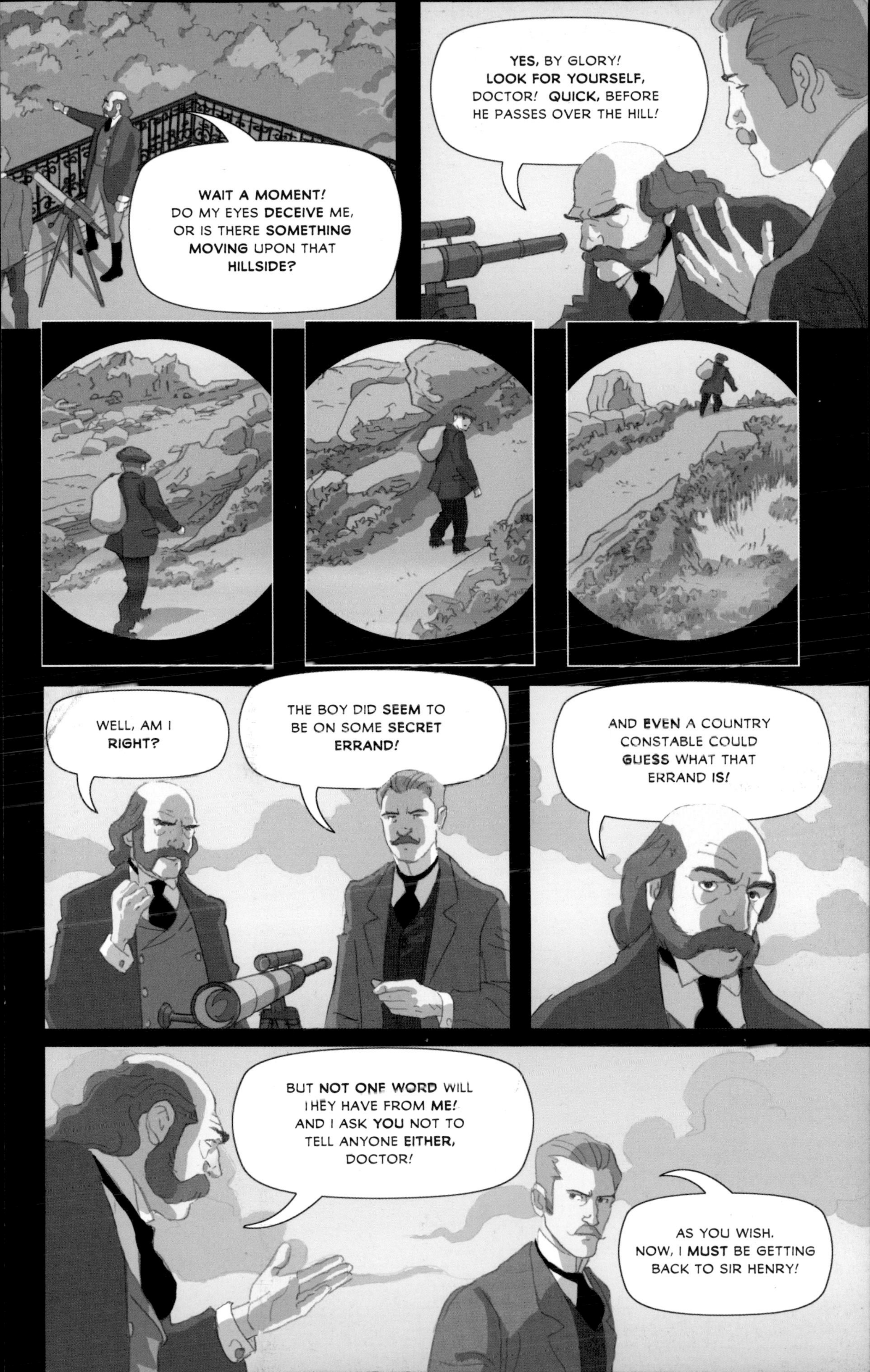
WAIT A MOMENT! DO MY EYES DECEIVE ME, OR IS THERE SOMETHING MOVING UPON THAT HILLSIDE?
YES, BY GLORY! LOOK FOR YOURSELF, DOCTOR! QUICK, BEFORE HE PASSES OVER THE HILL!
WELL, AM I RIGHT?
THE BOY DID SEEM TO BE ON SOME SECRET ERRAND!
AND EVEN A COUNTRY CONSTABLE COULD GUESS WHAT THAT ERRAND IS!
BUT NOT ONE WORD WILL THEY HAVE FROM ME! AND I ASK YOU NOT TO TELL ANYONE EITHER, DOCTOR!
AS YOU WISH. NOW, I MUST BE GETTING BACK TO SIR HENRY!

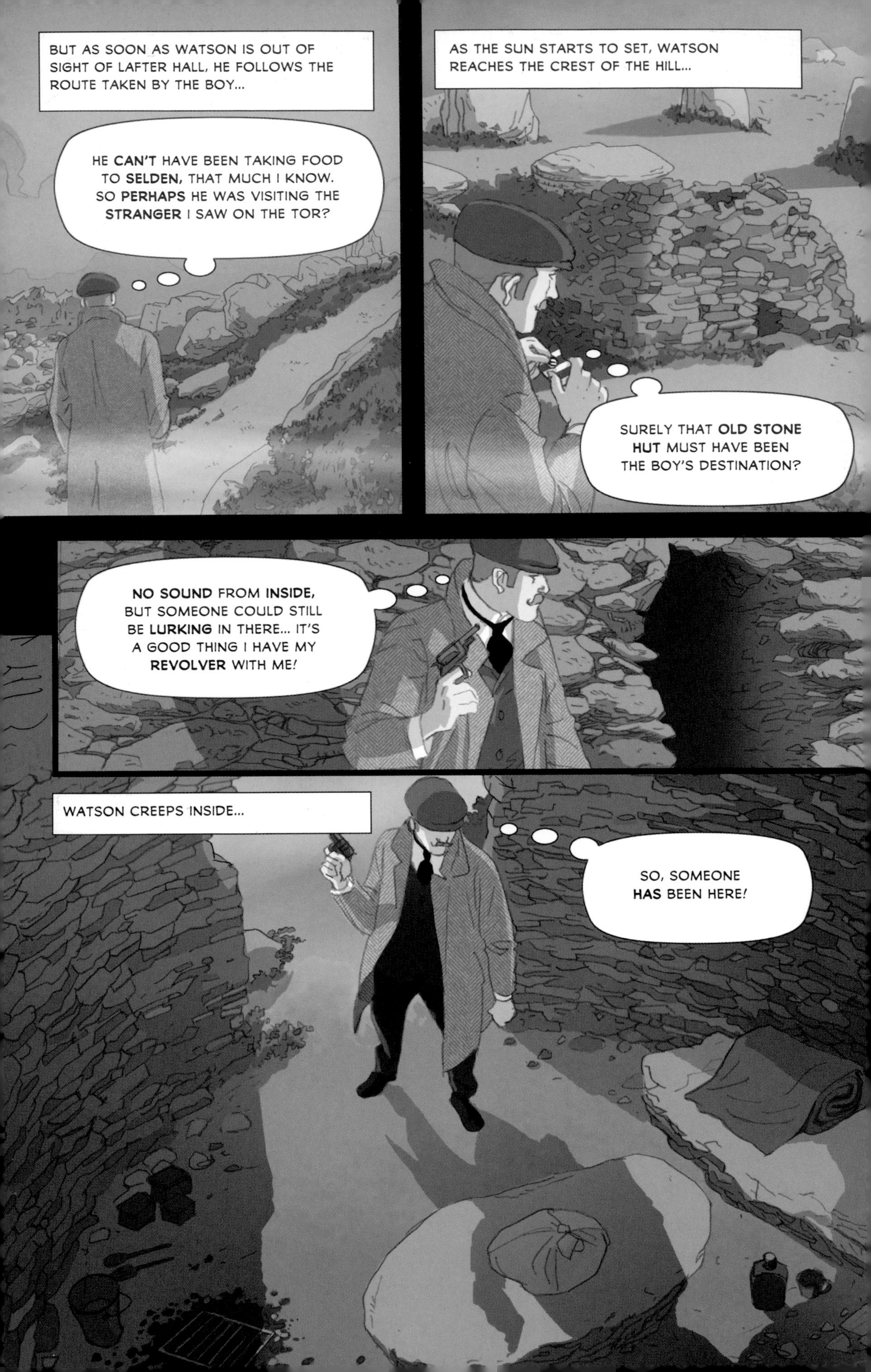
BUT AS SOON AS WATSON IS OUT OF SIGHT OF LAFTER HALL, HE FOLLOWS THE ROUTE TAKEN BY THE BOY...
HE **CAN'T** HAVE BEEN TAKING FOOD TO **SELDEN,** THAT MUCH I KNOW. SO **PERHAPS** HE WAS VISITING THE **STRANGER** I SAW ON THE TOR?
AS THE SUN STARTS TO SET, WATSON REACHES THE CREST OF THE HILL...
SURELY THAT **OLD STONE HUT** MUST HAVE BEEN THE BOY'S DESTINATION?
NO SOUND FROM **INSIDE,** BUT SOMEONE COULD STILL BE **LURKING** IN THERE... IT'S A GOOD THING I HAVE MY **REVOLVER** WITH ME!
WATSON CREEPS INSIDE...
SO, SOMEONE **HAS** BEEN HERE!

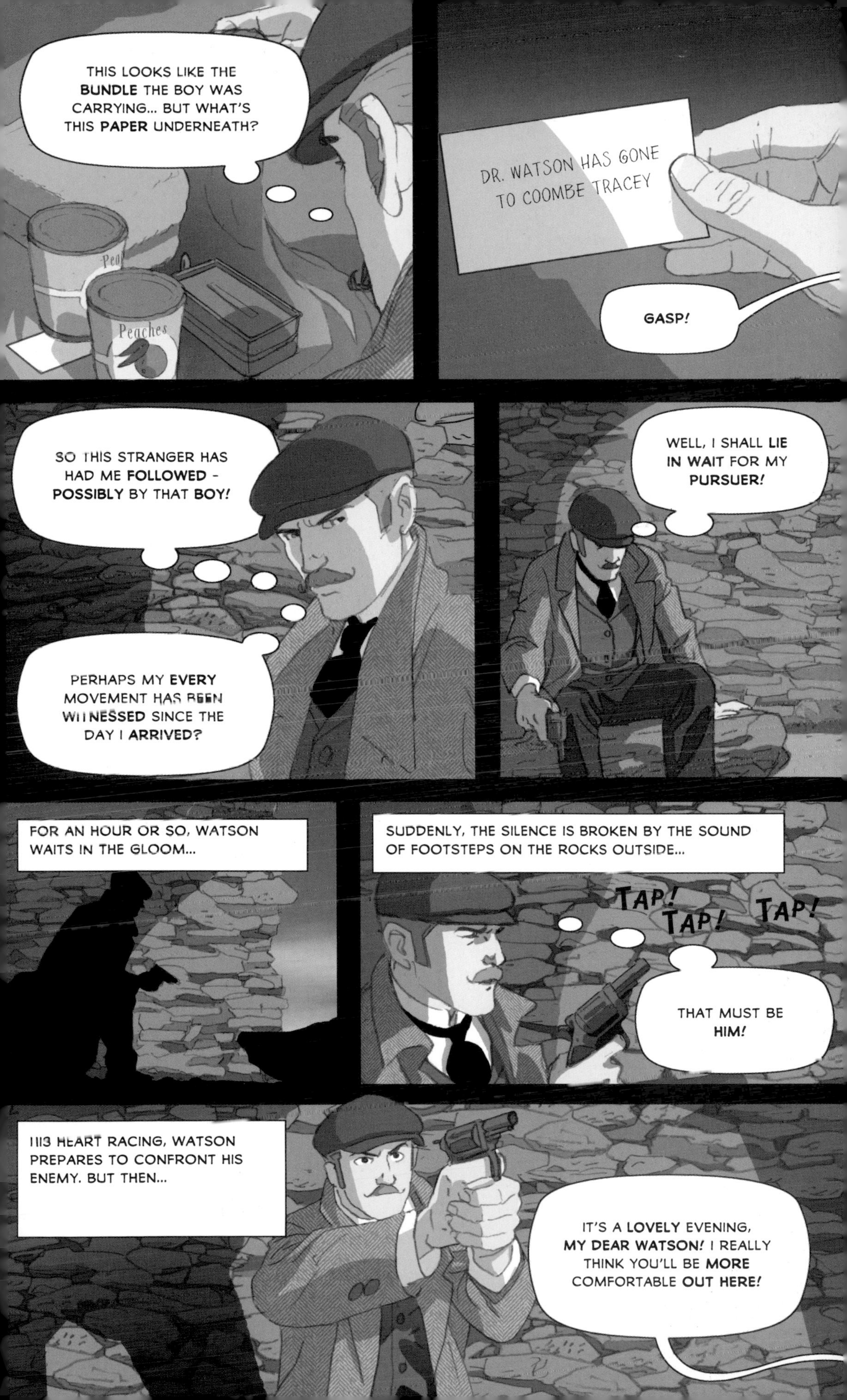
THIS LOOKS LIKE THE BUNDLE THE BOY WAS CARRYING... BUT WHAT'S THIS PAPER UNDERNEATH?
Peaches
DR. WATSON HAS GONE TO COOMBE TRACEY
GASP!
SO THIS STRANGER HAS HAD ME FOLLOWED - POSSIBLY BY THAT BOY!
PERHAPS MY EVERY MOVEMENT HAS BEEN WITNESSED SINCE THE DAY I ARRIVED?
WELL, I SHALL LIE IN WAIT FOR MY PURSUER!
FOR AN HOUR OR SO, WATSON WAITS IN THE GLOOM...
SUDDENLY, THE SILENCE IS BROKEN BY THE SOUND OF FOOTSTEPS ON THE ROCKS OUTSIDE...
TAP! TAP! TAP!
THAT MUST BE HIM!
HIS HEART RACING, WATSON PREPARES TO CONFRONT HIS ENEMY. BUT THEN...
IT'S A LOVELY EVENING, MY DEAR WATSON! I REALLY THINK YOU'LL BE MORE COMFORTABLE OUT HERE!

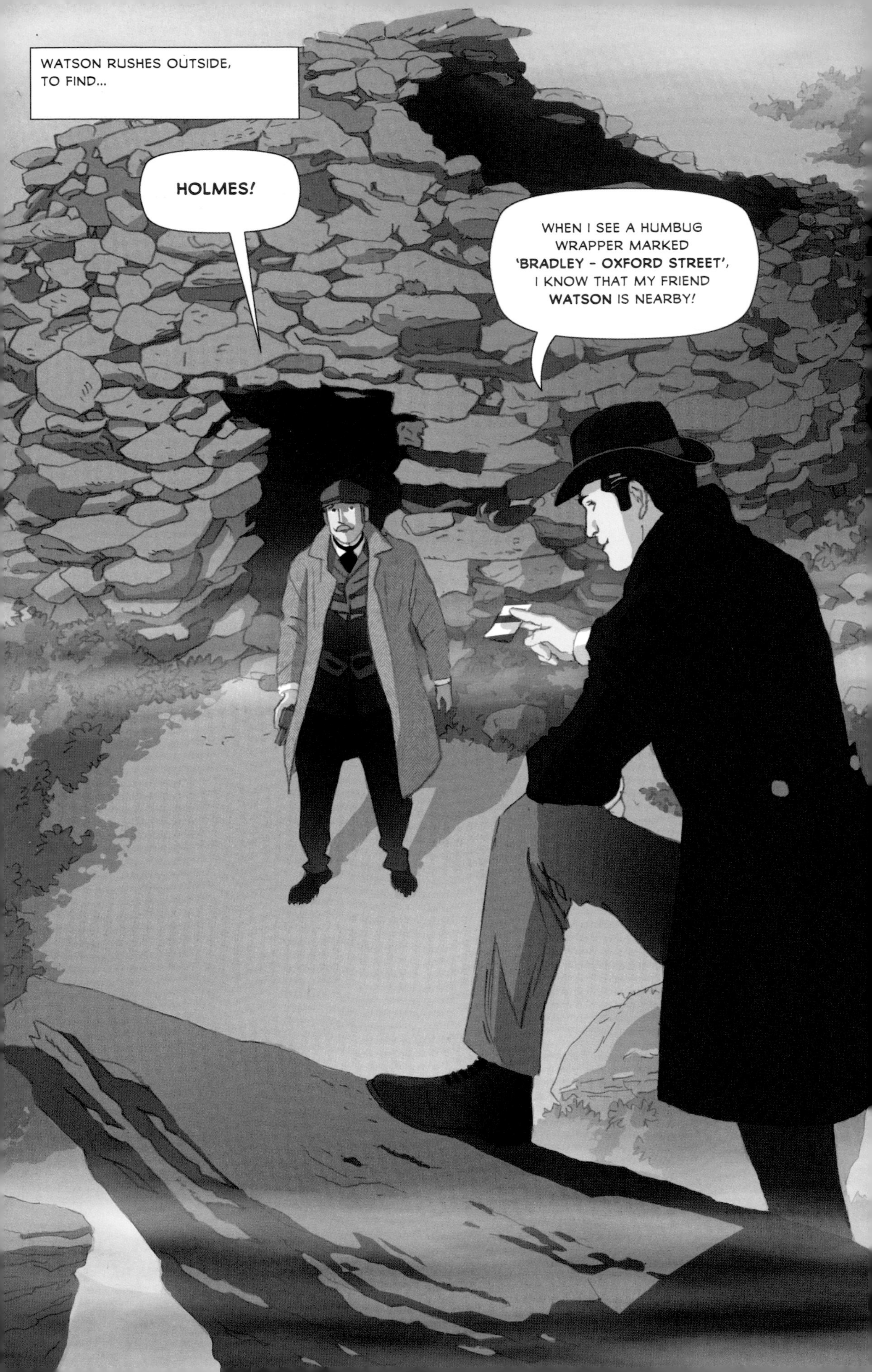
WATSON RUSHES OUTSIDE, TO FIND...
HOLMES!
WHEN I SEE A HUMBUG WRAPPER MARKED 'BRADLEY - OXFORD STREET', I KNOW THAT MY FRIEND WATSON IS NEARBY!

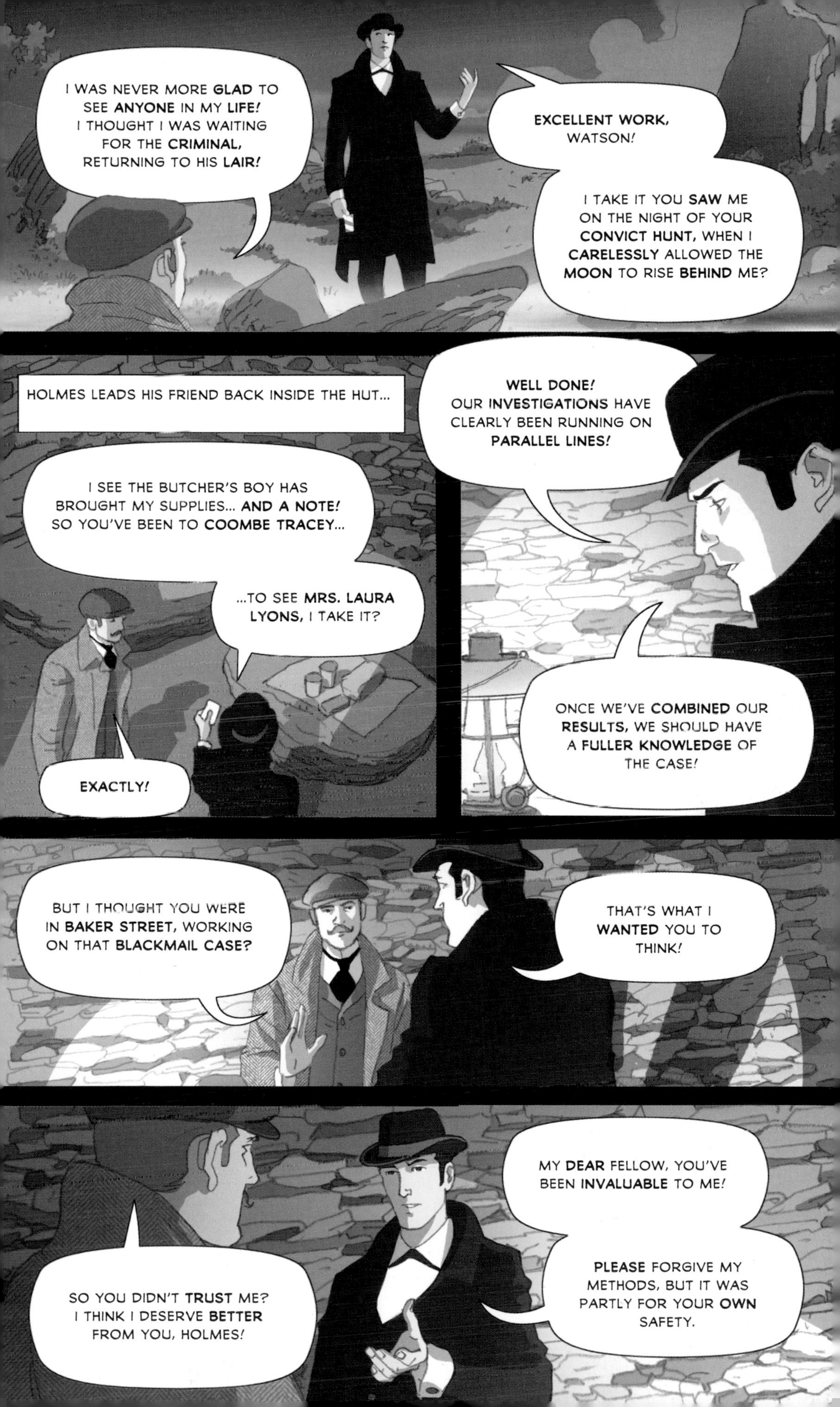

I WAS NEVER MORE GLAD TO SEE ANYONE IN MY LIFE! I THOUGHT I WAS WAITING FOR THE CRIMINAL, RETURNING TO HIS LAIR!
EXCELLENT WORK, WATSON!
I TAKE IT YOU SAW ME ON THE NIGHT OF YOUR CONVICT HUNT, WHEN I CARELESSLY ALLOWED THE MOON TO RISE BEHIND ME?
HOLMES LEADS HIS FRIEND BACK INSIDE THE HUT...
I SEE THE BUTCHER'S BOY HAS BROUGHT MY SUPPLIES... AND A NOTE! SO YOU'VE BEEN TO COOMBE TRACEY...
...TO SEE MRS. LAURA LYONS, I TAKE IT?
EXACTLY!
WELL DONE! OUR INVESTIGATIONS HAVE CLEARLY BEEN RUNNING ON PARALLEL LINES!
ONCE WE'VE COMBINED OUR RESULTS, WE SHOULD HAVE A FULLER KNOWLEDGE OF THE CASE!
BUT I THOUGHT YOU WERE IN BAKER STREET, WORKING ON THAT BLACKMAIL CASE?
THAT'S WHAT I WANTED YOU TO THINK!
SO YOU DIDN'T TRUST ME? I THINK I DESERVE BETTER FROM YOU, HOLMES!
MY DEAR FELLOW, YOU'VE BEEN INVALUABLE TO ME!
PLEASE FORGIVE MY METHODS, BUT IT WAS PARTLY FOR YOUR OWN SAFETY.

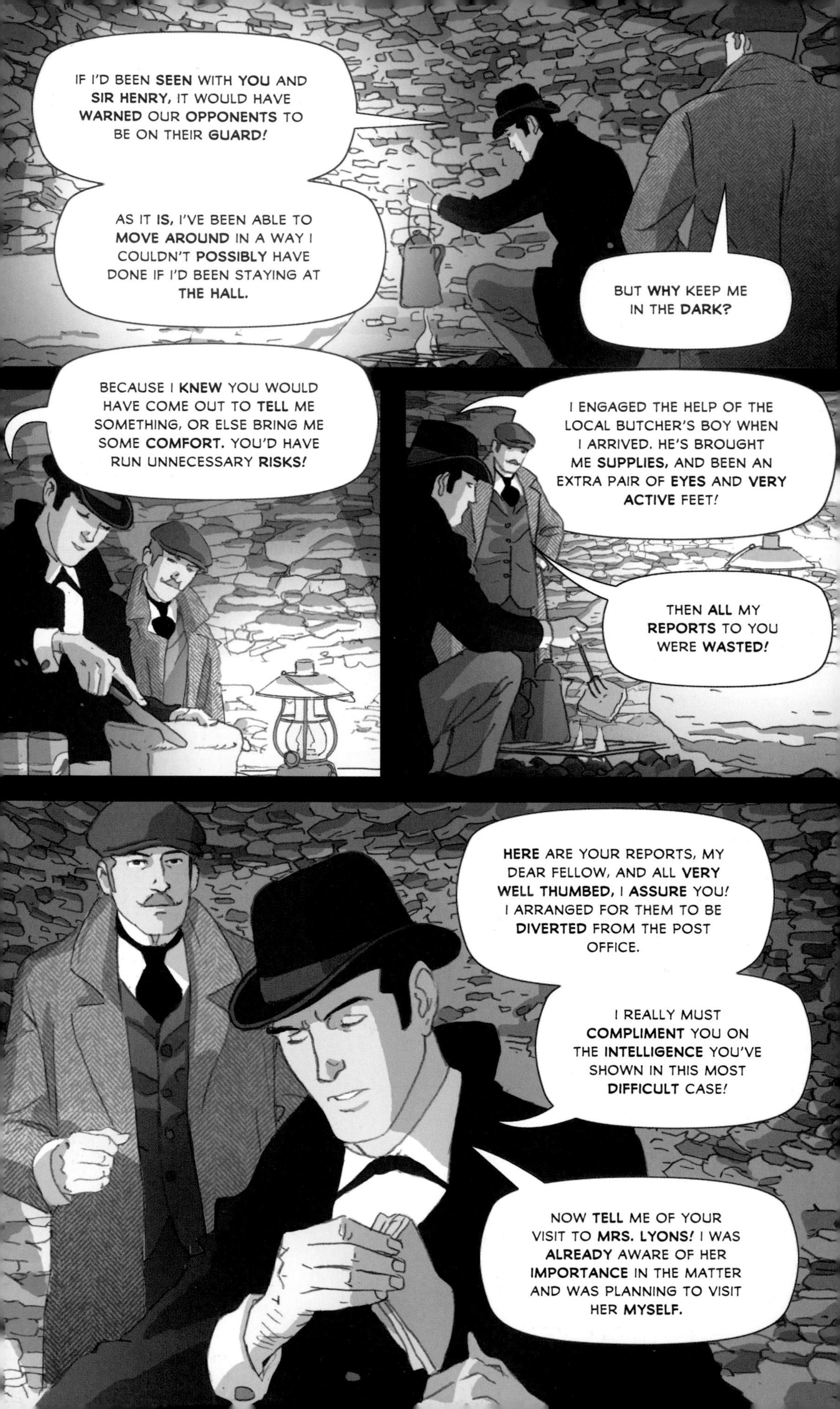
IF I'D BEEN SEEN WITH YOU AND SIR HENRY, IT WOULD HAVE WARNED OUR OPPONENTS TO BE ON THEIR GUARD!
AS IT IS, I'VE BEEN ABLE TO MOVE AROUND IN A WAY I COULDN'T POSSIBLY HAVE DONE IF I'D BEEN STAYING AT THE HALL.
BUT WHY KEEP ME IN THE DARK?
BECAUSE I KNEW YOU WOULD HAVE COME OUT TO TELL ME SOMETHING, OR ELSE BRING ME SOME COMFORT. YOU'D HAVE RUN UNNECESSARY RISKS!
I ENGAGED THE HELP OF THE LOCAL BUTCHER'S BOY WHEN I ARRIVED. HE'S BROUGHT ME SUPPLIES, AND BEEN AN EXTRA PAIR OF EYES AND VERY ACTIVE FEET!
THEN ALL MY REPORTS TO YOU WERE WASTED!
HERE ARE YOUR REPORTS, MY DEAR FELLOW, AND ALL VERY WELL THUMBED, I ASSURE YOU! I ARRANGED FOR THEM TO BE DIVERTED FROM THE POST OFFICE.
I REALLY MUST COMPLIMENT YOU ON THE INTELLIGENCE YOU'VE SHOWN IN THIS MOST DIFFICULT CASE!
NOW TELL ME OF YOUR VISIT TO MRS. LYONS! I WAS ALREADY AWARE OF HER IMPORTANCE IN THE MATTER AND WAS PLANNING TO VISIT HER MYSELF.

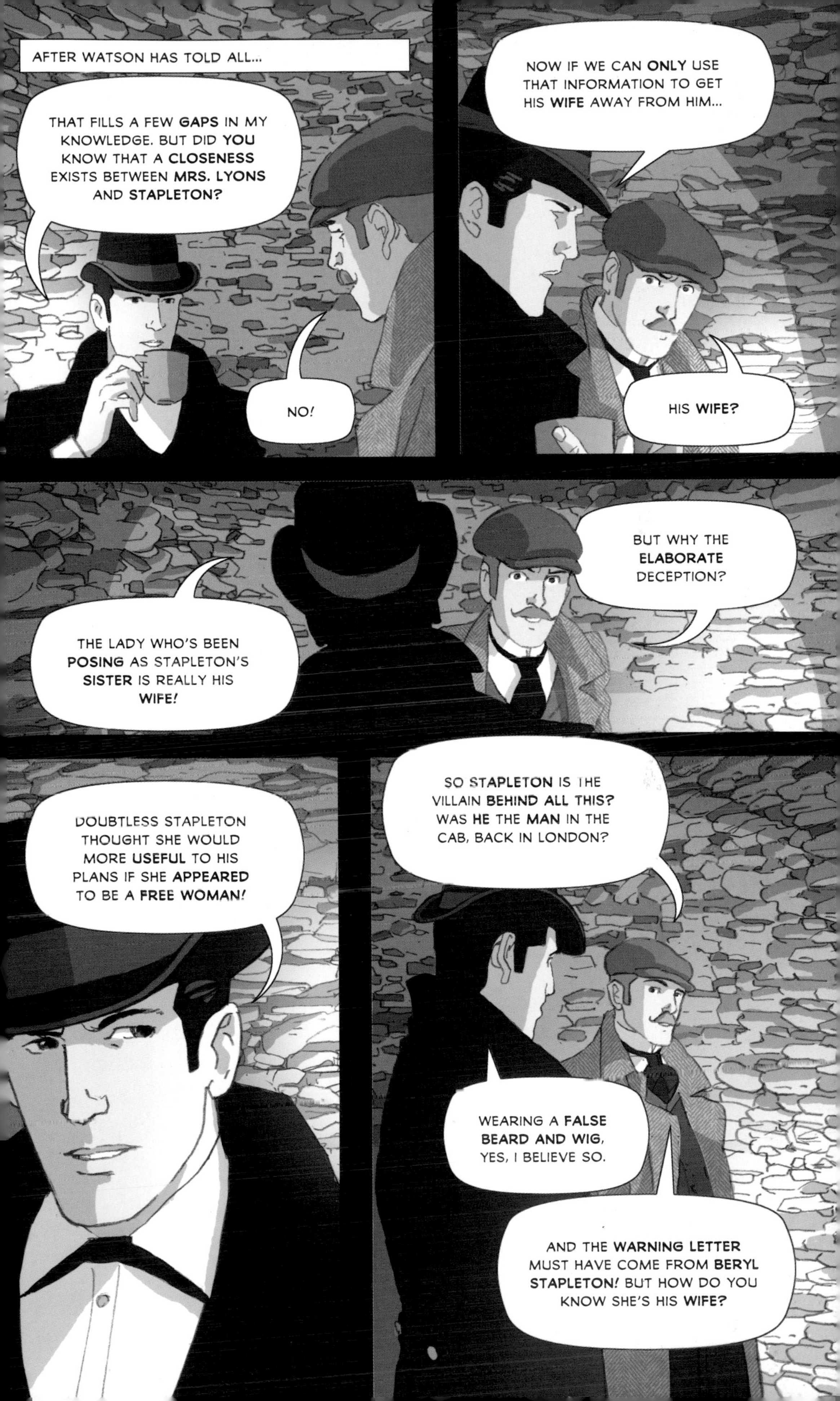
AFTER WATSON HAS TOLD ALL...
THAT FILLS A FEW GAPS IN MY KNOWLEDGE. BUT DID YOU KNOW THAT A CLOSENESS EXISTS BETWEEN MRS. LYONS AND STAPLETON?
NO!
NOW IF WE CAN ONLY USE THAT INFORMATION TO GET HIS WIFE AWAY FROM HIM...
HIS WIFE?
THE LADY WHO'S BEEN POSING AS STAPLETON'S SISTER IS REALLY HIS WIFE!
BUT WHY THE ELABORATE DECEPTION?
DOUBTLESS STAPLETON THOUGHT SHE WOULD MORE USEFUL TO HIS PLANS IF SHE APPEARED TO BE A FREE WOMAN!
SO STAPLETON IS THE VILLAIN BEHIND ALL THIS? WAS HE THE MAN IN THE CAB, BACK IN LONDON?
WEARING A FALSE BEARD AND WIG, YES, I BELIEVE SO.
AND THE WARNING LETTER MUST HAVE COME FROM BERYL STAPLETON! BUT HOW DO YOU KNOW SHE'S HIS WIFE?

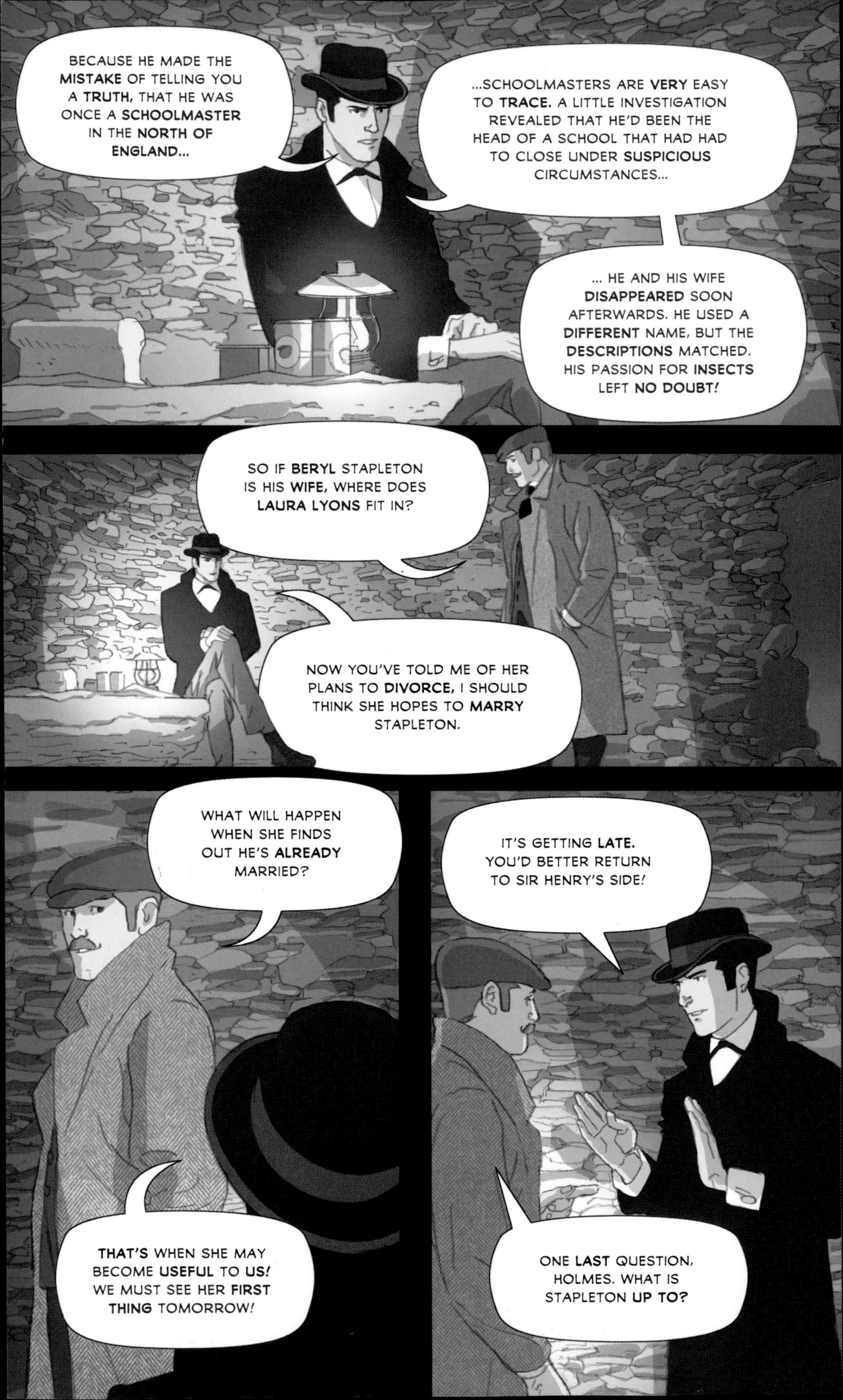
BECAUSE HE MADE THE MISTAKE OF TELLING YOU A TRUTH, THAT HE WAS ONCE A SCHOOLMASTER IN THE NORTH OF ENGLAND...
...SCHOOLMASTERS ARE VERY EASY TO TRACE. A LITTLE INVESTIGATION REVEALED THAT HE'D BEEN THE HEAD OF A SCHOOL THAT HAD HAD TO CLOSE UNDER SUSPICIOUS CIRCUMSTANCES...
... HE AND HIS WIFE DISAPPEARED SOON AFTERWARDS. HE USED A DIFFERENT NAME, BUT THE DESCRIPTIONS MATCHED. HIS PASSION FOR INSECTS LEFT NO DOUBT!
SO IF BERYL STAPLETON IS HIS WIFE, WHERE DOES LAURA LYONS FIT IN?
NOW YOU'VE TOLD ME OF HER PLANS TO DIVORCE, I SHOULD THINK SHE HOPES TO MARRY STAPLETON.
WHAT WILL HAPPEN WHEN SHE FINDS OUT HE'S ALREADY MARRIED?
THAT'S WHEN SHE MAY BECOME USEFUL TO US! WE MUST SEE HER FIRST THING TOMORROW!
IT'S GETTING LATE. YOU'D BETTER RETURN TO SIR HENRY'S SIDE!
ONE LAST QUESTION, HOLMES. WHAT IS STAPLETON UP TO?

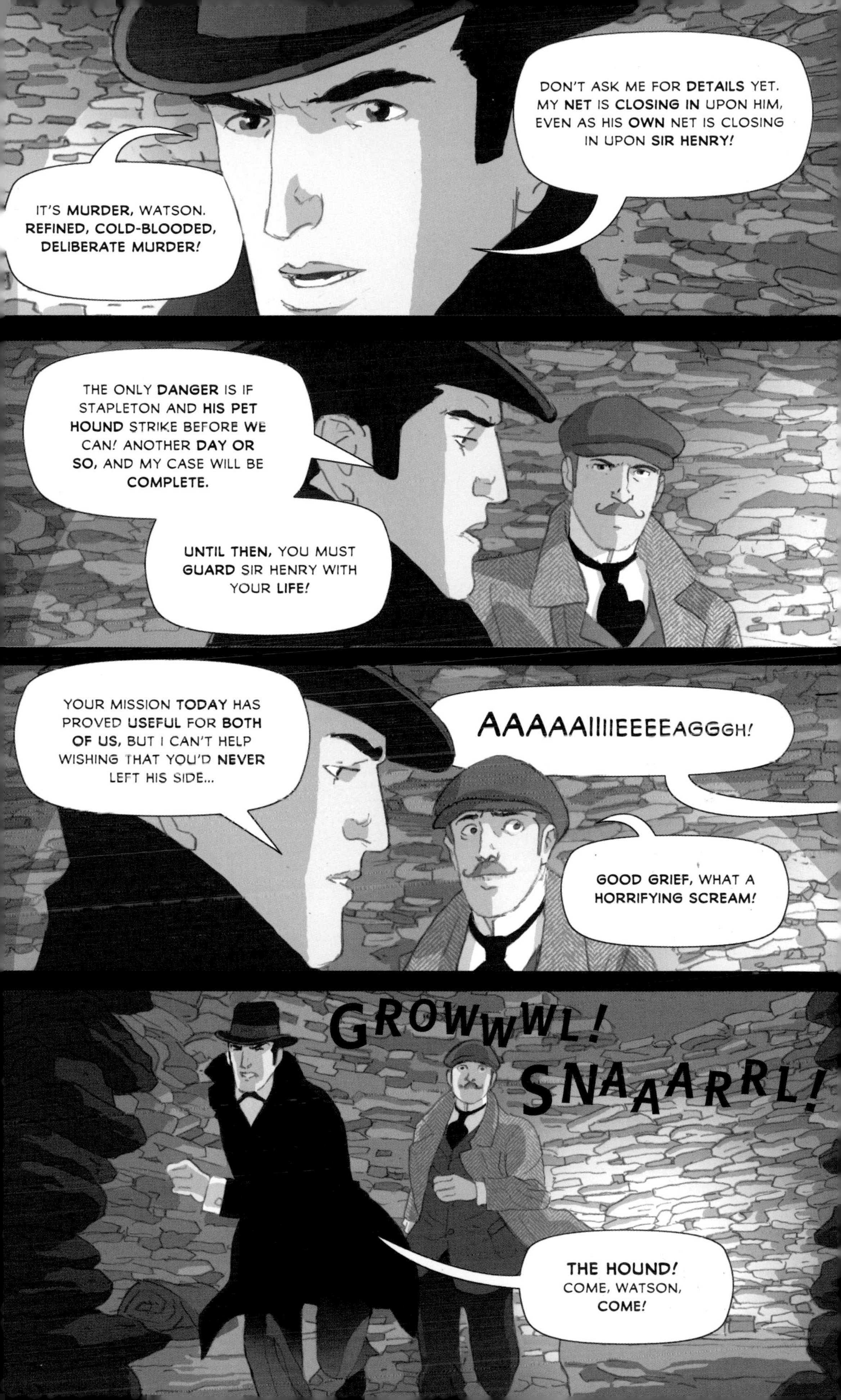
IT'S MURDER, WATSON. REFINED, COLD-BLOODED, DELIBERATE MURDER!
DON'T ASK ME FOR DETAILS YET. MY NET IS CLOSING IN UPON HIM, EVEN AS HIS OWN NET IS CLOSING IN UPON SIR HENRY!
THE ONLY DANGER IS IF STAPLETON AND HIS PET HOUND STRIKE BEFORE WE CAN! ANOTHER DAY OR SO, AND MY CASE WILL BE COMPLETE.
UNTIL THEN, YOU MUST GUARD SIR HENRY WITH YOUR LIFE!
YOUR MISSION TODAY HAS PROVED USEFUL FOR BOTH OF US, BUT I CAN'T HELP WISHING THAT YOU'D NEVER LEFT HIS SIDE...
AAAAAIIIIIEEEEAGGGH!
GOOD GRIEF, WHAT A HORRIFYING SCREAM!
GROWWWL!
SNAAARRL!
THE HOUND! COME, WATSON, COME!

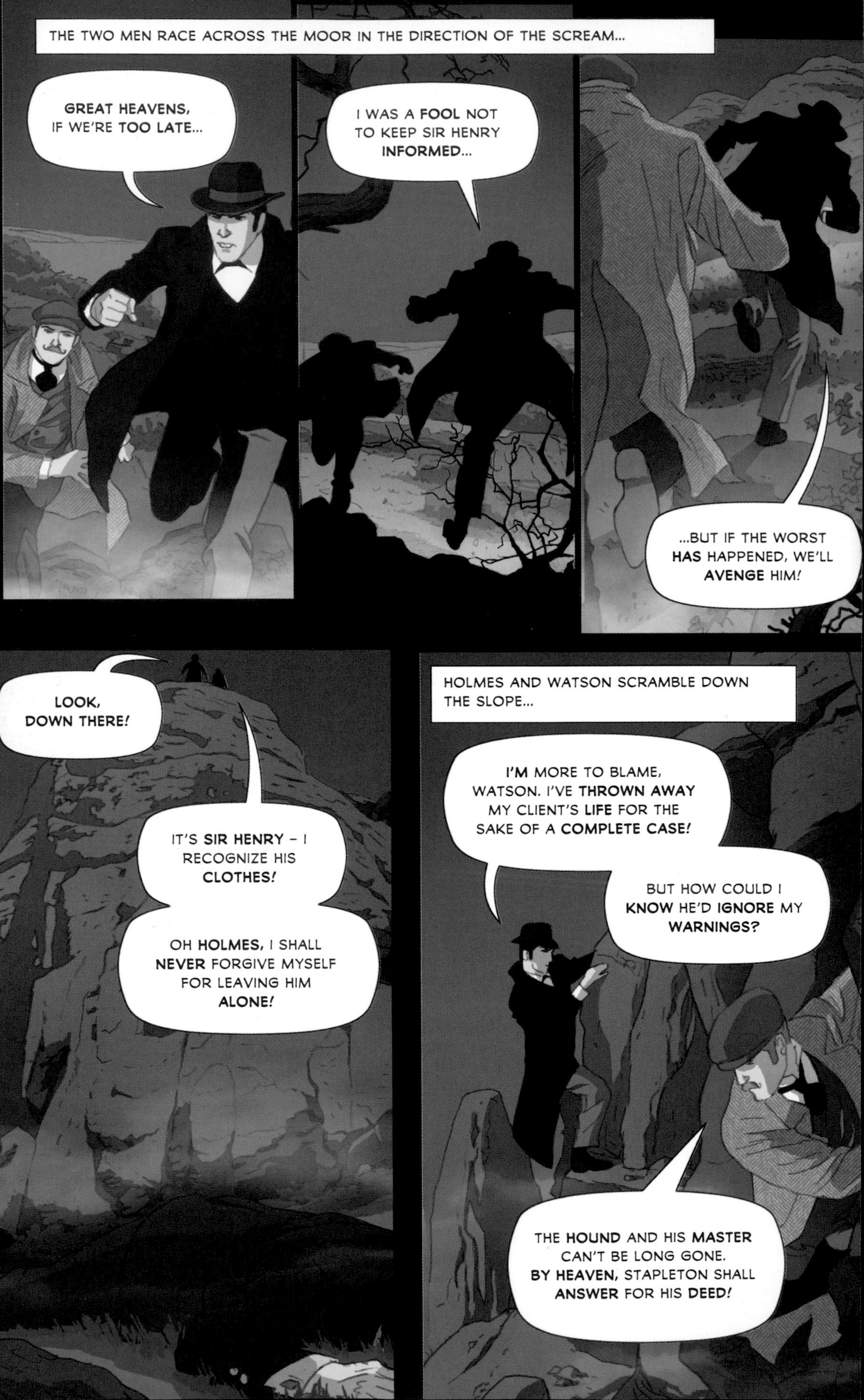
THE TWO MEN RACE ACROSS THE MOOR IN THE DIRECTION OF THE SCREAM...
GREAT HEAVENS, IF WE'RE TOO LATE...
I WAS A FOOL NOT TO KEEP SIR HENRY INFORMED...
...BUT IF THE WORST HAS HAPPENED, WE'LL AVENGE HIM!
LOOK, DOWN THERE!
IT'S SIR HENRY – I RECOGNIZE HIS CLOTHES!
OH HOLMES, I SHALL NEVER FORGIVE MYSELF FOR LEAVING HIM ALONE!
HOLMES AND WATSON SCRAMBLE DOWN THE SLOPE...
I'M MORE TO BLAME, WATSON. I'VE THROWN AWAY MY CLIENT'S LIFE FOR THE SAKE OF A COMPLETE CASE!
BUT HOW COULD I KNOW HE'D IGNORE MY WARNINGS?
THE HOUND AND HIS MASTER CAN'T BE LONG GONE. BY HEAVEN, STAPLETON SHALL ANSWER FOR HIS DEED!

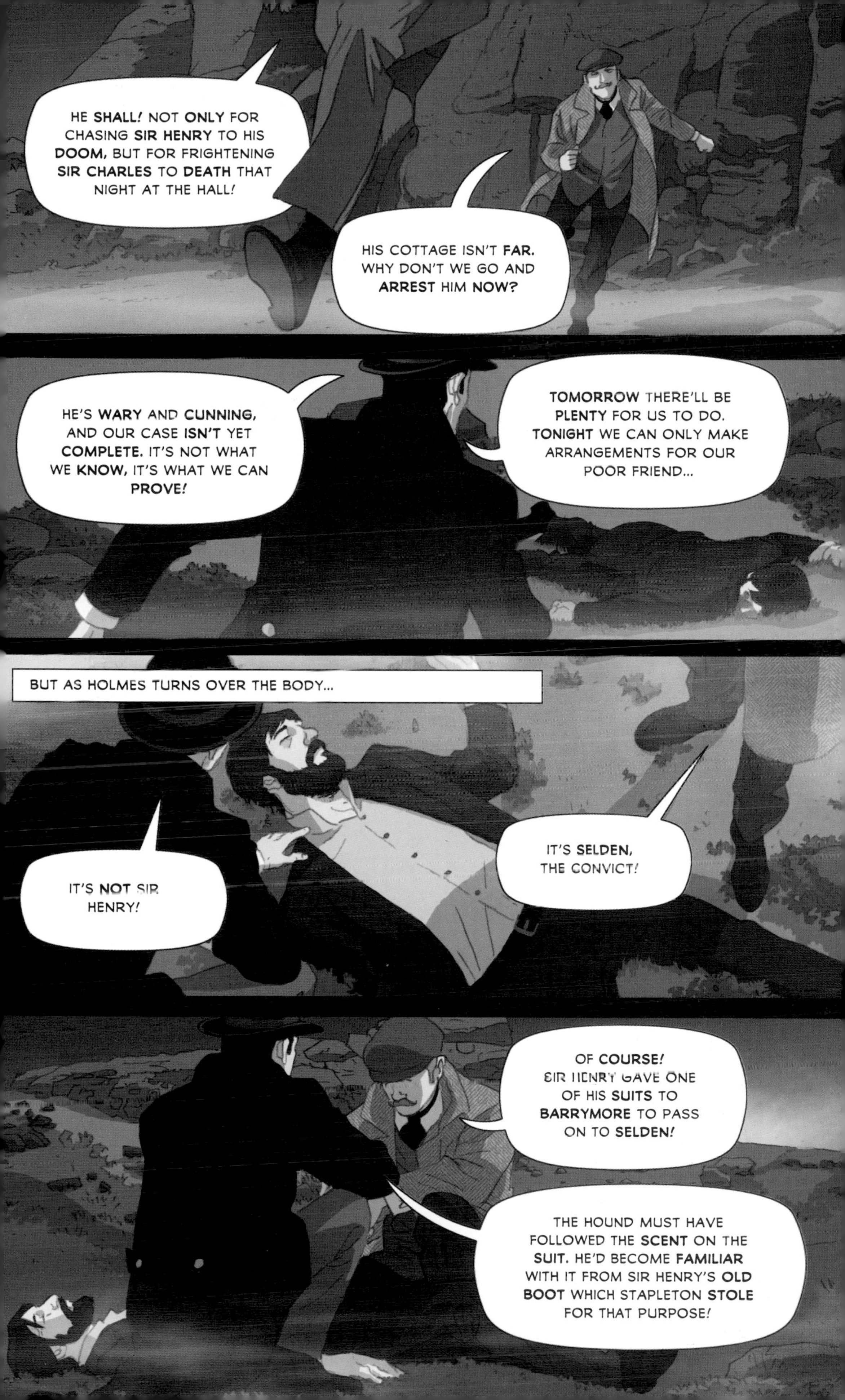
HE SHALL! NOT ONLY FOR CHASING SIR HENRY TO HIS DOOM, BUT FOR FRIGHTENING SIR CHARLES TO DEATH THAT NIGHT AT THE HALL!
HIS COTTAGE ISN'T FAR. WHY DON'T WE GO AND ARREST HIM NOW?
HE'S WARY AND CUNNING, AND OUR CASE ISN'T YET COMPLETE. IT'S NOT WHAT WE KNOW, IT'S WHAT WE CAN PROVE!
TOMORROW THERE'LL BE PLENTY FOR US TO DO. TONIGHT WE CAN ONLY MAKE ARRANGEMENTS FOR OUR POOR FRIEND...
BUT AS HOLMES TURNS OVER THE BODY...
IT'S NOT SIR HENRY!
IT'S SELDEN, THE CONVICT!
OF COURSE! SIR HENRY GAVE ONE OF HIS SUITS TO BARRYMORE TO PASS ON TO SELDEN!
THE HOUND MUST HAVE FOLLOWED THE SCENT ON THE SUIT. HE'D BECOME FAMILIAR WITH IT FROM SIR HENRY'S OLD BOOT WHICH STAPLETON STOLE FOR THAT PURPOSE!

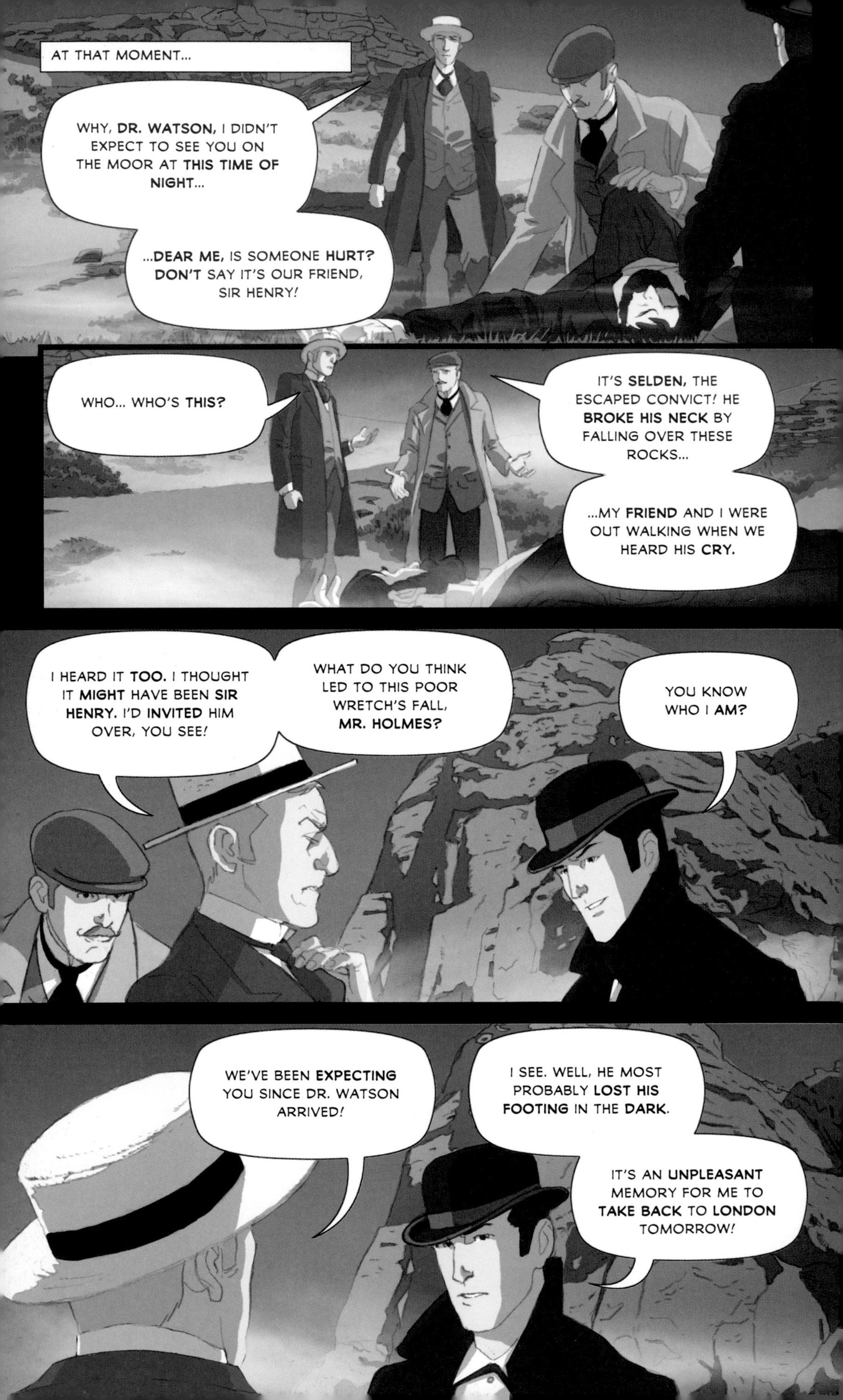
AT THAT MOMENT...
WHY, DR. WATSON, I DIDN'T EXPECT TO SEE YOU ON THE MOOR AT THIS TIME OF NIGHT...
...DEAR ME, IS SOMEONE HURT? DON'T SAY IT'S OUR FRIEND, SIR HENRY!
WHO... WHO'S THIS?
IT'S SELDEN, THE ESCAPED CONVICT! HE BROKE HIS NECK BY FALLING OVER THESE ROCKS...
...MY FRIEND AND I WERE OUT WALKING WHEN WE HEARD HIS CRY.
I HEARD IT TOO. I THOUGHT IT MIGHT HAVE BEEN SIR HENRY. I'D INVITED HIM OVER, YOU SEE!
WHAT DO YOU THINK LED TO THIS POOR WRETCH'S FALL, MR. HOLMES?
YOU KNOW WHO I AM?
WE'VE BEEN EXPECTING YOU SINCE DR. WATSON ARRIVED!
I SEE. WELL, HE MOST PROBABLY LOST HIS FOOTING IN THE DARK.
IT'S AN UNPLEASANT MEMORY FOR ME TO TAKE BACK TO LONDON TOMORROW!

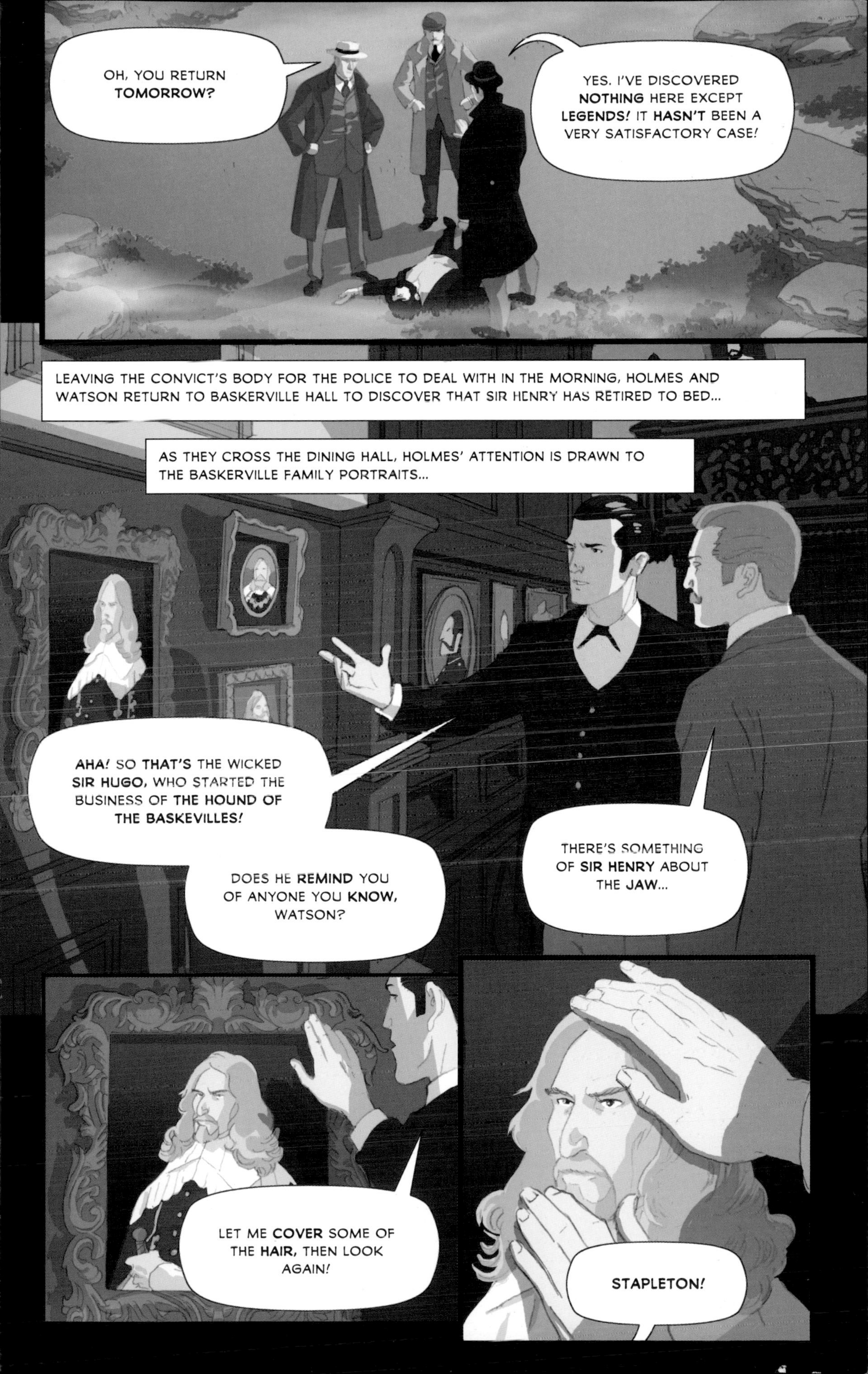
OH, YOU RETURN **TOMORROW?**
YES. I'VE DISCOVERED **NOTHING** HERE EXCEPT **LEGENDS!** IT **HASN'T** BEEN A VERY SATISFACTORY CASE!
LEAVING THE CONVICT'S BODY FOR THE POLICE TO DEAL WITH IN THE MORNING, HOLMES AND WATSON RETURN TO BASKERVILLE HALL TO DISCOVER THAT SIR HENRY HAS RETIRED TO BED...
AS THEY CROSS THE DINING HALL, HOLMES' ATTENTION IS DRAWN TO THE BASKERVILLE FAMILY PORTRAITS...
AHA! SO **THAT'S** THE WICKED **SIR HUGO,** WHO STARTED THE BUSINESS OF **THE HOUND OF THE BASKEVILLES!**
DOES HE **REMIND** YOU OF ANYONE YOU **KNOW,** WATSON?
THERE'S SOMETHING OF **SIR HENRY** ABOUT THE **JAW...**
LET ME **COVER** SOME OF THE **HAIR,** THEN LOOK AGAIN!
STAPLETON!

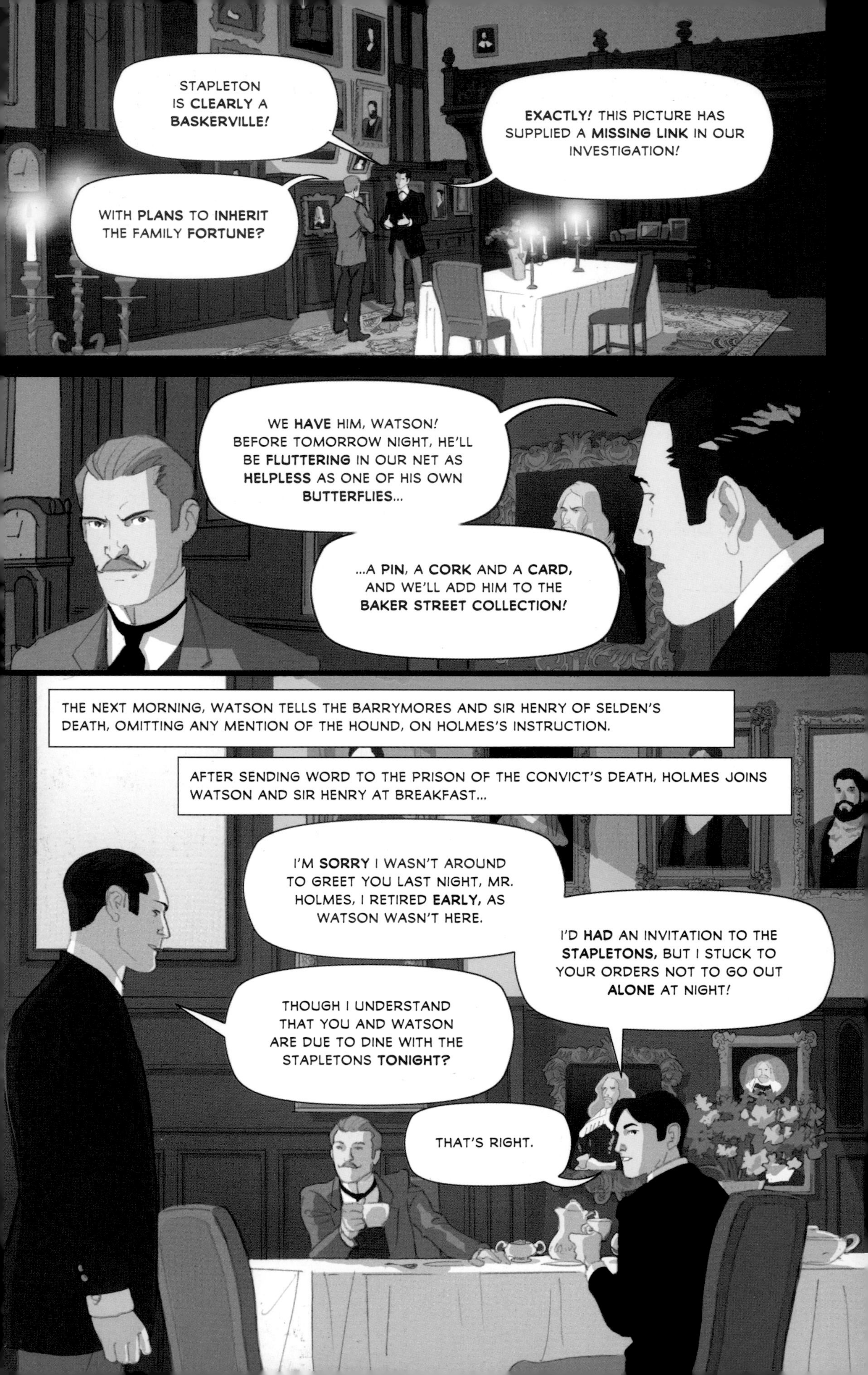
STAPLETON IS CLEARLY A BASKERVILLE!
EXACTLY! THIS PICTURE HAS SUPPLIED A MISSING LINK IN OUR INVESTIGATION!
WITH PLANS TO INHERIT THE FAMILY FORTUNE?
WE HAVE HIM, WATSON! BEFORE TOMORROW NIGHT, HE'LL BE FLUTTERING IN OUR NET AS HELPLESS AS ONE OF HIS OWN BUTTERFLIES...
...A PIN, A CORK AND A CARD, AND WE'LL ADD HIM TO THE BAKER STREET COLLECTION!
THE NEXT MORNING, WATSON TELLS THE BARRYMORES AND SIR HENRY OF SELDEN'S DEATH, OMITTING ANY MENTION OF THE HOUND, ON HOLMES'S INSTRUCTION.
AFTER SENDING WORD TO THE PRISON OF THE CONVICT'S DEATH, HOLMES JOINS WATSON AND SIR HENRY AT BREAKFAST...
I'M SORRY I WASN'T AROUND TO GREET YOU LAST NIGHT, MR. HOLMES, I RETIRED EARLY, AS WATSON WASN'T HERE.
I'D HAD AN INVITATION TO THE STAPLETONS, BUT I STUCK TO YOUR ORDERS NOT TO GO OUT ALONE AT NIGHT!
THOUGH I UNDERSTAND THAT YOU AND WATSON ARE DUE TO DINE WITH THE STAPLETONS TONIGHT?
THAT'S RIGHT.

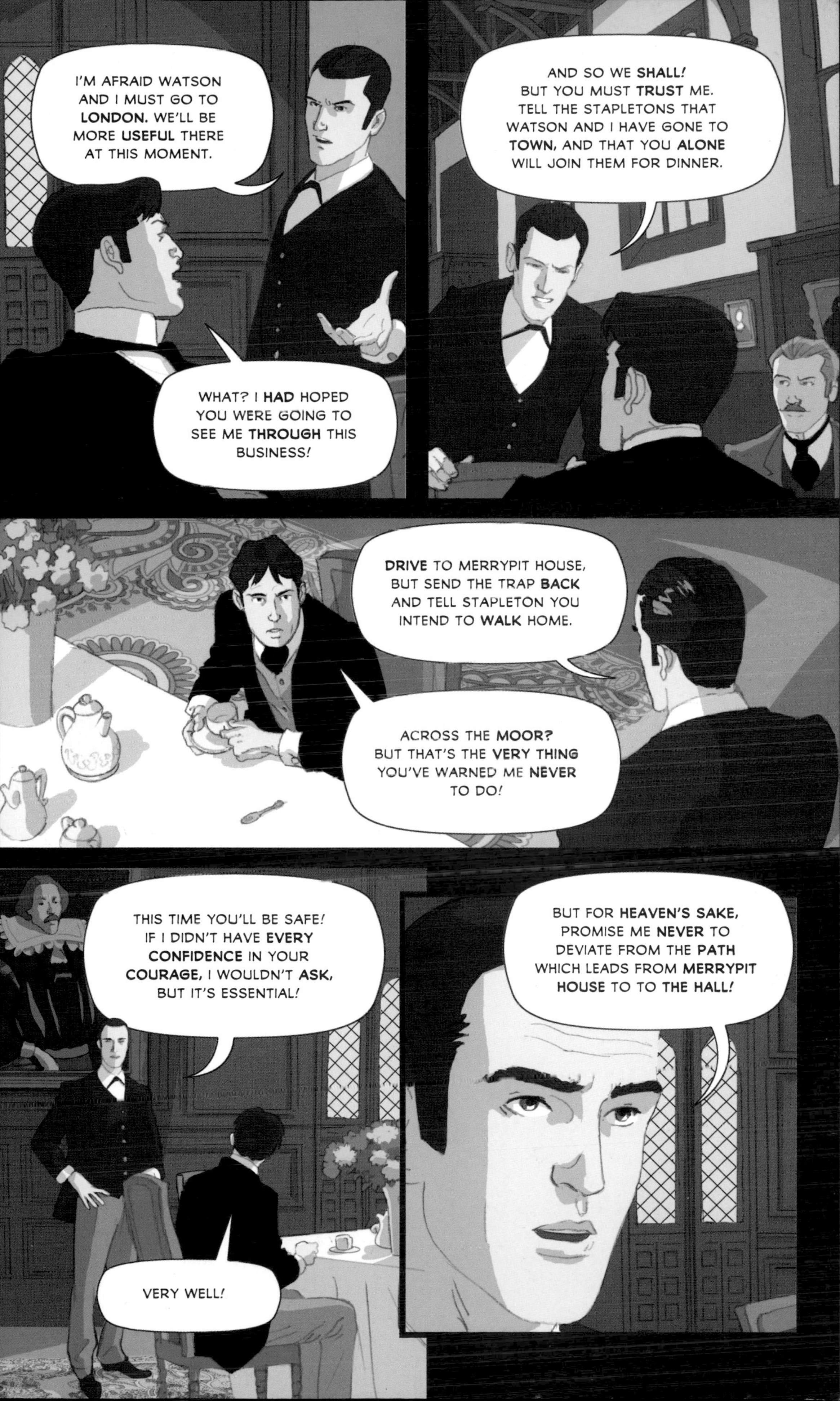
I'M AFRAID WATSON AND I MUST GO TO LONDON. WE'LL BE MORE USEFUL THERE AT THIS MOMENT.
WHAT? I HAD HOPED YOU WERE GOING TO SEE ME THROUGH THIS BUSINESS!
AND SO WE SHALL! BUT YOU MUST TRUST ME. TELL THE STAPLETONS THAT WATSON AND I HAVE GONE TO TOWN, AND THAT YOU ALONE WILL JOIN THEM FOR DINNER.
DRIVE TO MERRYPIT HOUSE, BUT SEND THE TRAP BACK AND TELL STAPLETON YOU INTEND TO WALK HOME.
ACROSS THE MOOR? BUT THAT'S THE VERY THING YOU'VE WARNED ME NEVER TO DO!
THIS TIME YOU'LL BE SAFE! IF I DIDN'T HAVE EVERY CONFIDENCE IN YOUR COURAGE, I WOULDN'T ASK, BUT IT'S ESSENTIAL!
VERY WELL!
BUT FOR HEAVEN'S SAKE, PROMISE ME NEVER TO DEVIATE FROM THE PATH WHICH LEADS FROM MERRYPIT HOUSE TO TO THE HALL!

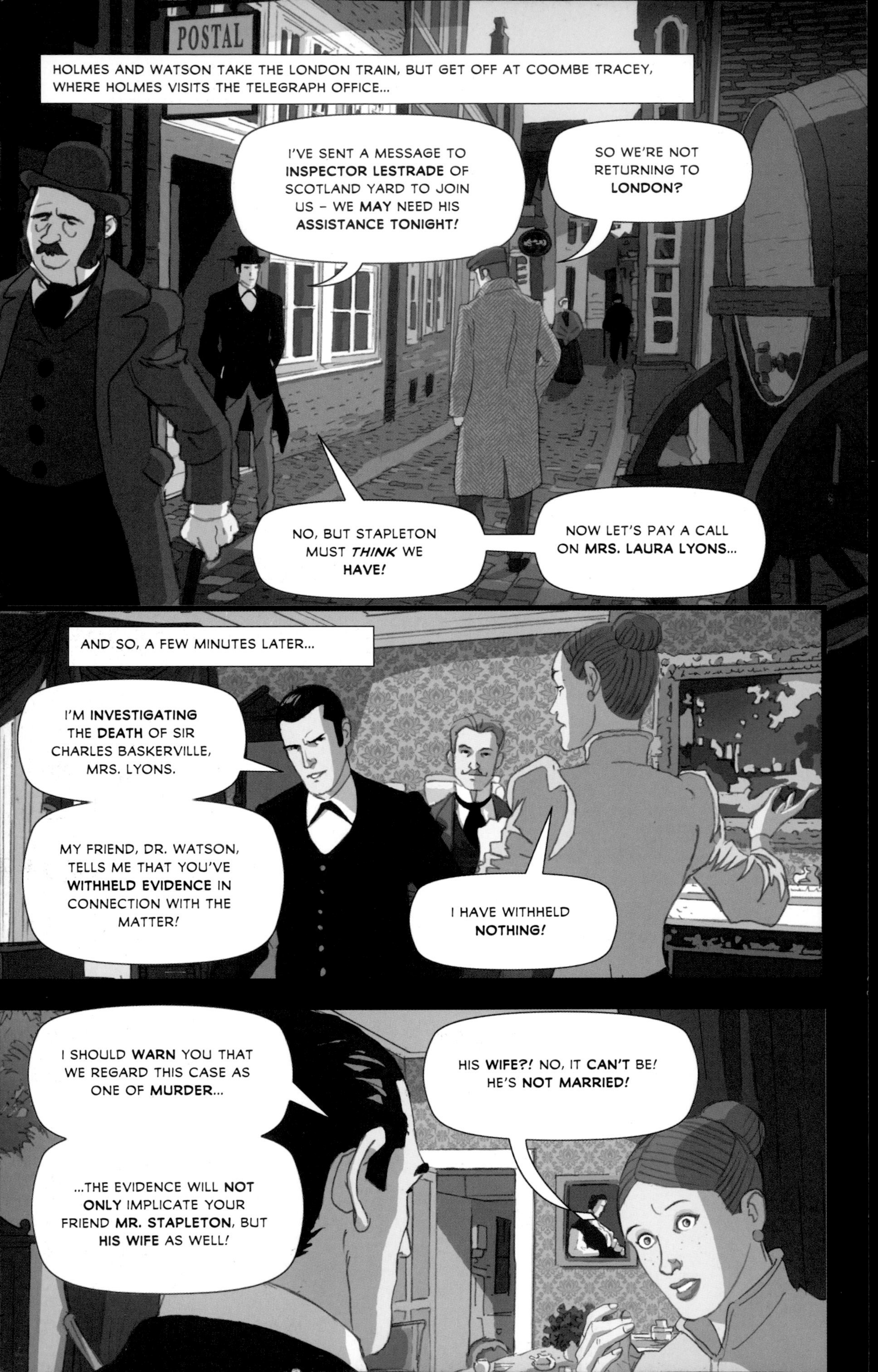
POSTAL
HOLMES AND WATSON TAKE THE LONDON TRAIN, BUT GET OFF AT COOMBE TRACEY, WHERE HOLMES VISITS THE TELEGRAPH OFFICE...
I'VE SENT A MESSAGE TO INSPECTOR LESTRADE OF SCOTLAND YARD TO JOIN US – WE MAY NEED HIS ASSISTANCE TONIGHT!
SO WE'RE NOT RETURNING TO LONDON?
NO, BUT STAPLETON MUST THINK WE HAVE!
NOW LET'S PAY A CALL ON MRS. LAURA LYONS...
AND SO, A FEW MINUTES LATER...
I'M INVESTIGATING THE DEATH OF SIR CHARLES BASKERVILLE, MRS. LYONS.
MY FRIEND, DR. WATSON, TELLS ME THAT YOU'VE WITHHELD EVIDENCE IN CONNECTION WITH THE MATTER!
I HAVE WITHHELD NOTHING!
I SHOULD WARN YOU THAT WE REGARD THIS CASE AS ONE OF MURDER...
...THE EVIDENCE WILL NOT ONLY IMPLICATE YOUR FRIEND MR. STAPLETON, BUT HIS WIFE AS WELL!
HIS WIFE?! NO, IT CAN'T BE! HE'S NOT MARRIED!

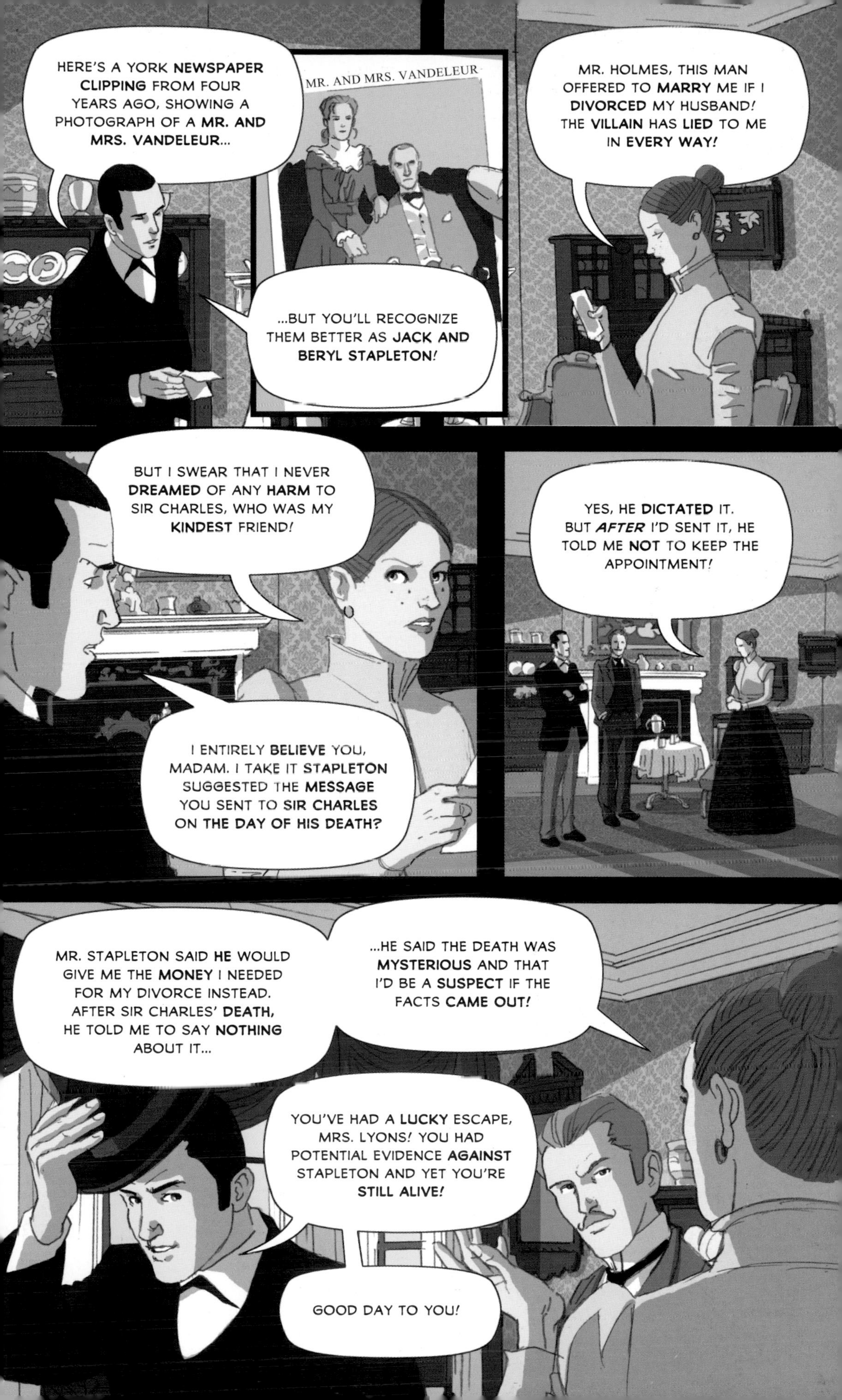
HERE'S A YORK NEWSPAPER CLIPPING FROM FOUR YEARS AGO, SHOWING A PHOTOGRAPH OF A MR. AND MRS. VANDELEUR...
MR. AND MRS. VANDELEUR
...BUT YOU'LL RECOGNIZE THEM BETTER AS JACK AND BERYL STAPLETON!
MR. HOLMES, THIS MAN OFFERED TO MARRY ME IF I DIVORCED MY HUSBAND! THE VILLAIN HAS LIED TO ME IN EVERY WAY!
BUT I SWEAR THAT I NEVER DREAMED OF ANY HARM TO SIR CHARLES, WHO WAS MY KINDEST FRIEND!
I ENTIRELY BELIEVE YOU, MADAM. I TAKE IT STAPLETON SUGGESTED THE MESSAGE YOU SENT TO SIR CHARLES ON THE DAY OF HIS DEATH?
YES, HE DICTATED IT. BUT AFTER I'D SENT IT, HE TOLD ME NOT TO KEEP THE APPOINTMENT!
MR. STAPLETON SAID HE WOULD GIVE ME THE MONEY I NEEDED FOR MY DIVORCE INSTEAD. AFTER SIR CHARLES' DEATH, HE TOLD ME TO SAY NOTHING ABOUT IT...
...HE SAID THE DEATH WAS MYSTERIOUS AND THAT I'D BE A SUSPECT IF THE FACTS CAME OUT!
YOU'VE HAD A LUCKY ESCAPE, MRS. LYONS! YOU HAD POTENTIAL EVIDENCE AGAINST STAPLETON AND YET YOU'RE STILL ALIVE!
GOOD DAY TO YOU!

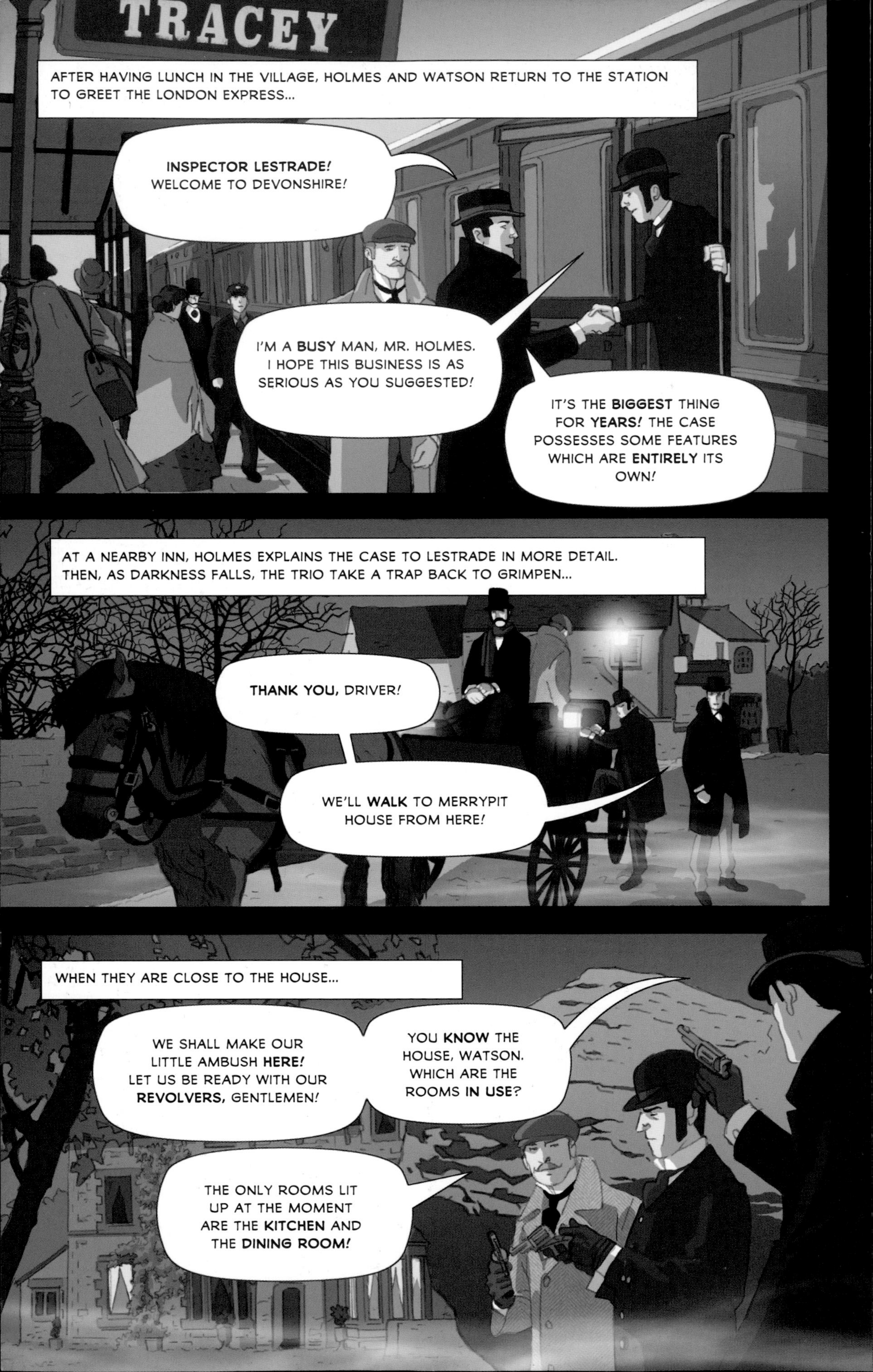

TRACEY
AFTER HAVING LUNCH IN THE VILLAGE, HOLMES AND WATSON RETURN TO THE STATION TO GREET THE LONDON EXPRESS...
INSPECTOR LESTRADE! WELCOME TO DEVONSHIRE!
I'M A BUSY MAN, MR. HOLMES. I HOPE THIS BUSINESS IS AS SERIOUS AS YOU SUGGESTED!
IT'S THE BIGGEST THING FOR YEARS! THE CASE POSSESSES SOME FEATURES WHICH ARE ENTIRELY ITS OWN!
AT A NEARBY INN, HOLMES EXPLAINS THE CASE TO LESTRADE IN MORE DETAIL. THEN, AS DARKNESS FALLS, THE TRIO TAKE A TRAP BACK TO GRIMPEN...
THANK YOU, DRIVER!
WE'LL WALK TO MERRYPIT HOUSE FROM HERE!
WHEN THEY ARE CLOSE TO THE HOUSE...
WE SHALL MAKE OUR LITTLE AMBUSH HERE! LET US BE READY WITH OUR REVOLVERS, GENTLEMEN!
YOU KNOW THE HOUSE, WATSON. WHICH ARE THE ROOMS IN USE?
THE ONLY ROOMS LIT UP AT THE MOMENT ARE THE KITCHEN AND THE DINING ROOM!

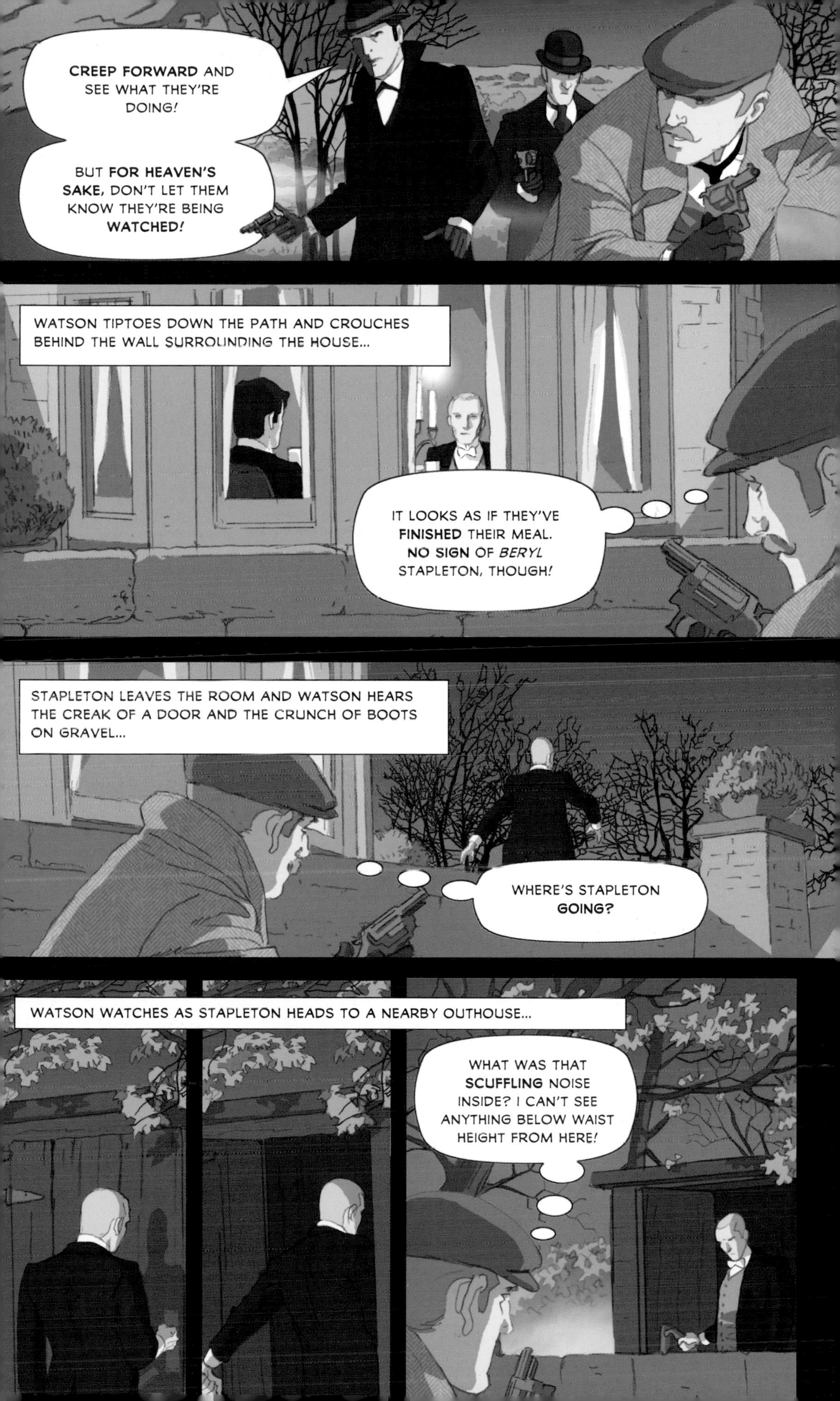
CREEP FORWARD AND SEE WHAT THEY'RE DOING!
BUT **FOR HEAVEN'S SAKE,** DON'T LET THEM KNOW THEY'RE BEING **WATCHED!**
WATSON TIPTOES DOWN THE PATH AND CROUCHES BEHIND THE WALL SURROUNDING THE HOUSE...
IT LOOKS AS IF THEY'VE **FINISHED** THEIR MEAL. **NO SIGN** OF *BERYL* STAPLETON, THOUGH!
STAPLETON LEAVES THE ROOM AND WATSON HEARS THE CREAK OF A DOOR AND THE CRUNCH OF BOOTS ON GRAVEL...
WHERE'S STAPLETON **GOING?**
WATSON WATCHES AS STAPLETON HEADS TO A NEARBY OUTHOUSE...
WHAT WAS THAT **SCUFFLING** NOISE INSIDE? I CAN'T SEE ANYTHING BELOW WAIST HEIGHT FROM HERE!

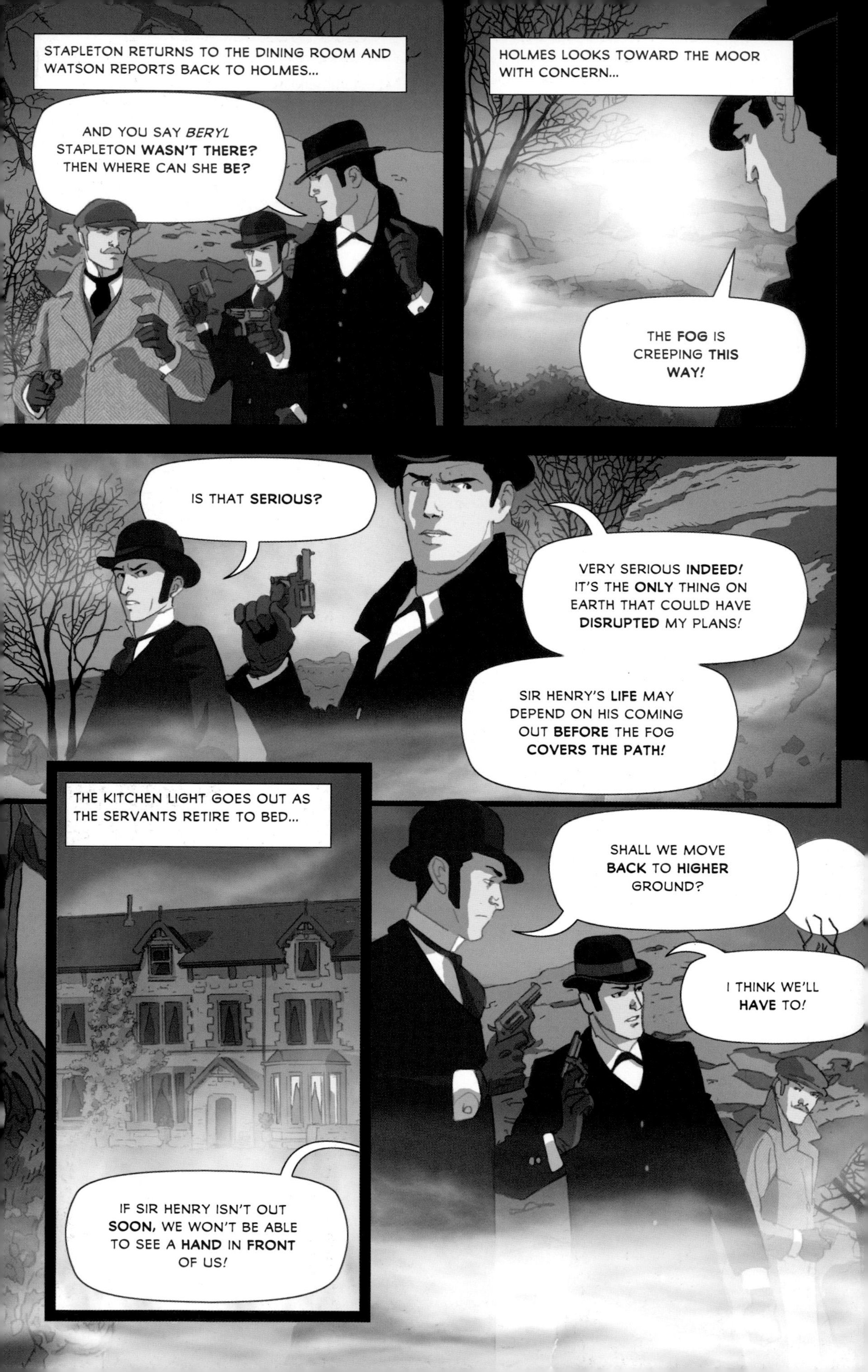
STAPLETON RETURNS TO THE DINING ROOM AND WATSON REPORTS BACK TO HOLMES...
AND YOU SAY *BERYL* STAPLETON **WASN'T THERE?** THEN WHERE CAN SHE **BE?**
HOLMES LOOKS TOWARD THE MOOR WITH CONCERN...
THE **FOG** IS CREEPING **THIS WAY!**
IS THAT **SERIOUS?**
VERY SERIOUS **INDEED!** IT'S THE **ONLY** THING ON EARTH THAT COULD HAVE **DISRUPTED** MY PLANS!
SIR HENRY'S **LIFE** MAY DEPEND ON HIS COMING OUT **BEFORE** THE FOG **COVERS THE PATH!**
THE KITCHEN LIGHT GOES OUT AS THE SERVANTS RETIRE TO BED...
IF SIR HENRY ISN'T OUT **SOON,** WE WON'T BE ABLE TO SEE A **HAND** IN **FRONT** OF US!
SHALL WE MOVE **BACK** TO **HIGHER** GROUND?
I THINK WE'LL **HAVE** TO!

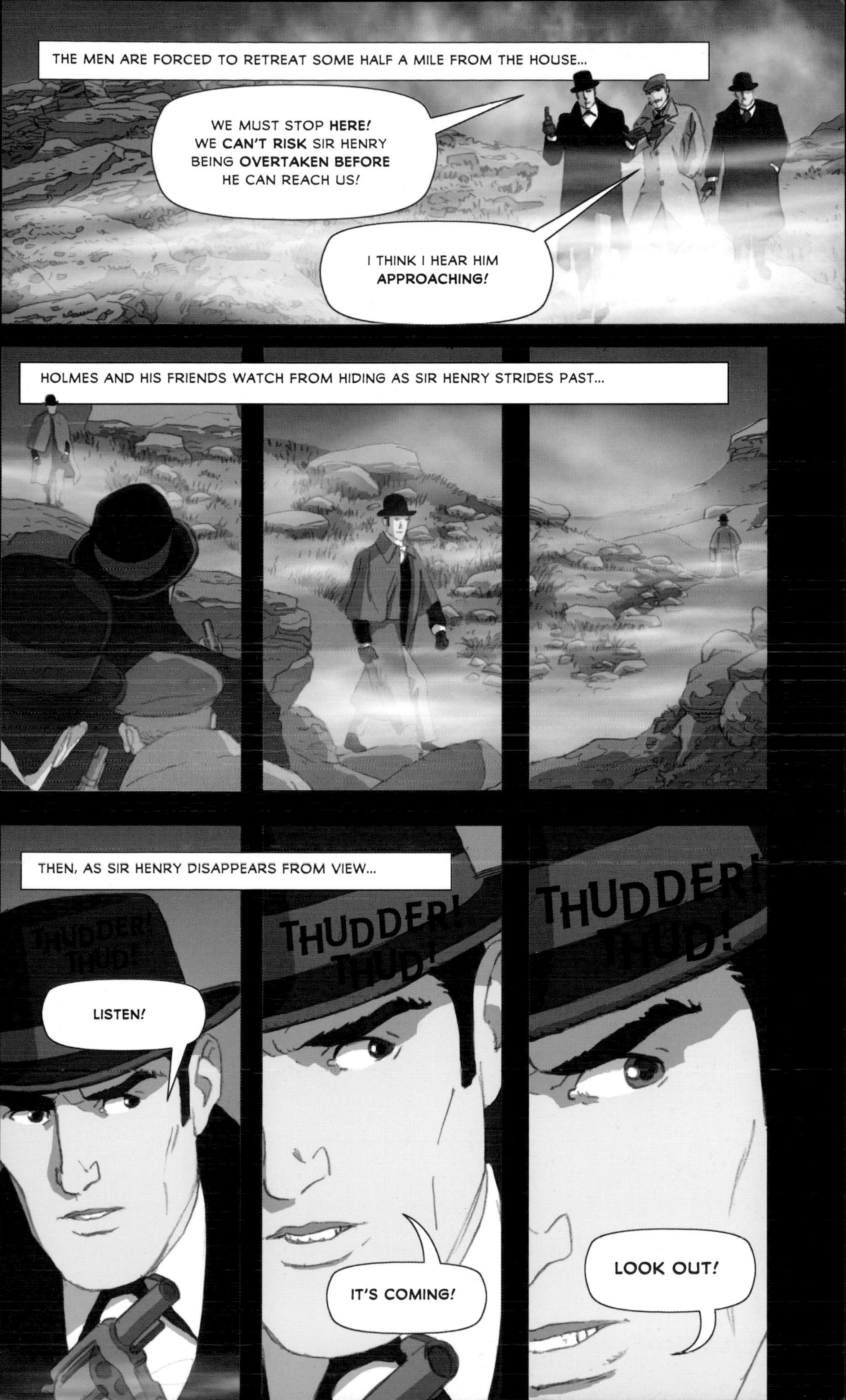
THE MEN ARE FORCED TO RETREAT SOME HALF A MILE FROM THE HOUSE...
WE MUST STOP HERE! WE CAN'T RISK SIR HENRY BEING OVERTAKEN BEFORE HE CAN REACH US!
I THINK I HEAR HIM APPROACHING!
HOLMES AND HIS FRIENDS WATCH FROM HIDING AS SIR HENRY STRIDES PAST...
THEN, AS SIR HENRY DISAPPEARS FROM VIEW...
THUDDER! THUD!
LISTEN!
THUDDER! THUD!
IT'S COMING!
THUDDER! THUD!
LOOK OUT!

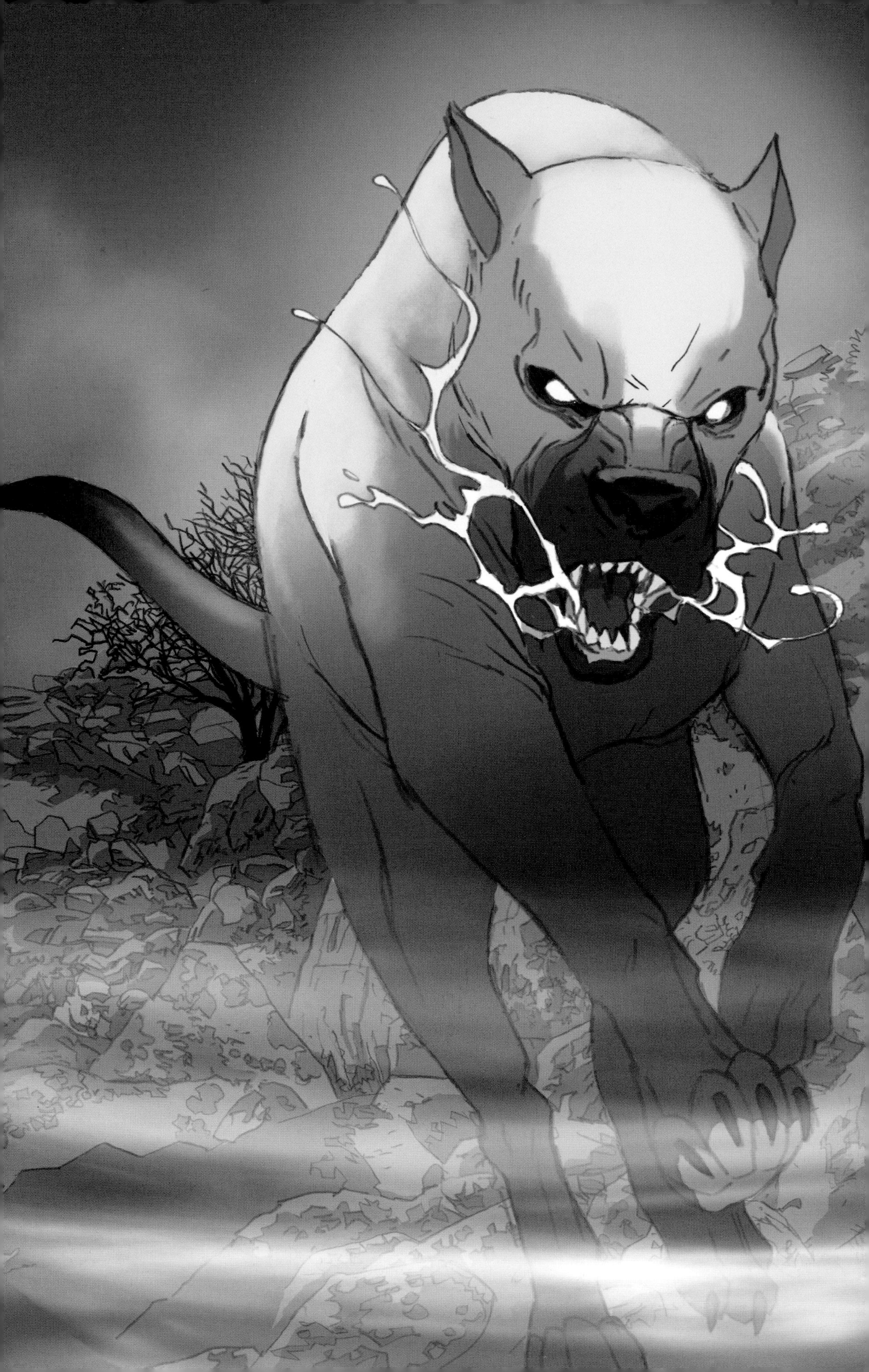

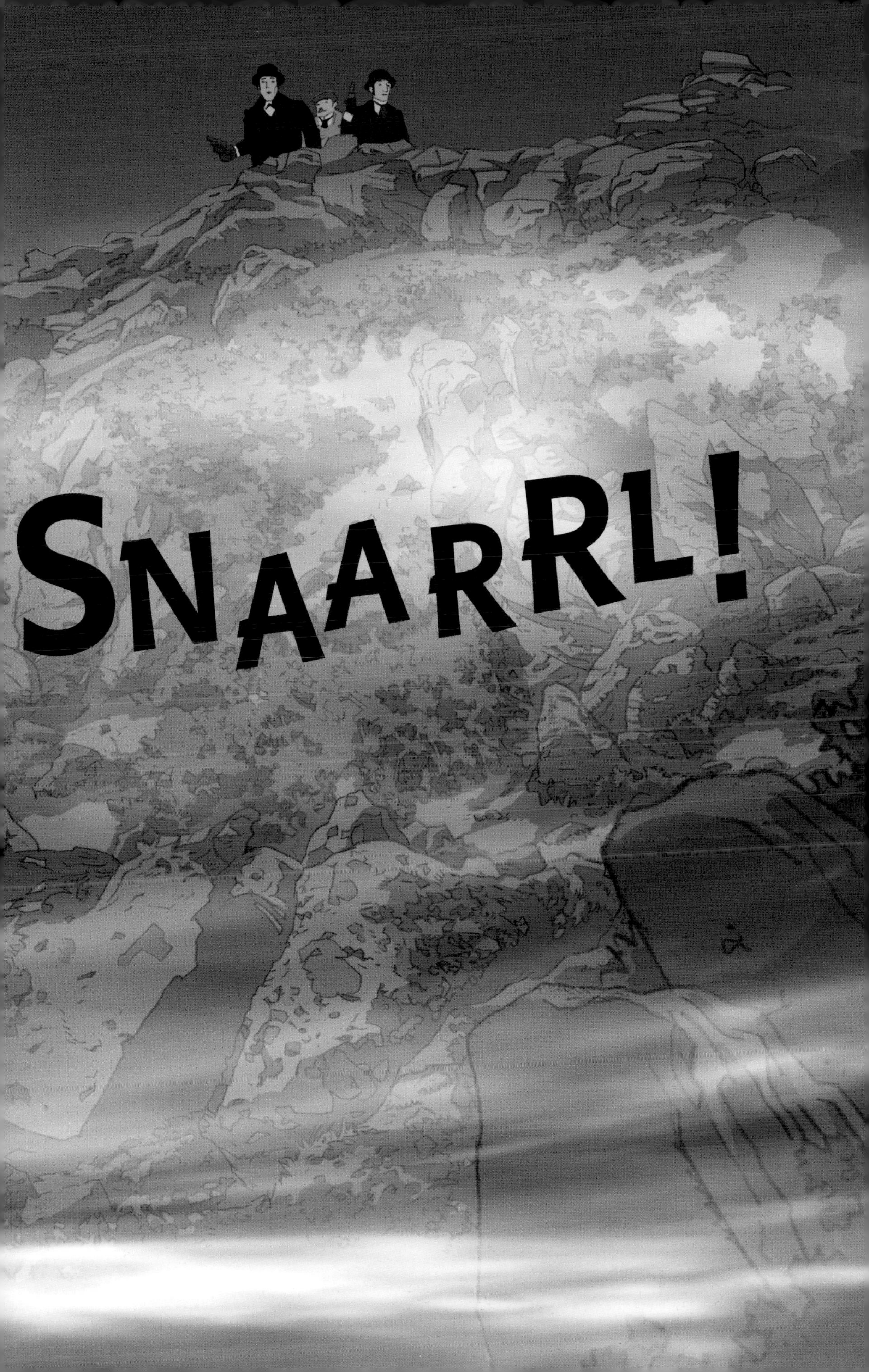
SNAARRL!

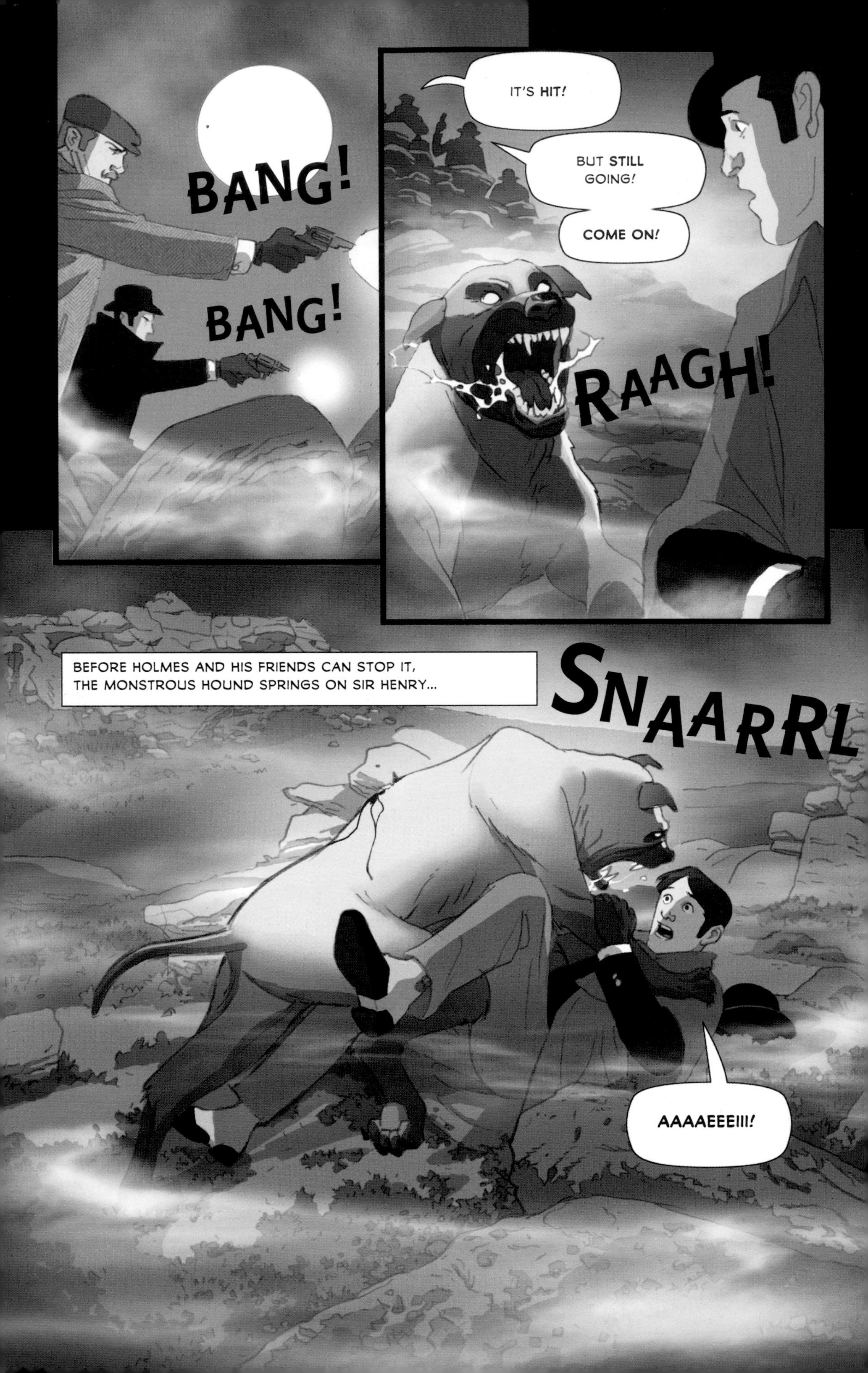
BANG!
BANG!
IT'S HIT!
BUT STILL GOING!
COME ON!
RAAGH!
BEFORE HOLMES AND HIS FRIENDS CAN STOP IT, THE MONSTROUS HOUND SPRINGS ON SIR HENRY...
SNAARRL
AAAAEEEIII!

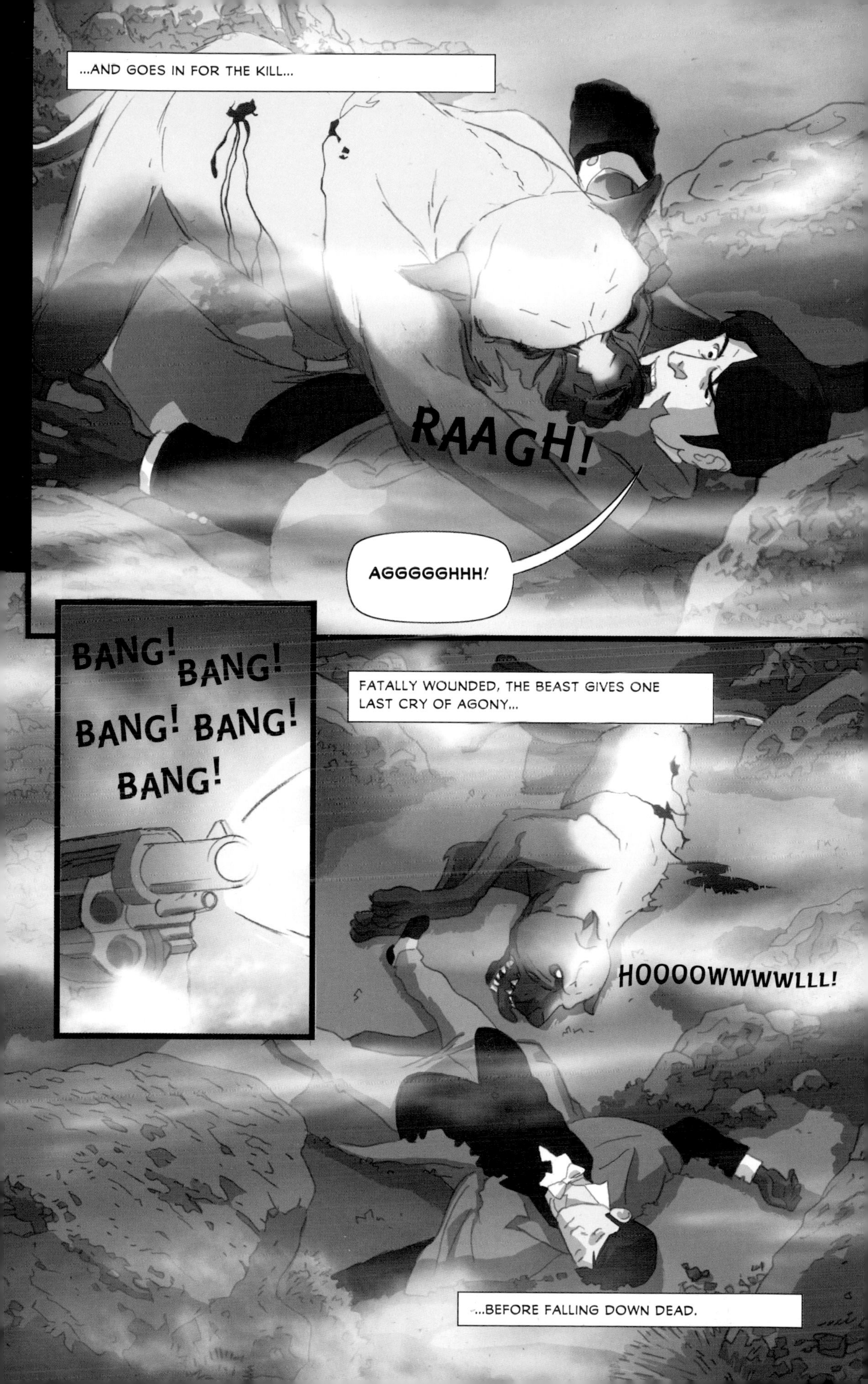
...AND GOES IN FOR THE KILL...
RAAGH!
AGGGGGHHH!
BANG! BANG! BANG! BANG! BANG!
FATALLY WOUNDED, THE BEAST GIVES ONE LAST CRY OF AGONY...
HOOOOWWWWLLL!
...BEFORE FALLING DOWN DEAD.

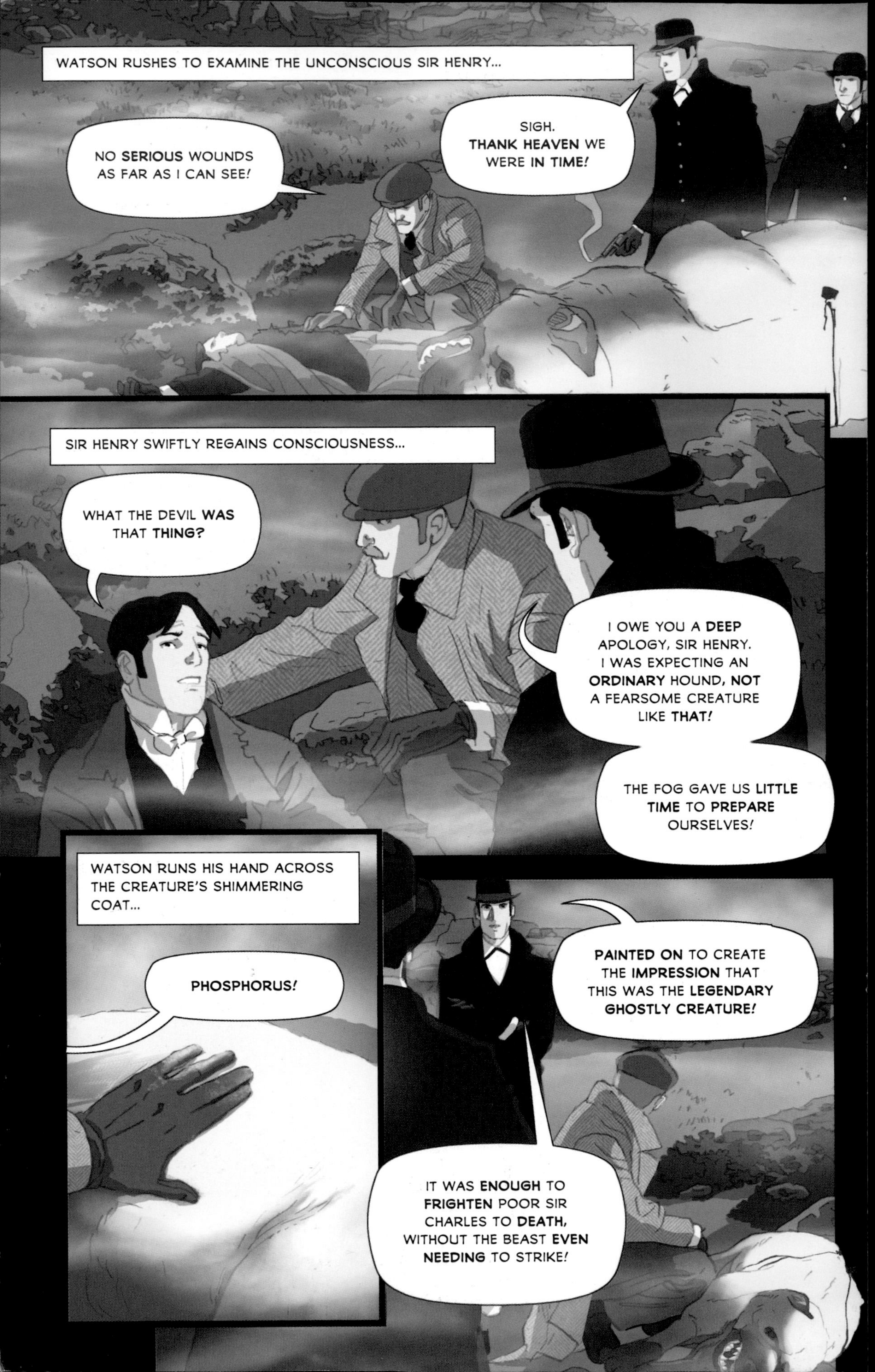
WATSON RUSHES TO EXAMINE THE UNCONSCIOUS SIR HENRY...
NO SERIOUS WOUNDS AS FAR AS I CAN SEE!
SIGH. THANK HEAVEN WE WERE IN TIME!
SIR HENRY SWIFTLY REGAINS CONSCIOUSNESS...
WHAT THE DEVIL WAS THAT THING?
I OWE YOU A DEEP APOLOGY, SIR HENRY. I WAS EXPECTING AN ORDINARY HOUND, NOT A FEARSOME CREATURE LIKE THAT!
THE FOG GAVE US LITTLE TIME TO PREPARE OURSELVES!
WATSON RUNS HIS HAND ACROSS THE CREATURE'S SHIMMERING COAT...
PHOSPHORUS!
PAINTED ON TO CREATE THE IMPRESSION THAT THIS WAS THE LEGENDARY GHOSTLY CREATURE!
IT WAS ENOUGH TO FRIGHTEN POOR SIR CHARLES TO DEATH, WITHOUT THE BEAST EVEN NEEDING TO STRIKE!

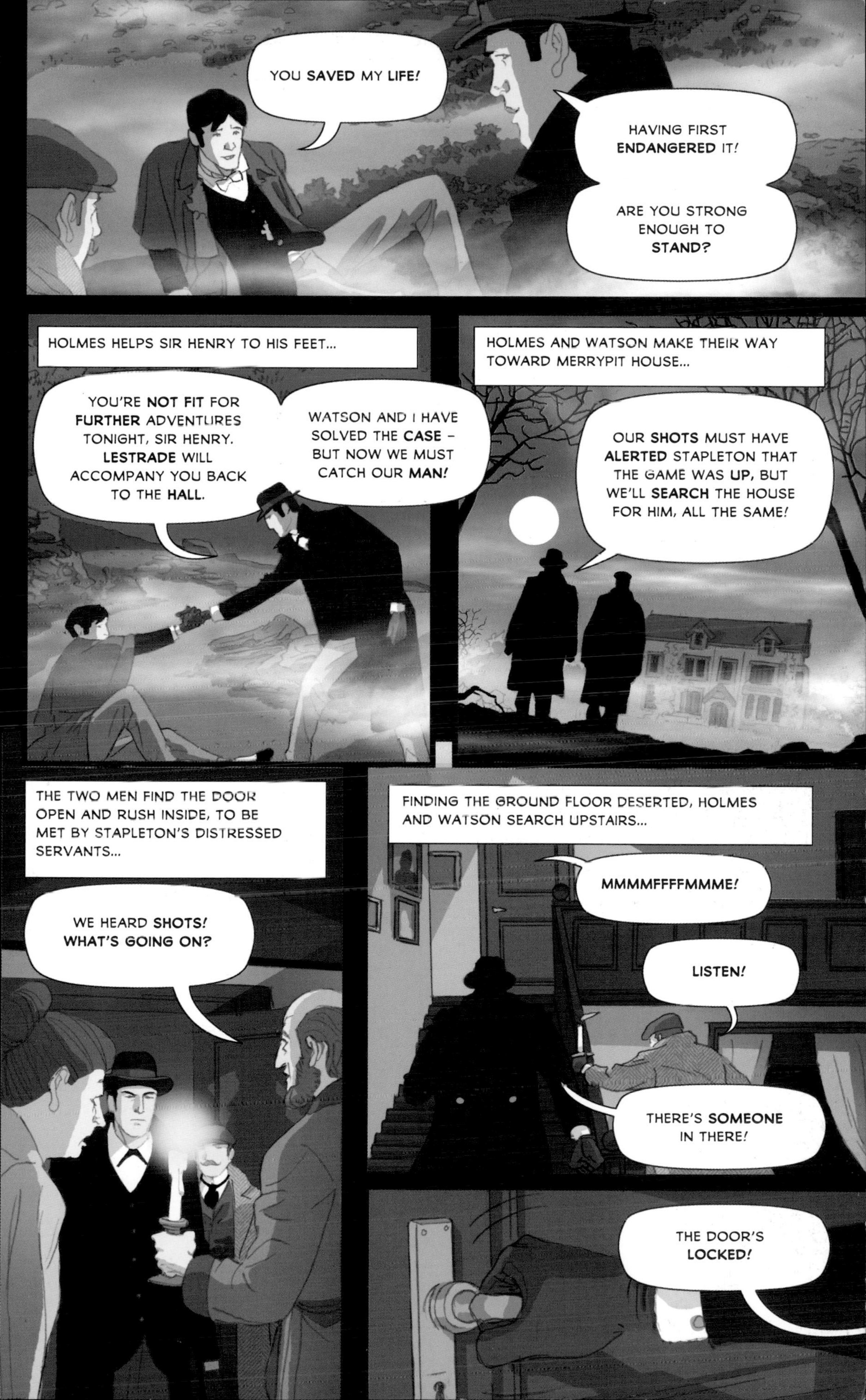
YOU SAVED MY LIFE!
HAVING FIRST ENDANGERED IT!
ARE YOU STRONG ENOUGH TO STAND?
HOLMES HELPS SIR HENRY TO HIS FEET...
YOU'RE NOT FIT FOR FURTHER ADVENTURES TONIGHT, SIR HENRY. LESTRADE WILL ACCOMPANY YOU BACK TO THE HALL.
WATSON AND I HAVE SOLVED THE CASE – BUT NOW WE MUST CATCH OUR MAN!
HOLMES AND WATSON MAKE THEIR WAY TOWARD MERRYPIT HOUSE...
OUR SHOTS MUST HAVE ALERTED STAPLETON THAT THE GAME WAS UP, BUT WE'LL SEARCH THE HOUSE FOR HIM, ALL THE SAME!
THE TWO MEN FIND THE DOOR OPEN AND RUSH INSIDE, TO BE MET BY STAPLETON'S DISTRESSED SERVANTS...
WE HEARD SHOTS! WHAT'S GOING ON?
FINDING THE GROUND FLOOR DESERTED, HOLMES AND WATSON SEARCH UPSTAIRS...
MMMMFFFFMMME!
LISTEN!
THERE'S SOMEONE IN THERE!
THE DOOR'S LOCKED!

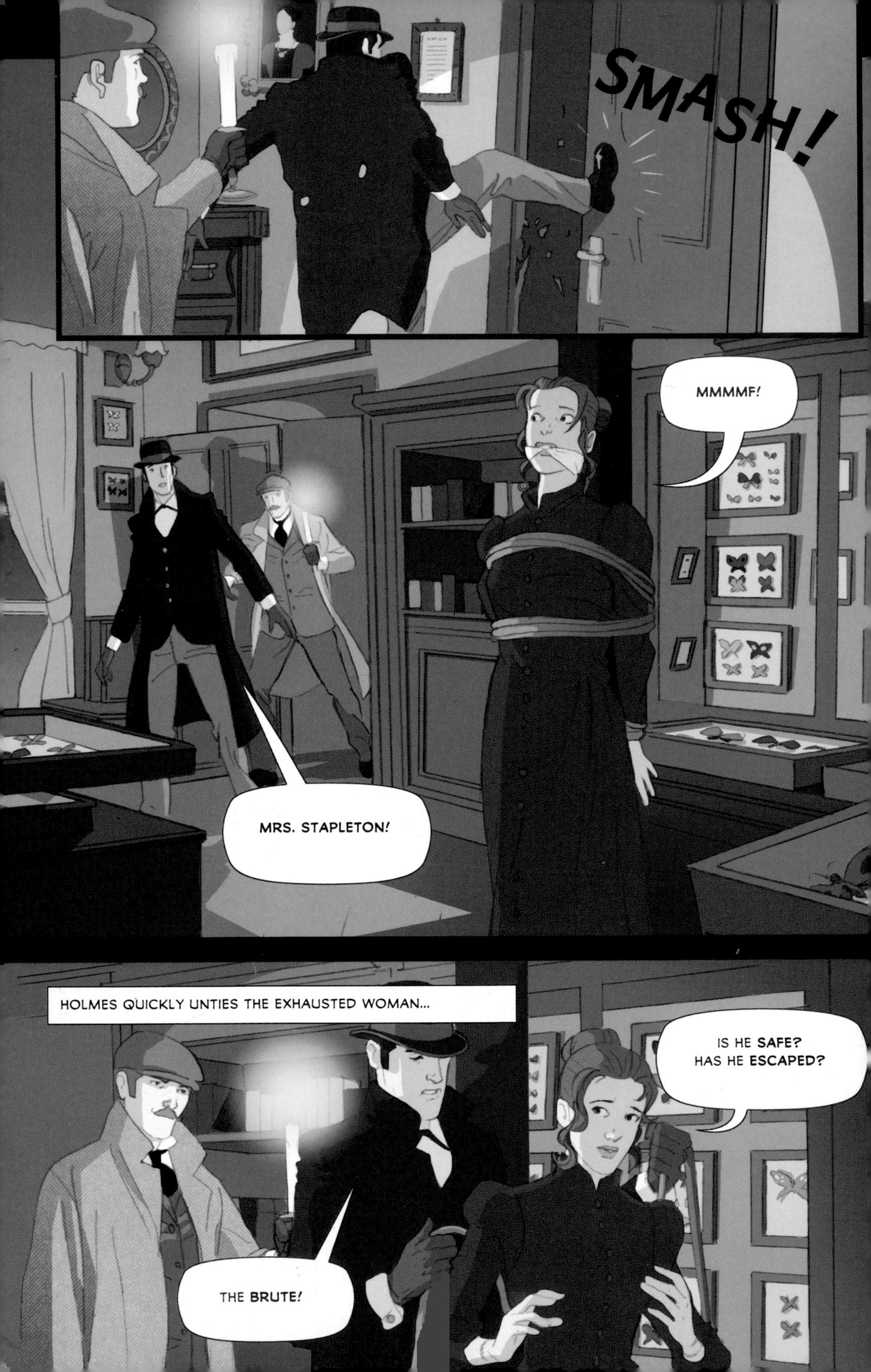
SMASH!
MMMMF!
MRS. STAPLETON!
HOLMES QUICKLY UNTIES THE EXHAUSTED WOMAN...
IS HE SAFE? HAS HE ESCAPED?
THE BRUTE!

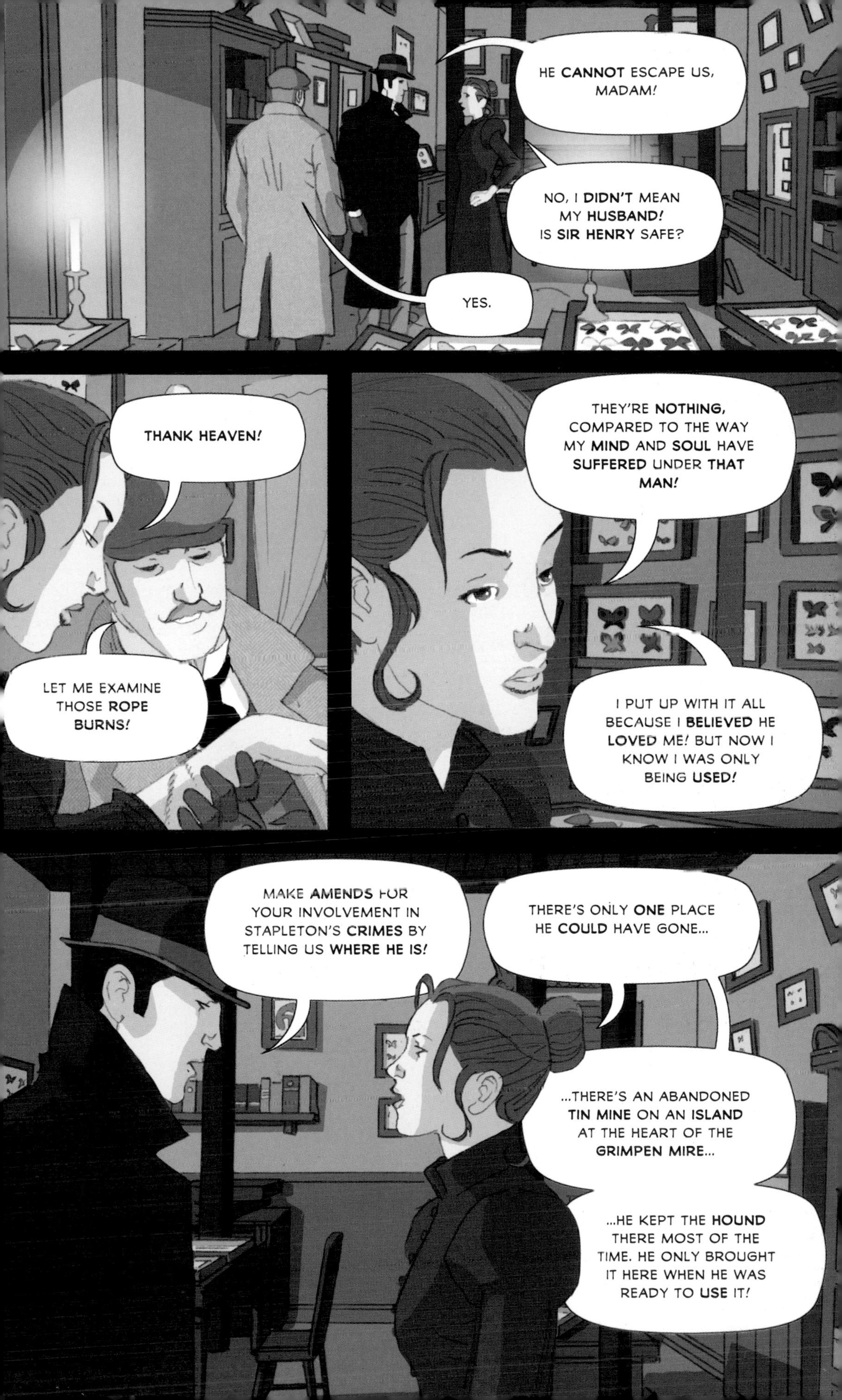
HE **CANNOT** ESCAPE US, MADAM!
NO, I **DIDN'T** MEAN MY **HUSBAND!** IS **SIR HENRY** SAFE?
YES.
THANK HEAVEN!
LET ME EXAMINE THOSE **ROPE BURNS!**
THEY'RE **NOTHING,** COMPARED TO THE WAY MY **MIND** AND **SOUL** HAVE **SUFFERED** UNDER **THAT MAN!**
I PUT UP WITH IT ALL BECAUSE I **BELIEVED** HE **LOVED** ME! BUT NOW I KNOW I WAS ONLY BEING **USED!**
MAKE **AMENDS** FOR YOUR INVOLVEMENT IN STAPLETON'S **CRIMES** BY TELLING US **WHERE HE IS!**
THERE'S ONLY **ONE** PLACE HE **COULD** HAVE GONE...
...THERE'S AN ABANDONED **TIN MINE** ON AN **ISLAND** AT THE HEART OF THE **GRIMPEN MIRE...**
...HE KEPT THE **HOUND** THERE MOST OF THE TIME. HE ONLY BROUGHT IT HERE WHEN HE WAS READY TO **USE** IT!

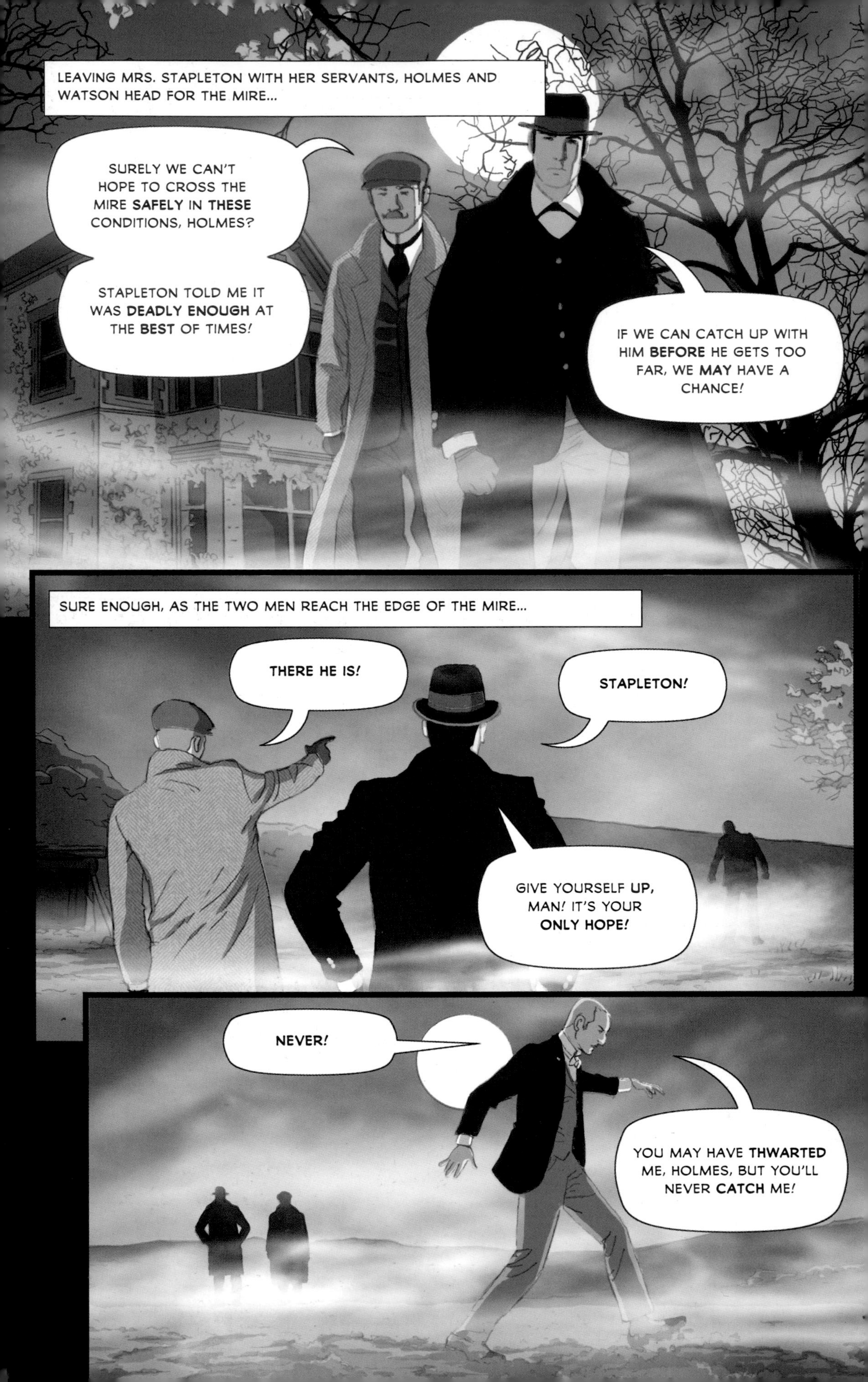

LEAVING MRS. STAPLETON WITH HER SERVANTS, HOLMES AND WATSON HEAD FOR THE MIRE...
SURELY WE CAN'T HOPE TO CROSS THE MIRE **SAFELY** IN **THESE** CONDITIONS, HOLMES?
STAPLETON TOLD ME IT WAS **DEADLY ENOUGH** AT THE **BEST** OF TIMES!
IF WE CAN CATCH UP WITH HIM **BEFORE** HE GETS TOO FAR, WE **MAY** HAVE A CHANCE!
SURE ENOUGH, AS THE TWO MEN REACH THE EDGE OF THE MIRE...
THERE HE IS!
STAPLETON!
GIVE YOURSELF **UP**, MAN! IT'S YOUR **ONLY HOPE!**
NEVER!
YOU MAY HAVE **THWARTED** ME, HOLMES, BUT YOU'LL NEVER **CATCH** ME!

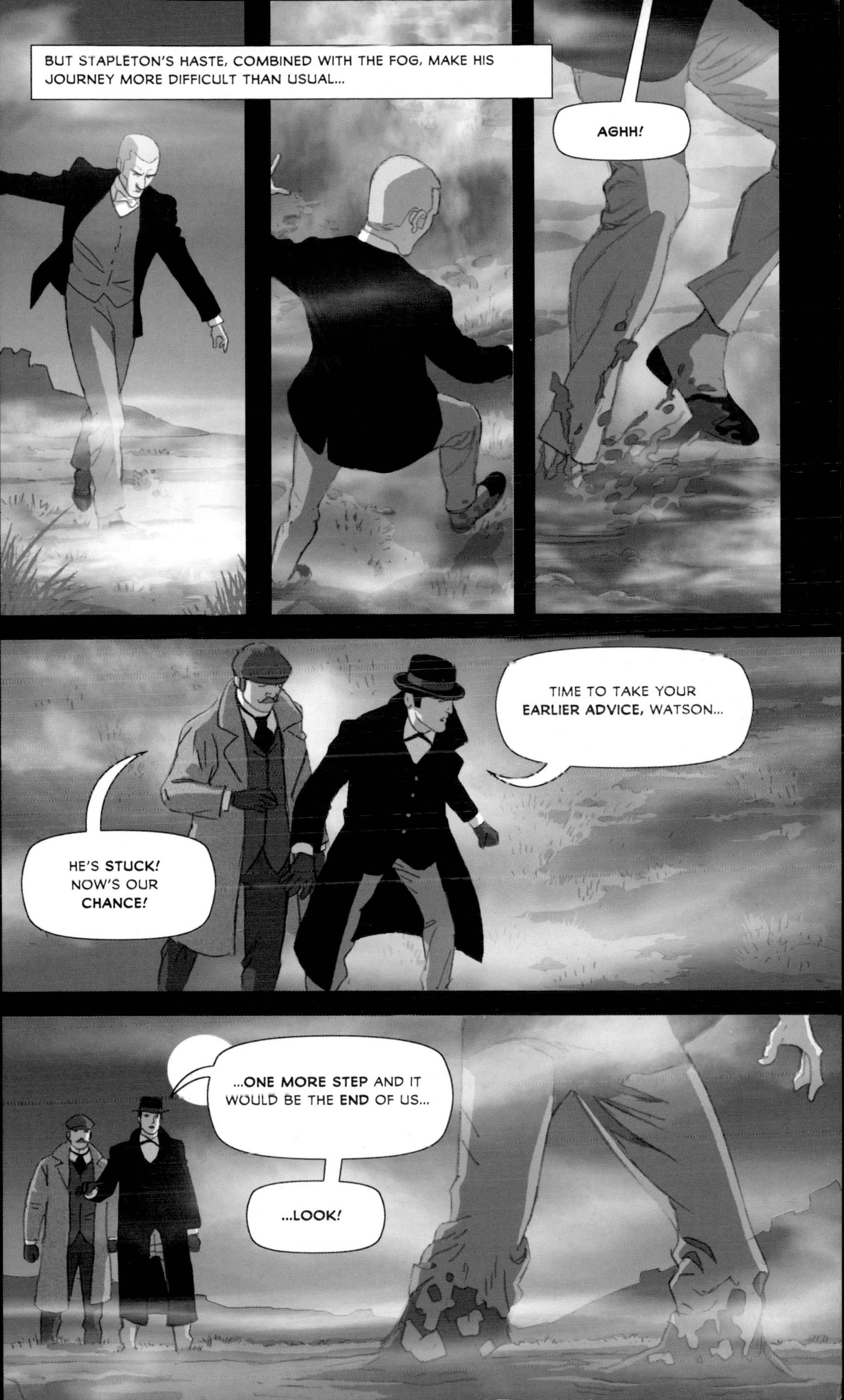
BUT STAPLETON'S HASTE, COMBINED WITH THE FOG, MAKE HIS JOURNEY MORE DIFFICULT THAN USUAL...
AGHH!
TIME TO TAKE YOUR EARLIER ADVICE, WATSON...
HE'S STUCK! NOW'S OUR CHANCE!
...ONE MORE STEP AND IT WOULD BE THE END OF US...
...LOOK!

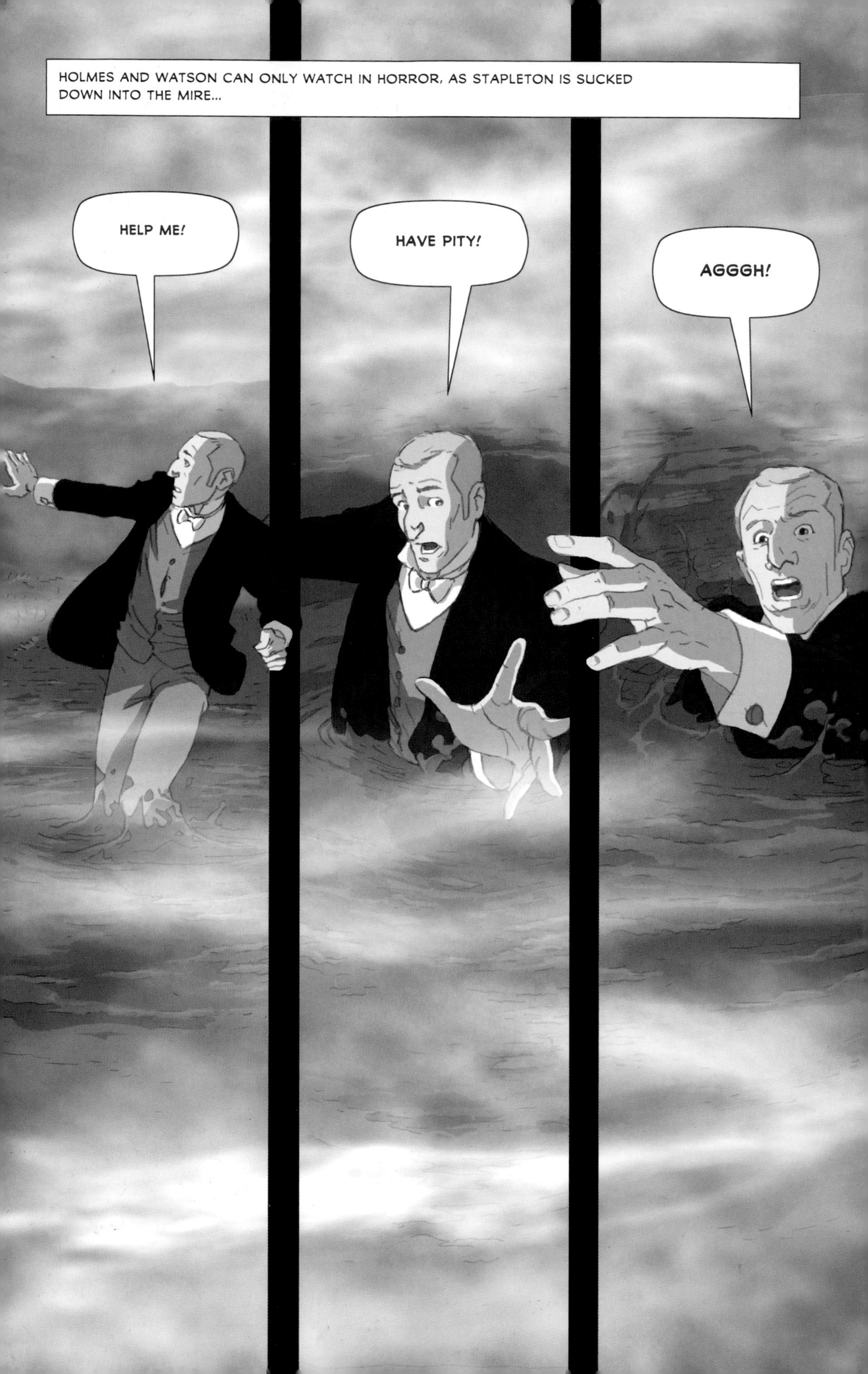
HOLMES AND WATSON CAN ONLY WATCH IN HORROR, AS STAPLETON IS SUCKED DOWN INTO THE MIRE...
HELP ME!
HAVE PITY!
AGGGH!

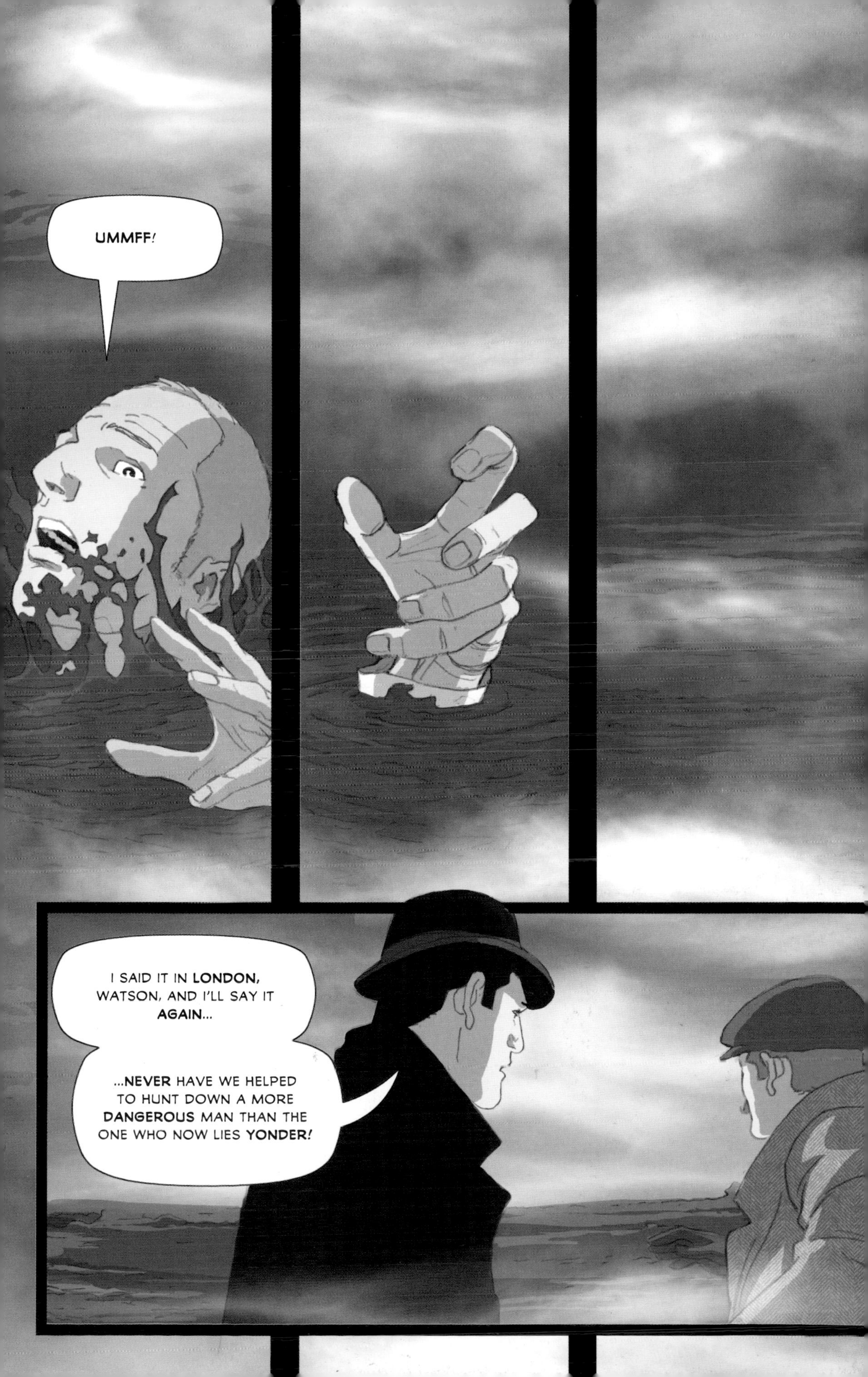
UMMFF!
I SAID IT IN LONDON, WATSON, AND I'LL SAY IT AGAIN...
...NEVER HAVE WE HELPED TO HUNT DOWN A MORE DANGEROUS MAN THAN THE ONE WHO NOW LIES YONDER!

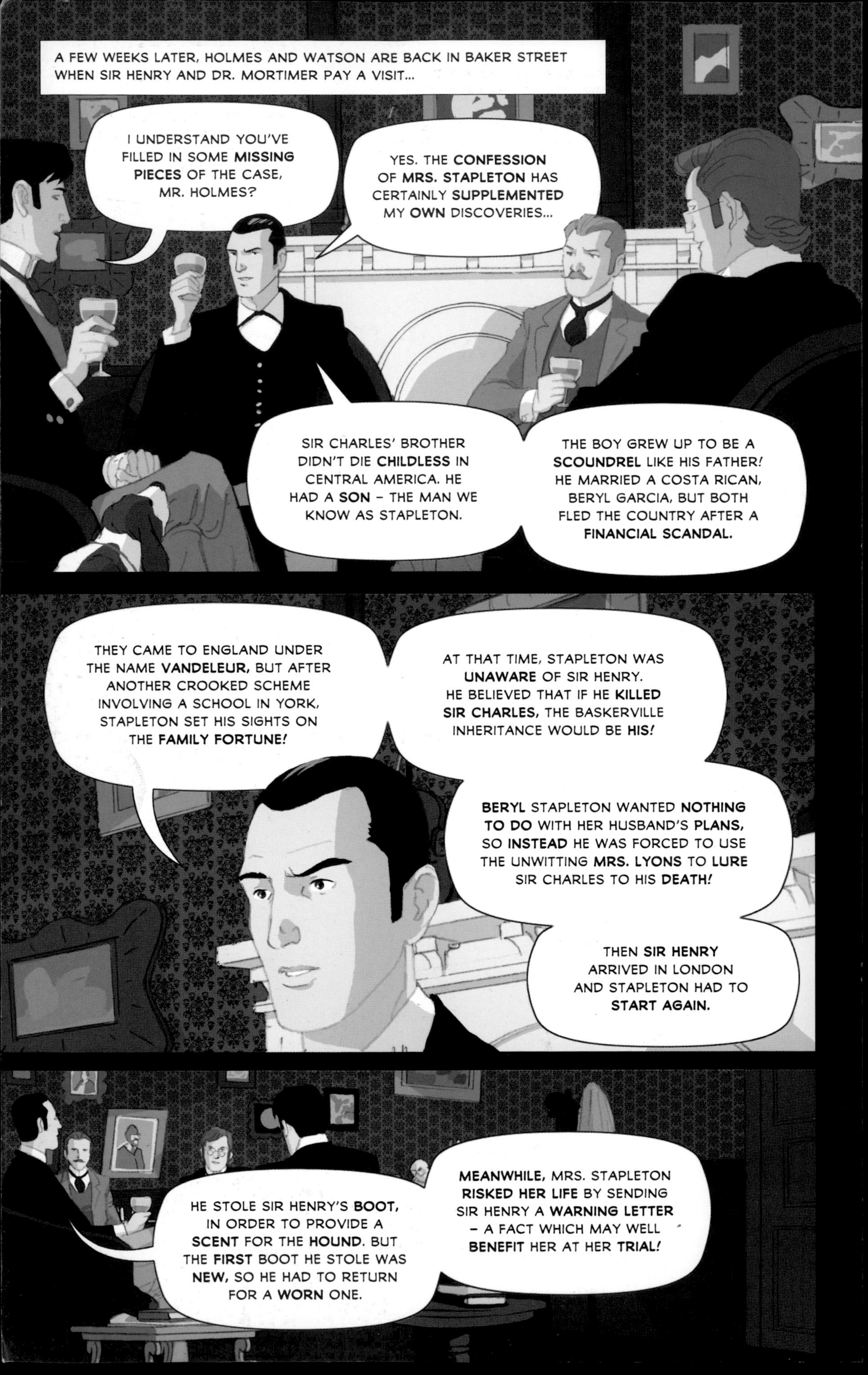
A FEW WEEKS LATER, HOLMES AND WATSON ARE BACK IN BAKER STREET WHEN SIR HENRY AND DR. MORTIMER PAY A VISIT...
I UNDERSTAND YOU'VE FILLED IN SOME MISSING PIECES OF THE CASE, MR. HOLMES?
YES. THE CONFESSION OF MRS. STAPLETON HAS CERTAINLY SUPPLEMENTED MY OWN DISCOVERIES...
SIR CHARLES' BROTHER DIDN'T DIE CHILDLESS IN CENTRAL AMERICA. HE HAD A SON – THE MAN WE KNOW AS STAPLETON.
THE BOY GREW UP TO BE A SCOUNDREL LIKE HIS FATHER! HE MARRIED A COSTA RICAN, BERYL GARCIA, BUT BOTH FLED THE COUNTRY AFTER A FINANCIAL SCANDAL.
THEY CAME TO ENGLAND UNDER THE NAME VANDELEUR, BUT AFTER ANOTHER CROOKED SCHEME INVOLVING A SCHOOL IN YORK, STAPLETON SET HIS SIGHTS ON THE FAMILY FORTUNE!
AT THAT TIME, STAPLETON WAS UNAWARE OF SIR HENRY. HE BELIEVED THAT IF HE KILLED SIR CHARLES, THE BASKERVILLE INHERITANCE WOULD BE HIS!
BERYL STAPLETON WANTED NOTHING TO DO WITH HER HUSBAND'S PLANS, SO INSTEAD HE WAS FORCED TO USE THE UNWITTING MRS. LYONS TO LURE SIR CHARLES TO HIS DEATH!
THEN SIR HENRY ARRIVED IN LONDON AND STAPLETON HAD TO START AGAIN.
HE STOLE SIR HENRY'S BOOT, IN ORDER TO PROVIDE A SCENT FOR THE HOUND. BUT THE FIRST BOOT HE STOLE WAS NEW, SO HE HAD TO RETURN FOR A WORN ONE.
MEANWHILE, MRS. STAPLETON RISKED HER LIFE BY SENDING SIR HENRY A WARNING LETTER – A FACT WHICH MAY WELL BENEFIT HER AT HER TRIAL!

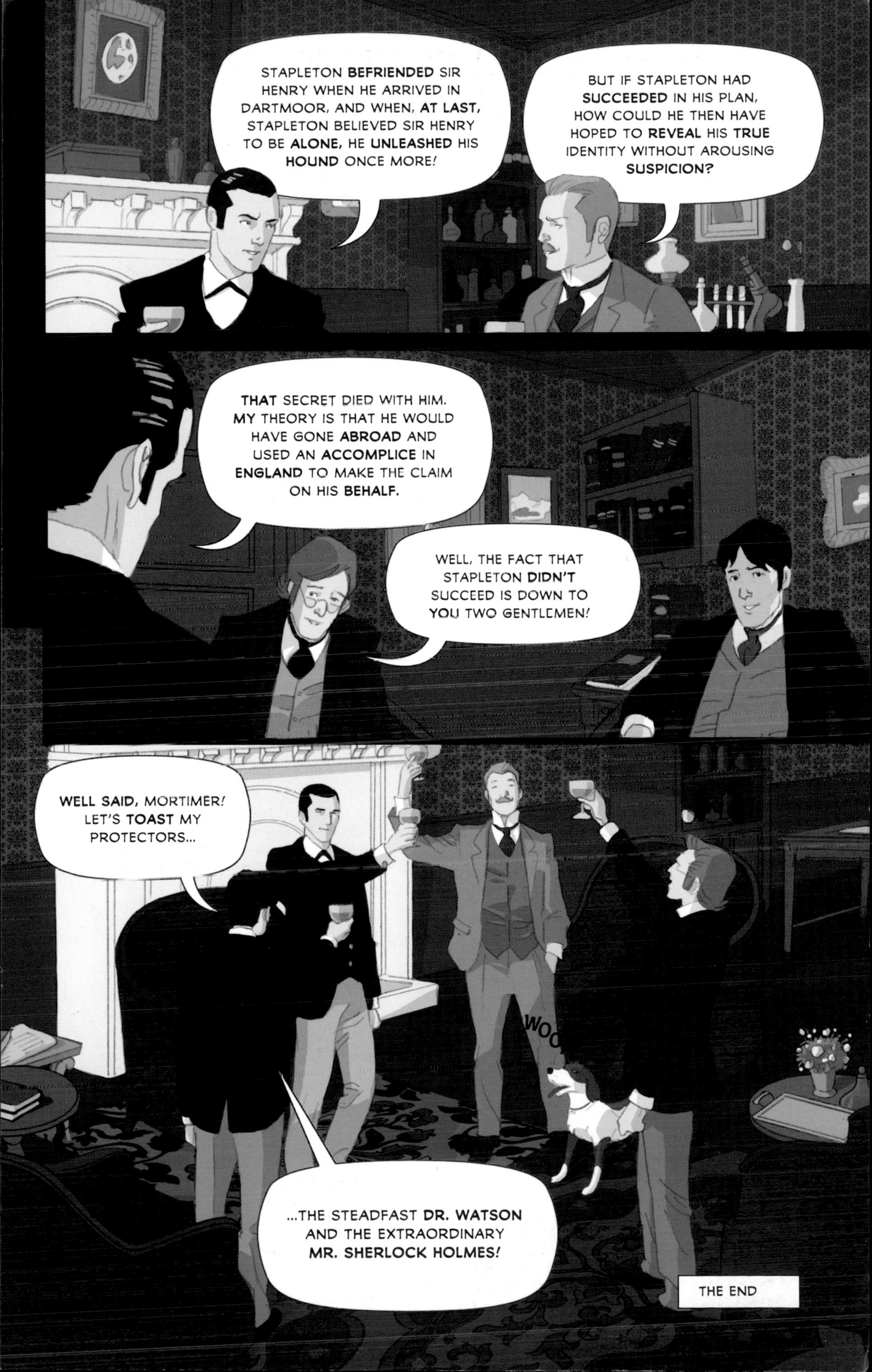

STAPLETON **BEFRIENDED** SIR HENRY WHEN HE ARRIVED IN DARTMOOR, AND WHEN, **AT LAST**, STAPLETON BELIEVED SIR HENRY TO BE **ALONE**, HE **UNLEASHED** HIS **HOUND** ONCE MORE!
BUT IF STAPLETON HAD **SUCCEEDED** IN HIS PLAN, HOW COULD HE THEN HAVE HOPED TO **REVEAL** HIS **TRUE** IDENTITY WITHOUT AROUSING **SUSPICION?**
THAT SECRET DIED WITH HIM. **MY** THEORY IS THAT HE WOULD HAVE GONE **ABROAD** AND USED AN **ACCOMPLICE** IN **ENGLAND** TO MAKE THE CLAIM ON HIS **BEHALF.**
WELL, THE FACT THAT STAPLETON **DIDN'T** SUCCEED IS DOWN TO **YOU** TWO GENTLEMEN!
WELL SAID, MORTIMER! LET'S **TOAST** MY PROTECTORS...
...THE STEADFAST **DR. WATSON** AND THE EXTRAORDINARY **MR. SHERLOCK HOLMES!**
THE END

The Story of The Hound of the Baskervilles

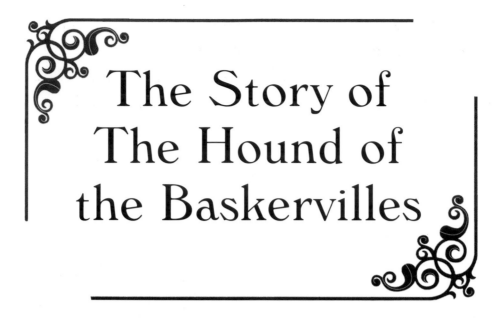

The *Hound of the Baskervilles* is the best-known case of Sherlock Holmes, without doubt the most famous fictional detective in the world. He was created over 100 years ago by Scottish doctor turned author, Arthur Conan Doyle. Doyle was born in Edinburgh in 1859. After leaving school, he studied medicine at Edinburgh University, where he began writing short stories.

It was here that he also encountered the man who would prove to be the inspiration for Holmes' methods: Dr. Joseph Bell, a surgeon at Edinburgh's Royal Infirmary who lectured at the University. In his talks, Bell described how it was possible, purely by observation, to deduce not only a patient's medical condition, but also very often his or her occupation and even their place of residence.

Joseph Bell

After graduating, Doyle was briefly employed as a ship's surgeon on vessels in Greenland and West Africa, before setting up a medical practice in Plymouth, England in 1882. To begin with, the practice was not successful, so Doyle returned to writing fiction in his spare time.

His first story featuring Sherlock Holmes and his friend and colleague Dr. John Watson was *A Study in Scarlet*, published in *Beeton's Christmas Annual* in 1887. An American magazine commissioned Doyle to write a sequel, and *The Sign of Four* appeared in *Lippincott's Magazine* in 1889. Two years later, a new English magazine called *The Strand* asked for six Holmes short stories. Over the next thirty-six years, it would publish every new Sherlock Holmes adventure.

Arthur Conan Doyle

Despite the success of the detective's exploits, Doyle himself soon began to tire of the character. In 1891, he wrote to his mother saying; "I think of slaying Holmes... and winding him up for good and all. He takes my mind from better things." In 1893, having penned twenty-five cases of the great detective, Doyle wrote *The Final Problem*, in which Holmes came face to face with the 'Napoleon of crime', the brilliant but immoral Professor Moriaty. The story ended in Switzerland, with a struggle between Holmes and Moriaty at the Reichenbach Falls, which supposedly led to both men falling to their doom.

The Yeth Hound

But there was public outcry that Doyle could have killed off such a popular character. Young men in the City of London even went as far as wearing black armbands as a sign of mourning.

Eight years later, Doyle was on a golfing retreat in Cromer, Norfolk, with his friend Bertram Fletcher Robinson. Robinson recounted the legends of ghostly hounds, specifically Black Shuck, who haunted the Norfolk coastline, and the Yeth Hound, said to terrorize Dartmoor. Doyle immediately realized that these legends would make the basis for a thrilling adventure story.

After drafting out the plot, he inserted the character of Sherlock Holmes, and in August 1901, *The Strand Magazine* published the first instalment of *The Hound of the Baskervilles*. The tale would go on to become the most famous of all Holmes' cases. At the time, Doyle was at pains to make clear that the story took place before Holmes' death in Switzerland.

However, bowing to public pressure, Doyle soon resurrected Holmes in *The Empty House*, published in 1903. He would go on to pen another thirty-two Holmes stories, with the final adventure, *Shoscombe Old Place*, being published in 1927. Doyle died three years later at the age of seventy-one.

The Hound of the Baskervilles has been adapted more times than any other Holmes story. The first known version is a German silent film from 1914 called *Der Hund von Baskerville*. British stage actor Eille Norwood played Holmes in a 1921 adaptation as part of a series of Holmes films which Doyle himself described as wonderful. Probably the most celebrated big screen Holmes, Basil Rathbone, played the detective in *The Hound of the Baskervilles* in 1939, alongside Nigel Bruce as a rather bumbling, yet likeable Dr. Watson. This was the first movie to retain the original Victorian setting and was successful enough to lead to thirteen more films starring the duo. Peter Cushing appeared in a 1959 Hammer Films adaptation, which was the first Sherlock Holmes film not made in black and white.

Cushing returned to the role on television in a two-part version of *The Hound of the Baskervilles* that aired in 1968. Further TV adaptations starred Stewart Grainger (1972), former Doctor Who, Tom Baker (1982), Ian Richardson (1983) and many people's ideal Holmes, Jeremy Brett (1988). *Sherlock Holmes and the Baskerville Curse* was a 1983 animated version of the tale, with Holmes voiced by Peter O'Toole. More recently, the TV series *Sherlock* and *Elementary* featured versions of the story respectively entitled *The Hounds of Baskerville* and *Hounded*.

It seems the public's appetite for the adventures of Sherlock Holmes and Dr. Watson will never be satisfied. The gas-lit, Victorian world in which the great detective and his friend existed may be gone, but the men themselves live on.

Sherlock Holmes and
Dr. Watson

Russell Punter was born in Bedfordshire, England. From an early age he enjoyed writing and illustrating his own stories. He trained as a graphic designer at art college in West Sussex before entering publishing in 1987. He has written over fifty books for children, ranging from original stories to adaptations of classic novels.

Andrea da Rold was born in Milan, Italy. He graduated from Milan's prestigious Academy of Fine Arts, and he still lives in the city today. He works as a cartoonist for Star Comics (*Samuel Sand*, *Lazarus Ledd*) and as an illustrator of children's books, working with, among others, Mondadori, De Agostini and Giunti. He illustrates the covers of the very popular *Geronimo Stilton* for Piemme and collaborates on Mondadori's *Focus Jr.* magazine.

Mike Collins has been creating comics for over 25 years. Starting on *Spider-Man* and *Transformers* for Marvel UK, he has also worked for DC, 2000AD and a host of other publishers. In that time he's written or drawn almost all the major characters for each company – *Wonder Woman*, *Batman*, *Superman*, *Flash*, *Teen Titans*, *X-Men*, *Captain Britain*, *Judge Dredd*, *Sláine*, *Rogue Trooper*, *Darkstars*, *Peter Cannon: Thunderbolt* and more. He currently draws a series of noir crime fiction graphic novels, *Varg Veum*. He also provides storyboards for TV and movies, including *Doctor Who*, *Sherlock*, *Warhammer 40K*, *Igam Ogam*, *Claude*, *Hana's Helpline* and *Horrid Henry*.

Cover design: Matt Preston

First published in 2018 by Usborne Publishing Ltd., Usborne House,
83-85 Saffron Hill, London EC1N 8RT, England. www.usborne.com
Copyright © 2018 Usborne Publishing Ltd.